RECKLESS SOUL

DIRTY SOULS MC - BOOK 2

EMMA CREED

Copyright © 2021 by Emma Creed

All rights reserved.

No part of this book may be reproduced or transmitted in any form or by any means, electronic or mechanical, including photocopying, recording, or by any information storage and retrieval system without written permission of the author, except for the use of brief quotations in a book review.

This is a work of fiction. Names, characters, businesses, places, events and incidents are either the product of the author's imagination or used in a fictitious manner. Any resemblance to actual persons, living or dead, actual events, or locales is entirely coincidental. The use of any real company and/or product names is for literary effect only. All other trademarks and copyrights are the property of their respective owners.

Cover design by: Rebel Ink Co
Interior design by: Rebel Ink Co
Photographer: Michelle Lancaster
Editing by: Sassi's Editing Services
Proofreading by Sharon Powell

For Angela
Who knew being stuck in a queue together could have led to this. You're the most beautiful soul and your love and support means the world to me.

Author Notes

Warning

Reckless Soul and all future books in the Dirty Soul's Mc series are all a work of fiction, and contain adult content. Due to the nature of the series you should expect to come across various subject matter that some readers may find disturbing.

Please contact the author if you require further information.

Reckless Soul is intended for readers 18+

THE STORY SO FAR

After his daughter, Hayley was killed by their rivals 'The Bastards' club Prez Jimmer Carson has been forced to dig up an old secret and is now putting all his faith in the club prospect Nyx.

Hayley, who had been in love with the club VP Jessie since she was a little girl, realized that he would only ever know happiness with her newly acquired best friend Maddy, and shocked everyone when she sacrificed herself to give them a shot at happy ever after.

Maddy is now adjusting to life with Jessie and the Dirty Souls, her hacking skills proving to be a valuable asset. While Jessie is coming to terms with the loss of Hayley and doing all he can to keep Maddy protected from the Bastards, she betrayed to be with him.

Skid is mourning the loss of his wife Carly, while struggling to come to terms with the fact that she was taken from him by his own brother, and former VP Chop.

With Chop and his son Tommy now on the run.

The club remain dedicated to getting Skid his revenge, while Nyx is about to undergo the ultimate test of loyalty.

'Bound not by blood but loyalty.
We live, we ride, and we die
by our own laws'

PROLOGUE

2003

As soon as I step out of the bathroom, I know something's off. First clue being the fact they're all smiling at me.

They never smile, not unless they've done something cruel.

I've been here a week and already I've figured out that this place is gonna suck even worse than the last hovel.

In this home, there are four other unwanted bastards just like me. Each inconvenient little wretch coming with a guaranteed paycheck.

All boys.

All assholes.

And I became their new plaything the moment I got dumped off by my social worker.

Toby's the worst of them. As the eldest one here, he's the ringleader, and the brains behind the cruel pranks and taunts. The other three are all just lickspittles, prepared to follow any order he gives them.

As I move closer to my bed, it doesn't take me long to realize why they all look so smug. My bottom sheet is smeared with something dirty, it's foul-smelling, and stinks a lot like… shit.

"What's wrong, didn't make it in time?" Austin fakes his best baby voice while looking up at Toby, pathetically craving his approval.

Austin's a chubby little shit, with a huge mat of ginger hair on top of his head and skin smothered in freckles. Being only a year older than myself, I'd stab a guess at him being the unfortunate victim before I showed up.

I don't react, keeping my head down and marching past them to strip the soiled sheets off my mattress.

"Oi. Austin asked you a question," Toby's voice grinds me to a halt. He uses his intimidation to his advantage, stepping around me in a slow circle before forcing his chest in my face. Since he's stronger than me I have no choice but to take a step backward, and the demonic sneer he looks down at me with has me curious…

What could he have suffered in his short life to make him so hateful?

"You think you're too good to be here, shit stain?" He prods his finger into my shoulder and I hold his stare, remaining silent. Refusing to feed him the fear he's trying to provoke out of me.

"You think your shit don't stink?" he taunts some more, his lips curling into a smile that displays his black stumpy teeth.

I manage to stop myself from struggling when his hand reaches around my head, gripping firm at the back of my collar. It doesn't take a mastermind to figure what comes next.

I fight against the urge to fight back when he starts to push me forward. Toby's bigger than me and much stronger, and in all honesty, I'd sooner get a taste of someone else's shit than give him the satisfaction of me begging.

I try so hard to deny him a reaction, but with my head just inches away from the bedsheet and the stench invading my nostrils, I can't help starting to retch.

The others roar with laughter as Toby edges me closer, his hand shaking from the pressure he's using to push my head forward.

"Tell me, does your shit taste any better than the rest of ours?" he grunts, pressing my face against the mattress. And I gag as the smell hits the back of my throat.

Toby's palm twists into the back of my skull, making sure I get a taste of whoever's shit I'm nasal deep in, his forceful pressure cutting off any air from entering my mouth or nostrils. I can't hold back my body's instinct to fight back anymore. I thrash against the mattress, my head straining to try and catch a breath. The laughter around me grows louder, and I hate myself for giving them all what they've been thirsting for.

Eventually, Toby lets me go, chuckling to himself as he watches me suck desperate gulps of air into my lungs, choking and gagging against the rancid taste clinging at the back of my throat.

"No? didn't think so," Toby shoves me hard in my back landing me in a heap on the floor, and from there I watch him and his minions leave the room.

Frustration turns the blood in my veins to lava. I know I should have stuck up for myself, but I'm too scared of getting into trouble. I can guarantee Bill's fist will come down harder than Toby's or any of the others if I got caught making trouble.

I wait until I can hear them all playing outside before quickly stripping my bed, balling up the sheets. Then I make sure there's no sign of Bill or Heidi before I sneak down to the laundry room. The last thing I want is to get caught by Heidi. I've already had a painful warning about bed-wetting after the cruel joke they all played on me the first night I got here. This would be so much worse.

After somehow managing to get the machine started by myself, I sit on the floor and wait patiently for it to finish its cycle. With the boys in the yard playing soccer, and Heidi still yet to rise from her pit, it's a relief to have some time to myself.

The rumbling machine slows to a stop, and I'm just about to

swap the sheets into the dryer when I hear voices coming from the kitchen.

The door is already slightly open, and when I risk taking a peek through the crack, I do a double-take when I see Bill cowering at the kitchen table.

I can't get a good look at whoever it is that's making him so fearful. I only have the back view of the tall dark figure that looms over Bill's quivering frame.

"The kid… you're taking good care of him?" the stranger asks Bill, with no tolerance in his tone. I shift my angle to try and get a better look but all I can see are black jeans and a black hooded top.

"Of… Of course. He's settled in real good," Bill's voice rattles with fear, it sounds strange, and I make a mental note to remember this moment the next time he clouts me.

"And the other kids? They give him any shit?" The man questions, leaning forward and resting his hand on the table in front of Bill.

"No. Never, we're one big happy family here," Bill proves that he can still be a good liar, even under pressure. "The older boys have taken him right under their wings."

The stranger relaxes slightly, easing back and reaching into the back pocket of his jeans. A heavy thud on the table has Bill licking his lips greedily, and when the stranger shifts his hand out of the way I see the brown envelope that he's put down.

"I've seen the kid, he looks a wreck. You send him to school dressed like that, he'll be a walking target. Hook him up with clothes. Decent shit, not thrift store crap. Make sure he gets everything he needs."

Bill's greedy fingers reach out to snatch at the envelope, his head nodding back enthusiastically, and my whole body jolts when the stranger's hand suddenly slams over Bill's. Gripping his fingers and crushing them awkwardly in his fist. Bill moans out in agony, and the man's free hand wraps around his throat forcing him silent.

The gurgling sounds have me shifting my position to get a better look, and I can't help smile when I see his petrified eyes bulging out from their sockets.

"I got eyes on you, Billy boy. The money is for the kid. You got that?"

Bill nods back like a pet monkey, gasping loudly when he's released and holding on to the edge of the table while he struggles to catch his breath.

"Of course... Understood Mr... um, sorry I didn't catch your name."

"I never fucking told you," the guy bites back, already making his way towards the door.

"Wait. You could see the kid if you wanted?" Bill calls after him, and his suggestion makes the stranger stop in his tracks, but he still doesn't turn around.

"You seem concerned about the boy's welfare. I know there are rules about visits, but I could make an exception, bring him in so you can see him. He'll be right outside playing with the others."

It's funny seeing Bill like this, a groveling creep ass, desperate to get on the good side of a man he's scared of.

"The kid's better off without me," is the last thing he mutters before leaving. And I swear I sense a little sadness in his rough tone.

Bill waits until the front door slams before tearing open the envelope and flicking his thumb through the impressive wad of notes. The chuckle he gives to himself suggests whoever the money was intended for won't be seeing it anytime soon.

"Heidi, wake up," he bellows. "Lazy fucking bitch," he mutters under his breath when she fails to respond. Getting up from the table, he takes the money with him.

I use the opportunity to bundle my wet sheets into the dryer, then I rush out of the laundry room, through the back door to join the others in the yard. I'm lucky I didn't get caught, I'd be in a whole heap of shit if Bill caught me listening.

Sneaking down the side of the house, I manage to make it to the front yard unscathed and take a seat on the broken bench. Picking up a stick, I scratch it into the crumbly earth around my feet and I can't help wondering who that man could have been. More importantly who had he come here for? Stupid as it sounds, I'm actually jealous of whoever it is. Doesn't matter that the guy was scary as hell.

"Hey, shit stain…" Toby calls at me from the other side of the yard. "You wanna play dodgeball?"

Knowing what that involves, I ignore him, moving out of their way and taking my stick with me. Their ball bounces off the back of my head, and I ignore that too. I take a few more hits from the ball to different parts of my body, and when they don't get the reaction they want from me, they start to use stones instead.

The boys laugh and call out all the same insults I've heard from them before, and I blank them out along with the hard stones that pelt against the backs of my legs.

I find shade under a tree, sitting down and resting my back against its trunk, they'll get bored eventually. Find a bug or stray cat that they can make suffer instead.

Closing my eyes to block them out, I try to imagine being somewhere else. I work my head until it throbs trying to remember what my life was like before all of this. But it's empty. I've been in the system for as long as I can remember.

A loud rumble from the other side of the street rings through my ears. The vibration, deep enough to rattle my ribcage, and when I open my eyes I catch sight of the motorcycle before it takes off. I only manage to get a back view of the rider, who's dressed all in black, it's the stranger from the kitchen. Only difference is, now he's wearing a vest over his hoodie, a leather one that has a hooded skull sewn into the back, and *D.I.R.T.Y S.O.U.L.S M.C.* arched over the top of it.

His bike is by far the coolest thing I've ever seen. I want one just like it, one that I could ride right out of this hellhole on.

Later that night, while all the boys scrap over who gets the remote for the TV, I draw from memory what I'd seen on the back of the rider's vest. Then, when we're sent to bed, I tuck the drawing inside my pillowcase so no one else will find it.

I've never been much of a sleeper, I learned from an early age to always be on guard. You never can be too sure when your next strike is coming and around these bunch of morons, I can guarantee there's always one right around the corner.

A few hours after lights out, when everyone is sleeping, I'm still wide awake. I lay with my eyes shut, making the most of the silence, until I hear the scraping sound that comes from the window. It's quickly followed by a muffled scream that comes from the bed to my left… Toby's.

I loosen my eyelids enough to see what's going on, and almost give myself away with a gasp of shock when I see him again.

The guy who threatened Bill is back, his hood pulled up over his head like the Grimm Reaper himself. He leans over Toby's bed, his gloved hand covering Toby's mouth and a sharp blade pressing beneath his chin.

It's too dark under the hood to see the guy's face, and I can't risk opening my eyes any wider.

"The kid…" I hear the stranger whisper to Toby and through my squint, I notice his head tip slightly in my direction. I almost choke on my breath. There has to be some mistake. Whoever this is can't be here for me…

I don't have anyone, that's why I'm stuck in this shithole.

"You back the fuck off," the guy warns Toby, who nods his head exactly the same way Bill had in the kitchen. I can just hear his faint terrified squeals muffled behind the giant hand that's covering his mouth.

"I'll be watching, and if you or any of your pals touch, talk, or even glance at him in the wrong way… I'll slit all your fucking throats. You understand that, Toby?" the stranger threatens, and I watch Toby's head bob up and down in agreement.

"Sleep with one eye open, kid." The stranger's fingers tap roughly at Toby's jaw before he releases him. Then he clambers back out of the window as quickly and quietly as he arrived through it.

All of a sudden, I find myself thankful for all those beatings I've woken up to. It's thanks to those times that I never rest easy like other kids do, my body has trained itself to function on limited sleep.

Without all those beatings I wouldn't have witnessed the color drain from Toby's face, or seen how fear had struck like matches in his eyes. Like all the others in the room, I would have missed him stripping his soaked bed and creeping down to the laundry room.

As I drift off into a peaceful sleep, I promise myself that when I grow up, I'm gonna be just like that stranger. Threatened by no one and feared by everyone.

One day when I'm old enough and tough enough, the Dirty Soul will come back for me and ride us out of here.

It was six months later when Bill never made it home. We got told it was a hit and run after he'd left a bar in town, but I figured it had more to do with the fact that I never did get those new clothes for school.

Heidi couldn't cope with us alone, so we all got moved to other homes. Where, for me, the torment started all over again.

I waited on the Dirty Soul to come again but he never did.

And it took me a few months, but I eventually figured that waiting around to be rescued wasn't going to solve my situation. So, I took fate into my own hands.

I stopped worrying about consequences. When I got beat, I fought back twice as hard. I made fear instead of friends, and I told myself that if the Dirty Soul wasn't gonna come for me, I'd find him myself.

And that's how I ended up in Colorado.

Chapter 1

NYX

"Mmmmm what's that noise?" a groggy voice purrs from my left and I'm as sure as Satan's a sinner that the hand covering my semi-hard cock ain't mine. I lift open one eye to check, and figure I'm still buzzed when I see two different sets of hands.

That hard pounding noise ain't going away either, and I quickly realize that it's the door, practically shaking off the hinges. I sit up, letting the two limp bodies slip off me. Turns out my head ain't fuckin' with me, there are two of 'em, one blonde, one red, both of them club hangouts.

"I'm comin'," I call out, scratching the back of my head and searching the floor for my clothes.

"Here," blondie tosses my pants at me with a sleepy seductive smile on her lips. I snatch 'em up and step straight into them. When I eventually open the door I'm greeted with a stern, unimpressed face.

The club Prez, Jimmer Carson, ain't a man that's used to being kept waiting. He tilts his head to look past my shoulder, shaking his head when he spots the two naked bitches spread out on the bed.

"Don't you got somewhere to be, Prospect?" His eyes focus back on me, and he raises one of his grey eyebrows.

"Sorry boss, must have forgot to set an alarm," I hit back

sarcastically, and two synchronized giggles ring out from behind me, along with a vague memory of both the little sluts taking it in turns to choke on my cock.

Club whores call it the 'Big Nyx challenge', and not one of 'em have managed to take me all the way without choking. Not even Mel, and that girl's a pro. She's been taking DSD in her mouth for as long as I've been walkin'.

"You've got twenty minutes before you need to be on the road," Prez shoves past me to step inside the rutting room.

We all have our own cabins here on the compound, but most of us choose to keep that space to ourselves. These rooms on the second floor of the clubhouse are used for one purpose only… For fucking in.

Red shifts over and makes space for Prez beside her. "Enjoy school, kid," he takes the time to snigger at me over his shoulder before he starts to unbuckle his belt.

I snatch up my prospect cut from the floor and locate my T-shirt before closing the door on my way out. My head's still thumping as I make for the stairs.

"Prez said you'd be needing this," Marilyn calls out from behind me, rushing out the kitchen and forcing a full plate under my nose. The smell of eggs makes my stomach roll.

Maddy's mom's been working here a while now, and I can't remember how we all didn't starve before her.

"Thanks, Mar." I grab the plate off her and take it down the stairs with me, heading through the foyer and into the main bar room. The place looks like a battlefield, bodies stretched out everywhere, some clothed, some not and I manage to find a clear space at the bar. One where I can eat without having to look at Squealer's naked, tattooed ass.

"You wanna coffee with that, Hunny?" Mel appears from the other side of the bar, and makes a start at clearing up some of the empty bottles.

"Best had," I lift my chin at her, stabbing some bacon with my fork and staring at it before I eat it.

"You flirtin' with that or eatin' it?" A heavy hand slams me hard on my back and when I glance over my shoulder, Tac's staring at my bacon and wetting his lips.

"All yours," I drop the fork from my hand and slide the plate to one side.

"Rough night?" Tac smirks at me, wasting no time loading his mouth with eggs. And when Mel places my black coffee on the bar, he helps himself to that too.

"Could say that." I scrub my face with my palm attempting to clear some of the grogginess from my head. Today's a big day, I need to be fucking with it.

"I gotta go," I tell him, checking the time. Tac shrugs his shoulders, and I leave him to fill his face as I head outside for some fresh air.

I make a quick dash up to my cabin for a shower and to change, and then I'm ready to go.

This is the earliest time of day I've seen in a long while, and as I pull out of the compound and take the road that leads to Castle Rock, a real weird feeling settles itself in the pit of my stomach. The type of feeling I haven't felt since I was a kid. One that stirs up your insides, and makes your heart beat a little faster.

I'm fucking nervous.

All the planning that's gone into this job for Prez, rests solidly on me now. That's a huge weight to carry.

Jessie and Maddy are the only other people at the club who know about Prez's secret daughter. The brown-haired, hazel-eyed creature who's claimed my thoughts since I first saw her photo last month. The girl is my ticket to getting what I've wanted since I was ten years old and that Dirty Soul showed up at my foster home. She's also the most beautiful thing I've ever set eyes on.

All Prez wants to know is that his girl is doin' okay, that the life he chose for her is treating her good. The man she's grown up believing is her father, is a federal judge, and recently Prez got his suspicions that he's stirring shit up for the club.

A few months ago, Judge Jackson granted a warrant for the CIA to search our compound, and Maddy struggled to find where that request came from. You better believe that if there's shit to be found, Jessie's old lady is the one who'll find it.

Prez doesn't trust Judge Jackson, and that's where I come in. All I need to do is make nice with Ella, check she's happy and find out what I can about the Judge. Easy enough work for someone who has basic social skills, but for me, this is gonna be a challenge. One made a damn sight worse by the fact I can't stop wondering how pretty Ella Jackson might look while she's being fucked… by me.

CHAPTER 2: ELLA

I walk into the kitchen and find the breakfast table laid out in the usual way. The only difference today being the neat bundle of envelopes propped up against my juice glass.

My father's head is buried in his paper, same as it is every morning, but today the space beside him is empty and instead of being in her usual position, Mom is flapping around the stove.

"Happy Birthday, Sweetheart." She plasters on a smile and stretches open her arms, waiting for me to go to her. I shuffle over and let her wrap me up in a hug.

"I can't believe I'm a Mom to an eighteen-year-old. I might have to start getting Botox," she jokes. I humor her, pretend that I don't know she started having Botox when I was fifteen. I'd looked up Dr. Stentil online when I found an appointment card in her bag hoping he was a shrink. *God knows she needs one.* As it turned out, Dr. Stentil is a specialist in cosmetic treatments who owns a private clinic a few miles out of town.

At least he does a good job. Mom still looks natural, and her lips aren't like the frankfurters Abby's mom seems to have acquired over the past couple of years.

"Sit down, darling. I've made your favorite… Vincent, the birthday girl is awake," Mom prompts Dad like he hasn't noticed I've been here all this time, and he just about manages to lift his head up from the current affairs to grumble me a 'Happy Birthday'.

Nodding back at him, I take my place at the table and begin opening my cards. The first one is from Mom and Dad. It's pink and pretty, with words that read *'To a dear Daughter'.* The second is from my grandparents, the ones on my mother's side who actually bother to acknowledge my existence. Enclosed is a cheque for 5,000 dollars, and the instructions to deposit it into my savings account.

My third and final card is from Penelope, our housekeeper. It's handcrafted, with my name and the number 18 made up out of different sized buttons.

Looking around the kitchen, I wonder where she is this morning. It seems brave of Mom to be attempting pancakes by herself, even if it is my birthday.

"There we go darling," Mom places the plate on the table mat, and smiles proudly. I look down at the smoked salmon and scrambled egg she's put in front of me, and don't have the heart to remind her that I hate salmon.

"Thanks, Mom." I smile up at her gratefully, digging in and detesting every mouthful I force myself to swallow.

After finishing up as quickly as possible, I stand up and drop my plate off in the sink. Penelope rushes into the room and I pretend not to notice the sly nod that she aims at Mom.

"Good morning, Miss Jackson, and Happy Birthday." Penelope lunges forward and gives me a hug, one from her never fails to warm me right from the outside in.

I've given up telling Penelope not to call me Miss Jackson. She's worked for us for years, practically raised me while my parents both maintained their busy schedules. Come to think of it, Penelope has hugged me more times in my life than both my parents combined. But despite me reminding her countless times that formalities aren't required between us, she likes to remain professional.

"Come, darling, we'll walk you to the door." Mom grabs my school bag from the back of my chair and rushes me out into the hall. Father doesn't bother getting up, or even say goodbye, but I don't expect him to. Like Mom often reminds me, Father isn't a 'morning' person. He isn't much of an afternoon or evening person either in my opinion.

Ushering me to the front door, Mom is failing to hide her excitement, and my eyes stretch wide in disbelief when I notice the shiny black Mercedes SLK convertible parked on our drive.

Forcing my eyes off the sleek looking car, I look back at Mom, and the nod of her head is all the confirmation I need.

This baby belongs to me.

"I love it. Thank you. Thank you so much." Mom's tiny frame almost topples over when I fling my arms around her neck and squeeze.

"Don't forget to thank your father," she reminds me, and I rush back through the house and find him sitting exactly where we left him.

"Thank you… for the car," I tone down my excitement, knowing how he likes things calm, and feel awkward as I gently place a kiss on his cheek. He stretches his neck slightly to receive it but doesn't take his eyes off the article he's reading. I thank him again, tell him it's the best present I've ever received.

"You're welcome," he responds, blank of any emotion, and so I leave him to his paper.

"Ella…" he calls out just before I make it out of the kitchen. I spin around and smile.

"Don't scratch it," he warns, again without bothering to look up, and I feel the smile instantly drop from my cheeks.

My dad is a hard man to understand, I've spent years trying to create a Father-daughter bond with him but he's just never seemed interested. He's a Federal Judge and I appreciate that he's under a lot of pressure. I can handle his detachment from me. What I can't tolerate is the way he constantly takes his shit out on my mom, she's become a pro at keeping up the pretense that everything is perfect. And I play along, mainly because I know it's me who she puts the act on for more than anyone.

Back outside, Mom holds out the keys to my new car. I take them from her hand, then squeeze her with another hug before opening the driver's door and getting behind the wheel.

"This is so exciting. I'm gonna call Abby, see if she wants to take a ride with me later. Don't worry I'll make sure I'm back in time for dinner." Mom will have organized for Penelope to work on some elaborate dinner for us all tonight. I don't want her worrying about me being home late.

"Oh darling, Daddy has a business dinner this evening at the Senator's. It's important. We were hoping you wouldn't mind celebrating your birthday another night." Her awkward smile reflects how terrible she feels, so I go easy on her.

"Sure, I'll see if Abby wants to go out for dinner," I shrug, convinced that I've done a good enough job of pretending not to be bothered.

"Great idea, sweetheart. I knew you'd understand. Wait right there…" Mom runs back inside as quick as her heels will allow, returning a few moments later clutching her purse.

"Here…" she takes out a few hundred dollar bills and holds them out to me, "…Our treat, go somewhere nice."

I take the money and let her kiss my cheek.

"Happy Birthday, Ella." She gives me her well-rehearsed smile, one that doesn't quite hide the sadness in her eyes, and I smile back as if I haven't noticed, because that's what we do for each other.

I start up the engine of my new ride, pulling off the drive of our perfect suburban mansion and head for another day of school.

I make it to my locker just as the bell rings for first period, and I grin to myself when I see that it's been decorated with pink balloons and an oversized pink bow. It has to be Abby's work, and I brace myself for a surge of energetic enthusiasm when I hear her loud screech come from behind me.

"Hey Birthday Girl." She throws her arms around my neck, leaving a thick film of lip gloss on my cheeks after she kisses them both.

With her deep red hair and bright green eyes, Abby never fails to stand out from the crowd. She's short, fiery, and has no filter, which is exactly why I love her.

"Sooooo, rumor going around is…" she beats out a drum roll on my locker door, "…there's a new guy started today, and he is hawwt. Trina saw him coming out of Kutcher's office earlier and apparently…" placing her hand on her chest she dramatically mocks Trina's southern drawl, "he is man in its finest form."

I snort a laugh back at her, but my mood rapidly changes when I notice Luke on the other side of the corridor, propped up against his locker surrounded by all his football crones, his usual scowl directed right at me.

Luke Robinson hates me, has done since he asked me out on a date last year and I actually dared to turn him down.

Unfortunately for me, the unwritten school code dictates that if the captain of the football team hates you, the rest of the team, the cheerleaders, and just about anyone else who cares about being popular hates you too.

It doesn't bother me. I have Abby, she's loyal and a better friend than any of the phony cheerleaders or football suck asses would ever be. What does bother me though, is Luke's dedication to loathing me. It's borderline obsessive. He still hasn't done anything serious enough to get himself into trouble, but I can tell he's thought about it. And I hate more than anything that I let that scare me.

I say goodbye to Abby outside the door to my English class and take my usual seat near the front, as far away as possible from the desks that Luke and his friends have all claimed at the back of the room.

Luke and his gang all pile into class together not long after me. With Luke stopping to casually rest his ass on the edge of my desk, his friends all surround him, doing an excellent job of making me feel claustrophobic.

"Happy Birthday, Ella." Luke looks down over his shoulder at me. I don't bother thanking him. Instead, I prepare myself for the insult that's evidently going to follow.

"You having a party?" he asks, and without giving me a chance to come back at him, he answers his own question. "Ah, that's right you haven't got any friends." His pathetic attempt to embarrass me earns him a roar of laughter from his buddies.

"Maybe you could ask Mommy and Daddy if they'd buy you a couple new ones for your birthday. Upgrade you on the skanky one you already got." He winks at me as the hyenas' chorus picks up again.

I'm about to speak up, asshole can say what he likes about me, but hell if I'm about to let him call Abby a skank. My mouth opens, but just as I'm about to say something the door swings open and someone unfamiliar steps inside, causing the words to get caught in my throat.

Straight away I know it's the guy Abby was getting excited about. And he brings a massive presence into the room with him, probably because he stands so tall and is built so solid. His shoulders and arms seem so much larger than any of the boys my age. Maybe he's older, repeating a year. He has to be, someone our age couldn't have acquired all the tattoos he's got in such a short time.

My head follows him as he strides across the room confidently, wearing blue jeans, black open laced boots, and a grey sleeveless hoodie that's unzipped. The tight white T-shirt underneath, drawing all my attention to his impressive chest.

His features are beautifully harsh, and there's a natural pout set on his thick bottom lip.

He glares at the group of boys crowded around me with eyes that aren't green or brown, but a unique shade of their own. Even his hair is perfect, shaved tight at the back and sides and graded into dirty blonde, messy spikes on top of his head. Whoever he is, he seems to be stealing my words and my breath all at the same time.

I watch him sit at the desk a row to my left, just in front of mine. His choice pleases me, it should allow me to look at him during the lesson without him noticing.

Mrs. Wallace hushes everyone as she comes through the door, dropping a tall stack of folders on top of her desk.

"Come on, take your seats. Books open. Time to enter the mind of Fitzgerald." She tries her best to draw enthusiasm from the loud groans and over-exaggerated eye rolls everyone makes as they disperse to settle at their desks.

Luke is the last one to move, narrowing his eyes at me as he pushes himself off my desk and takes a seat at his own.

I find it impossible to focus and spend the entire lesson entranced by the new guy. I scribble doodles instead of taking the notes I should be jotting. Towards the end of the lesson, he glances over his shoulder and catches me staring. I don't look away despite my head screaming at me to, I'm far too distracted by how much I like the silver ring he has pierced through his left nostril.

His eyes scan me, looking neither impressed nor disappointed with what he sees, and I feel my lips pull up into a wide smile that I'm sure looks embarrassingly desperate. One that quickly fades away when it becomes apparent he has no intention of returning it.

Not that I'm surprised, he doesn't seem the smiling kind.

His eyes continue to burn through me, it's intense and makes me feel uncomfortable and enthralled all at the same time.

Cassie Meadows wastes no time making her intentions clear, leaning over her desk she taps her finger on his ledge of a shoulder and he breaks our eye contact to turn to her. She fakes a blush as she passes him a folded up piece of paper. If I worried about my smile being shameful, she tops it with the high pitched giggle sound she makes as he takes the note from between her fingers.

I watch him smirk to himself as he reads her message, and I don't bother straining my eyes to find out what it says. It'll be some mindless compliment like 'you're hot' or an offer to 'make out' during free period.

Anything with a dick fancies Cassie Meadows, which is why I'm shocked when he crushes up her note in his huge fist, waiting until Mrs. Wallace isn't looking before tossing it with impressive aim into the wastepaper basket in front of her desk.

Cassie does a real shit job holding back the shock of her rejection. Her mouth opening like a tunnel, and this time a not so fake flush finds her cheeks. The girl isn't used to being turned down, none of the cheerleaders are.

The bell makes me jump, and clumsily I gather up my stuff and head out of class as fast as possible. Avoiding making eye contact with the new guy again, I don't want it to result in me smiling like an idiot at him for a second time. I also can't run the risk of Luke tripping me up or embarrassing me in front of him either.

When I get to science class, I take a stool at the station I share with Abby. Naturally, she wants to know everything about the new guy when I tell her he's in my class. I fill her in on the Cassie gossip. Then find myself describing his chiseled jaw and full pouty lips in way too much detail. Abby likes the sound of the nose ring and the tattoos. They're my favorite part too, though I don't admit that to her.

I pass through the rest of the morning without seeing him again. There's no sign of him in the lunch hall at lunchtime, and it's not until last period when I step into my math class that the sight of him stops me on the spot.

He's already seated at the back of the class, slouched back comfortably, with his arms crossed and his legs set wide apart beneath what everyone knows is Luke Robinson's desk.

I contemplate warning him, telling him that no one, ever, sits at Luke's desk. Not even if he's not here. But that would entail stringing a whole sentence together and I damn near struggle to breathe with him around me, let alone speak. Besides, I got a feeling the guy can handle himself if he needs to.

I hear the noisy crowd always led by Luke moving down the hall, and it's too late for warnings now. Stepping away from the door, I offer new guy an apologetic smile before I sit down myself.

Instant silence falls among them when all eyes settle on Luke's desk and the imposter sitting in his space.

Luke looks at Drew, his chief ring-rimmer, and they exchange a snigger. I swivel around in my seat to get a better view of the action, watching on with everyone else in the room. The showdown is inevitable, new guy is looking in no hurry to budge.

"Dude, that's my space," Luke speaks to him like he's dumb, and it takes the longest time before for him to get a response. New kid leans forward and slowly examines the desk, before a confused frown sets on his lips and he soothes his tattooed hand over its surface.

"Don't see the reservation," he says. It's the first time I've heard him talk, and I feel the vibration of each deep tone he releases.

Luke glances back at his friends and chuckles cockily. But I can sense his unease.

"I get it, you're new, right? I don't mind explaining this once for ya." Luke's eyes roll as he steps forward and holds out his hand. "Luke Robinson, captain of the football team."

The new guy stares at the hand in front of him, before raising his eyes up to stare right through him. His head nods slowly while the whole room holds their breath, waiting for his response. Luke's hand remains hanging between them, and new guy leans forward resting his impressively sized forearm across the desk.

"Nyx… and I don't give a fuck who you are, find somewhere new to sit," he says, without shifting his eyes away from Luke's.

The gasps of shock come in unison. And I watch in amazement as Luke's mouth moves, but words fail to come out of it.

"Yo, Luke, there's a seat over here," his buddy Drew calls over in an attempt to shade any embarrassment for his captain. And sensible enough not to challenge, Luke nods back, making his way over to join his friend. Nyx eyeballs Luke for his whole journey across the room, a detection of a smirk rising on his lip when he watches Luke take the desk beside Drew.

Nyx, his name is as edgy as he is, and although he looks a lot like trouble, I already like him… a lot.

CHAPTER 3

Ella Jackson. My golden ticket to getting a full patch at the club, and even damn prettier in the flesh. I've been staring at her picture for weeks now, waiting for Prez to have all the final touches in place before I could start my task. Those big hazel eyes had already etched a scar into my soul long before they'd stared back at me in an English class. She's tortured me through a photograph, and now, seeing her for real is much, much worse.

If those eyes ain't enough to drive me crazy, watching her smile is most definitely the finisher. Something as simple as a sweet, innocent smirk coming from her brings me to my fuckin' knees, and it takes all my willpower not to respond to it. Add to all that the fact that she's strictly off-limits, it just about makes Ella Jackson the most desirable creature fucking walking.

Once my first school day is finally wrapped up, I get out of the shit hole and head straight for my bike. Ella steps out a few minutes later, walking over to the far corner of the parking lot where her and the red-haired girl she hangs around with jump excitedly around a new model Mercedes.

Ella gets behind the wheel, her friend taking the passenger side, and when they drive out, I flick my unfinished smoke onto the tarmac, crush it under my boot, and set to following them. I hang far enough back to not get seen, managing to tail them all the way to the mall undetected. Then parking up, I watch them disappear inside, both of them without a care in their privileged little worlds.

I remain seated on my bike, cutting out the engine and lighting up another cigarette.

My ride is still far from being finished, but she's rideable. It's in the Dirty Soul Club rules that you have to build your own bike from scratch before making the cut—we're a motorcycle club after all.

I'm no mechanic, would never claim to be. Thankfully, Skid and Jessie, the club VP, has put a lot of time into helping me make the chassis of my Bobber roadworthy. It's been a hell of a lot easier without Chop being at the garage. That son of a bitch never liked me.

I've learned more about mechanics these past few months without him here then I have since I started hanging around the club. And I'm proud of what I've achieved. She's a classic, she's reliable, and when I'm finished with her she'll turn heads. I still prefer the dirt bike Tac gave me a few years back, but rules are rules and when it comes to the club, I usually stick by them.

Ella and her friend stay inside for the best part of two hours, and I start to grow impatient when I think about all the things I could be doing either back at the club or at the studio. Soul Inc is one of the legit businesses owned by the club and ran by Tac. This time of year we are always busy. Fresher's from Pines Peak College are always eager to get inked and Tac usually jobs me with all the lame-ass fraternity and sorority tattoos to lighten up his workload.

It may not be what I want to be doing, but skin is skin and if I want to get as good as Tac, I need the practice.

I sit up straight from resting on my handlebars when the girls came back into view. Ella and her friend are both walking towards her car, arms loaded with bags and huge smiles on their faces. I start up my bike while they're still far enough away for the loud rattle of its engine not to distract them from their chatting. Then stay on their tail when they leave the parking lot, making sure to keep a few cars between us. They drive back towards town, with the roof up and their music loud.

I have to think fast when Ella suddenly veers off and slides into a parking space outside one of the restaurants on Main Street. Taking a sharp left I head down a side street and park my bike, returning to the main street on foot, and shelter myself down an alley opposite the restaurant.

The place looks really fancy, the kinda joint I'd struggle to read the shit off the menus in. Both of them head inside and when the waiter shows them to a table out on the terrace I make myself comfortable, crossing my arms and leaning against the brick wall.

From over here I can take her in properly. Observe how she eats, and watch on as her friend makes her giggle until she's almost snorting. It ain't frustrating like it was when she was inside the mall. It don't matter that it takes her ages to place an order, or that when her food comes she takes such tiny, delicate mouthfuls from her plate. Not while I can study her movements and appreciate her smile.

It starts to get dark, and the neatly trimmed bushes that separate the dining area from the sidewalk light up, creating a soft glow that makes her look even more beautiful. The tips of her brown hair illuminating gold, and the highlights on her skin making my fingers twitch to sketch her.

After staring at the dessert menu for over ten minutes, she puts it down, picks it back up again, then eventually decides against the idea, quickly paying the check before she changes her mind again.

I continue to follow Ella as she drops her friend home, then on to her place. Of course, I already know where she lives, everything is in the details Prez gave me and I already scouted the place a few weeks ago. To lessen the risk of being spotted, I park my bike on a street nearby, pull my hood up, and walk the rest of the way.

The street she lives on is picture fuckin' perfect. All of the mansion-style homes are spaced wide apart, with immaculately kept front lawns and fancy cars on the drive. I'm careful to avoid any street lights and manage to find myself a space hidden in the shadows under one of the trees opposite her place.

Her car is the only one parked on the drive, so I assume she's home alone. It seems odd that her parents aren't around to celebrate her birthday with her, but then, what do I know about parents?

I wait for an upstairs light to switch on to indicate which of the rooms belong to her. That information may not be on Prez's need to know list, but it's sure as fuck on mine, and after a few minutes with no sign of movement I decide to check out the back of the house. When I'd scouted the area before, I found the best way to access the back of the house was to follow the tall red-bricked wall surrounding the property all the way round to the back.

The wall is too high to see over, so I climb the huge Oak tree that hangs over it that I already decided would be perfect for hiding and watching from.

There's light coming from one of the rooms upstairs, and despite the slight chill in the air now, the balcony doors are wide open.

I detect some movement and when Ella comes into sight, she's changed into a tank top and a tiny pair of PJ shorts. Even from way back here, they drag all my attention to the curve of her ass and her toned legs. I can't help think how incredible they'd look bouncing off my thighs.

She moves around her room, unaware that she's being watched, and it feels like I'm stealing something from her. Snatching away her personal space, yet I continue to watch as she ties up her hair messily on top of her head, and flops out on her bed to flick through a magazine. When she's done with that, she rolls on her front and scrolls through her phone. She's doing nothing of any relevance and looks bored as hell with it, but I can't take my eyes off her.

I'd happily sit in this tree all night watching her smile at her phone and twist stray bits of her hair around her fingertips. And I lose track of the time until her mouth opens wide with a long yawn, and her body stretches out. She reaches over and turns out her bedside light, and despite no longer being able to see her, I stay put. I wait at least another half an hour without any signs of movement until I assume she's fallen asleep.

The ride back to the club is a good forty minutes from here. I should be getting back. But there's something niggling at me that prevents me from leaving.

It's pathetic, but Ella falling asleep with her balcony doors wide open bothers me. I don't like the idea of leaving her vulnerable.

Prez wouldn't like it either.

I studied the place well the last time I came here, figured I'd be able to climb the wall with the aid of this tree without much effort, which means that someone else could too.

Scratching at the back of my head, I tell myself I should just leave. It's no big deal, the girl sleeps with her door open, I suspect in a neighborhood like this, most people do. But every time I think about jumping out the tree and leaving, I can't.

I tell myself I'm doing it for Prez when I stretch my leg out from the thick tree branch and hook it over the wall. He wouldn't want me leaving her exposed, especially with her being home all by herself. Sliding down the other side of the wall, my feet thud onto the ground below and I move quickly. Making sure to keep low as I run across the lawn, closer to the house.

I manage to get to the patio beneath Ella's balcony without setting off any alarm systems or outdoor lights, and I assess my options.

There's a trellis mounted to the wall, it'd be easy to climb it then reach across to her balcony, but I doubt it would be strong enough to take my weight. On the other side of her balcony is a wooden veranda. Green plants growing around the structure, creating a roof of leaves over an elaborate outside dining area. After inspecting it from the inside, I figure I can climb up on the table then up through the rafters and use them to get across. And just a few minutes later, I'm standing on Ella's balcony without even breaking a sweat.

I choose to ignore the comfort I get in knowing how easily I could do it again if I wanted to. This has to be a one-off.

Creeping closer to her doors I have every intention of closing them and leaving straight after. But my plan goes completely to shit when I hear a tiny faint moan come from her mouth and I step through the doors instead of closing them. It's a move that's risky, not to mention creepy as fuck. But she's drawing me in, just like those long inhales of breath she's continuing to make as I move closer to her.

She's sound asleep. And fuck… if she woke up and saw me, she'd be petrified. Yet I still take the chance. The moon provides just enough light for me to see her face. She's dreaming, her head moving, and her face creasing like she's hurting.

I feel an overwhelming urge to disturb her, to save her from whatever nightmare she's having. But I know that seeing me here like this would only be waking her up into a new one. So, instead, I watch her… My heart-beating faster, and my cock growing thicker inside my jeans.

Her covers are moving, her body struggling beneath them

and when they slide away from her, I realize that the expression on her face ain't been drawn outta pain.

Her delicate little hand is buried beneath the waist of her shorts, and her fingers are rubbing circles between her thighs

Ella Jackson is getting herself off.

Her teeth are sunk into her bottom lip, signaling she's close, and temptation replaces any sense when I step even closer.

The fact she's not actually asleep, or that if she is she could wake up any second becomes an irrelevant factor when her breaths become sharper, and her strokes get desperately faster. I want to resist. To back off, but there's no chance of that happening, not now that I no longer fear her catching me.

Missing out on feeling her pussy pulse as she comes seems like far too great a sacrifice.

Only the thin cotton of her shorts separates our skin when I gently cup my hand over hers. She's lost any rhythm, her body too needy, and too near climax.

Crushing my hand tighter against hers, I give her just a little more pressure, the pressure she needs to send herself over the edge. Her hips bucking, and her mouth opening wide. The relief in the moan she makes travels right through my body and causes my skin to shiver. Especially when she soaks right through the flimsy fabric and dampens my palm.

A beautiful, satisfied smile spreads across her mouth, and her eyes remain closed. Impulse overcomes logic all over again when I lean even closer and hold my mouth over hers. I skim the surface of her lips with mine to get a taste of her. The next shudder she makes causes one of her breaths to seep between my lips and fuck, I'm a gonner.

I keep my eyes open, waiting for her to wake, to be horrified when she realizes an intruder in her room just stole an orgasm right from beneath her fingertips. But she doesn't, her eyes remain closed, and her body relaxes.

Fighting every testosterone-driven urge in my body, I somehow drag myself away from her. Putting enough space between us for me to find some sense and back out onto the balcony. I allow myself a few more seconds to watch her. The wind picks up, whipping around the back of my neck and lifting up the white sheer fabric curtains on either side of her door, blowing them in front of me.

I notice her eyelashes began to flicker, and quickly close the doors. I can't lock them from the outside so I'm not fully satisfied, but they at least look secure. I jump the balcony wall back onto the veranda rafters. Then lower myself back to the ground.

This time I avoid the pristine green stripes of the lawn, staying tight to the wall, and use the storage locker beside the pool house to scale myself back over it.

My heart thumps and my cock throbs as I march back to my bike, pissed at myself for being so stupid. It's only day one and I've already crossed the fuckin' line with Prez's daughter. Hell, even if she wasn't his daughter, creeping into girl's bedrooms and watching them get themselves off isn't exactly chivalrous, even by my standards.

I beat myself up about it the whole ride back to the club. What would I have done if she'd woken up and seen me? How could I explain to Prez that I couldn't watch his girl anymore because she'd taken out a restraining order on me?

I pull up at the club and head straight to the back bar to get a drink. I'm done with being a high schooler today. Taking a stool at the bar, I immediately feel Mel's talons scratching at my back.

"Tough day, soldier, you wanna unwind?" she asks. The bitch has got even more desperate since Jessie got himself an old lady. Mel had convinced herself that she was gonna be the one riding the back of his bike someday. She'd even told me it herself one night after I'd finished fucking her. Not one for pillow talk, I bailed before she started crying on me.

"Not tonight, Mel. I'm tired," the lie rolls off my tongue easily. I never get tired, I hardly ever sleep. Real truth is, I don't want her erasing anything I have of Ella in my head, or from my fucking hand for that matter.

"Nyx, hop behind the bar, free up Stacey-Marie," a gruff voice comes from behind me, and I scowl over my shoulder at Squealer.

I've been the only prospect here since Tommy ran scared after his Pa turned traitor. I hate working the bar, 'specially when club bitches get in my way.

"Unless you wanna come over here and suck my dick," Squealer adds with a smirk, his hand grabbing his dick through his jeans and shaking it at me.

I stand up from my stool ready to step up to him, Prospect or not I ain't about to let him speak to me like that, but a heavy hand lands on my shoulder and holds me firm.

"Sorry Squeal, you're either gonna have to go blue ball or thirsty. I already got a job for the Prospect," Prez speaks up.

"Maybe Stacey-Marie should learn to pour and suck at the same time," I snigger back at Squeal as I pass him. A comment like that coming from the mouth of a prospect would have earned anyone else knuckles, but the brothers here know not to push me too far. I'm as big as most of them are, and I fight back.

He flips me the finger as I follow Prez out of the main bar and into the smaller lounge bar, the one where only members are allowed.

Once we're alone, just the low drum of music from the backroom vibrating through the walls, Prez picks a blunt up from the ashtray and blazes up. He sucks hard on the tip before passing it over to me and I take it, relaxing a little as that first deep toke filters into my lungs.

"How'd it go today?" he asks, eyes curious, "You manage to get close to her?"

Close enough that I can still smell her fucking cunt on my fingers… is not the reply I go with, and I feel the devil judging me as I leave that bit out.

"I had two classes with her, followed her on to the mall after school and then to a restaurant in Castle Rock. I kept with her until she got home."

I leave out the part about me locating her bedroom and climbing on her balcony. Think it's best I don't mention that her lips against mine tasted like cherries, or that I can still imagine her pussy pulsing against my fingertips. I don't want to end up being Grimm's latest problem.

"She turned eighteen today," he tells me, it almost feels like he's confiding in me or some shit. And he quickly clears out his throat. "The judge, you see him?"

"No sir, the girl was home alone. Well, that's what I figure anyway, there were no cars on the drive apart from hers."

Prez nods his head, and I can see he's thinking hard about something.

"The only way we're gonna know what's going on behind the doors of that home is by someone talking to her, or to someone who knows her well. You reckon you can get closer?"

"I'll do my best, Prez," I nod, it's a promise I know I can keep. I want to get closer. Close enough to know how that warm, wet pussy feels squeezing my dick. I'm raging hate for whoever she'd been dreaming about while she touched herself, I wanna slit the throat of whoever's hand she'd imagined sliding into those tight shorts to play with her clit.

"You keep your eye on that Judge, boy," Prez's warning snaps me out of the recollection I've got stored in my head of her. "Go to your cabin, get some sleep, I'll cover you with the brothers."

I nod at him before leaving, grateful for the opportunity of some space, after today and the restraints I've had to put on myself, I can't see myself having much tolerance for bullshit.

I ride up to my cabin. Thankfully I don't share with anyone anymore. Tac moved into the flat above the Studio last year which suited me fine, I like my own space. Inside my cabin is minimal, once a week I slip one of the club sluts a few bucks to keep the place clean, even though I hardly spend any time here. I'm always either down at the club or at the studio with Tac.

Tac had been my fuckin' salvation as a kid. I was only fourteen when I came here to Manitou Springs. It was the closest Dirty Soul's Charter to the foster home I ran out on, and Tac was the first member I came across.

Somewhere between the foster homes I was constantly being kicked out of, I'd convinced myself that the Dirty Soul who had checked in on me all those years before had been my Pa. I wanted to find him. So, I hung around outside the tattoo studio where the bald-headed, ink-covered biker worked every chance I got, watching and listening out for any information I could get.

Tac soon noticed me, took me off the street and fed me. He put a roof over my head, and I repaid him by working in the shop, cleaning equipment. Even helping a little with the under counter businesses for him and the club as I got older. Earning his trust was how I became a prospect with him as my sponsor.

At first, I'd seen Tac as a way into the club, but it was way before I became Prospect that I realized how valuable he was to me. And for a really long time, I really hoped it would be him.

I put off doing the DNA test for months in fear of disappointment, but in the end, curiosity won over, and I sent off for a kit. I managed to swipe a swab sample when he'd passed out one night at the club, and all that disappointment I'd sworn from the age of ten I'd never let myself be a victim of again, rushed back when the results came back negative.

Tac's a dirty bastard, he works, plays, and fucks hard, but he's had my back from the day we met, and he taught me a skill that expresses the only talent I possess.

I spend all my free time sketching, putting together tattoo ideas for the brothers and studio clients. I haven't done a lot of work on skin, but Tac is becoming more and more trusting. I've even inked him a few times. And after he saw the work I did on one of Jessie's less than willing volunteers a few months back, he was impressed. Slowly he's starting to give me more responsibility.

A few weeks ago, Jessie asked me to sketch him another design. He'd already trusted me to ink his old lady's name on his chest and wants his next one to be in memory of Hayley. Him and Prez's daughter had been like brother and sister. Everyone around here knows how deep he hurts from losing her. So there's a lot of pressure on me to do it justice.

I figure now is as good a time as any to get started. It might take my mind off Ella Jackson and the expression her face made as she shuddered against my lips and fingers.

If I'm gonna get this task done for Prez, and survive long enough to get my cut, I'm gonna need to get a grip. I've tried telling myself all day that the only reason I want her is because I can't have her. It ain't hard to dip your dick around here, even if you ain't a fully patched member. Females come far too easy.

But no one touches Prez's daughter, doesn't matter that her hair bounces as she walks, or that her hazel eyes burn into your soul, sucking you so deep that not even death scares you enough to resist her.

She is off fucking limits.

I throw my keys on the table and sit on one of the chairs, tracing my bottom lip with the finger I'd touched her with. I desperately seek out the taste of her, but any trace has vanished. So, picking up a pencil and flicking to a clean page in my sketchbook, I set to work.

When I look down at my sketchpad, it's her eyes staring back up at me.

Instead of the portrait of Hayley I should have been sketching for Jessie, I've etched out every flawless detail of Ella's face, captured every curve in the smile she'd shot me with in class this morning. I regret not smiling back at her now, but at the time it felt wrong. I don't deserve Ella's smiles. I'm the shadow of a lifelong lie that hangs over her perfect little world. The plague of a secret who has been sent to watch her and report the private details of her life back to a man she doesn't even know exists. Ella Jackson will probably never know who her real father is, and I take comfort in the fact we have at least that in common 'cause apart from that, we couldn't be any further apart.

CHAPTER 4: ELLA

He'd stood like an angel, white fabric blowing around his body while his eyes burned like hot embers. I don't want to wake up, my skin still tingles, and I feel strangely satisfied. I touch myself between my legs, and I'm… I'm wet. Jesus, I thought only boys had this kinda thing happen to them.

Shooting out of bed I strip out of my shorts and underwear, throw on a robe and head straight for the shower. My reflection blushes back at me from the bathroom mirror.

How am I ever gonna face Nyx now? It's hard enough as it is.

I've never really tried touching myself before, despite Abby telling me I should. I wasn't even sure exactly how you were supposed to do it. Clearly just the thought of the new guy had been enough to get me off in my sleep.

My dream had felt so real with his surprisingly soft lips touching mine. I'd sensed his fear, and that's how I know it was all in my head. I don't know anything about Nyx but I'm sure that he doesn't know anything about being gentle, and I'm certain that he fears absolutely nothing.

What I imagined last night must have been my own creative version of him. Yet the shiver that had climbed up my spine when his hand had touched between my legs had felt very, very real.

My cheeks flush, and I splash them down with cold water before I recollect any more of my dream. I blush just from the thought of seeing him at school, knowing I'm going to burst into the flames of shame the moment he walks through the door into English class. But thought of seeing him also stirs a strange kind of excitement in my stomach.

"You look pretty, Miss Jackson." Penelope smiles at me when I get downstairs, handing me a plate of eggs with some turkey rashers on the side.

"Thanks." I smile back taking a seat at the table. I'd hoped my extended efforts in front of the mirror weren't gonna be quite so obvious, but then Penelope does have a habit of noticing absolutely everything.

She's more than a housekeeper to me, she's a friend. It was her who took the time to explain what was happening to me when I got my first period and freaked out. My first instinct had been that there was something wrong with me, and I tried to hide it from Mom. I was ten years old, and even back then I didn't want Mom to worry about me. For as long as I can remember she's been on the verge of a breakdown.

Penelope noticed the change in me, and sat me down and explained that everything was normal.

She always has a way of knowing when I'm feeling down, and cheers me up either with my favorite breakfast or by rearranging a towel on my bed the same way they do in fancy hotels.

"The annual Mother and Daughter Luncheon at the club is only two weeks away, darling. I thought we could go to the mall this weekend and pick out something to complement each other." Mom looks at me across the table, popping a strawberry into her mouth from the fruit salad that Penelope prepares for her every morning.

"Do you really need me to go this year?" I sigh. Every year for as long as I can remember, Mom has dressed me up like a pretty doll and paraded me in front of the people at Father's gentlemen's club. I'd hoped that turning eighteen would have freed me of that kind of obligation.

"Darling, you love the luncheon. You have since you were a little. Besides it wouldn't be much of a Mother-Daughter Luncheon if I turned up without my daughter, now would it?" she laughs nervously, side glancing Father and expecting a reaction.

"It's just not really my thing anymore, Mom," I tell her. Immediately feeling guilty when her eyes sag in disappointment. Guilty enough to put my feelings aside and tell her that of course, I'll go with her. Just as I open my mouth to speak, I get silenced by a heavy fist slamming the kitchen table.

"You will do as your mother tells you." Father's voice is firm, and only raised a little more than his usual tone, it's his eyes that threaten. They dare me to argue back, and it isn't until he's convinced I'm not going to, that he releases me from his stare.

"Besides, who will keep Abby company if you don't go. You wouldn't leave her to socialize alone with those wretched Hannigan sisters, would you? Heaven knows how their father ever became a member of the club. It just proves that money can buy anything," Mom rambles, acting as if Father's outburst didn't just happen.

I pull together a fake smile especially for her.

"Of course I'll be there," I promise, getting up and kissing her cheek before I leave for school. I don't bother with a goodbye to Dad. He probably wouldn't respond anyway.

Arriving at school, I drop my books off at my locker and watch every girl turn their head and follow Nyx as he walks along the corridor. He doesn't react to their attention, either he doesn't notice them, or he's the most arrogant prick on the planet. I look down at the grey shaded rose he's got inked on his hand, and thoughts of him touching me like he did in my dream causes a shameful flutter between my legs and burning in my cheeks. He's wearing sunglasses so I can't see where his eyes are looking, and I quickly remember that the shades are sheltering his eyes and not mine. Whipping my head around quickly I yelp out loud when I accidentally clip my temple on the corner of my locker.

"Shit," I curse, pressing the heel of my palm against where it hurts. When I pull it away again, I see blood.

This can't get any worse and I'm just thankful there's no sign of Nyx when I make an embarrassed check back over my shoulder.

I keep my fingers over the cut, attempting to stop any more bleeding while taking out my English book with my free hand. When I slam my locker door shut, he's standing right behind it and I jump in shock, making another pathetic noise. His arms are crossed over his chest, his back resting against the locker beside mine and I swallow back hard trying not to stare at his huge biceps.

He doesn't speak, his mouth is set straight, and his eyes are still hidden behind his shades. And when he raises that rose inked hand, the same one that owned my dreams the night before, I realize he's clutching a bunch of tissues inside his fist.

I stare at him for far too long. Mostly at his lips, they look edibly soft, and I swear I can almost taste them pressing against mine the way they had in my fantasy.

With a nervous giggle I reach out and take the tissues, subtly brushing over his knuckles with my fingertips at the same time because I have to know if they feel as rough as they look.

"Thanks," I smile, focusing hard on the tissues in my hand. Too afraid to look up now that he's pushed the glasses on top of his head and his eyes are exposed to me.

"They're for your head." His voice is low and raspy, and his forehead scrunches slightly as he looks to where our hand's touch. Probably wondering why I'm still staring at the bunch of tissues he's grabbed for me instead of putting them to use.

"How hard ya hit it?" he smirks, and as beautiful as it looks on him, I can't pinpoint if he's genuinely concerned or mocking me with sarcasm.

"Oh, this… It's nothing. I'm fine… and thank you." I pull away quickly, holding up the tissues to awkwardly wave them at him before pressing them against my graze.

He must think I'm batshit crazy.

Nyx tips his head at me before casually walking off in the direction of our English class. I hear Luke and his posse coming down the corridor, so quickly scurry after Nyx, entering the room just a beat after he does. He doesn't look up from his seat at the back of the room, and I'm not at all surprised that he's taken the desk Luke usually occupies.

I keep the tissue tight to my head. Already hating the fact I won't be able to look at him without turning around, he proved his point in math, why did he have to move desks in English? Where he'd sat yesterday had given me the perfect view.

Luke stares over me and straight at Nyx when he walks into class, but he doesn't challenge him. Instead, he takes a seat on a desk a few spaces away.

At least today I get some work done during lesson time, although I swear I feel Nyx's eyes burning through the back of my head.

There's something mysterious about him that has me desperate to know what he does with his time out of school. I wonder if he comes from a good family? He's too young to have so many tattoos. His parents must be pretty cool. My father would have a coronary if I ever got one.

"My mom's started talking about the luncheon already, wants to go to the mall for coordinated outfits," I tell Abby when we meet up in the canteen at lunchtime.

"Don't… my mom's been going on about it for weeks. At

least we have each other to pull us through it." She rolls her eyes before stabbing a plastic fork into her Caesar salad.

"True," I shrug, as Nyx chooses the exact moment I look up to enter the canteen. Sitting in the corner alone, he pulls a pad out of his bag, props his foot up on one of the benches and slides down the pencil from behind his ear. Whatever it is in front of him has his full attention, and I watch his hand moving fast over the page as he sketches, stopping now and again to smudge his finger over the paper.

"I heard that his parents travel a lot, apparently he never settles in one place for too long," one of the cheer girls' comments to her friend as they move past us.

"Maybe that's why he's not very friendly. I'll bet his cock is huge," the girl she walks with adds, and they both giggle.

Abby and I both smirk. My best friend is a lot like me, just a little more experienced in the fact she's actually got to second base with a guy.

It's obvious she likes Nyx too. Every girl in the school likes Nyx. He acts and looks so much older than anyone else, and doesn't seem the slightest bit bothered by what anyone thinks of him. Since he came into my English class yesterday, he's owned every thought in my head. Which serves as a nice distraction from worrying about Mom.

My mom seems to have one purpose in her sad excuse for a life, and that's to keep Father happy. Which is a tireless mission considering the man is never satisfied. She does her best to keep everything to his liking, attends all the dinner parties they get invited to, always makes sure she looks in prime condition. She encourages me to behave the way the daughter of a well-respected judge should, and forgives him countlessly for taking every hard day or bad mood out on her.

Joanne Jackson is the perfect wife, but I've long given up aspiring to be the model daughter. I have a rebellious streak inside me, one that I choose to keep secret. I do things subtly and solely for self-satisfaction. That way Mom doesn't get in trouble.

Petty little actions that have no purpose other than to piss Father off. Like last week when I snuck into his office when he was at work and took his favorite crystal tumbler. I knew it would irritate him to think he'd misplaced it. Judge Jackson isn't clumsy like that… Which is why three days later I returned it to his office, placing it somewhere I know he would have already looked.

I've had to watch for years as he's slowly driven my mom to the brink of insanity, and gradually I intend to do the same to him.

Hating your own flesh and blood isn't easy. Detesting the person who is half responsible for giving you life brings with it a disgruntled guilt

I've known from a young age that despite the image my father portrays to others, he's a cruel man. There is nothing about him that hints at empathy for the way he hurts my mom, and so I struggle to find any in my actions towards him.

PE is straight after lunch, and the only reason I look forward to it is because Abby is in my class. It's no shock that the class conversation continues to center around Nyx. What the girls usually gossip about isn't an interest to me, but today I find myself doing my stretches a little closer to them so I can listen.

I even agree with what they say on this occasion, the boys are running track, and Nyx in a tight vest and shorts is hard not to notice. His thighs are thick like his arms, the muscles in them straining tight as he sprints around the track.

More rumors come in as the lesson goes on. Apparently, he's been expelled from every school he's attended. There's a theory being thrown that he's in the witness protection program. And my personal favorite is the story about him recently coming out of juvie for almost killing a kid from his last school.

By the end of the lesson, I've decided that one way or

another I want to find out what his real story is. I know it's not gonna be easy but I do like a challenge now and again.

When school finishes, I head straight out to my car. Nyx is on the other side of the parking lot, walking towards a bike. It's a classic sort, not like the racer bikes Luke and his friends brag about owning and tear through town on at the weekends.

No, Nyx's bike is rustic and rough. It suits him perfectly. I watch him balance a cigarette between his lips, then use a zippo to light it up. When his eyes flick up from the flame, they focus on me, and even with the vast distance between us, I feel the intensity in his stare.

All sense wills me to look away from him, and yet my eyes continue to participate in the stare-off, watching him straddle his seat and grab the handlebars. Suddenly, I realize how pathetic I must look, and shake myself back to reality before hopping inside my car. Even then I find myself angling my mirrors so I can still see him.

"Whatcha doin'?" Abby startles me when her hand slams against my window.

"Jeez, you scared me." I breathe slowly to calm myself back down.

"You weren't gonna leave without me, were ya?" She laughs.

"Of course I wasn't. I was just…" I give up on trying to explain. "You know I wouldn't have left without you. Come on, we're hanging out at yours tonight."

I start the ignition and pull out of the parking lot, noticing how Nyx's head moves to follow my car as we pass him, his lips parting just enough to blow out a long stream of smoke.

"That guy is something else," Abby rolls her head back in the seat.

"I don't get what all the fuss is about." I shrug, pretending to concentrate on the road while I tell my best friend a blatant lie. "And if the rumors are true, he won't be with us for much longer. So it's pointless getting yourself excited."

"Well, one person will definitely be glad to see the back of him." Abby raises her perfectly plucked eyebrows at me. "Luke hates him. Whatever that new hot bod did the past two days has really rubbed him up the wrong way."

"Well, then I guess the guy's good for something after all." I smirk, pulling out onto the main street and driving us back to Abby's so I can avoid my parents right up until curfew.

CHAPTER 5

NYX

Ella almost knocking herself out wasn't exactly how I planned on making the first verbal contact with her. Still, I grabbed the opportunity by the balls and went in.

The blood that seeped out of her wound was the sweetest shade of red I've ever seen, glistening like a ripe red apple as it trickled down her temple. Somehow I'd managed not to get distracted, keeping our encounter brief. But I still analyzed it over and over in my head after, wondering if she'd picked up on the tension in me. The last thing I'd wanted to do was scare her, or have her thinking I'm a weirdo.

I'd almost forgotten how shit high school could be, the same, pathetic hierarchy system is still in place, the one that I have no real place in. I've quickly, and without even trying, become the kid everyone avoids again. Not that I'm bothered, I ain't here to make friends.

Ella goes straight to her friend's place after school. And even though Prez doesn't expect a report on her every night. I follow her there anyway.

I wait across the street, hiding out of sight the entire time she's there, then I follow her back home, keeping a safe distance. The whole time telling myself that I'm just doin' a thorough job for Prez.

When she pulls up on her drive and lets herself in. I know

she's safe. I could leave, but instead, I find myself repeating the same actions as the night before. Leaving my bike out of sight, and sprinting around the back of the house to climb the tree.

From the thick branch on the other side of the wall, I watch Ella move around her room. She gets some homework done. Which reminds me that I have fuckin' homework to worry about too now. She searches through her wardrobe, deciding on an outfit that she hangs on the door. I assume it'll be what I see her in tomorrow, and already I can't fucking wait.

It isn't long after she finishes that she turns the light out, and satisfied that her balcony doors are shut tight I prepare myself to leave.

As I go to jump back to the ground, I notice another light on downstairs. It's over on the other side of the house, and much dimmer, but the pitch-black surrounding me allows me to see him clear enough.

The judge, sits at his desk, reading through what looks like a file, completely unaware that he's being watched. Judge Jackson is a large man, with a stern face and thin blonde hair that sweeps back from his forehead. I watch him sip from his crystal tumbler until it's empty and then top it back up again.

Looking at the house from back here it reminds me of the Dolls house one of my foster moms had. We were never allowed to touch it, only ever to look. That never bothered me, I didn't want to play with it anyway. It was far too perfect.

Instead, I'd sit and stare at it for hours. Making up in my head the normal family that lived inside it. A Dad who came home from work and cut the lawns, a Mom who fussed and made sure you ate all your greens before you got dessert. The family my head invented had three kids. Two older brothers who fought like shit, but the minute someone else turned on the other, they unleashed hell. And a sister who wound up her older brothers tirelessly. I feel stupid when I think of the hours I'd wasted making up stories for them. I haven't thought about that family in a long time. Not at all since I'd found my own fucked up family at the club.

And on that thought, I leave Ella in her perfect little house and get back to where I belong.

I wake up in a shit mood. When I got back from Ella's last night, the club was busy and I ended up working the bar till early hours after all the girls got occupied. Usually, I don't need much sleep, but lately, I've been feeling exhausted.

I attempt to wake myself up in the shower before I leave my cabin, but I still feel spaced when I step out onto my front porch. Tac's waiting on his bike, staring at me like he's expecting some kinda explanation out of me.

"Mornin'," he tips his chin at me, looking pissed as fuck.

"Mornin' yourself," I reply, fixing my bag in place before throwing my leg over my saddle.

"Ya thinkin' of showing your face at the studio anytime soon?" Tac asks before I get a chance to start my engine.

"Been busy," I tell him, hoping he ain't gonna press me on it. I haven't come up with an excuse to give the brothers yet, and even if I had one, I don't want to bullshit Tac.

"You've been busy," he scoffs a laugh, knowing damn well how much I like being at the studio.

"Nyx, there ain't been a single day in four years that you haven't come by the shop, the last two days I haven't seen a trace of ya. What's up?"

"He's been keepin' eyes out for Prez," a voice cuts in from behind me, "Prez has let Tommy going AWOL lie for too long. We got Nyx here chasing up some leads." Jessie's hand lands on my shoulder, and Tac nods acceptingly at Jessie's explanation.

"I almost feel sorry for the little bastard," Tac snarls.

He has a point, Tommy's in some deep shit, but hell if I feel sorry for him. The kid's always been an asshole in my opinion.

Tommy's Pa, Chop, had been VP before he turned on the club and killed Skid's wife. The Dirty Souls would never judge a man by another man's actions, but the fact that Tommy skipped town straight after didn't scream innocence. Since then, Jessie's pieced some shit together that indicates Tommy was in on the whole thing. So Tac's right, things ain't looking good for him.

"I got to get to the shop." Tac looks over at me. "Don't worry I got shit covered, you just focus on finding Tommy so we can get Skid some fuckin' answers." He starts up his engine, saluting us both before he rides off.

Jessie waits till he's gone, then checks around the yard for any more bodies before he speaks.

"You need any help covering up your absence around here, let me know," he slaps my back before hopping on his own bike and heading in the direction of the clubhouse.

I'm grateful for Jessie's help, but it doesn't stop me feelin' guilty for leaving Tac to cope at the studio. Soul Inc is the only place for miles where you can get inked. Likely due to the fact no one local is ballsy enough to set up a rival studio.

We're always busy, and I hate that after all Tac has done for me I'm having to let him down.

I have to focus on why I'm doing all this. I want the respect of a fully patched member. And when all this shit is over with, I'll make it up to Tac by putting all my efforts into becoming a kick-ass tattooist and freeing up some time for him.

I arrive at school just in time to see Ella get out of her car. She's wearing a massive smile on her face as she walks inside with her friend. And it almost forces my own lips to lift. I follow them inside, trying not to stare too hard when I pass her at her locker. That smile that looks fucking incredible on her quickly fades the second she hears Luke and his fuckwit followers walking towards her from the other end of the corridor.

It's only taken me a short time to realize that Ella's scared of him, and I hate him just for having that kinda power over her.

Luke Robinson is that jock asshole that every high school has. To me, he's a joke, but to anyone who gives a shit about what people think of them, he's venom. Everyone wants to be friends with the captain of the football team, and the whole school practically suck the kid's dick.

The way he glares at Ella with such spite gets me fucking twitchy, and I hope the reason he hates her so much is that, unlike most of the girls around here, she hasn't sucked on his fuckin' dick.

When I get to class, I purposely sit at Luke's desk at the back. Ella arrives a few minutes later, offering me the awkward little look that never fails to get a reaction out of my cock, before she sits herself down three desks in front of me.

She always seems so focused during class, I, on the other hand, have no clue what the fuck is going on. Not that it matters, I'm not here to learn about Scott what's 'is name and his long assed book.

The only subject I have to take in is her, and so far I'm excelling at that.

Luke struts inside the room like he owns it. Narrowing his eyes at me when he sees me sitting at his desk. I respond with a sarcastic smile, refusing to back down from his intense glare. He proves that he knows exactly how to rile me, when he slips his hand over Ella's head, taking one of her glossy brown curls and yanking it as he passes her.

My hands grip tight to the edge of the desk, trying to hold back a reaction. Luke touching her pisses me off more than it should. But the fact he might have hurt her in the process makes me want to stomp on his face. If the motherfucker has caused her any pain, Ella doesn't let it show, and for that, I'm proud of her.

Luke continues to wind me up all period, either by throwing scrunched up paper at her or whispering a snide remark under his breath every time she speaks up in class. I make sure he notices the silent warning I glare at him because my tolerance is rapidly upping and fucking off.

When the bell rings, I don't wait to be excused, grabbing up my shit and making sure I'm the first one out the door. My fist slams hard into the first locker I come too, driven out of pure frustration.

What the fuck am I doing? Why am I getting so defensive of her? My job is simple. Get enough information to assure the Prez she's happy. Ella isn't my problem. I'm not supposed to care about her, and I'm complicating the shit out of things.

What I should be doing is telling Prez about Luke Robinson. Guarantee that slimy prick a fucked up, Jessie style warning to back off. But it doesn't seem like justice.

I want to be the one to make Luke pay.

I want to be the one who keeps Ella safe.

I'm fucking pathetic.

Aside from PE, Art is the only subject I'm actually any good at, and I manage to relax a little once the lesson gets started. Ella's friend, Abby, takes the same class, and that girl can chat. In fact, she never stops chatting. Annoying as she is though, I see what Ella likes about her. She has good energy. Granted a little too much for me, but I'm glad Ella has someone like her in her life.

"That's real good, ya know." Abby leans over my shoulder to get a better look at my sketch. "What is it?"

"It's just something I'm drawing up for a friend," I tell her. Skid asked me last night if I'd draw him some wings to have put on his shoulder. I know they're for Carly so I wanna make them perfect for him

"Oh, so you do have friends then?" Judging by the sudden look of embarrassment on her face I'm guessing that her mouth just ran before her brain had a chance to filter.

"Yeah, I got friends." I smirk to myself, still focusing on the sketch I'm doing for Skid.

"So where are you from?" she asks. In another attempt at starting a conversation with me.

"Right now, I'm from here," I answer, unsure what to say. I didn't think to make up a backstory because I hadn't intended on talking to anyone.

"Okay…" she trails off, and for a moment I think I might actually get some peace.

"Your ink's kinda cool," she starts up again. Christ, the girl's persistent.

"Thanks." I put a stop to the conversation by putting my headphones in and burying my head back into my sketch.

There's something about drawing that calms me, it takes me out of the real world. I don't think when I sketch, not about anything important anyway. I zone out, my only focus being to get the image in my head onto the paper.

Once Abby has shut up, the lesson seems to go faster. I don't have the chance to finish up Skid's tattoo, but I've managed to get a good start on it. The lunch bell rings, and when I step out of class the corridor is already busy. Everyone's eager to rush and meet their friends, while I'm just desperate for a smoke. I manage to locate Ella without realizing I was looking for her, she's walking straight to me, more than likely on her way to meet Abby. And striding towards me she looks so fucking beautiful.

She's my calm among the chaos. A calm that quickly snaps when Luke passes her, his hand flicking up under the pile of books she's carrying, sending them crashing to the floor. Throwing his head back he roars out a laugh, turning himself around and walking backward so he gets full pleasure from her reaction. His friends laugh, and cheers follow him as he moves on.

I tense my fists to prevent myself from making a Luke

shaped dent in one of the lockers, and when he steps past me, he gives me a side glance that confirms he knows exactly how much his actions get to me. I swear to Satan if I wasn't trying to keep a low profile I'd tear the skin right off his face.

Ella flushes pink, ignoring all the cruel jibes as the group travel towards the canteen. She quickly stoops down to her knees and starts picking up her books. I think about going over to help, but don't trust myself to be that close to her. I can't promise myself that I won't touch her again.

When she's done gathering her books, she stands up and pulls her dignity back into place. Keeping her head held high as she carries on walking towards me. I'm weighed down to the floor, my eyes unable to pull away from her and Ella does everything to avoid looking back at me. Her feet rushing, and her gaze remaing on the floor as she passes. I have to clench my fists even tighter when the temptation to reach out and grab her becomes even stronger than my desire to cause Luke Robinson severe pain.

I stomp away in the opposite direction, towards the quad. There's a quiet spot under one of the trees where I can get some more drawing done. Taking a seat against the trunk, I pull out my pad and get back to working on Skid's sketch. This time I can't lose myself. There's no zoning out from my frustration. I'm too mad that Luke gets away with treating Ella like trash, and that she does jack shit to defend herself.

My cell vibrating in my pocket distracts me from thinking out all the things I could do to fuck him up. When I pull it out, I see a message from Tac asking if I can spare him a few hours later. I don't want to refuse, I've spent no time at the studio lately. So I reply, telling him I'll stop by around four.

I'm slipping my phone back in my pocket when I hear Luke's voice again, and when I look up from my pad I see him standing in front of the bench where Ella and Abby are now sitting. How did I not notice them come out here?

"What's up, Ella, you look sad?" Luke goads.

"Do one, Luke," Abby snarls at him like a mamma bear protecting a cub. It makes me like her a little more.

I'm not sure how much more of Luke Robinson's shit I can tolerate, especially with Ella sitting there, staring at the ground and looking so helpless.

"That pretty little mouth of yours not got anything to say?" Luke ignores Abby, aiming straight for his target. I stand up and step closer. Close enough to see how repulsed her face looks when he speaks up again.

"Maybe you should put those lips around my cock, and show me that you're good for something."

The light tap his fingers make against her cheek is the final trigger to me losing my shit.

I make the three strides that are left between us so fast the fucker doesn't see me coming, and Ella's disgust turns quickly to shock when I pull back my elbow and land my fist hard into Luke's jaw. His cheek wobbles against my knuckles, and a mouthful of bloody phlegm shoots from his mouth landing on the concrete path before he falls back and lands on his ass.

A sharp gasp from Ella is the only sound among everyone else's silence when I reach down and grip the collar of his shirt. I use it to drag him back to his feet, then throw him into the gang of people that follow him around like he's some kind of god.

I glance back at Ella and see the shock frozen on her face.

"You shouldn't let him speak to you like that." The words come out of me much harsher than I intended them to and her mouth hangs open. She looks like she's about to say something, but a shrill voice comes from behind me before she has the chance.

"Nicolas. My office. Now." I ignore it at first, forgetting that thanks to Jessie's old lady, Nicolas is actually me. Maddy is good at what she does, Prez assured me she's made everything tight, fixing me up with fake IDs and making me up a school history report.

I turn around and look down at the stern-faced Principal I met on my first day. I'd known within a few seconds of being in her office that she didn't like me.

Looking back at Ella, I hate how guilty she looks as she watches me follow Principal K back inside the building.

Sharp clips from her heels echo off the corridor floor as she escorts me back through reception into her office. Then making an over-exaggerated gesture with her arm, she shows me to the seat in front of her desk, slamming her door shut as soon as my ass sits down.

With her cold blank stare fixed on me, she moves towards her filing cabinet and takes out one of the brown files. Mrs. K has a 'not to be fucked with' type face, and despite her five-foot fuck all frame I can see how some might find her intimidating.

Sitting behind her desk, she clears her throat before her bony fingers begin flicking through the pages.

"Nicolas Anderson," she speaks my name like it tastes sour, and the way her eyes peer at me over her glasses makes me paranoid that she might have figured me out. If she hasn't already, she's about to… Prez told me to read the file Maddy made up for me, but I haven't. I have no idea what background she made up for me.

"Transferred from Utah." She nods her head looking surprisingly impressed. "Good grades." I shift in my chair when her eyes widen even more. "With a keen enthusiasm for… drama." She looks at me like she expects an explanation but I lift up my shoulders and fake her a smile, internally cursing Jessie's old lady for showing that she's got a sense of fuckin' humor at a time like this.

"This is only your third day here, and you already seem to be causing trouble. There's nothing in here to suggest you had this problem at your last school. So, tell me what makes you think violence is acceptable in mine?" She slams the file shut. There's a long silence, and I wait until her forehead has stretched so high that the creases in her brow disappear completely.

"Guess I just lost my cool, Miss," I respond, with another shrug.

"Well, if you plan to get on here, you're going to have to find a way to keep a lid on that cool, Mr. Anderson. Do you understand?"

I nod my head to satisfy her, and she lets out an aggravated sigh.

"I'm happy to issue a warning on this occasion. Don't let yourself down again." Her peephole eyes shift to the door in a silent dismissal and I waste no more of our time, standing up and leaving. I storm back through reception and onto the corridor. I shouldn't have let Luke get under my skin. The last thing I need is to draw attention, me and my hot head could have just blown this whole fuckin' cover-up.

The corridors are empty, everyone already back to class. I go straight to my locker to take out the chemistry textbook I need before I get to mine. Slamming the door shut I rest my forehead against the cool metal, hoping it might take some of the heat out my blood. I close my eyes and try to focus, to figure out a way to carry out this shit without fuckin' forgetting why I'm here.

"I'm sorry." The softly spoken voice forces my eyes open, and when I twist around. Ella is standing in front of me, teeth digging into her bottom lip guiltily and her hands fidgeting like she doesn't know where to place them.

Undoubtedly, it's the cutest thing I've ever seen.

"What ya sorry for?" I ask, not meaning to sound so agitated, but my voice is the last thing I worry about controlling when I'm around her.

"About what happened… I'm sorry you got in trouble for me." Her eyes fall from mine and settle on the floor, and I miss their contact instantly.

"He had it coming," I tell her, using my shoulder to push myself off my locker. I need to get away from her before I grab at that chin, force those eyes back on to mine, then bite down on that peachy lip myself.

"Thank you," she calls out when I've gotten a few steps away from her. The desperateness in her tone causes me to stop, and I take in a deep breath while I fight the urge to turn around. If I do it will only make me want to go to her. To take her hand and walk us both the fuck out of the door, put her on my bike, then ride until I come up with a way to have her.

I quickly shake that thought away and keep walking.

It unnerves me how in such a short time, one girl has the potential to ruin every dream I've ever had. At the same time, it makes me understand a little better why Jessie always seems so obsessed over his old lady.

CHAPTER 6
ELLA

A whole week has passed since Nyx punched Luke, and it seems Nyx has barely looked in my direction since. I miss his icy stares—the ones that make my bones shudder and cause heat to pool in my stomach—the way he defended me, gave me a little hope that he might actually like me. Although it's much more realistic that he just really hates Luke, and took an opportunity to prove how much.

Father is in a terrible mood at dinner, I get that vibe from his stern expression and the fact he poured himself something strong the minute he arrived home from work.

Mom is trying her best to make conversation over the table, while he arrogantly ignores every single one of her attempts. I ask to be excused as soon as I finish eating, heading straight up to my room and away from the atmosphere. I have more homework to catch up with than normal as I'm finding it impossible to get anything done in the classes I share with Nyx. He has a habit of unwittingly sending me off topic and into a dreamy haze.

I get started on my English assignment, throwing myself into it for a good few hours, and increasing the volume on my iPod as the argument downstairs becomes louder. I call it an argument, but considering Father's voice is the only one I hear, it seems much more like a scolding.

Vincent Jackson is a bully, he does a great job of hiding that part of his personality, and I really hope Mom isn't getting blamed for something petty that I've done. This week I've been so distracted by Nyx, I haven't done much to piss him off. I may have swapped over a few documents from one file to another in his cabinet, but surely he couldn't be blaming her for that…

I wait for the shouting to stop before sneaking down to the kitchen for a drink. Trying my best to stay quiet as I creep across the landing. I almost leap out of my skin when I bump into Mom coming up the stairs.

By the looks of it Father has gone all out tonight, her right cheek is burning red and her eyes are swollen from tears. She quickly moves her hand to her cheek, attempting to shield me from my asshole father's handy work.

"You surprised me, darling." She swallows back any pain she's feeling, painting on the 'everything's okay' smile that over the years I've come to know better than her genuine one. "How's that essay coming along?" The tears are still in her eyes, and I want so much to hug her, but if she senses that I see right through her act I know she'd hurt even more.

It seems ironic that she works so hard to protect me from what she goes through, and that my only way to comfort her is to play along with it.

"It's going good, almost finished." I manage a false smile for her.

"That's terrific, sweetheart. I'm going to get myself an early night. I have another headache." She rolls her eyes like it's no big deal, her hand still trembling as she taps me lightly on the arm and carries on towards their bedroom.

"Mom…" I don't turn around, but I know she's stopped when the floorboards stop creaking beneath her feet.

"Those headaches seem to be coming a lot more often lately. If you keep getting them, maybe you ought to speak to someone."

Without waiting for her to respond, I continue to move down the stairs and into the kitchen.

Opening the fridge, I pour myself a glass of water, then stare out the window across the back lawn that Father pays a gardener to keep looking pristine. It must have been freshly cut today, I can smell that cut grass scent lingering.

Needing some fresh air, I step out the back door, making sure to turn off the automatic light on my way out. Last thing I want is to disturb Father in the mood he's in. His office may be on the other side of the house, but he doesn't miss a thing.

The evening is chilly, but I sit out on one of the patio chairs anyway. Other than the occasions when I sit out here with Penelope on her breaks, our garden rarely gets used.

Our patio stretches the whole width of the house, and the outdoor dining table beneath our veranda could seat at least fifteen people. I can't remember a time when it's ever been used for socializing like it should be.

We also have a pool which I'd probably use more often if it wasn't located right outside Father's office window. Too many times I've caught him glaring at me coldly through the glass. The man seems opposed to me having any kind of fun while he's working. Or at any other time for that matter.

I gave up a long time ago trying to understand him, he's incapable of emotion. The upstanding family man people see outside this house is a complete stranger to me.

Sitting back in my chair, I inhale the fresh evening air and enjoy the silence for a while.

Some movement in a tree on the other side of the wall catches my attention. At first, I suspect some kind of night creature, an owl perhaps. But the loud, heavy rustles of the branches suggest something much larger.

My heart crawls inside my throat when a frame becomes clearer, and I realize what I'm seeing is a human shadow.

I always figured the massive wall Father had built around the perimeter of our house was for privacy. Pretty naïve of me, considering I know what my father does for a job. Being a federal judge, he's responsible for sending a lot of people away. There would of course be people who held grudges against him.

Confident that the veranda is providing enough shadow for the intruder to be unable to see me, I watch the huge figure settle itself between the trunk and a thick branch that hangs over our wall. They sit motionless, so still, that if I'd come out here just a few moments later I would have never known they were there.

For a while, I sit and watch out of curiosity, and slowly a sick thought enters my head. One that I try to dismiss yet can't help being attracted to. What if whoever this is, is here to hurt my father? If this someone has come here to serve him a taste of his own justice?

My bedroom light is still on, shining above me and illuminating a patch of lawn. It highlights the different shades of green the gardener has taken time to stripe to perfection. As soon as I go upstairs, the person in the trees will likely be able to see every move I make. But I know from up there I'll be able to get a much better look at who it is. Quietly, I creep back inside the kitchen, making my way up the stairs and to my room. Then making sure I'm nowhere near my window, I change into my pajamas.

I do my best to act normal, settling into bed and turning off the lamp beside me. My room turns black, and I dare to glance out at the tree.

I'm still too far away to make out anything clearly, so I keep my eyes open and wait. Hoping that the figure will move out of the shadows so I can catch a glimpse of them in the moonlight.

Eventually, the branch shakes, and the figure stretches out from the tree to clamber over the top of the wall.

I realize too late that my balcony door is still open, and I wonder how the hell I could forget to close it knowing that a creepy stranger is watching the house.

The figure rushes out of sight, and a sound of movement just below my window tells me they're closer. Panic hammers in my chest while I helplessly lie and wait. I hold my breath in my lungs when the tall frame climbs onto my balcony and freezes me to my mattress with fear.

It never once occurred to me that this person might be here to hurt me, and my thoughts immediately go to Luke.

Gripping hold of my blanket, I close my eyelids enough to make it look like I'm sleeping, leaving a tiny gap for me to peek through my lashes. The figure steps towards my door and my pulse beats, fast and uncontrollably, the urge to scurry from my bed suddenly taking over my limbs.

From the height and broadness of the shoulders, I'm certain it's a man. One who wears black jeans and a dark hooded jumper. And now, even with limited vision, I realize who they belong to.

There are no shadows for him to hide in up here, and when the moonlight shines on the large hand that wraps around my balcony door. I almost choke out loud when a rose tattoo confirms my suspicion.

Nyx.

I have no time to react, because what he does next shocks the tiny bit of life I still have left out of me. Reaching inside for the other door he carefully pulls them together, holding both the handles in his hand and rests his forehead on the seal between them in the same tortured way I found him at his locker the day he punched Luke. It looks like he's angry at himself, or holding himself back from something. He looks like he's hurting.

Nyx eventually turns around, but instead of leaving like I expect him to, he slides his muscular back down the doors and sits on my balcony floor like he's guarding them. I want to climb out of bed and go to him, but instead, I stay put and try to understand why he's here.

He's made no attempt to wake me up, and I know he's not here to hurt me. The way he's shut me in feels protective.

He protected me from Luke.

Thinking about it, ever since Nyx showed up at Castle Rock High he's been there when something has gone wrong for me. I wonder now if all that is a coincidence.

Nyx remains on my balcony for some time, arms resting over his knees, and his head hanging between them. I watch his sturdy shoulders rise and fall as he breathes, desperate to know what's going on inside his head.

Him being here is so confusing, and yet I find it oddly comforting at the same time. I don't know how long I watch him sitting out there in silence but my eyes feel heavy and I drift off. The sound of rustling leaves disturbs me again and when I open my eyes, Nyx is gone. I bolt out of bed just in time to catch him jogging across the lawn, scaling back over the wall and disappearing back into the night.

Maybe I should be freaked out that the new, mysterious, kick-ass kid from school has been watching me. But, I'm not. What I feel is unfamiliar. It's warm and exciting, and as I drift back off into a deep, restful sleep, I dream about what might have happened if Nyx hadn't shut the doors, but let himself in instead?

Chapter 7

Moping over Ella like a fuckin' idiot is getting me nowhere. I've gone to her house every night since I followed her home that first time, and now it's become my routine.

She has some crazy power over me, one that keeps drawing me back to her. She's on my mind every damn second, day and night. And I can't relax until I know she's safely asleep, with those fuckin' balcony doors shut.

It's ridiculous, especially considering I can't lock them anyway.

I want to pin her down and ask her why she does it. Why she insists on leaving the damn things open every night? It exposes her to predators—Predators like me—and it bugs the shit out of me.

Ella getting an early night gives me the chance to spend time at the club. Yeah, it means I'll get bitched around, but I need normality. I drop my homework to Maddy before heading down to the clubhouse. She's that excited, she practically snatches the shit outta my hands.

Things turned dangerous for Mads when she took her hacking skills away from our rivals, the Bastards, and brought them to us. Now Jessie's bitch is stuck here on the compound until we figure what to do about the Bastards being after her blood.

"The Great Gatsby. I loved doing this one." Maddy's eyes spark with genuine excitement. "I have my old paper somewhere at home. I got an A-plus."

"Like my lit teacher is gonna believe I could come up with an A-plus essay, keep it real, Mads." I roll my eyes at her, then look down at the plate of Meatloaf and veg she places in front of me.

"What's this?" I look up at her.

"Jeeez, Nyx, I know my culinary skills aren't great but come on. It's meatloaf."

Her happy smile turns into a sad one. "Skid gave me Carly's recipe book."

"I can see it's meatloaf, it looks great. But what's it doing in front of me?" I ask, confused.

"I figured you'd be hungry, so I saved you some. You haven't stopped to breathe these past few weeks." She smiles, nudging the plate a little closer and handing me a knife and fork.

"Thanks," I manage, making sure my voice sounds as grateful as I feel. Tac's the only person who's ever really looked out for me and he's done it in a unique way of his own. This is just Maddy being kind and thoughtful, but it puts a hard ball in the back of my throat which I have to quickly swallow before I grow a fucking pussy of my own.

"You're welcome." Maddy smiles again, settling opposite me and putting on her glasses before she starts on my homework.

I finish every scrap on my plate not just because it's delicious, but because I suddenly realize I'm starving. Thanking her again, I take my plate over to the sink.

"Guess you'll be heading down the club?" she says, lifting her head out of my textbook.

"Yeah, you need anything?" I offer, because it feels right to.

"No, thanks anyway. If you swing by in the morning. I'll have all this ready for you."

"Appreciate that, Mads," I nod, before walking out to my bike and making the short ride down to the club.

Years ago, our compound used to be some fancy vacation complex. Secluded up in the mountains, it's perfect for our needs. There are plenty of cabins for the brothers who choose to live here, and a huge clubhouse that's always got a fully stocked bar. The Dirty Souls open their doors to the people they trust. Prez and his members have connections everywhere. It's how they run this town, and to do that, we need allies. Crime rates are low, and there's never much trouble to deal with in Manitou Springs... Not for the Police anyway.

Roswell and his deputy are leaving the members only bar after a meeting with Prez. I know the town sheriff has been bringing his second man up to speed on how the department's relationship works with the club. Danny Foster isn't an idiot, he's worked under Roswell for enough years to know the score. But Roswell ain't getting any younger, and it's in everyone's best interest that we keep our arrangement moving into the future. I nod my head at them as I pass them in the foyer. Danny's a regular at the studio and has almost got a full body suit underneath the uniform he wears. He's as professional as Roswell but he also knows how to kick back. He's got high with me and Tac a few times after we've shut the shop.

Jessie and Troj arrive back from town about half an hour later, they look pacified so I assume they've just roughed someone up who's been dealing too close to our turf.

I'd worked with them with them on some of the names Rogue supplied us with a few months ago, but new ones keep popping up. I know that Rogue gave Skid a few more names last week, she's good at that shit. I occasionally get a few leads from keeping my ear to the ground, but I never do as good as her.

The club is fixed on keeping our town clean. We're no neighborhood fuckin' watch, but the last thing we want here is trouble; with trouble come authorities, and we don't want ATF or CIA sniffing around and getting in our business. The Bastards can have their dealers distribute on their own territory much as they want, but if they try pushing that shit on ours, their runners are gonna feel the consequences.

"Prospect, get over here." Prez raises his hand, calling me over to where he's sitting at the bar. There're females everywhere tonight, the room already stinks of sex. Haven, current queen of club sluts, is positioned between Prez's legs, her massive tits already out on display. He's having a conversation with Brax, the nomad who rode in a few months ago. Rumors are flying that he's looking to patch into our Charter permanently and from what I've heard about him, he'd be a welcomed asset.

I head straight over. It's been a while since I've given Prez a report back on Ella, not that there's much to report back. Beside the fact she gets harder to resist every damn fucking day.

"How's it goin', kid?" Prez asks, holding up three fingers to the whore behind the bar. She fills up his glass, then Brax's, and gets a fresh one for me. I'm about to head around and give her a hand. It's busy and nothing pisses a brother off around here worse than having to wait on a drink.

"It's good." Prez slams his strong arm across my chest. "You been workin' hard lately, you deserve to kick back for a few hours… You want Haven here to help you unwind?" he offers, moving his eyes onto the blonde that's sliding between his legs to the music.

No one can deny that Haven's pretty. She wouldn't look twice at a guy Prez's age if he didn't have the cut and the money. Prez is smart enough to know that too. But I'm sure he gives no fucks about that when she's riding his cock.

"Thanks, Prez," I nod gratefully, watching Haven's eyes open wide. I don't know if it's out of shock or pleasure, but she sure ain't disappointed. I haven't fucked Haven before. Prez is picky about who he shares her with. Which makes it too much of an honor to refuse.

I down the drink that's been poured for me, then let her take my hand and lead me out towards the foyer.

"You gotta be yanking my dick." Squealer pulls his mouth away from the nipple he's biting on as we pass him. "I've been wantin' in on Haven for months."

The bitch bouncing herself up and down on his lap slaps her hand hard across his cheek, and he growls back at her like a feral animal. His hands gripping at her hips and thrusting her deeper onto his cock. He snatches a fist full of her raven-colored hair and after using it to tilt her head back, shoots a mouthful of spit directly at her face. The girl responds by giggling at him darkly, then uses her palm to spread his saliva all over her skin, sucking her fingers clean when she's done. His twin Screwy, sits beside him, unfazed as he passes him the spliff he's been smoking. Squeal takes a long, deep toke and exhales it straight into his whore's mouth.

Squealer likes 'em a little tapped, and has a real knack for finding the psychotic ones.

"You ain't never gonna make it into Haven, Squeal, not with hell waitin' on ya for such a long time," Prez calls out at him across the room before getting back into his conversation with Brax. Squealer holds out his hand for me to smack as I move on past him.

"Fill ya boots, kid," he cackles like a hyena and gets straight back to business.

Haven keeps a firm hold of my hand, dragging me up the stairs, into one of the unoccupied rutting rooms. Turning me around, she forces me to sit on the edge of the bed and wriggles her way between my legs. I lift my head up to look at her. There's got to be something fuckin' wrong with me. She's the hottest bitch the club's got to offer, and yet the way she looks down on me, attempting to be seductive… ain't doing nothing for me.

"Can you keep a secret?" her fingers flex over the tops of my arms. "I've wanted to fuck you for a real long time, Nyx," she whispers.

Without waiting for me to answer, she pushes my prospect cut off my shoulders and climbs onto my lap. Her inner thighs resting on the outer-edge of mine. There are at least a dozen men downstairs that would kill to be in the position I'm in right now, and yet my cock is being picky. Comparing her to everything I want back in Castle Rock.

"Me and you are gonna have a good time, baby," she promises, sliding her fingers under my tee and scratching over my abs. It feels irritating. I don't want her touching me.

Her lips find their way to my neck and she slides her tongue from my collarbone to my ear. I want for it to be Ella, and I try so hard to imagine that it is.

"Mel tells me you're fuckin' hung," Haven breathes against my ear. But she gets no response outta me. I've already decided she won't be finding out for herself if that's true or not.

"It'll be nice to have some young blood. Keep pleasing Prez and I'll bet he'll let you have me again," she giggles, and I'm done being polite.

I slide my hand around her throat, and she smiles back at me, hissing an excited little breath at the same time. Those seductive eyes soon turn fearful when I stand up and force her into the back of the door.

"I don't want your overworked pussy anywhere near me. Far as I'm concerned, Prez can keep it," I warn. Haven looks back at me confused, and my guess is the girl doesn't get refused cock all that often.

"When we leave this room, you are gonna let Prez and everyone else downstairs think that we fucked, and if you don't, I'll relay to Prez everything you just said to me. Prez will replace you with another whore, and you'll be back working the bar and entertaining Squealer to keep your nose powdered. You understand that?"

I wait until she nods back at me like a scalded little puppy before I release my grip. Stepping back, I pull a chair from the corner of the room and point for her to sit. Then laying out on the bed, I shove my hands behind my head and try and find some calm.

"You gay?" she asks, her voice a lot less confident than before. Looking up, I tip my head to the side.

"What? You don't believe that there's a straight guy who just doesn't wanna fuck you?"

"Not in this universe," she bites back, attempting to pull her pride back together.

"You just found one. I ain't gay, darlin'."

"Who is she then?" Haven pushes for more but I ignore her, staring up at the ceiling. My obsession for Ella has gone too far. I should be slappin' my balls against Haven's cherry shaped ass right now, but instead, I'm lying here pining over some pretty little rich girl I'll never have, one whose Daddy would kill me for even thinking about her the way I do. And what scares me most is that I don't know how to stop myself from wanting her.

I stop by Jessie's cabin before school and find my homework stacked neatly on the table with a brown paper lunch bag beside it. Jessie and Maddy are sitting eating breakfast, and they both greet me with huge grins when I let myself in.

"What?" I ask, wondering if they're gonna let me in on their joke.

"Heard Prez gave you a pass with Haven last night," Jessie speaks first. "Jeez kid, Prez only shares his toys with his favorites."

"Oh, really VP?" Maddy smacks him hard on his chest, but the big smile she wears suggests she's messing with him.

"Now, what would I want with rancid club pussy when I got perfection right here?" Jessie grips his woman around the waist and pulls her onto his lap.

"Besides, you ain't got nothing to worry about," Jessie nods his head in my direction. "Prez's clearly got a new favorite now," he smirks at me with his eyes while his lips kiss Maddy's cheek.

"This for me too?" I pull the Brown bag off the top of my homework.

"Yeah, I made you lunch," Maddy says proudly, and Jessie buries his head into her shoulder to try and hide his snigger.

"There's an apple in there for ya to give your teacher too," he teases.

Maddy's head whips around to him. "Your lunch bag's in the refrigerator," she tells him looking a little wounded.

It's my turn to smirk when a vision of Jessie, mid interrogation, pulling out the lunch bag that his old lady made him pops into my head.

"It's not exactly like I have a lot to do around here," Maddy reminds us, and I notice how quickly the smile drops off Jessie's face. I understand now why he hates not being able to guarantee her safety on the compound and Jessie, like me, isn't the kinda guy who deals with helplessness all that well.

"Nyx, you reckon you could spare a few hours after school to help out at the garage?" he quickly changes the subject. "Rogue's doing her best but she's got to shoot off early. We got an exhaust to weld and I could use some help putting an engine in a corvette."

"Sure," I nod, remembering that Ella usually hangs back at the library on Wednesdays after school. "Maybe Mom here could write me a note and get me out early?" My eyebrows waggle at Maddy, and it makes them both laugh again.

"Get out of here." Jessie chucks something off his plate at

me, shifting Maddy's position on his lap so she's straddling him. I pack my lunch and homework into my bag and leave them to it.

Ella's car is already in the lot when I get to school, and I park my bike two rows behind, scrunching my forehead when I notice all the chaos in the corridor. I push my way through the crowd of kids until I get to the front of the semi-circle surrounding Ella's locker.

Ella stands in a space of her own, staring forwards with her hands covering her mouth. I read the words ELLA JACKSON IS A SLUT that are in huge black letters across her locker door and feel all my muscles tense. It doesn't take a lot of brainpower to figure who's responsible for this and my hands twitch to find Luke Robinson's head so I can slam it into the metal locker and make him eat his words one by one. Luke strolls through the entrance a few seconds later with a couple of other players, stopping to casually ask one of the other students what all the fuss is about.

His acting skills are almost as good as his ability to be a huge fuckin' cunt. A hard shove in my back makes me turn, and I start raising my fist until I realize it's Abby, rushing past me to comfort her friend.

"Come on, let's get out of here." Abby pulls Ella into her arms, trying to drag her through the crowd, but Ella stands firm.

"I'm fine," she insists. Taking a deep breath and stepping towards her locker to open it. She puts her bag inside, takes out the book she needs, then slams it shut again.

"What's all this?" Miss Wallace claps her hands, dispersing the crowd of teenagers, and hurrying them on to their classes. Principal K joins her, helping her to usher everyone along.

"I'll have Hilary add this to the caretaker's job list," she mutters under her breath, looking at Luke's insult before clipping her heels back down the corridor towards her office.

I have Calculus first period, which means I don't see Ella again until Lit in third and I'm wound up like a fucking screw all morning. When third eventually comes. I waste no time getting to class, sitting at my desk, and waiting for her to arrive. Ella doesn't show, and I'm forced to listen for almost an hour to Wallace's drivel until I can find out why.

I make sure I bump into Abby by hanging around near her locker in between lessons and as I stomp towards her, I can't figure if she's afraid or surprised to see me.

"Where's Ella?" I cut to the chase, by now I'm seething, ready to tear off limbs.

"She went home, couldn't stand all the whispering behind her back. Apparently, everyone thinks she slept with Luke Robinson." Her answer enrages me even more, I hadn't considered that being the reason he's so vile to her. I always figured it was because she'd rejected him, that she was different to all the other wannabe football player's girlfriends.

"Why do you care anyway?" she adds, a tiny smirk on her narrow lips.

"I… We…" Shit, I'm stuck for an excuse. "She's in my Lit class and offered to help me, I'm falling behind, need the help." I impress myself with the lie I manage to pull out of my ass.

"Well, you're gonna have to wait till tomorrow. Unless you want me to give her your number. I'm sure she wouldn't mind." Abby's eyes roll over my chest and shoulders before looking back up, judging me like I'm a prime bull at a cattle fair.

"It's fine. I'll just catch her tomorrow." I nod, leaving for my next lesson and wondering how the hell I'm gonna make it through the rest of the day without forcing Luke's skull down into his chest cavity.

I don't head back to the club after school, instead, I message Jessie warning him I'll be late. Then I wait inside the toilets for the school to empty. When the halls fall silent, I break into the janitor's closet and help myself to everything that I need. I spend the next few hours scrubbing Maddy's locker clean and just as I'm finishing up, I hear the familiar sound of heels approaching behind me, and I curse under my breath before turning around to face Principal K.

"I hope you're not doing this due to a guilty conscience, Nicolas," Principal K speaks sternly.

"We both know who did this." I drop the cloth into the bucket. "I just thought I'd save your janitor a job," I bite back sarcastically, fast losing my patience with the hard-faced bitch who claims to run things around here.

"Mmmm." She peers at me over the rim of her glasses, unconvinced. "I hope we won't be seeing any… retaliation," she warns, and the look I hit her back with makes no such promise. She leaves me to get back to scrubbing, and I don't leave until all traces of Luke's cruel words have vanished.

It's nearly six by the time I make it back to the club, and when I pull up outside the garage Jessie is looking pissed at me. I park my bike and head inside, Jessie doesn't say anything, just tosses the spare pair of overalls at me before I have the chance to explain.

"I'm sorry, okay," I tell him, scrubbing at my face in frustration.

"You know how important this place is to the club. This and the studio are legit businesses, Nyx, they have to stay running. And while Skid's off finding fucking God or whatever he's doing at that church, this place is going to shit.

We can't expect Rogue to cope on her own. It's too much"

What Jessie's saying is true, since Skid's old lady got killed he's been helping out at some local church. None of us know what's going on in his head. But he's always busy helping soup kitchens, he even had us all help him fix up some rambleshacked house in town last month so a single mom could move in.

We're all being patient with him 'cause we know how bad he's hurting. Far as we're concerned, it doesn't matter what it takes to pull him out of the giant ass abyss he's fallen into, just so long as he fights his way back out.

"Yeah, I get it, but I'm stretched, Jess. I'm trying to get as much info about the girl as I can so Prez can rest easy, but it ain't happening. Me and her, we're so different. She ain't gonna talk to me… and I need this. I need to get my cut so I can pick up some fuckin' respect around here." I pick up a spanner from the workbench, but all I can do slam it back down again out of pure frustration.

Jessie's head shakes, and he lets out a long sigh before he sits down on one of the stools.

"Look, Tac loves you like a son. You've had my respect from the day you set foot on this compound, Troj's too. And the fact Prez trusts you with all this shit proves that you got his."

"Come on, Jess, he was kinda forced into trusting me. It ain't like he could send Squealer to fucking high school, ain't no lawyer out there good enough to dodge that lawsuit." I'm being serious, but Jessie makes the situation lighter by huffing a laugh at me.

"He could have sent Grimm," Jessie shrugs. "That kid probably got about as many hairs on his balls as Tac's got on his fucking head." That makes me chuckle, Tac's as bald as a snake's ass.

"Look, Nyx, I know things are tough right now, and I get the pressure you're under, but you gotta remember that the others don't know what shit's goin' on. The way I see it, the sooner you can get what Prez wants, the sooner you can move on."

"Jess, I don't know what he wants. Does he want her to be happy, or does he wanna have to save her so he gets a second shot at being a dad?" I don't know what's going through our leader's head. All I can be sure of, is that he wouldn't like me having the thoughts that go through mine.

"He just wants to know she's safe. Judge Jackson's fuckin' shady. Find out what you can, how he treats her and shit. Prez just wants to know his girl's doin' and that he made the right decision all those years ago, okay? Then we can move on."

"She drives a fuckin' brand new Mercedes, he can't be treating her that bad," I point out.

"Yeah, well a lot goes on behind closed doors, things men like Jackson don't want people to know about. We don't know if he knows that he ain't Ella's father, and I can guarantee you if he does, he'll resent her for it."

The thought makes my pulse tick.

"Once Prez knows that she's safe and taken care of, he'll pull you off this shit and we can set on making you a fuckin' brother." Jessie stands up and picks up the spanner, holding it out to me. "Now, this engine ain't gonna fit itself, shithead. Let's get those pretty hands dirty."

It's gone nine by the time I finish helping Jessie fit the engine. Realizing the time, I race back up to my cabin to shower, not bothering to grab anything to eat before I jump on my bike and drive out to Ella's place.

I stick to my routine, parking my bike up the street, then jogging behind the house. I climb the tree effortlessly now and swing myself on to the branch that I always watch from.

Ella's bedroom light is off and her balcony door is wide open. I let out a frustrated huff, this girl will seriously be the death of me.

I assess the rest of the house, every room seems to be in darkness. I already suspected she was alone when I saw that only her car was on the drive. Jumping out of the tree to the other side of the wall. I prepare to make my journey across the lawn. What I don't prepare for are the hands that cover over my eyes when I land.

I'm close to spinning around and throwing whoever it is over my shoulder until I hear a soft sweet laugh, and instantly know I've fucked up.

How the fuck am I gonna explain this?

"You know you shouldn't sneak up on people in the dark, you could cause a heart attack." I manage to keep any emotion out of my voice.

"This, coming from the night ninja who scales walls and climbs trees." Her hands slide away and I quickly spin around. Ella's arms are folded across her chest now, unintentionally pushing her tits together and making them look even more fuckin' tempting.

"Why you stalking me, Nyx?" she asks before I have the chance to speak.

"I ain't stalkin' ya," I snigger, remaining calm and swiping my finger across my bottom lip.

"Oh, so you weren't in this tree last night, you didn't climb on to my balcony, and you aren't standing in my garden in front of me right now?" She stares back at me, the tiny smirk on her mouth making me want to push her against the wall and wipe it away with my lips.

"I was gonna see if you could help me, I'm falling behind." I stick to my original lie. Abby has the biggest mouth in Castle Rock High so no doubt Ella already knows about our earlier conversation.

"Most people would try the front door approach, maybe send an email or maybe try talking to me at school," she suggests.

"Yeah, well I ain't normal," I tell her, placing both my hands in my pockets and kicking up some dirt at my feet, suddenly I feel fucking shy.

What's with that shit?

"You can come in, you know, no one's home." Her saying that catches me off guard, and I quickly look up to check I'm hearing her right. She doesn't give me a chance to think about it, her delicate warm hand grabbing at mine and tugging me towards her house. I don't put up a fight, following her lead and letting her lead me until she stops at the back door.

"You sure you're gonna be okay coming through the door? You could use the balcony if you'd be more comfortable."

"Funny," I humor her, trying hard not to blush as I let her pull me through a utility room and then into a kitchen. It's almost the same size as one of the lounge bars at the club.

"You want something to drink?" she offers, opening up the fridge and looking over all the items.

"Sure," I shrug, still not really sure what the fuck's going on here. She doesn't seem scared, or mad at me. What's wrong with her?

"You know what?" she smiles a devilish smile over her shoulder, "we can do better than this. Follow me." Slamming the refrigerator door shut, she breezes past me out into the hall, looking fuckin' edible with her hair plaited either side of her head and resting on her shoulders. She's wearing a tank top, light-colored jeans, and a pair of worn-out sneakers. I know she could afford a new pair whenever she wanted, but I stab a guess that she likes these because they are worn in perfectly.

We pass through a huge open spaced hallway, complete with a large ornate staircase just like the ones in the movies.

"Come in here," she tells me, opening a door on the other side of the room and disappearing inside. I follow her, crossing the hall into the room and closing the door behind me. The room is dark inside. Pitch fucking black in fact. But I can sense she's close from the sound of her breathing.

"Boo," she giggles as she flicks on the switch, lighting up another impressively sized room that's something between a library and an office. The walls are lined with shelves full of books, and a huge mahogany desk sits proudly in the center of the room. There's an old-style green leather chair behind the desk, and two not so comfortable ones on the other side. Even with the light on, the room remains dark, and there's only one narrow window in the whole room. I'm in Judge Jackson's office!

"Have a seat," Ella extends her arm, pointing to one of the chairs and putting on a voice that's even fancier than her own. I look at her with a raised eyebrow but still do as she requests. I may not be giving it away, but I love seeing her act playful.

She walks over to a cabinet on the far side of the room and opens it up.

"So, what will your poison be?" she looks over her shoulder to ask. The cabinet is full of choice, but I doubt Judge Jackson is a Jack drinker.

"Lady's choice," I shrug.

"Very well, he keeps the good stuff at the back," she winks, reaching up onto her toes, pulling out a bottle, and walking back towards me.

She places a very expensive looking bottle of scotch on the desk between us and then sits in the judge's chair.

"You wanna play a game?" she asks sweetly. Like she's asking me to participate in a game of chase or red fuckin' rover. But the way she kicks her feet up on the surface of the desk suggests that's not what she wants at all.

"I ain't really a game kinda guy."

"You're right, stalking's clearly much more your thing. Promise we can play hide and seek later." She tips her head to the side and raises one of her eyebrows. Her smart little mouth and sass, doing fuck all to calm my cock down.

"I wasn't stalk..." I start, but gave up halfway through, flinging my arm in the air in defeat. "What's your fuckin' game?"

"You tell me something about yourself that no one else knows," she says quickly.

"That's a real lame game," I laugh, watching as she unscrews the cap of the scotch and takes a sip straight out the bottle. Her face creases when the burn of liquor hits her taste buds, pissing all over her hard ass performance. I hide my smirk behind my hand to spare her some embarrassment.

"I hate my father," she says without any trace of emotion. Passing the bottle over the desk to me. Her admission shocks me but makes me realize the advantages of playing along... Jessie and Prez know there's something suss about the judge, and this is a good way of finding out what. So, for the sake of the club, not the heavy ache in my balls, I decide to play Ella Jackson's game.

"Why d'you hate your dad?" I ask.

"Nah ah, that's not the game, no questions. Your turn." She shakes the bottle, reminding me to take it.

Taking the bottle from her hand, I down a good mouthful and wonder what she was flinching at, the stuff slides down your throat like liquid gold.

I don't know where to start, I've never had to do this kinda shit with anyone, not even Tac. The club is a need to know kinda place, brothers don't ask each other questions, no doubt because everyone there has their own secrets.

"I never knew my parents," I admit, watching everything widen on her face. She stays in that shocked state for a good ten seconds, before pity makes its way to her eyes. I fuckin' hate how it looks on her. There's the reason I don't talk about this shit.

"So you're an orph—"

"Nah ah, no questions remember," I point out.

Ella twists her lips into a pout when I remind her of her own rules, and I hand the bottle back over. I want more of Ella Jackson's secrets, all of them in fact. Even if that means having to give up a few of my own.

After another huge swig of her father's expensive scotch, she wipes her lips with the back of her hands and scrunches up her eyes, placing the bottle back on the desk.

"I'm a virgin," she blurts out, quickly shutting her eyes again and cringing like she regrets her words. My cock stretches against my jeans even tighter at the confirmation of what I've been pretty sure of since I cast eyes on her. Luke Robinson obviously knows jack shit.

"I ain't," I take my turn straight after. Ready to move on to her next confession.

"I don't think you understand the concept of the game Nyx, you're supposed to tell me something I don't already know." Her eyes roll and her sarcastic smile drops when she pulls the bottle to her lips again. Only this time she speaks before she drinks.

"Luke Robinson scares me," she confesses before swallowing another huge mouthful. "I try to tell myself that he doesn't and I hate that he makes me feel weak, but it's the truth." She lifts up her shoulders, seeming disappointed with herself. I can see how hard this is for her to admit, even if I already know it. I've known it since that first day I arrived, because with her I notice every little thing, including the way she cowers whenever he's close to her.

I pick up the bottle from the table and drink a little more, leaning forward and making sure I have her full attention before I take my turn.

"I'd never let Luke Robinson hurt you," I rasp, upping the intensity of the game by admitting that I care. My dick stretches even more when a sweet little smile finds its way to her lips. She's so fuckin' cute, and clearly a little tipsy.

She rounds the desk, clumsily dragging the bottle with her, then sits on its surface right in front of me.

"I feel safe when you're around," she whispers without taking her eyes off mine. She takes another swig, then her smile turns a little dopey as she moves forward, her ass leaving the desk as she rests a hand on the armrests each side of me.

Fuck, she's gonna kiss me. Ella Jackson the Prez's daughter is gonna kiss me. This is a cardinal sin, but as her hot lips move closer to mine, I already know they're gonna taste too delicious to resist, especially now they're laced with expensive scotch.

I know I shouldn't let it happen. But I want it to happen too much to stop her. Luckily, her hand loses its grip on the armrest and she slips onto my lap. I quickly catch her, feeling the giggle that she lets out vibrate against my chest before I stand up, taking her with me. Turning us around, I place her steadily in the seat and her head lolls to the side sleepily.

Damn, she's a lightweight.

I set to work tidying up the judge's office so she won't get in any trouble, putting the scotch in the back of the cabinet where she'd got it from, and erasing any traces that we'd been here. Then I scoop Ella's small sexy as fuck frame into my arms and lift her up. She stirs slightly, nestling her head between my shoulder and neck. Having her close, holding her in my arms, actually hurts me, and I question why I'm doing this to myself.

Heading back out to the hall, I kick the door closed behind me then climb the stairs. It doesn't take me long to locate her room, and when I do, I lay her down gently on her mattress before taking off her sneakers and covering her with a blanket. I sit on the edge of her bed facing away from her, my elbows resting on my knees, while my hands grip together just to prevent myself from touching her.

It's impossible not to turn and look at her, to take in every single feature on her beautiful face. She's fast asleep now, knocked out in a scotch coma, but it's still my turn…

I could tell her anything I wanted; her sleepy state won't remember it in the morning. So, soothing away the long strand of hair that's fallen over her nose, I tuck it away behind her ear and tell her the thing I want her to hear the most.

"I think you're the most beautiful thing I've ever seen," I whisper, taking the opportunity to stare at her up close for a little longer.

I silently laugh at myself for being so ridiculous, standing up and being gentle not to disturb her as I creep my way out to the balcony.

"I've dreamt about you every night since you came to

me," her sleepy voice responds from behind me, and when I turn my head back around and find her still fast asleep, I release the breath I'm holding.

Maybe I'm hearing things, or maybe there's a chance that I was the vision that Ella Jackson had in her pretty little head when she got herself off that first night I came here.

And if I got nothing else in this cruel, unforgiving world. I got that.

Chapter 8

ELLA

I'm scared to open my eyes. My head feels thick and fuzzy. And slowly, memories start to filter back to me.

Mom and Dad leaving the house, helping myself to a few glasses of wine from the cellar. Deciding that waiting for Nyx by the tree would be a good idea.

Father's office. Expensive Scotch... that will explain the pounding. *The game I thought would be a good way to get to know him.*

I was going to kiss him... Why didn't it happen? Did he stop me?

Nope... I slipped onto his lap, I'm sure I remember him catching me. I was definitely wrapped up in those strong arms at some point.

I slam my palm over my face, and give up trying to remember any more.

School today is going to be horrific enough, everyone will still be talking about what Luke wrote on my locker, and now I'll have to face Nyx too.

Another vague memory surfaces, and I struggle to recall if it was him telling me I was beautiful or me telling him.

Pulling my groggy ass out of bed, I walk lazily to the shower and look at the sorry state staring back at me in the mirror. I'm still wearing yesterday's clothes for Christ's sake.

Firing out a quick text to Abby, I ask her to pick me up. I'm in no state to drive.

Nyx must think I'm a complete lightweight, I'd only shared a few sips of Father's scotch with him before I turned into a blabbing rag doll. He had no idea that I'd drank nearly a whole bottle of overpriced wine to help me find the confidence to confront him before he got here last night.

I do my best to make myself look human again. At least the braids I had in all night gives my hair a curly bounce when I take them out.

"You look like shit," Abby informs me as I lower myself into the passenger seat of her car. I don't even bother to pull her up on her lack of tact, my head hurts too much. And she's way beyond any help in that department anyway.

We arrive at school and I follow her along the corridor, waiting to see Luke's cruel words again and all the sniggers that will no doubt follow. When I arrive at my locker, I see that the janitor has already scrubbed my locker clean and I breathe a huge sigh of relief.

I hear a few pathetic girly noises come from behind me and when my head turns around, I see Nyx heading towards his locker. The confidence in his stride is like he's walking the runway. He's wearing another tight white tee, and his denim jacket has its collar standing up and the sleeves rolled partway up his colorful forearms. I swear I almost melt into the ground when he slides his shades down the bridge of his nose and directs a wink at me. Like he wants to remind me that we share a secret.

If I'm remembering last night accurately, we share a few.

"Mornin'," he nods as he passes, and my mouth moves to reply, but no sound comes out. Instead, I follow him shamelessly with my eyes, my mouth wide open as I watch him put his bag inside his locker and take out his books for Lit. Shit, we have that class first period. I turn back around and quickly scramble through my own locker, locating my books and ignoring the gob-smacked look on Abby's face. I slap a kiss on her cheek and thank her for the ride before scurrying off to class.

Nyx is already at his desk when I walk through the door, slouched back lazily in his seat with his legs stretched open. My palms feel clammy, like my books are going to slide out of them, as I stand and stare at him for an uncomfortable amount of time before I eventually pluck up the courage to talk.

"Nyx, about last night. I'm…"

I'm interrupted by the sudden rush of bodies filling up the room. And it's kind of a relief, I hadn't figured what I was gonna say to him anyway.

I spend the entire lesson having to resist the urge to turn my head to look at him. He looks dangerously handsome today, and I wonder if he's done it on purpose. The flutter in my tummy whenever I give in and look over my shoulder, dances all the way to my panties. I guess it's a distraction from the hangover.

Thankfully we have no more lessons together for the rest of the day, and I don't see him during break. My last period is PE, and despite the fact my head has cleared I'm not feeling very focused. Nyx is kitted up in that tight vest again, his shorts short enough to show off all the muscles in his thick thighs.

"Ella Jackson." Miss Mortimore's stern voice interrupts me from watching him stretch. "Are you planning on throwing that Javelin?"

"Yes, Miss." I tear my eyes away from him begrudgingly and launch myself into a ridiculous attempt at a throw.

I never have been very athletic.

After a few more attempts to redeem myself, without success, our session is finally over. The boys have already left the field for the locker rooms and I try not to lose myself to a vision of Nyx soaping up in the shower. I'm chatting to Abby as we walk back inside the girls locker room, and start searching the benches for my gym bag. It's not where I left it. It was definitely on the bench when I went out onto the field, and no one else's stuff seems to be missing.

Abby helps me look, and as the room slowly empties, so does any hope of finding my bag.

"You know who did this, don't you?" Abby crosses her arms over her chest looking furious. "I'm telling you, Ella, he can't keep getting away with it. Someone needs to teach him a lesson. What did you ever do to him anyway?"

I shrug my shoulders and sit on the bench while she changes into her regular clothes.

Abby's right, Luke has to be behind this. Why can't he cut me a break, what could he possibly get out of tormenting me?

"I hate to bail on you, hon, but I'm already running late. I'll meet you out in the lot in an hour," she says, reminding me that she has an extra tuition session after school. Abby has a creative mind, not an academic one, luckily for her, her parents have money, so they can afford extra tuition for her. And it looks like I'll be stuck in this flimsy athletics uniform until she's done because she's my ride home.

I usually go to the library and do homework while I wait for her, but I can hardly go there dressed like this. Abby kisses my cheek, offering me a guilty smile before dashing out of the locker room.

I wait a little while longer to be sure the boys locker room is completely empty, then after heading out to the corridor I call out a warning before stepping inside. The room is steamy but from what I can tell, empty.

I choke on all the overused aerosol, despite the smell of sweat still lingering, and do a quick scan of the benches. I'm not at all surprised when I find my white gym bag resting on the far side of the room. I'm so relieved I can change back into normal clothes, until I open the zip, and a strong smell of ammonia suddenly attacks my nostrils.

Urine.

I stand and stare at my sodden clothes, shocked and fucking speechless. Luke has taken it too far this time. He's actually pissed on my clothes.

I try, but fail miserably to stop myself bursting into tears. My loud, ugly sounding sobs echo from the walls and I'm just thankful there's no one here to witness them.

When I get the feeling someone's watching me I sniff my tears back, forcing them to stop, and spin around to see Nyx leaning against the doorframe watching me. I don't know how long he's been there but his eyes are venomous and his crossed arms are clenched so tight I can see the white of his knuckles bleeding through his tattoos.

"Too fuckin' far." His head shakes slowly before he pushes his shoulder off the door and disappears. I don't chase after him, I haven't got the energy to. Instead, I slump down on the bench and cry into my hands.

I remember admitting to Nyx last night that Luke scared me, Nyx told me he'd never let him hurt me and I remember believing him on that. Something tells me that Luke is about to get that lesson Abby said he needs. I can tell by the way Nyx stormed out of here that he isn't gonna let this go, and he's already in so much trouble because of me.

I stand up and dry my eyes, rushing to the door of the boys locker room to try and stop Nyx from doing something stupid. But I'm too late. The footsteps are already approaching. Hard, heavy ones that thunder towards me. At first, I worry that they belong to Luke and when I see that it's Nyx who steps into the room, I don't have time to be relieved, because he has Luke with him, dragging him across the floor by his collar like a child throwing a tantrum in the grocery store.

Every part of Nyx's body is tense as he tosses Luke into the middle of the locker room floor.

"Nyx... I..." He ignores me, slamming his boot hard into Luke's stomach and releasing all of the air from his lungs. I step back and watch, knowing I should try and stop him. He's going to get himself suspended, but the look of determination Nyx has shadowing his eyes makes me doubt God himself could stop him.

"You had a warning…" Nyx grabs my bag and thrusts it hard into Luke's chest. Then gives him no chance to react before pulling his helpless body towards the toilets. I follow them, watching on as Nyx kicks open the cubicle door with such a rough swing it almost comes off the hinges. And then I cringe because I know what's coming. Nyx is gonna give Luke Robinson a swirly.

A real bad move if he ever planned on graduating Castle Rock High.

"Nyx don't, you'll get into trouble," I call out, but Nyx doesn't seem to be hearing me. Or if he does, he's choosing to ignore me. He throws Luke to the floor and wedges his open laced boot between Luke's neck and shoulder, forcing his head to rest on the toilet seat. I can't stand here and watch Nyx fuck up, not when all this is because of me. I turn and run out of the changing rooms, into the gym. There's nothing I can do or say that is gonna stop him. Something untamed has taken over inside him and now he has tunnel vision on hurting Luke.

The gym is already set out ready for the basketball game tomorrow. All the bleachers are pulled out around the court. So I sit on one of the benches and try to breathe. I wonder if I should get some help, maybe even call a teacher before things go too far. Nyx looked capable of murder when I'd left them. But I'm too scared of getting Nyx in any more trouble.

Tapping my foot against the metal grate flooring, I wait anxiously until the door bursts open and Luke runs out. He's soaked from the chest down and I wonder how Nyx managed to swirly him and keep his head dry. Luke doesn't even notice I'm sitting watching as he runs through the gym and out of the door that leads to the corridor. And I'm not sure if I should wait here for Nyx or leave, but guilt weighs me down, fixing me to the bleacher I'm sat on.

Nyx swaggers out from the locker room not too long after, as if nothing's happened, and he stops when he sees me like he's surprised I'm still here. Standing up, I drag down my embarrassingly short gym skirt and jog my way down the stairs to meet him in the middle of the court.

"You know, that was a really dumb thing to do," I scold him, trying hard not to smile. As satisfying as it felt seeing Luke get what he deserves, this is serious. Nyx could get in a lot of trouble.

He just shrugs back at me in response.

"How did you manage to swirly him and keep his head dry?" I bite my lip to stop myself from laughing at the image of Luke Robinson with his head down the toilet. I kinda wish I'd hung around to see it now.

Nyx stares at me confused, his eyebrow raising slightly and lifting the nostril he wears the ring through.

"I didn't swirly him…" he shakes his head at me and for a second I feel kinda relieved for Nyx's sake. "…I did to him what he did to your stuff," he tells me casually, and my mouth falls open in shock.

This is bad.

"I warned him, and he didn't listen," Nyx explains as if that makes it all okay.

"Nyx, you can't do things like that around here." I bury my head in my hands, and he grabs at my wrists and wrenches them away again.

"But he can do what he did to you and expect no consequences?" His head shakes at me again. "That's bullshit, Ell." I sense all his anger building up again but I love the fact that he just shortened my name. Nobody does that anymore.

"You need to start sticking up for yourself or he's always gonna piss on you one way or another," he snaps, and my lips lift when I note the irony in what he's said. Nyx must notice that too because he closes his eyes before sniggering himself.

I don't hold back, letting myself giggle out loud and feel the mood instantly lighten. Then just as things are about to turn serious again, we're interrupted by the sound of muffled voices.

Nyx snatches up my hand and drags me under one of the bleachers. Forcing my back against the cool steel, he lifts up the arm that's holding my hand above my head, pinning me so there's no escape.

His breaths are heavy, and we're so close I can feel each beat from his chest. His eyes are searching inside mine, as if he's waiting for me to tell him to stop what's coming. And when I do absolutely nothing, he growls in frustration, closing the small space between us and pressing his lips hard onto mine.

I'm not sure how something can feel so overpowering and yet so soft at the same time, and as his mouth moves against mine I feel my whole body prickle with heat. His palm crushes my hand inside it as his lips claim more and more of me, and when his tongue pushes inside my mouth and dances around mine, it sparks flames in the pit of my stomach.

If there's a moment I'd want to last forever it's this one. Him consuming me with his mouth, tongue and the weight of his body.

I'm not even sure if I'm doing it right, in fact, I'm not really doing anything except let him own my mouth, and I worry I've messed up when he pulls his lips from me slightly. His forehead presses into mine and I'm not sure if the long sigh he breathes is out of relief or disappointment.

"I shouldn't have done that," he whispers closing his eyes and swallowing deep.

"Nyx. I…" His tattooed hand suddenly slams across my mouth, and he touches a finger from his other hand over his own lips to silence me.

"Ssssshhhh." His warm breath heats my skin.

The sound of shoes squeaking against the gym floor, and the tapping of heels come from behind me.

"I could have sworn they were still in here, Miss," Luke's voice echoes around the gym as he leads the Principal on a hunt to bring Nyx to justice. I panic, and a wicked smile puckers on Nyx's lips like he's enjoying every second of it.

He waits until the doors swing shut before reaching into his bag and pulling out a hoodie, the same hoodie he'd worn when he'd come to my balcony a few nights ago. "Put this on, you need to cover up that ass." He tosses it at me. "I'll walk you to Abby's car."

"How did you know I came with Ab…" Nyx gives me a look that suggests I shouldn't bother asking, and all I can do is shake my head and smile. "Abs is having tuition, she's gonna be another half hour. I was gonna wait in the library."

"Well, then I'll walk you to the library." He picks up his bag and flings it over his shoulder, while I put his hoodie on. It's so big that it covers my ass and the tops of my thighs too, making me feel a lot more comfortable. I'm following him out into the corridor when I reach out and grab at his hand to pull him back.

"Next time, I'll try sticking up for myself. You're gonna get in some real trouble for this." All the excitement I've been feeling fizzles to dread when I think about him taking all the blame.

"If there's a next time, Ella. I'll kill him," Nyx says, and his flat tone and the look in his eyes is enough to suggest that his threat isn't empty, and for the first time in my life I actually feel a little sorry for Luke Robinson.

CHAPTER 9

She's Prez's daughter.

Jimmer Carson's fucking daughter.

And whatever shit I just tried pulling is suicide. My head tries to remind my cock of that fact as I keep a firm grip of her hand in mine and walk her to the library. I need to pull my head out of my ass and tell myself that none of this is real. I don't come from a world where high school kids make out in gyms.

It's just gonna be hard to accept, now I know how good it feels to have her lips on mine.

Ella finds a seat in a quiet corner, and I join her, sitting in awkward silence while she pulls her books from her bag.

"You don't have to stay with me," she speaks up first, sounding shy, and all I wanna do is kiss her again.

"I know I don't." I can't look up from the spot on the table I'm staring at. My head is still trying to catch up with how stupid I've been, and looking at her isn't gonna help me regret what just happened.

"Luke won't bother me again today and Principal K is looking for you. You should probably get out of here. She'll have already rung your par…" Ella quickly stops herself when she suddenly remembers what I told her last night. "Sorry," she shrugs, biting her lip awkwardly and making me want to sink my tongue between them all over again. I shake my head, let her know it's okay. I have thick skin, fucking bulletproof. It'll take a lot more than words to hurt me.

"Mr. Anderson," the icy tone snaps from behind me, and I'm pissed with myself for being too distracted to hear her coming.

"Time to face the music," I breathe out, standing up and slowly turning around.

Principal K stretches her neck so her slanted eyes can square up to mine. Bitch don't look impressed.

"Follow me. Now." She spins on her heels, and her little legs march off hella faster than I expect them to. I take long strides to keep up with her, following her all the way to her office and when she opens the door, I make sure I take a seat before giving her the pleasure of telling me to.

"Well Mr. Anderson, it seems that you couldn't heed my warning," she starts with a satisfied smirk slightly loosening the tightness of her lips.

"No Miss, Luke Robinson didn't heed mine," I correct. The time for ass licking is long gone.

Principal K rounds her desk and sits down on her chair, keeping her back straight and tweaking the photo frame containing her family a touch to the left.

"You know I'm going to have to exclude you for what you did today. You can't urinate on fellow students and expect to get away with it." She purses her lips together but soon slackens the tension in her face when I give her a wide, fake smile.

"I take it Luke Robinson will be joining me then?" I keep my eyes focused on her as she stares back at me blankly. "I was only giving him a taste of his own shit. Did he tell you that he stole Ella Jackson's gym bag and pissed all over her stuff?" Her lack of response gives me the answer to my question.

"No… well, I assume that now you do, he'll get the same punishment as me." She closes her eyes while she tries to form words.

"I… um… Mr…"

"Let's cut the fucking shit, shall we, Miss?" I watch her eyes double in size as I continue. "The reason Luke Robinson walks around this school like he fucking owns it, is because he pretty much does."

"I don't know what you're suggesting… but…"

"I'm not suggesting anything." I stand up from my chair and make my way to the other side of her desk, resting my ass on its surface just to her left. I look at the photograph of her family and fake a laugh. I have plenty of shit to worry about, but being suspended isn't one of them. Prez isn't stupid enough to have sent me here without a plan B, and thanks to Maddy, plan B is gonna be what keeps me here for as long as I need to be.

"Mr. Robinson Senior is generous ain't he. One of the board of directors, I hear he's made some impressive financial contributions to this place, am I right?" I tilt my head to the side and watch her start to panic.

"It isn't a secret that Mich… Mr. Robinson has funded certain aspects of the school in the past, but that wouldn't be a cause for me to treat his son any more favorably than any other student."

I shake my head. "No, I guess it wouldn't, would it, Miss?" Leaning forward, I make sure I'm so close that her expensive perfume itches at my nostrils and that I'm causing her unease. "The fact that you're fuckin' his father might though," I whisper.

She freezes, stunned into silence and as I pull back, I reach behind me to pick up the framed family photo. "Such a happy lookin' family, where was this taken? It looks like a nice place."

She snarls back at me like a caged tiger. "And Mr. K looks like a decent guy, what's up with him? Doesn't he do it for you anymore, Miss?"

"Nicolas, I suggest you stop there, what you are insinuating is not only ridiculous but impossible to make evident." There's a nervous quake in her voice now, all her authority completely vanished.

"Your daughter, she's in 9th grade here, right?" I check. "I can only imagine the shit she'd have to take if your dirty little secret crawled its way out of the gutter." I place the photograph back where it belongs, tweaking it myself into a perfect position.

"Tell you what, Mrs. K, I'll privilege you with the same advantage you gave me. A warning. You won't suspend me for what I did today, but you will punish Luke for what he did and for any more trouble he causes Ella Jackson. And as a thank you, I will assure you that the evidence I got that backs up my impossible allegations remains hidden. You get to keep your career, your reputation, and your flat fuck attempt at marriage all intact."

Principal K stares back at me like she wants me dead, I don't blame her for that, right now I really do have her wedged between a rock and a hard place. I stand up and make my way to the door, letting myself out and leaving it open.

"Was there anything else, Miss?" I ask in an all-American preppy boy voice making sure her receptionist hears. "No? Guess I'll be seeing you tomorrow then."

I wink at Rita the receptionist on my way out—she seemed to take a shine to me on my first day—before I walk back to the library feeling pretty fuckin' smug. I can't wait to put Ella's worries about getting me in trouble at ease, even though I won't be able to tell her how I fixed it.

When I get there, she's already gone. And my bag is still on the table, a note sitting on top of it.

I hope you didn't get into much trouble. I'm sorry, I kept your hoodie to save me the shame of leaving in my gym kit. Will return it to you tomorrow. Unless you want to come get it tonight. (That's an invitation BTW)

Ella x

She's even gone out of her way to draw a winky face after her sarcastic comment, which makes me smile.

I head straight to the club to shower, then check in at the garage before I leave. Rogue has her head buried under a hood when I get there.

"Nice of you to show ya face," she calls out over her music.

"I actually came here to see if you needed me for anything?" I bite back.

She straightens up and stares at me blankly, reminding me that Rogue has never needed anyone for anything in her life. Not from what I can gather anyway. There ain't no denying the girl's fuckin' hot. In a totally psychotic, fuck with your head and your man business kind of way. Her blonde hair and makeup are always perfect, while her hands and pink colored overalls are usually covered with oil.

She's a total contradiction of herself.

"In that case, I'll head over to the studio."

"Save your energy. I saw Tac head inside the club about an hour ago," she informs me before getting back to work. Looking at the time, I realize how late it is. I must have spent longer jacking in the shower than I realized.

Heading across the yard to the club, I go in search for Tac. The last thing I want is for him to think I've abandoned my responsibilities at the studio, and I find him talking to Prez in the member's only bar.

"Hey kid," he looks up when he hears me come in.

"Tac, I'm sorr…"

"No explanation needed. Prez has just been speaking to me, I can manage at the studio while you got eyes on Tommy. Getting Skid that fucking brother of his is more important. You keep hard on that fucker and don't worry about me, kid." He wraps his hand around the back of my head and pulls me closer. "Jessie mentioned summit about it the other week, but you never told me how stretched you were," he adds before he pulls away and lights up a smoke. "I'ma go get my dick polished, I'll catch up to ya later."

Prez waits for Tac to close the door before he speaks.

"How's it goin'?" he asks, his face suddenly turning serious.

"It's actually goin' okay. I asked her for some help studying, thought it would be a good in. She's already let it slip that she doesn't like her father. I'm hoping to find out why soon."

"Good work, kid." He nods back, impressed.

"You free tonight? Club got something that needs takin' care of, we could use you. But if you need to study, I'm sure we can cover it."

I think about taking the opportunity to take Ella up on her invitation. I could go to her tonight, maybe we could even hang out like regular teenagers do. But I don't trust myself around her. Not now that all I can think about is kissing her again.

Normality is what I need to get me thinking straight again. And this is my normal.

"I'm free, could use some action." I tip my chin at Prez.

"Cage leaves in an hour," he tells me with a smirk, his head gesturing towards the door signaling for me to leave. I step out into the foyer and take a breath, hoping that whatever job Prez has for me tonight involves me getting my hands dirty.

An hour later, I'm sitting in the back of the cage opposite Squealer and Screwy. Brax is beside me while Grimm's behind the wheel. The fact he's come along is enough to suggest things are gonna get messy.

"You good, kid?" Brax asks me, sliding his black leather gloves over his hands.

"Yep," I nod, knowing that all the tension inside me is soon gonna be relieved. For a while at least.

"Should be an in and out." Squealer smiles, spinning the silencer onto the end of his Glock.

"You're covering us from the back," Brax gives me my order and it immediately pisses me off.

"What? No. I want in."

"Don't argue, kid, you're still green and Prez has put me in charge of this little excursion. We got Grimm covering upfront, and you're watchin' the back, end of discussion."

"I ain't green." I snap back the slider on my semi-automatic to load its chamber. I've taken out more than one man for this club, probably nowhere near the number Brax has, but that don't mean I ain't capable of pulling this off.

"Leave the killing to the big boys." Squealer winks, flipping the toothpick he's holding between his teeth.

Asshole.

"We're here," Grimm calls back at us. We pull the balaclavas down over our heads.

"Remember, nobody takes out Nelson, we promised Declan we'd take that fucker back breathing."

"But the rest, they're fair game, right?" Squeal checks.

"Have at it." Brax smirks before Grimm slides the side door open, and we all pile out.

I dart off into the tree line behind the house. When I see it's all clear, I give them the signal. And then have nothing to do but listen to the sound of wood splintering, followed by muted ping gunshots. I'm pissed as hell; I didn't come here to be fuckin' look out. I want in on the action, and I can guarantee if I had my patch that's exactly where I'd be. I've proved on more than one occasion that I'm handier for more than being a pair of fuckin' eyes.

The back door suddenly flies open and a man stumbles out. He starts picking up pace and I can't see through the dark whether it's Nelson or not. I point my gun aiming for the fucker's knee cap, and after I pull the trigger he only manages to make another few meters before he hits the deck. I race over to him, checking he ain't armed before I press my boot into his throat and keep him grounded. Fucker looks familiar, with a shaved head and an angry-looking scar that cuts from his eye to the corner of his mouth. I remember serving him drinks at the club when the Utah Charter last visited.

"Fuck," he shuts his eyes tight, and tries to suck in air from underneath my foot. The traitor knows he's in fuckin' trouble.

I reach down and haul the asshole up by his scruff, placing him on to his feet and pressing the chamber of my gun against his temple. Brax comes racing out the back door, slowing down when he sees that I've caught his mark.

"This what ya looking for?" I toss Nelson forward, landing him in a heap at Brax's feet. The fucker can carry him back to the van himself.

"And that's a wrap." Squealer appears behind Brax along with his mute brother, Screwy's face is splattered with blood and the dripping knife he's holding in his hand suggests that tonight he went for blade over bullets.

I ain't surprised. Screwy likes to make them suffer. He'd make an excellent executioner if he had a fraction of the patience Jessie or Brax do.

"Your boys back home wanna speak to you, brother." Brax kicks Nelson hard in the ribs.

"Load him up," he orders, looking up at me, his eyes daring me to argue. I glare back at him, holstering my gun and stepping forward, lifting the guy by his scruff and dragging him back to the cage where Grimm is waiting.

"Ya got three turning stiff back there, Grimmy." Squealer looks pleased with himself as he steps up into the back of the cage and gives Nelson a hard shove in the back, forcing him onto the bench seat. Grimm nods his head thoughtfully, before pulling a huge duffle bag off the front seat.

"See you back here when you've dropped them off," he tosses me the keys. "And bring shovels."

Great, looks like I'm spending my night shifting fuckin' stiffs.

I take the driver's seat and wait till everyone's loaded before I pull off.

"You fucked up, Nel," I hear Brax snarl.

"It ain't what you're thinkin'," Nelson argues back, and I glance over my shoulder when I hear a loud thud. Screwy's just cuffed the sorry motherfucker in his jaw, I wouldn't be surprised if the force that came from behind his fist hasn't dislocated the thing.

"Oh, so we didn't just find you cozied up, sharing flake with five of Yardley's goffer's?" Brax mocks. "You know, my instructions were to take you back in one piece so your own Charter can serve you your punishment. But I'm struggling to see what I'm gonna get out of that," he threatens.

I'm just glad I'm not in Nelson's position. Nobody fucks with Brax, he's a different breed of Dirty Soul.

"I can explain," Nelson pleads. Brax has a reputation for being merciless, and I don't hold out a lot of hope on this fucker making it back to his Charter whole.

"You wanna tell us why you're so far away from home, cuttin' blow with those dead motherfuckers?" I watch Brax calmly light up a smoke in the rearview mirror, its cherry glowing and illuminating the fear on Nelson's face. And I'll bet he's wishing I'd shot that bullet into his skull right about now.

"Come on, man, I got a family to feed. Club back home ain't doing so well, I was trying to make some connections for the club," Nelson stutters his lame-ass excuses.

"You getting a whiff of that, Screw?" Squealer sniffs the air in front of him. "Smells like fuckin' bullshit to me."

"Those fucking cowboys have had feds sniffing up their ass for months. There's a reason we've stayed clear of them and their business, you stupid fuck." Brax stubs out the end of his cigarette in the space between Nelson's eyes and I hear him hiss out in pain.

"I didn't know that, I swear, take me back to Jimmer and let me explain, please, Brother, you got to believe me."

"I ain't your fucking brother no more," Brax tells him before I hear a painful scream come from behind me.

"That was your spleen," Brax speaks to him calmly. "You keep that knife in place, you might survive long enough to make the journey back to the club. Our doc can fix you up and I'll get to keep the promise I made Declan to get you back to him alive. Piss me off with any more of your bullshit, I swear I'll pull that knife out myself and let you bleed out right here in the back of this cage. To fuck with promises."

I flick my eyes back there again and catch Squealer snorting a line off the arch of his hand. "Rest in peace, Yardly, ya cut some good shit." His eyes look up at the truck roof before he looks at Nelson and laughs like a fucking psychopath. "Ya know, it's been a while since I watched someone bleed out. What about you, Nyxy boy?" he callss out at me.

It's gonna be a long assed fuckin' night.

CHAPTER 10
ELLA

It's the Mother-Daughter Luncheon day and, same as every year, Mom's insisting that I dress to standard. Today's choice isn't as bad as some of the previous years' choices, but I still look like a Stepford housewife in training.

My white summer dress tapers in at the waist, the floaty skirt section finishing respectably a few inches above my knees. My look is finished off with a yellow cardigan and matching pumps. I protested against having my hair pinned in a French pleat, reminding Mom that I'm eighteen and not forty. Instead, I compromised and agreed to wear a yellow headband behind a subtle quiff.

"You look great," I assure Abby when her and her mom arrive to pick us up. Abby's eyes roll in her head, unimpressed. She's also been dressed to resemble a china doll, looking completely out of her comfort zone in a baby blue dress cut below the knee with a matching jacket.

The luncheon is exactly the same boring fiasco that I remembered it to be last year. The Hannigan sisters attempt to gossip, and Abby and I smile sweetly, making polite conversation back. When we're seated at our tables, I'm pissed off that I've been separated from Abby. It's all part of the club's attempt to network, and I'm suddenly surrounded by fake, mindless women incapable of talking about anything besides their husband's career and how exceptional their children are.

I sip tea, and engage in a dull conversation with the senator's wife who's been positioned beside me. She persistently brags about her son and how he's heading for law school once he finishes his bachelor's degree. Meanwhile, I can't get the image of Nyx out of my head, his plump bottom lip and how his eyes spark a thrill inside me. The skin on my arms tingle when I think of his fingers touching me yesterday, and the inappropriate flutter between my legs seeps into my panties when I think about the dreams I've been having about him lately.

I excuse myself from the table, picking up my clutch, which of course matches my cardigan, and make my way to the bathroom. Locking myself inside a cubicle, I take out my phone and stare at the message Nyx sent me last night. I'd fallen asleep before it came through and when I opened it this morning, it made my chest beat like it was caging a thousand butterflies.

Night x

That's all it said. Nyx doesn't seem like the kind of guy who puts kisses after his messages and it makes me feel special. I hadn't had time to message him back earlier, not with mother flapping around like a chicken trying to get us ready, so decide to type a message back to him now.

Hope you slept okay. I'm at the most boring luncheon at my father's club. You up to much?

I keep it casual and return to the table. The senator's wife picks the conversation straight back up, and Abby gives me an unimpressed glance from across the room where she's been seated beside Mrs. Hannigan herself. I feel my phone vibrate on my lap and can't resist taking a look.

Guess being an orphan has its perks after all.

I try to hide the giggle that I snort behind my hand, and earn myself a sharp look from Mom. Then, keeping my hand under the crisp white table cloth I write back a quick reply.

And here was me hoping you might live up to your reputation and come rescue me.

"I'm sure Ella would love to meet Ruben when he next visits, wouldn't you, dear?" I feel a sharp kick at my ankle and look up to one of Mom's fake smiles, her wide eyes peering at me expectantly.

"Ruben? Ruben…"

"Mrs. Bennet's son," Mom speaks through her teeth, but I'm too distracted by another vibration against my thigh that I know is another reply from Nyx.

"Sure, why not." I smile at the woman beside me. Then quickly flick my eyes down to my phone.

On my way, princess.

Dread seeps from my preppy headband all the way down to my toes. Because with Nyx, I know anything is possible and a few minutes later, when the harpist's soothing strings are drowned out by a very loud, gravelly engine, heat floods my entire body.

It can't be him, how would he know what club my father is a member of? And even if he did know, he couldn't have gotten here this fast.

I smile a nervous smile across the table, and find the confidence to raise my eyes and look out the patio doors at what everyone else is staring at. Sure enough, it's Nyx that's caused the disturbance.

He skids up the flagstone, gravel beneath his tires as he rides around the fountain at the front of the building. The bike he's riding is different to the one he usually rides to school and he pulls it to a stop on the other side of the lawn from the glass doors that separate us. He looks sinful saddling the leather seat, his hand twisting the throttle and making his engine rev.

He's staring at me through the glass, willing for me to go to him and I pull away from his intense glare to look at Abby. She claps her hands together excitedly until a side glare from her mother causes her to quickly look back down at her plate.

"Whatever's this?" Mother asks with one of her snooty laughs, her eyes focused on the senator's wife.

"That's my ride." I take a deep breath as I stand up, leaving any sense I claim to possess at the table with the dullest group of people I've ever met in my life.

A horrified gasp leaves Mom's mouth as I dash around the tables and push open the doors to the patio. Adrenaline pumping frantically into my veins and ignoring the *please do not walk on the grass sign* as I race across the lawn.

Nyx smiles at me, revealing a tiny dimple in his left cheek that I've never noticed before.

"Hey." I smile back at him, blanking out all the chaos I've left behind me.

"Princess." His smirk spreads wider as he gestures his head over his shoulder, daring me to hop on behind him.

"Ella Rose Jackson... I forbid you to get onto that motorcycle," Mother's distressed voice calls out from behind me and when I turn around, I see a crowd has gathered on the patio. Mom's hand cups her mouth, her knees turning inwards like she's about to collapse and I mouth a sorry to her before throwing my leg over the seat and straddling behind Nyx.

"Hold on tight, darlin'," he warns me as he pulls off, and when I clench my arms tighter around his solid middle, he does something that makes the engine screech louder and speeds us out the gates of my father's precious club.

My grip doesn't loosen for the whole journey. I don't ask where he's taking me, I don't care. All that seems to matter is the fact he came. I can't think about the consequences, not while I'm on such a high.

It feels like I'm soaring as he rides us through the mountains and as I breath in the fast flowing air around me, I don't care how harsh my punishment will be. The rush of being bad with Nyx feels too good to be worrying about them.

Nyx surprises me when he veers off the road into some woodland. This bike is much rougher and louder than his normal one, I don't know if it's even road legal and I hold on a little tighter as we bounce over the rougher terrain. He cuts the engine when we come to a clearing, waiting for me to climb off before he gets off himself and props the bike against one of the trees.

He remains silent, threading his fingers through mine to grip my hand and leading me deeper into the forest until we reach a shelter hidden amongst the trees and bushes.

"What's this?" I ask as he tugs me closer.

"This is my kick-ass hideaway." He shoots me with that boyish grin again, and it looks so good on him I'm desperate for him to kiss me again.

"You have a hideaway?" I can't help laughing at him.

"Built it when I was younger." I catch a touch of pride in his tone and suddenly feel bad for mocking him.

"It's impressive." I keep the smile on my lips as we step closer to the barely held together structure, complete with a rusty tin roof.

"I ran away from my foster home when I was fifteen and lived here for a few weeks before I met Ta…" he quickly stops himself from sharing more than he intended with me.

"Why have you brought me here, Nyx?" I ask. He keeps so much of himself hidden away, maybe he finally wants to share something with me.

"I brought you here because I know no one will find us here," he answers, keeping us moving forward.

"Wow, that sounds a lot like the kinda thing a serial killer would say before he slices up the girl and leaves her for bear food."

Nyx laughs, and it warms the pit of my stomach.

"Don't be stupid… there ain't no bears out here." His voice

turns deadly serious and he totally deserves the punch I lay into his shoulder. Even if I do have to pretend the impact with his solid muscle didn't hurt my knuckles.

"So, you gonna show me inside?" I ask, getting impatient, and Nyx answers my question by opening up the old refrigerator door that serves as an entrance.

"You really built this yourself?" I check, actually impressed with the skills of fifteen-year-old Nyx. Judging by the conditions inside, the shelter's roof hasn't let in any water. There's a hammock hanging from one tree trunk to another, and an old bus chair in the corner. It really is a kick-ass hideout.

"What's this?" My fingers touch the hooded skull that's carved into the wood. I think I recognize it, I just can't make out where I've seen it before.

"That's nothing…" Nyx spins me around and forces me to sit on the bus seat. "Listen, we got to talk." He sounds serious all of a sudden.

"Talk about what?" I try not to sound disappointed, I was kinda hoping he'd brought me here so we could make out like we did in the gym yesterday. And then I start to panic when he scrubs his hand over his face like something's worrying him.

"I… I don't know," he sighs, frustrated.

"Nyx, you picked me up from my father's club on a dirt bike and rode me all the way out to a secluded forest to talk, and now you don't know what you want to talk about. Do you realize how crazy that sounds?" I snort a tiny laugh, hoping it might ease some of the sudden tension.

"Yeah," he shrugs back unapologetically, and all I can do is shake my head back at him in confusion.

"I wanna play a game," Nyx blurts out after a long thoughtful silence that I thought was never going to end.

"I thought you weren't a game kinda guy," I remind him.

"Yeah, well this time I'm making up the rules." He crouches down and sits on the floor opposite me, crossing his legs. "You get to ask me any question you like and I'll answer, but after, I get to ask you whatever I want and you can't ask me why." I take a deep breath because this game he wants to play sounds appealing, especially since I know so little about him.

"And I get to go first?" I check before committing.

"You do." He dips his head slowly, like he's psyching himself up for something.

"Okay," I agree to play along. "Why have you been following me?" I shoot straight to the most important question of all, the one that I can't sleep thinking about.

"I like knowing that you're safe," he responds quickly, not taking a single second to think about his answer. "My turn… Why do you hate your father?" Nyx seems so focused on what I'm going to say next, it's making me wonder if this question is the whole reason he brought me here.

"I hate him because he's a horrible person." I put it as simply as possible "He's mean to my mom, and I don't know what I've ever done to make him hate me the way he does. He's a controlling malicious asshole…"

I'm starting to wish we had whiskey here too.

"Where do you live?" I fire another question at him, not liking his chosen subject. It makes me think about the trouble I'm in back at home.

"About a forty-minute ride from school…" he answers vaguely, moving on to his next question.

"Has your father ever hurt you… physically?"

"Not yet." I keep up with his fast pace. Hoping to divert my answer. It's a scary truth, but I always wonder if that day will come. For now, Father seems content to take everything out on Mom.

"Why are you so reckless?" I'm not letting Nyx off lightly. He never seems to worry about his actions and seems to thrive off getting into trouble.

"I'm not reckless, darlin'." He shakes his head stubbornly, a tiny grin on his face suggesting I've amused him.

"You so are. You're always acting before you think, it's like nothing scares you," I argue back.

"I guess I gave up fearing shit a long time ago," he shrugs. "What happened between you and Luke?" he immediately shoots me with another question.

"Nothing, I think that's why he's so mean to me. He asked me out once, I didn't want to go, and he's hated me ever since. That's the whole story."

Nyx nods slowly, but he doesn't seem convinced. I use my tongue to wet my lips, they feel dry all of a sudden, and the air is really stuffy in this small space we're in. Then, feeling brave I decide to jump to the question I've been dying to ask.

"You ever gonna kiss me again?"

Nyx shifts off his ass and onto his knees, his face leveling with mine. And when he leans into me, I don't just hear his words, I feel them.

"If you keep tempting me, I might not be able to stop myself." It would be easier than breathing to edge forward and help myself to him, but I want him to kiss me like he's hungry for me. Just like he did in the gym.

"So, you really think I'm reckless, huh?" he snaps me out of my recollection, putting space between us and resting his back against a weathered filing cabinet that's missing a few drawers.

"I don't think it, Nyx, you are reckless. You act first and think later."

He chuckles to himself as he lifts his ass off the ground to pull a packet of cigarettes from his jeans pocket, and I watch him casually slip one between his lips before he lights it up.

"If that's your definition, then you're pretty reckless yourself," he points at me with his cigarette, releasing a mouthful of smoke at the same time.

"Absolutely not," I disagree, I'm many things, reckless certainly isn't one of them.

"Did you think before you jumped on the back of my bike in front of your mom and all her friends back at your daddy's fancy club?" He cocks an eyebrow at me smugly, reminding me what a huge storm of shit will be waiting for me when I get home.

"You're a bad influence." I move, standing up in front of him. His eyes slowly lift up my body. Looking up at me from under his hooded eyes, his mouth is just inches away from the place that sparks to life whenever I'm around him, and I can't help wondering how it might feel to have him kiss me there too.

"What did I tell you about tempting me?" he warns, his eyes following a path from between my legs all the way to my pupils and I feel wound up so tight, I swear I'll combust if he doesn't do something physical to me.

"Obviously you're not as reckless as I thought you were," I huff, moving to pass him to get some air and I gasp out loud when his hand shoots up and snatches at my hip, preventing me from leaving.

"You really want me to kiss you again?" he asks, stubbing out his smoke in the ground before he flicks it away. His other fist gripping so tight at my dress I can feel all the tension in it.

"Yes," I answer him back way too fast and likely sounding desperate. But I'm so past pretending with him.

"But today, I really want you to kiss me here." Bravely I place my palm over the hand he's got hold of me with, and slowly guide him to where I crave his touch. The pressure of his fingers as they touch me through my dress making my pussy ache for something it's never had before. And when Nyx's eyes snap up to mine, he looks shocked and scared all at the same time.

"Ella Jackson… You're are gonna be the fuckin' death of me," he rasps darkly.

CHAPTER 11
NYX

One second she's innocently asking me if I'm ever gonna kiss her again, the next she's got my hand on her pussy, telling me that's where she wants it.

When I tell her she'll be the death of me, she has no idea how literal I'm being. There's no doubt she will be now, especially when there's no way I'm gonna refuse her.

Standing over me looking so prim and pretty, with her white sundress as pure as she is. And that fucking yellow band she's wearing adding to the whole virgin straight out of prep school kink that's got my dick steel fuckin' hard.

Her hand trembles over mine as she holds it where she wants me. She has no idea that this isn't the first time my hand has touched her there, or that the last time I'd been the one controlling the pressure. And when her smooth palm presses me tighter between her legs, I swear I feel her pulsing beneath my fingertips again.

I keep my eyes on hers as I trail my middle finger over the cotton of her dress. And watching her head roll back as she's finding relief has my cock growing thicker in my jeans.

Cupping her pussy in my palm, I pull her closer and put her in the perfect position for me to take her with my mouth and devour her like my last fucking meal.

The way things are shaping up, it's looking like she might be.

Ella steps one leg over mine, her thick hazel iris's holding on to mine and begging for me to give her what she's asked for. I wrap my free hand around her ankle, and her skin feels silky smooth beneath mine as I slide the arch of my hand all the way up to her toned thigh. Fisting her dress, I scrunch the fabric and raise it over her waist revealing the cutest lace panties I've ever seen, with a damp patch growing right in the center of them.

All my senses are set on fucking fire by what I'm seeing. Her little breaths flooding my ears. The blood under her skin heating my fingertips, and that fucking flowery scent of hers driving me wild. I hook a finger inside her panties, let her slickness coat the tip as I trail it slowly through her neat little slit to that spot that's craving all my attention.

I massage her there with tiny circles, and her hand's fist at my hair as her hips dance to the rhythm of my fingers. When her hand grabs at her dress, freeing up my hand, I'm tempted to rip her panties the fuck off. But instead, I steadily peel them past her knees, I should keep hold of them, request they get fuckin' buried with me. If this pussy is gonna be my one-way ticket to hell, I want to make sure the memory of it lingers with me forever. Ella lifts a foot from the floor so I can slide them all the way down her legs and out of my way.

"Kiss me, Nyx, please." Her hips coax me, rocking closer to my mouth, and I do what any other *reckless* person would do in my situation. I take that innocent little pussy to my lips and I kiss the ever-living shit out of it.

I taste purity in its sweetest form as I explore her with my tongue. Spreading her pussy with my fingers, and licking straight through her center. I look up her body and watch her. She looks so beautiful taking pleasure from me and I can't resist teasing her entrance with the tip of my finger.

"Fuck, yes," she curses breathlessly, I ain't ever heard her swear before, and Ella's filthy little mouth turns me the fuck on. So much, that I can't resist pushing my middle finger inside that sacred little hole. She's so tight, her pussy puckering around me as she takes me to the knuckle. I want to fill so much more space inside her, but worry it'll hurt her. And I can't help wonder what the fuck my cock would do to her.

It's exactly the point I'm letting myself forget about me and her. I ain't supposed to fit… We ain't meant to fit together. Things were never meant to go this far. But I push all that shit to the back of my mind, my tongue continuing to flick against her clit while I fuck her with my finger.

When her hand grips my hair tighter and her breaths get heavier, I slide both my hands behind her knees, forcing them forward so her legs bend. At the same time, I slide down onto my back.

"Ride my face, Ell," I tell her, my lips already missing the taste of her pussy.

"What?" she looks down at me, all wide-eyed and open mouthed, like the thought terrifies her

"I want you ridin' my fuckin' face," I repeat myself. Desperate to get her back on my mouth.

"I don't know how," she whispers, shaking her head, her cheeks flushing with embarrassment.

She's too fucking perfect…

"There ain't no right or wrong way to do it, princess. Just sit that pretty little pussy on my mouth and take what you need from it." I smirk up at her and Ella bites her lip before nodding back at me with newfound confidence. Placing her thighs on either side of my head she saddles my face so I'm reacquainted with that already soaked snatch.

Pressing an outstretched palm against the filing cabinet in front of her she steadies herself as she slides back and forth over my tongue. At first, she seems timid and unsure, but it doesn't take her long to discover how she likes it, and finally, she lets go.

My fingers indent her thighs as she increases her speed, digging so deep into her flesh I'm sure I'm gonna leave bruises. And I'm not about to pretend I don't like the idea of leaving my mark on her. Ella does something territorial to me. I want everyone to know she's mine, despite the fact I know I'll never really have her.

Her dress falls over my eyes, blocking my view of her face. She's so close to coming apart for me, I can tell by the way she's trembling and I ain't prepared to miss that.

I pull the fabric that's in my way taut against her stomach, and get ready to watch her come for me while I fuck her with my tongue.

She moves faster and I feel her fuckin' throbbing. She's almost there, and fuck, it feels like I might be too, I swear the girl's gonna have me coming in my boxers like a needy virgin just from tasting her.

She's holding back on me, slowing down her pace every time she gets too close. So I take some control back, gripping both my hands at her hips and driving her thrusts against my mouth.

"Shit… Nyx," she shouts out my name like she's crying for help, her palm slamming hard into the rusty cabinet behind my head.

"Come on my tongue, Ell, give it up for me." I tear myself away for a second to tell her what I want, and as soon as my tongue returns to her needy little clit, she soaks it with all that pleasure I've been fuckin' begging for.

She wriggles her hips against my hands, her hips trying to escape the intensity of it all. But I hold her firm, making sure she gets the full experience.

Her scream is so loud it disturbs nesting birds from the trees outside. And she damn near crushes my head between her thighs as she tries to squeeze them together. She finally flops forward, sucking in a long deep breath and I can't pull my eyes off her face. She's resting her forehead against the cabinet, her long hair falling like shelter over both of us. And while her legs tremble and her chest seeks air, I take one last, long lick through her pussy, and I feel the shiver dance its way through her body.

We stay like that for a while, her hair tickling my face and neck, my fingers stroking over her thighs while our heartbeats find a normal beat. Eventually, Ella makes the first move, sitting back on my stomach, and smiling sweetly as she repositions that cute little headband like a princess whose tiara just slipped.

"We. Are. Doing. That. Again," she tells me in between breaths. And all I can do is smile back at her and nod her a silent promise.

Fuck it, I already crossed the bridge to hell and set it on fire when I decided to kiss her. All I can do is stand and watch it burn. It's only a matter of time before all this catches up with me and Satan comes to collect. I just hope he can wait a little longer, because I'm nowhere near done with Ella Jackson yet. And right now, I can't see that I ever will be.

Chapter 12
Ella

My legs shake the whole ride home. I wonder if Nyx feels them, or if the vibration from his engine dulls it out for him.

A cold, sickly feeling grows heavier in my stomach the closer we get to home.

It's much more than just nerves. Now that reality is hitting me, I'm petrified. Mom was furious when I left with Nyx, and I'm certain Father will expect nothing less than an internal organ as a sacrifice for bringing scandal to our family. And at his precious club of all places.

"You want me to come in with you?" Nyx frowns as he looks over his shoulder at me. He's pulled up a few houses down from mine and we've been sitting here in silence for a ridiculously long amount of time.

"No!" the answer comes out sharp as a razor, I can't have Nyx fighting me on this, I'm in enough trouble as it is.

"Ella…"

"Nyx, please. I'll be fine. It'll be so much worse if you come in with me," I beg, hoping he understands.

He doesn't look impressed, his eyes narrowing, and his nostrils flaring the way they always do when he's pissed about something.

"Fine… but I ain't going far. You know where I'll be, if you need me flick your bedroom light a couple of times." He twists his body around, his finger tipping up my chin to give him access to my mouth. His lips brush softly across mine and I can still taste myself on them. Even the shit ton of trouble I'm in doesn't stop me from smiling at that.

"Thanks," he whispers against my mouth. And I wonder what he's thanking me for? Surely, I should be the one thanking him.

"What you thanking me for?" I give in and ask, laughing nervously.

"For being reckless with me today." The soft tone of his voice and the hint of shyness in his expression makes whatever punishment I'm about to receive from my parents totally worth it.

I smile back at him before sliding myself off his bike and Nyx nods his head at me, for reassurance. He stands up from his seat, sliding his sunglasses back over his eyes, then kick starts his engine. The loud roar shakes through my bones, and I watch as he rips down the street, turning onto one of the side roads so he can access the back of the house.

It's a comfort knowing he won't be far away as I make the journey to my front door, my hand trembling as I pull down the handle and let myself in.

The large hall, or the reception as Mom likes to call it, is disturbingly silent, and I slip out of my pumps, picking them up to tiptoe as quietly as I can towards the stairs.

"Your fucking daughter has ruined this family's reputation." Father's voice comes booming from his office. It's typical that I'm always referred to as "her" daughter when I do something wrong.

"I won't tolerate it, Joanne. The girl's growing to be a desperate little slut, just like her mother." I seethe with anger, especially when I know the loud slap that follows his cruel words will have landed on Mom's face. This is all my fault.

Mom is suffering all because of my selfishness. I knew when I got on Nyx's bike that there would be consequences, I should have guessed that it would be Mom who'd be made to suffer them and I won't let her endure it a second longer.

Running across the hall, I burst through the doors into my father's office. And what I see in front of me is far worse than anything I imagined. The slap I heard wasn't aimed at mother's cheek, it's her back that he's struck, and it's his belt, not his palm that he's made the strike with.

Mom is on her hands and knees in front of his desk, her blouse rolled over her shoulder and I count at least five angry welts that have been thrashed against her skin. Black tears streak through her thick layers of foundation, and she turns her head from me in shame when she realizes that I've seen what he's done.

"What is this?" I ask, pure rage the only thing suppressing my tears.

"Ahh, your little slut returns, darling." Father's eyes roll over me in disgust. His lip snarling at me like an aggravated dog. "Look at the state you're in. Your dress is creased, your knees are grazed… Did you fuck that boy?" he spits out at me harshly, making me cringe.

"Vincent, please," Mom begs through her tears, and Father silences her with another sharp crack against her sore skin.

"You should be punishing me for what I did. Not Mom, none of this is her fault," I scream at him, growing the balls I should have years ago.

"Your mother should know better, she should have raised you better… Look at her, Joanne. Look at your slutty wreck of a daughter." He grabs Mom's cheeks in his podgy hand, squeezing them tight and forcing her to look at me. "Tell me, darling, are you proud of her now?"

Mom shuts her eyes tight, but not before I see the disappointment that they hold for me.

"You will receive your punishment when I'm finished here. I suggest you go and clean yourself up... I will call you down when I'm ready."

"Mom?" I call out at her, urging her to stand up and fight back. To take me and leave this house and this wicked man behind us.

"Please Ella, just do as your father tells you." She puts on a familiar brave face. Even on her knees with her bare back exposed and bleeding in front of me, she's still trying to maintain her dignity.

I turn and run up the stairs to my room. Slipping out of my dress to take a shower, I drench myself in the warm sprays allowing the water running through my hair to drip onto my face and disguise my tears.

Mom steps inside my room an hour later and judging by the state of her face, he hadn't finished with her when I left. She won't be leaving the house for a good few days, not even the most expensive cover-up makeup is gonna hide his marks this time.

"Your father wants to see you." Her voice sounds cold, and I ignore the wrench in my gut as I force myself off my bed. It's dusk outside and there's every chance Nyx is still watching. I contemplate flicking the switch as I pass it like he told me to. But it won't help. Him coming in here will only make Father angrier. I stop in front of Mom and pull her into my arms, being careful not to touch her back. I hate myself for what she's been through and it takes a while but eventually, her arms lift enough to hug me back.

"I'm so sorry, Mom," I cry into her shoulder.

"Ella, just take your punishment gracefully," her voice is emotionless as she offers me an apologetic smile, then backs away and walks across the landing to her room.

After a few deep breaths, I take the steps down the stairs one at a time while torturing my mind with the thoughts of what he might do to me. Dad's never raised a hand to me before. Up until now, he's seemed satisfied in knowing how much I hurt when Mom pays for my actions.

When I'm outside his office I wipe away any tears before I tap my knuckle against the door, waiting for his voice to permit me to enter, and when it does, I step inside.

The atmosphere is different from earlier. Father seems unnervingly calm, and is waiting behind his desk with a large drink poured in front of him, he almost seems pleased with himself.

"Close the door behind you," he orders and I do as he asks, the thud of the oak against its frame feeling like the final beat of my heart as I step closer towards him. The curtains are drawn across the windows so if Nyx is watching he won't be able to see me now. I stand in front of Father's desk, feeling his eyes judge me in disgust. There's no visible sign of the belt, at least I have that to be grateful for.

"You have embarrassed me and our family beyond any redemption, do you understand that, Ella?" he tells me calmly. My head bobs up and down in response, but I can't look him in the eyes.

"You have forced me to take action, and your mother has had to suffer the price for your decisions." Again, I nod, trying so hard to hold back my tears. This man doesn't deserve them, he's already gotten enough pleasure out of hurting Mom, I'd seen the sick satisfaction on his face as he struck her.

"I'll ask you again, did you fuck the boy?" He's getting impatient, and I don't need to look at his face to see how much the thought repulses him.

"No," I shake my head.

"And why, Ella, should I believe a single word that comes out of that lying whoring mouth of yours." His leather chair creaks when he stands up, and he slowly rounds his desk, prowling towards me until he's so close that I smell the whiskey on his breath.

"Did you give him your pussy, Ella?" My stomach clenches in disgust hearing those words come from his mouth as I shake my head again.

"Did you let him take your virginity?" he whispers heavily into my ear, his lips so close to touching me that it makes my skin crawl.

"No," I repeat.

"Come on, Ella, you don't honestly expect me to believe that you didn't let him touch you, especially given the state you came home in."

"He didn't. I promise." I focus so hard on holding in my tears.

"Is that why you had the doctor prescribe you those birth control pills, how long have you been sexually active, Ella?" He questions me harder. I have no idea how he could know any of this. I haven't even told Mom about my visit to the Doctor last year. It was Penelope's suggestion for me to ask for birth control as a way to steady my periods and so far, it's been working.

"No. That's not what they're for. I take them for my…"

"I could check for myself, you know."

His words chill the marrow inside my bones. I couldn't have heard them right, he couldn't be suggesting…

"You're my daughter and if I think you have been tampered with, I have every right to make sure that you're still intact."

"Please," I beg, trying to remain calm, but it's useless, a wet tear drips free and trickles slowly over my cheek. I'm beyond holding them back now. I'm too scared.

"Pull down your shorts, Ella… your underwear too," he commands so calmly it sounds like he's asking me to pass him the salt at the dinner table.

"No," I refuse. I can't let him do that, this is wrong on so many levels. I can't let my own father touch me there, he shouldn't even want to touch me there.

"Do as I ask, or I will drag your mother back down those stairs and beat her until the sun rises tomorrow morning," he threatens, closing his eyes like he's holding back his anger.

"Please, I'm not lying." I won't let him hurt her again, up until today I've only ever seen the aftermath of what he does to her. It's way worse than I thought, I've never seen her broken like the way I have tonight.

"You have lost my trust. I have no reason to believe you anymore. Now do as I say or go fetch your mother." He's losing his calm, practically foaming from the corners of his mouth, and I've never felt so helpless or hollow.

"Beat me. Take off your belt and lash me until daylight if it's what you need. I'm the one who did this not her," I beg him through sobs, and he responds by smiling back at me darkly.

I look to his window, wondering if Nyx is out there. I know he won't see and knowing what I'm gonna have to do next, a part of me is grateful for that. I can't imagine the damage he'd do if he saw my father touch me like he's suggesting.

"Listen to yourself, slut. Needy and begging for my fucking belt. Is that how you like it. Is that how you let him fuck you, like a dirty whore?"

"No," I croak, sliding down to my knees and grabbing at his ankles. "Please, you can take me to a doctor, let them give me a check-up. You don't need to do this."

I squeal when he snatches a fistful of my hair, tearing it from the scalp as he pulls me from the floor.

"You're my daughter. Slut. You're my responsibility. Now take off your underwear and let me check if you're lying to me or not." His spittle lands on my cheek as he talks. And my body goes numb as I pull myself back together and steady myself on my feet.

Humiliation melts me from the inside out, as my hands

tremble to force my shorts down to my ankles. I focus on the wall in front of me, sniffling back tears while I wait for what comes next, because there was no way Mom is gonna suffer for me a second time tonight.

"Sit," Father pats his hand on his desk surface. "If you're telling me the truth this is going to be uncomfortable for you." The sound of concern in his voice makes me retch, and I decide the only way I'm gonna get through this is if I blank everything out. I sit down where I'm told and my knees protest against his hand when he uses it to try to pry them apart. The warning look he gives me makes me think of Mom and how she's already had to suffer, and I slowly ease the tension in my muscles allowing him to spread my legs, while resisting the urge to kick him in his ugly face.

His cold fingers touch at my thigh before they taint everywhere Nyx's tongue had given me pleasure earlier. He prods and pokes further, sharp stabs of pain stinging me inside and making my mind scream so loud I want to crawl out of my body.

I blank out the sounds of my painful whimpers and his grunts, and turn my head to the side to focus on the huge acrylic painting of the scales of justice that hangs on his wall. I stare at it until it becomes blurry through my tears, tears that fill up my eyes and drip onto his desk. He takes his time, choosing to be thorough with his examination and I can feel myself shattering piece by piece.

I'm dry and sore against his fingers. And want to rip the heart out of my own chest just to make this horror be over. When he's finally satisfied that I'm telling the truth he pulls his fingers from inside me, and wipes them on my T-shirt.

"Seems you were telling me the truth after all." There's a hint of relief in his voice that makes me shudder. "But how do you explain these bruises on your thighs, Ella." He picks up his tumbler and takes a swig of its contents.

"Gymnastics..." I blurt out, thinking fast. "Me and Abby

have been practicing extra during break. We've been doing lifts." The voice speaking the lie back at him sounds like it belongs to someone else. I'm still an empty shell.

"You can call her and check if you need to," I add, needing to sell my story better.

"No need, precious. You've earned some of my trust back. We can work on the rest another time." The hand he strokes over my cheek is steady as a rock and I freeze under his touch.

"You're still my pure little princess," he whispers. I realize it's the most affection he's ever shown me in my life and it makes bile burn the back of my throat like acid. "Bedtime now." He moves out of my way and I quickly slide off his desk and pull my shorts back into place.

"Ella…" that warning tone returns to his voice again and I look up at him. "If that boy or anyone else thinks that they can break what's mine. I assure you, I will make sure it's the last thing they ever do."

My head screams at me to launch at him, to find that paperweight I've hidden from him countless times and use it to smash his skull to a pulp. But I'm weak, I feel like my body's been destroyed. I can still feel his fingers scraping inside me.

My own father. How will I ever get over this?

I nod my head solemnly before walking out of his office. I can't find the energy to run up the stairs like I want to, and when I eventually reach my room and lock my door, I dash straight to my ensuite. Lifting the toilet seat, I manage to gather up my hair just before the contents of my stomach come hurtling up.

I retch and I sob, gagging until my throat feels like it's bleeding raw. Then I turn on the bath, making sure the water is near scalding and hope it will burn any trace of him from my skin. I don't know how long I lay there staring at the white tiles but when I eventually force myself to get out of the water, just a look at my reflection causes me to throw up into the basin again.

I wrap the towel tight around me, and switch off my light,

making sure my balcony doors are open before I get into bed. I breathe a sigh of relief when I hear the familiar sound of the leaves rustling and then see him appear on my balcony. He must think I've gone to sleep because he's about to shut my doors and leave. So I sit up, grateful that it's dark and he can't see how puffy and swollen my eyes are.

"Nyx," I say his name so softly I don't know if he'll even hear it.

"Ell, what have I told you about keepin' these damn things shut." I hear the frustration in his whisper back at me, and it takes me out of my misery for just a moment when I think about what he told me earlier.

Nyx likes to know I'm safe. He cares about me in a way I've never experienced from anyone.

"You don't know who's out here," he adds and I even manage a snigger at the irony in that statement, he doesn't know it, but he's shutting me in here with the biggest monster of them all.

"Nyx, can you come and lie with me, just for a little while?" I ask, hoping he'll agree. I need to feel something again. I want so much for it to be him. He doesn't reply for twenty long, drawn-out seconds, and just when I think he's gonna say no he steps inside and looms over my bed. Cool air hits my back as he lifts up my covers, he replaces the heat when he slides in behind me and pulls me tight to his chest. His heart beats soundly against my back, steady and grounded. I feel safe again, just like I knew I would, and never want him to leave.

"You ok, darlin', was your dad angry?" he keeps his voice low but the concern in it.

"It wasn't so bad," I tell the biggest lie of my entire life because as much as my father scares me, what I suspect Nyx is capable of scares even me more. Something tells me he could crush a man like my father in the palm of his hand, and I won't lose him for that.

"Will you stay with me until I fall asleep?" I ask, a helpless plea in my tone that I hope he doesn't pick up on.

"Sure." He places a kiss on my temple like what I've asked of him is the simplest thing in the world. But to me, him being here means everything. He must have been waiting out there for me for hours and he's still prepared to stay for as long as I need him.

And God I need him right now.

He holds me tight against him, his lips and nose buried into my hair while his fingers draw shapes under the towel on the outside of my thigh. It soothes me, I want him to touch me everywhere, to wipe away all traces of my disgusting father's hands ever touching me. But I'm too sore, mentally and physically, I recall the discomfort of the whole ugly process and it causes more tears to soak into my pillow. I just hope Nyx doesn't notice them.

"Nyx, will you promise me something?" I whisper, trying to hide the tremble in my voice.

"If I can give it to you, I will," he replies softly and everything inside me trusts that he means it.

"Promise me, that it will be you." I turn in his arms and look up into his eyes. They're open wide, staring right back at me. His thumb swipes away a tear that's fallen beneath my lashes so gently that it makes my heart ache. "I want my first time to be with you. Promise me, it will be you." I cling to his chest, needing to hear him say the words. If I'm gonna come out the other side of this horror, he's gonna be my reason. I want to belong to Nyx Anderson. A part of me feels like I already do.

"I wouldn't have it any other way, princess." He kisses my temple again, and continues to draw those soft lazy shapes on my skin until I drift off to a place where only me and Nyx exist.

And those scales of justice actually balance.

CHAPTER 13

I stay with her long after she falls asleep. The sound of her breaths and feeling her chest against mine, far too satisfying to miss.

I know I'm not being fair to her, I'm leading us both down a false path to hopelessness. She just asked me to be her first. Even I know enough about bitches to know that to a girl like Ella, that's a big deal. Would it still be what she wanted if she knew who I really am, or why I'm here?

I'm not some mysterious kid who just rocked up at her school and suddenly became obsessed with her. I'm a selfish fuck up, sent here on an errand by her real father, who, yeah, has pretty much become obsessed with her. And lying here with her in my arms, I realize I'm completely fucked because I have no idea how I'm gonna let her go when this whole lie is done with.

Carefully, I slide out of her bed and creep out of her room. I'm starting to feel like I might fall asleep myself, it's the first time in a long time that I haven't had to try to. I can't risk that, I've got her in enough trouble for one day.

It kills me to leave her, especially when she's lookin' so fuckin' pretty, and all I can think about is the promise I just made her and how much I wanna see it through.

I make it back to the club just before 2am and I'm relieved that it's quiet. Jessie is talking to Skid around the fire pit, they look like they're having some kind of deep and meaningful thing, so I give them a nod as I pass.

"What's up?" I ask Grimm, he's got his back to the bar, his elbows propping him up, and an almost empty bottle in his hand.

"Just thinkin'," he answers me, his eyes focusing across the room at the girl who's sucking Screwy's cock, while one of her hands pumps hard at Squealer's cock.

"You wondering which one of 'em is gonna jack first?" I snigger, taking the joint he offers and dragging it between my lips. I hold on to the smoke in my chest until it burns and when I offer him it back, he shakes his head for me to keep it. Grimm gets weird about that kinda shit, if something's touched someone else's lips it ain't touching his. Maybe it's why he rarely gets himself laid around here. He seems to prefer to watch.

"My money's on Squeal," I say after exhaling.

I feel a hard squeeze on my shoulder and I know without turning around that it belongs to Prez.

"Grimm, give me and the prospect five, will ya," he nods him a dismissal and Grimm pushes his body off the bar, taking the bottle with him and heading out into the foyer.

"You got anything to tell me?" Prez asks, the look on his face unreadable. It's unnerving, but there ain't no way he could know about what happened this afternoon, if he did, I'd already be dead.

"We spoke some today. About her da… about the judge," I correct myself, referring to the Judge as Ella's Dad is gonna hurt him. "She really hates him, apparently he treats her Moma bad." Prez's eyes flare but I continue. "I asked if he'd ever hurt her, you know, like raised a hand. She said no, but I don't think I can say the same for his old lady." I don't miss the slight hiss that comes from between his teeth, and wonder if maybe a long time ago that black heart of his may have held some feelings for the bitch he knocked up.

He leans in closer, his voice dropping so that no one in the room can hear.

"You know how important the girl is to me, Nyx. I'll crush the life out of anyone who dares lay a finger on her. And I'm relying on you to make sure nothing is happening to the only thing I got left to fucking breath for."

"I got ya, Prez," I assure him, almost convincing myself.

Prez ain't one for showing emotion. When he lost Hayley, we all saw a weakness in him. I understand why he chooses to keep face for everyone, he's our leader and holds everything together around here. With nothing left to lose, he's feared now more than ever by our rivals. He ain't about to let Ella become a chink in his armor, and neither am I.

I finish up the joint and say my goodbyes, before I head somewhere to try and release all my tension before I attempt some sleep.

Halfway up the track to the cabins is an outbuilding we use as a gym. This time of night the place should be empty. Even Troj doesn't train this late. I'm proved wrong when I hear the dull sound of leather against leather from outside. Troj does have a fight coming up, maybe he's still going at it.

The thuds get louder and when I open the door, I'm surprised to see Brax pounding the shit into the punch bag. Brax has been a nomad for years and has the same twisted talents as Jessie. He's a great enforcer because, like Jessie, he gets a kick out of what he does.

He's been hanging around for a few months now, and I've heard whispers that he might be sticking around for good. The club sure as hell could do with him, we've already lost a member in Chop, which despite being good fuckin' riddance, is still a drop in numbers. The club is at a constant threat from rivals, and an extra pair of hands, especially skilled ones, would be welcomed.

"What ya doin' here kid?" Brax stops his assault on the bag

and throws an unimpressed look in my direction. He's drenched in sweat and sucking hard through his nostrils for breath, but I still wouldn't fuck with him. I've seen for myself what he's capable of.

"Same as you," I tell him, stepping forward and reaching over my shoulder to pull my tee over my head. Brax rips the Velcro on his glove open with his teeth and pulls it off, and after freeing his other hand he tosses both gloves at me. Then he surprises me when he picks up a pad and holds it up for me to punch. I've never really taken the time to speak to Brax, he's a loner, and where he sure has a voice, he don't often use it for making nice.

Still, he's dependable, strong, and has a no fucks attitude. Everyone likes him, but no one's close to him. Like me, he keeps himself to himself.

Once I've gloved up I get straight to work, throwing my fists at the pad he's holding, I can tell by the way Brax shrugs and nods at the same time that he's impressed. He's got nearly ten years on me, I stand taller and I'm built broader than he is, but I still know he could take me. He knows it too. I think the only person who could make him sweat is Troj.

"So, what's got under your skin?" he asks after one of my sharp blows pushes him backward. I consider ignoring him, ain't like I can tell him the truth.

Prez's secret daughter just offered me her virginity and I'm seriously considering fuckin' taking it.

"You been prospect a while now, right?" he keeps pushing.

"Yeah," I answer brashly. I ain't in the mood for a heart to fuckin' heart.

"Bet you're ready to wear that cut, huh?"

I hit the pad harder. I don't need a reminder of how close I am to getting what I want, it only reminds me how close I am to fuckin' it all up.

"Yeah," I give him another one-worded answer that's full of attitude.

"I see how bad you want it," he goads. "You got a fuckin' flair in ya that fuckin' screams it. You wanna tell me why you want in so bad, Nyx?"

I shrug before landing a solid punch into the pad, forcing him to take another step backward.

"Come on, tell me. I wanna know what drives your determination to fucking be here," he yells at me, and it's clear he's intentionally trying to aggravate me. It's working too. My blood is already scorching beneath my skin. "Come on, fuckin' tell me," he shouts, the veins in his neck standing out and his eyes deadly serious. I slam the pads so hard that my heart rate overtakes my ears. "Say it. Tell me why you want to be part of this club." I keep hitting until my fists become too heavy to hold up.

"Why do you fuckin' need in so bad?" he asks again, and I finally drop my guard.

"Because I got to fuckin' belong somewhere," I scream back at him, shoving all my weight into the pad he's holding. This time he's ready for it and he stands firm. I'm breathless and fucking furious that the fucker in front of me shares nothing of himself with anyone and he's somehow managed to get a weakness out of me.

Years of being passed from one foster home to another, never knowing my parents or having a family made me feel worthless. And if I don't have a place in this fucking world. If I don't belong, what's the purpose of existing in it?

That Dirty Soul who came to my foster home is the only clue I ever got into the life I should have had. Whoever he was, he gave me a purpose that day, he gave me a place to exist.

He'll probably never know it but he saved me. I stopped being a victim because of him.

I belong here, I feel it in my fucking blood.

"Well, you need to keep that in mind while you're dealing with whatever shit fuck you got goin' on beyond this compound." Brax drops the pad to the floor, picks up his white tee from the bench, and pulls it over his sweat covered torso. Then snatching up his leather cut, he makes for the door out of here.

"Hey Brax," I call out after him, I'm curious, he must have something keeping him here too, as a nomad, he chose not to belong anywhere, so why here, why now?

I'm surprised when he stops to look over his shoulder at me.

"What about you, why do you wear the cut?"

He stares at me long and hard before he speaks. I get the feeling he's either never been asked the question before, or he's spent a real long time avoiding answering it.

One word comes out of his mouth, sharp and unforgivingly before he turns back around and marches out.

"Vengeance."

CHAPTER 14
ELLA

I hate it when I come down the stairs and everyone is acting like today is a normal day. Mom, despite having a huge shiner on the side of her face, is sitting at the table wearing a wide phony smile and Dad is reading the newspaper. Penelope is the only one who contributes any normality to the situation, by offering me a sympathetic smile as she passes me my breakfast.

"Morning sweetheart," Mom chirps at me, and a newly formed irritation for her begins to root inside me. She could have taken us away from all of this years ago, but she made the decision to stay. And for as long as she's happy to ignore the fact Father is psychotic, I'm expected to go along with the whole charade too.

"Morning Mother." I know she hates it when I call her mother, and it brings me a tiny pleasure to know she will have to make her smile a little more fake than it already is. I finish up breakfast and throw my bag over my shoulder, desperate to leave and get to school.

"Where do you think you're going?" Father doesn't raise his head from the paper when he speaks but just his voice stirs unease in my chest.

"School," I reply sharply.

"I'll be taking you to and from school from now on," he informs me. I feel the dread creep its way onto my face and I'm pleased he isn't looking up, because I wouldn't want to give him the satisfaction of seeing it there.

"But…"

"No buts, Ella. You're grounded. I think you've gotten off lightly for your behavior, don't you?" his eyes lift from the paper, and when they gesture to Mom's swollen face it takes every strength inside me not to launch at him and gauge them out of their sockets.

Our journey to school is silent. My skin itches the entire way and I flinch every time his hand moves. I feel like I could throw up and I've never been more grateful to get to school when we finally arrive. I need to escape this stuffy car, it smells so strongly of air freshener that I can taste it on the back of my throat. I move to open the door, and he grabs at my knee, his fingers digging into my flesh and making me freeze.

"Remember what I said. You stay away from the boy. Unless you want to make those examinations a regular occurrence," he threatens.

The sound of my scream pierces my ears but no sound leaves my mouth. I open the door and jump out, rushing into school as fast as I can. Abby is already waiting at my locker for me, bouncing on her toes like the floor is made of hot coals.

"Morning." I manage a smile, opening my locker and dumping my bag.

"Morning? Morning…? You're kidding me, right?"

"No. last time I checked it's still morning." Rolling my eyes, I grab my physics textbook.

"You need to tell me what the fuck happened yesterday after hunkasaurus picked you up from the club on his bike. That was totally awesome. Tell me he kissed you. Tell me he fucking kissed you, Ella Jackson." She shakes my shoulders in her hands. But I blank her out completely when I see Luke glaring at me across the hall and turn my back.

"Morning," he calls out to me, and I ignore him.

"I said, good morning." He's standing beside us now, making it impossible for me to avoid him.

"Waiting on your boyfriend?" he asks with a smug grin that I'm so tempted to scratch off his face.

"What's it to you?" Abby bites back at him, we both know that the minute Nyx shows up, Luke's cocky act will be over.

"I'm just hoping you enjoy it while it lasts," he taunts, begging for me to retaliate. Instead, I search around the corridor impatiently. Nyx should be here soon. "I don't know what you see in him, but if I'd known that the bad boy vibe was what got in those panties, I wouldn't have been so nice to you," he whispers as he leans in too close.

"Why don't you fuck off, Luke?" Abby crosses her arms over her chest and Luke snarls at her before he flicks his eyes back to me

"I'm gonna find out what your shady boyfriend's hiding, what has him thinking he's got so much power over everyone. And when I know his dirty little secrets, I'm gonna crush him and run him out of town. Then…" his hand reaches up and tucks my hair behind my ear. It feels nothing like the time Nyx did it. "…everything can go back to how it was." He smiles a dark smile at me before he crosses back over the hall to his locker. The chill of Luke's final words thaw when I spot Nyx walking through the entrance, his bag hanging off his shoulder and looking wickedly delicious

"Mornin' darlin'." He lifts his head at me, reaching around my shoulders and pulling me under his arm. I'm still unnerved by what Luke just said. Worried about what he might actually find out if he does do some digging.

"You're in a good mood," I look up at him.

"Yep." He kisses the top of my head, leading us towards my first class and quickly making me forget all about Luke and his threats. The hall is chaotic as always and Luke remains at his locker watching me with that smug look on his face, one that suggests he has the power to make my world come crashing down.

Nyx is waiting for me by my locker between second and third, and I smile at him when he shifts his shoulder out the way so I can open it to switch books. Taking out my textbook, I ignore Luke's eyes burning a hole into the back of my head. A loud crash makes me jump, and I know shit's about to get ugly when I realize it's Nyx's palm connecting with the locker beside mine. The calm, content look he had on his face moments ago completely vanished.

"I'll fuckin' kill him," he growls, already storming across the hall towards Luke.

"Wait." I chase after him, tugging at his arm, and pleading for him to come back. "Please don't."

"You expect me to stand there and let him look at you like you're a piece of shit, I'ma wipe that snigger right off his face." He rips himself from my grip and carries on moving in on Luke.

"No, Nyx." I rush in front of him, blocking his path and preventing him from taking another step forward.

"Ell, I ain't gonna let him stare you down like that." He looks down at me like I've lost my mind.

"Jesus, Nyx, why do you have to be like this all the damn time. Sometimes it's like you go around looking for trouble," I yell at him, and I don't care that everyone has stopped what they are doing and are staring at us. I can't risk him getting suspended before we graduate.

He looks back at me like I've physically hurt him, and I wish he understood why I can't have him going off at Luke and making the situation worse. Luke has a vendetta, he's used to getting what he wants. I can't lose Nyx over him.

Nyx holds up his hands in surrender, shaking his head and

backing away from me. I feel like shit for killing his happy mood. Hurting his feelings puts a lump in my throat and a sting in my chest.

"What was all that about?" Abby appears from behind me, her hand resting on my shoulder.

"Nyx was gonna pound Luke for the way he just looked at me," I say, realizing how pathetic that sounds.

"He's so dreamy," Abby sighs dramatically.

"I swear Luke does it to get a reaction, he spoke to me this morning, says he's gonna find out what Nyx's deal is," I explain.

"And you're worrying what he might actually find out," she guesses. I hate her for always being so accurate.

"No," I lie.

"Oh, come on, you can't fool me. You've fallen for him hard and you're scared whatever secrets he's got are bad ones."

I shrug back at her.

"Ella, we're young, we only have a few months left till graduation. Live a little, have fun, And tell Mr. fucking Macho, from me, if he hurts you it won't be just his secrets biting him on the ass."

"I doubt I'll be telling him anything, you saw how he just looked at me," I point out.

"You're so silly," she shakes her head amused, before kissing both my cheeks and rushing down the hall towards her class.

I sit at my desk in calculus and Luke winks at me as he walks past to take his seat. I can't focus all lesson, I need to speak to Nyx, to tell him I'm sorry. I love that he worries about me. But he doesn't understand how dangerous Luke can be. He's clever and his dad holds a lot of power around town, not to mention the school itself. He's chair of the board.

Nyx thinks he's untouchable, physically he probably is, but with Luke Robinson, he's playing in a different league.

I find him sketching under his tree at lunchtime and watch him for a while, too scared of rejection to approach him. Then after a few deep breaths I waste no more time and make my way over to him, his eyes lift up from his pad as if he senses me coming.

He shuts up his book, putting it in his bag and I smile at him awkwardly, feeling horribly distant from him when he doesn't respond.

"Can I sit?" I ask.

"You're a big girl you can do what you like," he bites back sarcastically, and I sit down beside him, despite his frostiness.

"Whatcha drawing?" I ask, hoping to ease him into a conversation.

"Ella I…"

"I'm sorry," I interrupt before he can finish. "What I said. I didn't mean it. I just couldn't let you hurt Luke again."

"But why?" he shakes his head at me like he fails to understand my logic.

"Because you can't just go beating on everyone who hurts me, the world doesn't work like that, Nyx."

"And there lies our problem, Ell, because that's exactly how the world works for me. The thought of someone hurting you, or looking at you like Luke thinks he can, I don't just want to hurt him. I want to kill him. I want to take care of you, and this the only way I know how," he admits, his eyes dropping from mine to focus on the blades of grass he's ripping out the ground.

"That's sweet, but you can't…"

"Sweet." He laughs bitterly. "Ell, there ain't nothing sweet about it. This is who I am, you can't change me, that's how I deal with shit. And it makes me so mad that you want to protect him."

"Nyx, I'm not trying to protect him. I'm trying to protect you. You underestimate Luke, he could hurt you if he wanted to."

"No one can hurt me," he says, all his focus on me now. "Except for you." His voice fades and he looks down shyly when I place my tiny hand over his.

"Why do you shut me out of your world? I feel like you don't want to let me in and it hurts?" I ask him.

"You ever wonder…" he slips his fingers through mine and scoops my hand up to his mouth, placing a firm kiss where we link, "…that maybe I'm protecting you from it?"

"Protecting me from what?" I ask, hoping this will be the time he chooses to open up to me.

"Everything," he tells me sadly. "It's a big nasty world out there, Ell, I'd much rather keep you in this one." His hand squeezes mine a little tighter.

"Are you mad that I yelled at you in front of the whole school?"

"No, I'm mad that you won't let me stand up for you. That you don't trust me when I tell you that Luke can't touch me."

"You're not invincible, Nyx, no one is," I warn him.

"That's what you think." He suddenly grabs at my waist, that handsome smile from this morning finding his lips again.

"Nyx," I squeal, as his fingers dig into my ribs and force me to giggle. He's laughing too, his teeth nipping at the skin on my neck. We both stop when a pair of feet land in front of us and I look up and see that they belong to Luke, I tense, my heart sinking to the pit of my stomach.

He doesn't say anything, just laughs smugly, smug enough to make Nyx raise to his feet in a matter of seconds.

"Please," I reach up to tug on Nyx's hand and Luke flicks his eyes down on me then back to Nyx, doing nothing to hide the satisfaction on his face.

"Look," Nyx's nostrils flare as he takes a calming breath. "For some reason, my girl doesn't want me to wipe that look off your face. I figure you only got a short time left on that privilege." Gripping at my hand, Nyx pulls me up to my feet and starts moving us away. I let out a long relieved breath as I move alongside him.

"I'm gonna find out what you're hiding, Anderson, and I'm

gonna ruin you," Luke calls after us, and I panic for a moment when Nyx stops walking, his body turning rigid.

"Do ya worst," he dares Luke over his shoulder, at least pretending to be calm as he moves us back inside the building.

"Nyx, you know there's nothing you could tell me about yourself that would make me like you any less, don't you?" I tell him when we get to my locker. I can't remember if I'd told him that before or not, but I want him to be sure of it.

"I wish that was true." He touches his lips to my forehead and smiles sadly at me, before dragging me towards our next class.

Mom calls me down for dinner at eight and we sit around the table like a normal family. She asks mindless questions in an attempt to create conversation, which I answer as simply as possible. As soon as Father finishes his meal, his chair scrapes against the slate floor and he walks away from the table towards his office without excusing himself. Mom doesn't speak for ages, the silence between us sharper than a knife's edge before she sips her wine and clears her throat.

"You must make more of an effort to make conversation with your father, darling. He does so much for us. It wouldn't harm you to show him a little more respect." She dabs the corner of her mouth with her napkin, being careful not to ruin her lipstick.

"Are you kidding me?" I grip the edge of the table to stop myself from launching something at her. "You try and talk to him every time we sit at this table together and he blatantly ignores you. He humiliates you, he beats you and you sit there and ask me to show him my respect." I slam my napkin onto the table and stand up.

"I will not let you ruin this family over a stupid boy," she warns me, standing up herself and walking towards me. "Boys like him will never make you happy, Ella."

"And what the fuck would you know about happiness, Mother?" I bite back at her before turning on my heels and storming out of the room. My heart beats wildly as I pass through the hall and up the stairs. I've never spoken to my Mom like that before, I've never sworn at her either. I'm not worried she'll tell father, not unless she wants to be punished for it too.

Nothing I've said is untrue, I can't remember a single time during my whole life when I've ever seen her look truly happy.

I shower and catch up on some homework. Unable to focus or stop myself from glancing out to the tree and hoping to see a sign of him. It's just after ten when I turn off my light and get into bed. I leave my balcony door open hoping he might come and close it like he usually does.

Chapter 15

After school, I ride straight to the studio to help Tac out for a few hours. The studio isn't as busy as I expect it to be, so I manage to find some time to finish up the sketch for Jessie's tattoo.

"Officer," Tac looks up from the blunt he's rolling when the door opens and Roswell's second man steps into the shop. Danny Foster's been a deputy for over a year now, and Roswell's not far off retiring. Lucky for us, Danny here doesn't just agree with the way we run town, he appreciates it.

"Got something for ya." He tosses a small baggy onto the desk in front of Tac, "Roswell wants to know where that's come from, someone he busted for a DUI had it on him and he ain't talking."

"Happy to assist." Tac grins, pulling a hand mirror up from under the desk. Carefully he taps some of the bag's contents out onto its surface, and Danny gives me a friendly nod while Tac sets to work examining the product.

Deputy Foster's a handsome guy, from what I hear he's got half the women in town figuring how to get themselves arrested. He's stopped by the club a few times since Roswell decided to bring him in deeper and I know some of the girls already have a wager down on who's gonna drag his ass down to Sluts sanctuary first.

"Ain't Mexican or Russian," Tac tells him straight off. "Ya see that slight yellow tinge, this shit's probably been cut with meth and that ain't their style." Wetting his finger with his tongue, he dabs it into the powder and rolls it between his thumb and finger then rubs some into his gums. "Yep, you definitely got some crank mixed in there."

"Didn't Jessie handle a meth situation last week with those college kids?" I point out.

"Yeah, and they didn't get their shit from Bastards' runners either," Tac answers.

"You don't think this has come from The Bastards?" Danny frowns.

Bastards are usually the only fuckers dumb enough to push their shit in our town. Tac shakes his head, and I can see that he's thinking.

"Last I heard, Bastards were getting supply from a triad crew running out of Nevada. That shit comes at a heavy price and it's pretty clean. Either Bastards got themselves a new supplier or we got ourselves a new problem." Tac takes one of the shop's business cards from the plastic holder and cuts himself a small neat line on his tray before he hoovers it up his nostril.

I watch Danny watching him, he doesn't seem fazed. Perhaps there's hope for him yet.

"I'm sorry, officer, how rude of me," Tac clears out his airways and passes him the mirror.

"I'm on duty," Danny shakes his head.

"Nyx?" Tac offers, and I shake my head. I ain't in the mood for a buzz tonight, especially not off whatever shit that is.

"Ever heard the phrase, don't eat yellow snow. I'm thinking the same thing applies here," I smirk at Danny, and Tac shrugs his shoulders before he buries his head back into the mirror.

"Well, anyone who knows what they're snorting, ain't gonna pay a high price for this. It's cut too heavy," he tells Danny when he's finished.

"I got an appointment due in any minute, but if you want my boy here to come with you to the station, I'm sure he can get whoever you're holding to loosen their lips." Tac tips his head towards me.

"He already lawyered up. So, probably not a great idea. Tell Jimmer we'll let you know if we get a name. Thanks for the help."

"All part of the service, Officer." Tac smiles. "I'll keep a hold of this for further investigation and bring the situation to the table at church tomorrow." He winks, tucking the baggy in his back pocket.

"I'll leave this with you guys," Danny places a card of his own on the table. "Anything else comes to light, you give me a call." Officer Foster leaves and Tac picks up the card and checks it out.

"You really think we can trust him?" I ask, the club doesn't let outsiders in easily, especially those involved with law enforcement. Roswell and Jimmer go back years.

"Prez had Maddy check him out, he's sound. Besides he's got an edge. I like that in a person." Tac moves from the stool he's perched on and starts setting up his station.

We finish up around eight, and I help Tac pull down the large shutter door before we both saddle our bikes.

"Fucking hands are killing me today," Tac says grabbing his bars.

"They pulled off some sick shit though, the horse you put on that chick's ribs looked insane," I tell him.

"That was your sketch, kid," he reminds me. He doesn't start up his engine like I expect him to, instead he leans his arms over his bars. "You know, soon as we find a replacement prospect, Prez is gonna give you your cut." I don't know why Tac decides now is a good time to bring this up, but it only reminds me of the position I'm in and how I have no idea how to get out of it.

"You think?" I test, wondering if he knows what the other brothers' thoughts were.

"Yeah, why wouldn't he? You're a good kid, you do a shit ton for the club, and you may have a stinking attitude, but name one of us who doesn't." He nods at his own point. "Let's unwind tonight, get some liquor and pussy, smash 'em both. Club should be quiet, you might be able to catch a fucking break."

I wonder what Ella's doing tonight, if she's hanging out with Abby or just by herself.

"Come on, whatcha waitin' on?" Tac asks, getting impatient.

"I got to check something out first. I'll catch you there," I tell him, deciding to stop by and check in on her. Tac gives me a confused shake of his head before he starts his engine and heads off towards the club. I'm about to take off myself and head for Ella's place when I notice a guy stumble out of the station across the street. I watch him take out his cell, his hands shaking as he dials. I recognize him from somewhere. Then when I realize where it's from, I push the kickstand on my bike back down and turn off my engine.

"Toby," I call out at him to be sure, and when he looks up at me I know I've got it right. His eyes still look cruel, even when squinting to try and make a recognition.

He doesn't seem to have grown much over the years, and now that I'm at least a foot taller than him he doesn't seem intimidating at all. His clothes are dirty, and he walks with a limp. It seems life ain't been kind to him.

"Do I know you?" he asks, looking agitated as I move across the street towards him. My guess is he's on a fucking comedown and I wonder if he's the DUI driver who Roswell busted earlier.

"Yeah, we go back. You remember Heidi and Bill's foster home?" I put on a friendly tone and his expression changes.

"Nyx." He pulls together a fake, toothless smile.

"Yeah," I nod.

"It's good to see ya, man. I could really use some help, just a couple of bucks. I just got released and I need to catch a bus back to Colorado Springs."

"A DUI, huh?" I check, because this is too fuckin' good.

"Yeah, fucking assholes busted me before I pulled on to the interstate."

I laugh at the sorry son of a bitch and watch the hopeful look on his face turn to fear when I grab his arm, twist it around his back and slam him face first into the florist shop window.

"Where you get that shit from?" I ask crushing his wrist in my fist and lifting it higher up his spine.

"I don't know what you're…" I pull the knife from my belt and press it against his throat.

"Toby, now ain't the right time to be testing my patience," I warn. Christ this fucker stinks.

"I got it from a friend of a friend, I don't know his fucking name."

"I don't believe you." I push him harder into the glass and increase the tension I've got on his arm.

"He's new, but the cheapest around," Toby manages through the pain I'm causing.

"You're gonna give me his contact details, then you are gonna fuck off back to wherever you came from," I tell him. "And if I ever see your face in this town again, you'll leave it with a fucking tag on your toe."

"He's just a kid," Toby says releasing a long breath.

"And he's dealing here in town?"

"He deals fucking everywhere," Toby manages a laugh and I release him, spinning him back round so he's looking up at me.

"How do I contact him?"

"If you're lookin' for a fix, Nyx, you should have just asked, no need for bad manners and blades. I slam my fist into his face and he stumbles back.

"Jesus," Toby spits some blood streaked phlegm at the sidewalk before he fumbles inside his pockets. "Here," he holds up his cell to me. "I got him saved under Mom," he laughs as he drags himself up off the floor.

I pull up the contact on his phone and take a photo of the number with mine. Prez will want to deal with this quickly before it gets out of hand.

I throw the cell back at him and just as I'm heading back across the street, I hear someone call my name. It's Officer Foster, he's out of uniform, running on the other side of the street covered in sweat from working out. He jogs over to catch up with me and flicks out his earphones.

"I see he got released." He looks over the street at Toby, who's still pulling himself back together. "I saw you talking to him, there a problem?" he checks.

"Not anymore, looks like I got a contact number for the dealer. I'm gonna head back to the club and fill Prez in now." I really wanna get to Ella, but I have a responsibility to the club.

Danny nods back at me, but something's off, he looks disappointed.

"What's up?" I ask.

"Nothing, good work." He smiles back at me but it ain't genuine.

"What's on your mind, Officer?" I look at him suspiciously.

"It's just…" he sags his shoulders and rolls his eyes. "I was kinda hoping I'd get the info. I want Prez to trust me. I want Roswell to believe I can do this. When he retires he gets a huge say in who takes his place. He's gonna want someone who can work with the club."

"Believe me, if you didn't work with the club, Prez wouldn't have you on the compound." I snigger, it would have taken a lot of persuasion from Roswell for him to trust Danny. He's got nothing to worry about when it comes to Roswell. I've never seen it before but me and the deputy ain't so different.

"You're right, I just wanted to prove myself. What the club and this department got goin' on works." I look up at the town clock, it's already gone eight fifteen. I really wanna get to Ella, and if I'm being honest I wanna avoid seeing Prez. I hate the guilt of betraying him.

"I got something I need to take care of. It's gonna be awhile before I get back to the club, Prez is gonna wanna set to work on this fast. What's say you swing by the club and offload the information I got to Prez. Tell him you cracked him in the interview room."

"You don't have to do that." Danny looks down at his feet, and I can see that his pride's a little hit.

"You can owe me one." I take my cell back out and pull up the picture of the contact number I took before passing my phone over to Danny. "Send that to yourself so you can show Prez. Apparently he's just a kid. Probably just a runner, but Jessie will know who he's working for by the time he's done with him."

"I appreciate that, Nyx." Danny hands my phone back to me when he's done. "I stored my number in your contacts, you let me know when I can return that favor." He nods his head at me and then jogs back towards the station where his patroller is parked.

We both set off in our separate directions. Danny towards the club, and me heading for Castle Rock.

CHAPTER 16
ELLA

It's amazing how much joy a simple gesture can bring to someone.

I can't remember ever wanting material things. My parents both come from rich families and my Mom likes to shop… A lot. It's always been the small things that have brought me the greatest delights. Like Mom reading me a bedtime story on Christmas Eve when I was a kid, or the way Penelope arranges the chocolate chips on my pancakes into a smiley face when she knows I've woken up in a bad mood. But none of that compares to Nyx climbing into my room at night. He came last night and we made out on my bed then he waited until I fell asleep again before he took off.

Feeling fresh, I leap out of bed and quickly shower so I can take my time picking out something pretty to wear to school. The thought of Nyx coming last night keeps a smile on my face the whole way through breakfast. It gives me a focus during the agonizing journey to school with Father, and it makes me practically bounce into Lit class first period.

Nyx is already sitting at the back of class, and he offers me a shy smile as I walk in and sit at my desk. Despite my excitement. We're given a new assignment by Mrs. Wallace, and when the bell rings I wait for the rush out of class to die down before making my way to the door. I try to hide my smile when I feel his hand wrap around my wrist and drag me out to the corridor, caging me against the student noticeboard beneath his strong arm. He smells of tobacco and danger. I've missed him.

"Ella." The way he breathes me in as he says my name makes my legs quiver. "You miss me?" he asks, like he can read my mind.

"Nyx, it's been hours not days." I attempt sounding cool but I'm rubbish, who am I kidding. His head tips sideways and the way his large frame hunches over me and his eyes hold onto mine make it really difficult not to kiss him right here in the corridor. Before I embarrass him in front of everyone, I duck under his arm and start walking to class.

"Oi," Nyx calls after me, and when I flick my head around his lips slam hard onto mine. His kiss isn't long or drawn out, it's merely a quick peck, but it sends all my nerves into overdrive.

"I'll be seeing you later." His promise sounds much more like a warning as he backs up a few strides, his tongue rolling around in the corner of his mouth as he watches me. He turns around and disappears into the crowd and I stand rooted to the spot, ignoring the shoulder barges and chaos of the hall during class change.

The rest of the school day passes quickly but the feeling of dread soon pits in my stomach while I stand and wait for Father to pick me up. When he arrives, I take out a book from my bag and start reading whilst Father drives. There's never any conversation between us and it will be far less awkward if I have something to focus on.

I only end up reading the same line over and over though because all I can think about is Nyx and his promise to see me later.

We're just pulling on to our street when something catches my eye, and I recognize the hooded skull straight away. It's the same one that had been carved into the tree back at Nyx's shelter in the woods, only this time it's on the back of a leather vest, worn by a guy on a motorcycle and parked on the corner.

Father grunts something under his breath as we pass the rider. I use the wing mirror to look back at him. The guy looks menacing and possesses the exact same kind of danger Nyx does. It's too much of a coincidence for them not to be linked. Still, I manage to stem my curiosity and act normal as Father pulls on to the drive.

"Your Mother and I are out for dinner with the Hendersons tonight. Your mother is already dreading it after your latest little fuck up, she doesn't need anything else to worry about. Penelope will be sticking around tonight to make sure you don't do anything stupid." His eyes look me over like I'm something he just stepped in. I respond the way he'd want me to, nodding submissively, then head straight up to my room.

I shower and change, then do all my homework. Anything, I can to make time go faster. Penelope knocks on my door around seven to ask what I want for dinner and I tell her I'll make myself a sandwich later. I'm too excited to eat. Tonight could be the night. My parents are out, and even though Penelope is 'babysitting', she'll soon be so transfixed in her crocheting she won't care about what's going on up here.

I've been craving that feeling I get when me and Nyx are together all day. No amount of showers or baths can take the feel of Father's hands from my skin. Every time I close my eyes I see him hovering over me, grunting as he examines inside me. It makes my stomach churn and my skin turn cold. I know from experience that Nyx has the capability to make everything go away. When Nyx's hands are on me nothing else matters, there is no past or future, only us in the present.

I want Nyx to be who I see when I close my eyes, it feels like he's the only person who can fix me. And it doesn't even scare me that my father threatened to kill him. When it comes to Nyx, fear has never been a factor. He holds a threat in his eyes that I know could protect me from anything, even memories.

My very own hero, but instead of armor and a stead, he's got ink and rides a motorcycle.

My father picks on weak people, and Nyx is anything but weak. As long as I've got Nyx, he won't be able to hurt me either.

I'm starting to lose hope of him coming when darkness falls and it gets late. But when I hear a rustle from the leaves outside, relief settles my nerves.

Chapter 17

She doesn't look happy when I climb on to her balcony, and the way she glares at me with her arms crossed and a pout on her lips makes my cock hungry.

"Took your time," she huffs, sounding unimpressed.

"I had clu…" I stop myself before I fuck up, "…stuff to take care of," I whisper, creeping in through her balcony door. "You ain't mad at me, are ya?" I try being playful, the same way Jessie is with Maddy when she gets mad at him, though I know that shit doesn't suit me.

"Depends." She rolls her eyes before shifting up her bed and resting her back against the headboard.

"I was thinking shit over," I admit. I didn't go to the studio after school. I went to the gym and spent some time going over stuff before I rode out here.

"What kind of shit?" she asks, looking worried.

I can't exactly tell her the truth. That she's unknowingly destroying every chance I have of being a member of a club that has been my whole life focus since I was eight years old. Or that I'm juggling with daggers wanting to do all the things I want to do to her. Instead, I give her another reason why us being together is a real bad idea.

"I feel selfish for wanting you." I move to sit on the edge of her bed, my fingers fiddling with the lace trims on her white comforter blanket. "Me and you, we were never supposed to be a thing. We're from two completely different worlds. You don't belong in mine and I sure as shit don't belong in yours." I take a look around her luxurious bedroom. Light, fresh and pure. "I can't see no middle ground for us, Ella," I admit honestly.

"So why are you here?" She leans forward, crawling across the mattress to me, and when I turn my head around and catch her eyes, the way they stare back fucking breaks me.

"Because I ain't about to let it stop me," I admit.

Her mouth doesn't move, but her eyes smile. They twinkle with hope and excitement for the future, one I know we'll never get. But I'm selfish enough to let her think differently because I want to be her hope. I like how good that feels too much to give it up.

I stare at her for a real long time before I give in and kiss her, trying so hard to be soft and gentle. It's never been this way before, but with Ella, it comes like a second sense. My hand slides up her neck to cup her cheek, and I hold her in my palm like she's the most precious thing to ever touch my skin.

Ella releases a relieved little sigh into my mouth when my tongue slips between her lips and her petite body curls around mine, her legs wrapping around my waist and squeezing me between them tightly. She must feel my cock straining between us, rubbing against my denim and pushing against the flimsy cotton of her sleep shorts. She grips at my T-shirt, dragging it up over my ribs, and I lift my arms to aid her as she strips it from me. Then grabbing her ass cheeks in my hands, I squeeze them tight and force her to grind deeper onto my lap. Her lips break away from mine, and she places delicate kisses all over my jaw and neck. Driving me fucking insane for her.

"Nyx, you remember what you promised me?" she whispers.

How could I fucking forget, it's all I've thought about since she asked me. That, and how the fuck I'll ever survive it.

She sits back on my thighs waiting for my response, and I

nod my head back at her, still stunned that she'd ever want to give me something so precious.

"It's time," she says, trying real hard not to look nervous. And as much as I wanna tear the shorts from her and fuck her through to next week. I know I gotta take some care with this. This is her first time, I want her to remember it forever because when all this is over, memories like these will be all we have.

There's a determination in her eyes, warning me not to argue with her and I can't figure out exactly what it is, but something tells me she really needs this.

"Sure," I tuck a loose strand of her hair behind her ear and brush my thumb over the apple of her cheek. She stands up and moves towards her bedroom door, turning the key in the lock while I strip out of my jeans.

I feel that strange feeling in my stomach, worse than the nerves I felt the first time Tac put a gun in my hand. I don't want to fuck this up for her.

There's never been emotion or feelings involved with a female before, half the time, Tac or one of the other brothers have been fucking in a chair next to me.

This is just as new to me as it is to her. She stands with her back against the door, staring back at me a little helplessly. She looks so adorable, her hair plaited to one side, the T-shirt she's wearing a little too short and showing off the lower section of her stomach. She doesn't know what to do next. So I make the first step, right towards her.

I wrap my arms around her tiny waist and slide the T-shirt up over her tits, she raises her arms so I can take it off her body completely, and I toss it away. My fingers brush back down her arms, soothing over her ribs to the waistband of her shorts. She looks down between us, watching as I push the shorts over her perfectly formed ass and guide them down her thighs.

The sight in front of me actually fucking hurts. Ella naked, wanting to give herself to me. A blank canvas for me to leave my mark on, and that's exactly what I do as I trace my fingers all over her body, drawing shapes and circles delicately over her flawless skin. I study every curve and angle of her with my fingertips, storing them inside my memory, knowing that when this night is through, I won't be able to resist going home and drawing her. When my fingers reach her lips, she gently kisses my fingertips and smiles.

I let my hand fall into hers, guiding her over to her bed and sitting her on the edge of the mattress. Her pretty eyes widen even more when they drop to my underwear, and she looks back up at me with an awkward smile that breaks my heart.

When her fingers reach for my elastic waistband and she peels it down, my cock bounces free, damn near slapping her face, and she blushes when she sees it for the first time. Long, thick, harder than it's ever been and already leaking for her.

Ella slowly reaches her hand out and wraps her palm around me. I look up at the ceiling and let out a groan because the touch of her fingers on my sensitive skin surpasses anything I ever imagined. And when her tongue comes out from between her lips, and delicately swipes over my tip, my cock jolts in her hands. She looks up at me with those pretty green eyes before returning her attention to my cock, her warm tongue rounding my tip. When she takes me a little inside her mouth, I have to fist my hands to stop them from grabbing her head and forcing myself all the way down her throat.

Her tongue exploring me is the most pleasurable thing I've ever experienced. There's no rhythm to her movements, no fluency. I have no idea where her inexperienced tongue will go next, but I fuckin' love it. The more of my cock she attempts to take inside her mouth, the sloppier she becomes. Her saliva coating my shaft and dripping over my balls as she clumsily gags around me.

It's incredible, but I'm far too close to firing my load to

allow her to carry on. When I quickly pull away from her, she looks up at me disappointed.

"Sorry..." she shrugs, her cheeks flushing pink. "That's the first time I've done that."

Fuck me, she's worth the price I'm gonna pay for this.

"It was perfect, I just really gotta be inside you now, Ell," I admit, and she nods her head in agreement as she starts to shuffle backward on her bed.

"Will it fit?" she asks, looking down her body at the biggest fuckin' erection I've ever had.

Leaning my body over hers, I carefully part her thighs with my knees "You'll stretch to fit me, darlin'," I assure her, settling my hips into the space I've made between her legs. Though, when I feel her tight entrance against my tip, even I start to doubt she'll take me. I circle her with my finger first, slowly pushing inside her, just like I had a few days ago, and when she moans I add another finger to stretch her a little more. She's already wet for me, making it so easy to slide in and out of her.

"Make it go away, Nyx," she breathes, her arms wrapping around my neck and her hips rocking to the rhythm of my fingers. I look between us and watch her getting off on me, my cock now sliding between her pussy lips, stroking over her clit while my fingers work her from the inside. Her hands move to grip at her bedsheets, and her mouth opens like she's gonna scream and alert the whole fucking neighborhood that she's about to come. I silence her with my free hand, cupping it over her mouth and muffling the cry that tears from her throat.

Her hips buck wildly against my hand and cock, making it impossible to hold back any longer.

"You ready?" I check, and her head nods enthusiastically against my hand before I slide it away from her mouth and press it into the mattress behind her. Holding my weight off her body as I pull my fingers from her pussy and wrap them around my cock. Her fists tense into the sheets even more as she anticipates me, and slowly I guide my tip inside her.

I push inside a little more and she gasps painfully, so I stop and give her some time. I hate the thought of her hurting, and me being the one to cause that pain stabs me right in my chest.

"Don't stop, Nyx, I can take it," she winces and I force myself to give a little more to her. Her trembling hands wrap around my biceps, clenching me tight, and I feel guilty for feeling this damn good to be inside her. Her tight little channel trying to resist, clamping so tightly around me.

"I want it all. Don't worry about it hurting. I'll stretch for you, Nyx," she assures me being brave, and her words force me deeper inside her. I give her all of me, and her whole body tenses as she grips her fingers into my skin.

"I'm yours now, right?" she manages, her eyes filling up with tears, and her pussy throbbing around my cock.

She's killing me, slowly fuckin' drowning me.

"You're mine," I whisper back, wiping away the tear when it spills onto her hot cheek. And I mean every fuckin' word. Ella Jackson is mine, and now I really do have to figure out a way of keeping her.

CHAPTER 18
ELLA

Nyx owns me. He's stolen my heart, possessed every thought I've had since I first saw him and now, he's inside me. Hard, thick and throbbing. He stays still inside for the longest time, wiping away my tears and kissing at my cheeks. He's so gentle as I stretch around him and I forget what the emptiness of not having him inside me feels like.

I wrap my arms around his neck, and when I nod he begins to move again. Slow, steady movements that cause discomfort and pleasure all at the same time. I feel whole, complete. I'm his now, no one can hurt me, well only him, and my heart screams to trust him.

His hand slips down my thigh, gripping me tight and guides it around his hips. It opens me wider to him, and I feel him even more. When I open my eyes I'm met with his, he usually holds back so much from me but he can't keep this from me. I see too many emotions there. Nyx is feeling what I'm feeling. An overwhelming pleasure roots deep inside me, outweighing the pain, and my stomach clenches, my skin prickles, and for a moment I worry I might pass out.

This level of intensity can't possibly last forever, but with Nyx slowly rocking inside me I can't ever see it ending.

"Fuck Ell," Nyx growls, burying his head into my neck. "You covered?"

I can't speak. My breath keeps catching in my throat every time I try. "Ell, I'm about to fucking shoot my load inside you. Are you covered?" Nyx repeats, his voice strained and uncontrolled.

"Yes," I manage, before letting go of everything that's been building inside me. His cock suddenly feels bigger and as I throb around it, Nyx growls low into my ear, his body turning rigid as I feel him spill inside me.

We're both breathless, his head buried into me and his lips touching at my skin. It takes him a while, but eventually he pushes himself up. His long arms supporting him as he hovers over me.

"That was pretty fucking awesome, princess," he smiles down at me and God, I love it when he smiles and have the sudden urge to kiss that sexy mouth of his. So I shift up onto my elbows and help myself to it.

"Can you stay?" I ask him, then notice how his eyebrows crease together. "Tonight I mean, could you stay here with me? My parents are out and the doors locked. If anyone came you'd have time to sneak back out." His eyes follow mine over to the balcony doors. "You don't have t…"

"I'll stay," he interrupts me, slamming his lips onto my mouth, this time hard and possessively. His cock flexes inside me and I look down between our sweaty bodies to where we're still joined.

"Maybe we could go again," I suggest, and he huffs a laugh at me.

"Let's see how you feel when I pull out," he winks, causing a flutter between my legs which I wonder if he notices. He pulls out from me slowly, and I hate the instant emptiness and then…

Wow. Sore. Very fucking sore.

I move to sit up and it hurts.

"Fuck." Nyx's face looks worried as he stands up straight and pulls up his underwear.

"What?" I follow his eyes to where they've settled between my legs and curse out loud myself when I see the red blood streaks all over my white cotton duvet cover.

"I'm so sorry, Ell. I didn't think. Are you okay?" I'm still staring in shock. Sure I was expecting something, but not this. How the fuck am I going to hide this. "Ell." Nyx grips at my shoulders and forces me to look up at him. "You alright? You need a doctor or summit? I don't know what's normal. I've never…'"

"I'm fine, a little sore but okay." Moving to stand up, I wobble on my feet, and when I go to take a step forward. A pain shoots through my center and I try not to yelp.

"Come on." Nyx scoops me off my feet and carries me into the bathroom. He places me on the surface beside the sink and then surprises me when he turns on the faucet, filling the bath. While the water fills up the tub he comes back to me, standing between my legs and kissing my cheek, neck, and shoulders. I swear I hear him whisper a sorry after each touch his lips make against my skin.

When the bath is ready, he carries me over and gently submerges me into the warm bubbles. Then taking a sponge from the basket he starts moving it over my skin. We both stay silent as he washes me. Him looking mad at himself, while I try and think of a time where I've ever felt more cared for.

"I can't hurt you, Ell," he speaks so quietly that I barely hear him, his eyes remaining focused on the sponge as he squeezes warm water over my back.

"I think it's like that for everyone the first time." I reach behind me and take his hand with mine, pulling it in front of me and kissing his knuckles. I can't have him feel bad about this. Not when I'm so happy.

"Don't trust anyone, Ell. You gotta learn to be strong and take care of yourself." His eyebrows tense together. He wraps his hand around my jaw, holding my face up to his so I can't look away from him. "And know that no matter what happens, I never would intentionally hurt you, okay." He kisses me hard on the lips and I nod my head back at him despite feeling a little haunted. Not just by what he's said, but how he's saying it. It's as if he knows something that I don't and it's a cold reminder that I really know nothing about his life.

"Rest here for a while," he tells me, pressing his lips to my forehead, before standing on his feet and leaving the bathroom. I hear him fumbling around in my room for a while and then silence.

I wait as long as possible before curiosity wins over and I get myself out of the bath before grabbing a towel from the rail and wrapping it around me. I'm scared to step through the door into my room in case he's left, and I breathe a heavy sigh of relief when I see him. He looks huge sitting on my vanity stool, his shoulders hunched forward, and hands hanging between his knees. My bed has been stripped and remade, the dirty sheets balled up in the corner of the room. He's fully dressed and it makes me want to cry. I really don't want him to leave, not after what's just happened between us.

When he looks up from the floor, he looks destroyed. Any trace of the smile he wore before has completely vanished. I hope he doesn't regret what just happened. What if this is all too much for him, I go to him, standing myself between his legs and he rests his head against the soft towel I'm wearing, wrapping his arms around my hips and holding me tight to him.

"I got some real feelings for you, you know that?" he tells me without looking up. "Just the thought of anyone hurting you… I need to protect you. Always." I run my fingers through his hair and nod my head even though I know he won't see me do it.

"I hurt you, Ell, I was selfish." Pulling his head back he looks up at me and his eyes look heavy with guilt.

"Nyx. I wanted that. I needed it. It was always going to hurt the first time and, well, you're a little above average down there." My attempt to make things a little lighter between us fails.

"I'd kill anyone who ever hurt you," his jaw clenches tight. "I mean it, a life would mean fuck all to me if it was a threat on yours. Even if I thought they'd hurt you just a little bit. I can't be the person that hurts you."

"You could never hurt me," I assure him, placing a kiss on the top of his head as he grips my body tighter. "What just happened with us was the most amazing thing that's ever happened to me. I want to do it over and over with you. Well not right now, cause well I am kinda sore but…" Nyx quickly stands up, lifting me off the floor.

"You're the fucking cutest thing," he tells me, the teeniest hint of a smile back on his lips that makes my heart soar. "You're mine, Ella Jackson. No matter what happens next, I need you to remember that this is fuckin' real."

"How could I forget? I'll be feeling you for fucking days." I roll my eyes at him, and he gently nips the lobe of my ear with his teeth as he carries me over to my bed and tucks me inside.

"You're not leaving, are you?" I ask, worried that this is goodbye. Nyx looks at me like I've grown an extra head.

"You asked me to stay, didn't you?" he asks.

"Yeah," I nod.

"Then I'm staying," he speaks as if I was crazy to assume otherwise, snuggling in beside me and wrapping me up in his arms.

"You gonna sleep with your clothes on?" I ask, exhaustion making my voice lazy.

"I don't sleep all that much, and I might have to make a fast exit." That makes sense, I guess. At least one of us is thinking straight.

"Nyx, will you make me a new promise?" I yawn, feeling my body shutting down on me.

"If I can give it to you, I will," he answers me, exactly the same way he did the last time I asked him to promise me something.

"Promise me you'll never leave me?" I feel his body turn rigid and when he takes the longest time to answer, I wonder if I've pushed him too far. I mean, way to scare a guy off, Ella, you've only just slept with him.

"Promise," he says, his lips touching my hair. Warmth spreads inside my tummy as I start to drift off to sleep. I remind myself to ask him about the guy I'd seen on the bike wearing the hooded skull on his back, but my brain switches off too soon… I'll ask in the morning.

I'm stirred awake by soft kisses at my temple and I peek my eyes open. My curtains are still open and it's barely light outside.

"I got to go, darlin'." I hear Nyx's voice and I stretch out against his body like a needy kitten.

"What time is it?" I yawn.

"It's almost six. I got to change before school and I wanna get out of here before anyone wakes up." He slides out of bed and I miss him instantly.

"Nyx."

"Yep?"

I look over my shoulder and see him pulling on his shoes.

"We have to keep us a secret. I don't want my father finding out about us, not yet."

"Okay," he says with a smile, leaning down and placing another kiss on my lips. I close my eyes feeling the mattress move as he pushes away from me. I'm just starting to drift off again, and suddenly he's back. His body on top of mine and his legs straddling either side of my hips. He takes my hands, pinning them above my head then kisses me, long, hard, and almost as roughly as you'd expect a guy like Nyx to kiss you.

"That should keep me going till later." I open my eyes and catch him licking his lips before he jumps off me and darts out onto the balcony.

I would bounce down the stairs weightlessly, if it wasn't for the dull ache between my legs. And I say a good morning to everyone. Including my father who huffs a disgruntled response back at me. I wear a smile the whole drive to school, because all I can think about is Nyx and how as soon as I graduate, he can take me away from all this bullshit.

Father drops me off at the entrance and I make my way inside.

"Hey." I hear his voice come from behind me and quickly spin around. "Still grounded, huh?" Nyx lifts his head as he catches up with me.

"Yep," I sigh.

"How's your…?" his voice lowers and he looks down between my legs. Just his eyes focusing there does something to me.

"Like hell walking," I tell him, and he suddenly looks hurt.

"Jeez, I'm kidding. It's still a little sore but fine. I guess that's what you get for playing with the big boys," I tease.

"There will be no fuckin' boys, plural, just me. Mine, remember?" his eyebrow lifts in a warning.

"How could I forget? I'm reminded every time I take a step," I roll my eyes.

"If it's that bad, I'll carry you inside."

I laugh and then squeal loudly when I go to move forward and I'm pulled back. Nyx's shoulder dipping low and pushing against my stomach as he lifts me off my feet. My fists slam against his back in protest, and I try to ignore the tingle in my panties when he places a firm slap on my ass and jogs up the stairs into the hall with me on his shoulder. I love it when I hear him laughing too.

"Mr. Anderson." I hear the stern voice in front of us and I know who it belongs to before I even stretch my neck around Nyx's body to look. "Please would you and Miss Jackson reserve these kind of disruptions for outside of school hours?"

Nyx carefully lets me slide down his broad body and back to the ground. His face now a deadly kind of serious that sends a chill through my bones.

"Sorry Miss." He walks slowly towards her, speaking calmly as his huge body overpowers her. "I didn't hear the bell." He holds her under his stare until a perfectly timed sound of the bell rings through the halls and I haven't noticed the crowd that's gathered around us until they start to disperse.

"Classes everyone," Principal K claps her hands together, escaping from Nyx's glare, "Come on." She hurries off towards her office in a fluster.

Luke and his buddies walk past. But Luke doesn't bother to look in our direction. "See ya in Lit, darlin'." Nyx winks, touching his lips to my cheek as he makes his way off to first period.

CHAPTER 19

I didn't even try to sleep when I got back to the club early this morning. Instead, I sat out on the deck of my cabin, chain-smoking and trying to come up with a plan. The conclusion is, that I'm gonna have to pick one or the other.

Ella or the club.

Of course choosing Ella could also cost me my fuckin' life, but I reckon I could convince her to run with me.

I don't want to take her away from the perfect world she's used to. I couldn't offer her what she has here. The money, security, a chance at a decent education. I just have to decide if I'm really selfish enough to take all that away from her?

And am I prepared to give up on something I've worked so hard at?

Being a prospect hasn't been easy, I've had to get my hands dirty in more ways than one. I'm almost there, weeks away from being patched an official Dirty Soul, to belonging to a family.

"Whatcha doing?"

When I look up from my sketch pad, Ella is standing over me with a huge smile on her face, I can't think of a time when I've ever seen her look so happy, and I fuckin' love that I got somethin' to do with it.

"Nothin'." Quickly shutting my pad, I stand up on my feet and tower over her tiny frame.

"I'm just about to go grab some lunch with Abby, you wanna come?" she asks.

"Nah, I'm good," I lower my eyes at the brown paper bag Maddy packed for me this morning. She's bored at the club, and her taking care of me is fast becoming a habit.

"You wanna show me what you're drawing?" Ella points her head at the sketchpad wedged under my arm.

"It's just scribbles. Nothing that would interest you."

"Why don't you let me be the judge of that?" She snatches it away from me and sits with her back against the thick trunk of the tree. Slowly, she turns the pages, I really don't want her to see what's in there. It feels like an invasion of my privacy… And yes, I get the irony in that.

"Just give it back, Ell, come on, I'll walk with you to meet Abby." She waves me away, continuing to turn the pages.

"These are beautiful. You're really good, Nyx." She passes the tattoo I drew up for Grimm a few months back, then pauses when she turns the page onto a sketch of herself.

"This is me." She looks up surprised.

"Yeah." I scratch at the back of my neck, suddenly feeling real fuckin' embarrassed.

"You drew me?"

"Yeah, I drew you, okay." I snatch the pad out of her hands and shove it back inside my bag.

"Nyx, you're amazing, you should do something with these"

"I do," I snap back, too fast to consider the consequences of opening my big fat mouth.

"Oh yeah, what?" Ella crosses her arms over her chest. Being all sassy and making me want to tug at her waist and kiss that smug little smirk right off her lips.

"It doesn't matter." I sling my bag on my shoulder and grab her hand, urging her towards the canteen.

"No, Nyx, tell me. I feel like I know nothing about you. We only ever talk about you if we're playing silly games. So, I demand you tell me." Ella might as well stomp her foot into the ground with her little strop, and I take a quick glance around us before I step forward, forcing her back against the trunk of the tree.

"You demand, huh?" I look down my nose at the pretty hazel eyes staring back up at me.

"I do," she nods back at me, with a daring glint in her eye. And all I can think about is how much I want to be back inside her.

"They're tattoos." I watch her expression turn into shock. "I sketch up tattoos for people, sometimes I even ink 'em on too." I give her a little bit of information about my other life, despite knowing that I shouldn't. It's too easy to keep forgetting the reason I'm here.

Who the fuck am I kidding, I forgot that shit the moment I caught fucking feels and allowed myself to kiss her.

"Why are you acting ashamed? That's really cool." Her arms slide behind my neck, and her head lifts towards mine like she's gonna kiss me. I divert it, brushing my cheek past hers and whispering into her ear.

"You're about to break your own rules, darlin'." I remind her that she's worried about her father finding out about us and suddenly realize how sloppy I've been myself. I'm hardly hiding what's going on between us. I've kissed her a few times now in public. The last thing I want to do is get her into trouble.

Her arms quickly drop and when I take a step back, she's blushing.

"What's up?" I hate that I've killed her excitement.

"It's hard to see you and not to, you know," she shrugs, looking adorable.

"Look, I got some shit to take care of after school, but I could come to see you later, around nine. Your folks gonna be in?"

"I don't know yet. I'll message you as soon as I get home. Hopefully, I won't be grounded for much longer."

I nod in agreement and manage to resist taking her hand as I walk her back inside.

I'll see you in calculous," she says, before moving on and giving me a glance over her shoulder that weakens me even more. I quickly pull her back and tug her under the fire escape stairs, out of sight.

"You can't give me looks like that and expect me not to react," I warn her, licking my lips as I watch hers pull up in a smile.

"Do you have any idea how hot for you I am right now?" she whispers, and there's nothing I can do to stop my hand sliding up under her skirt. My finger skimming her panties and touching her through the fabric, she's soaked.

"So, you are," I smirk slowly pulling away then heading to my next lesson.

She hits me with that same look a few times during calculus, and by the time school finishes, I'm desperate to have my hands on her again.

I lean against the wall at the entrance and watch her father pick her up in his flashy car, then once she's out of sight I get on my bike and ride straight to the studio.

"Nice of you to show your face, we were starting to forget what you looked like." Tac chuckles to himself. He's got some bitch bent over his station, her ass up high. The ash is about to drop from the cigarette he's holding between his lips onto her back but he doesn't seem to care,

"This is some real good work, kid, you should come take a look," he winks at me. I do as he suggests, stepping closer and taking a look. Tinkerbell is hitching up her little green dress and showing an ass cheek. There must be at least fifty of the same inked on asses all over Manitou Springs, and this is usually the kinda basic shit Tac entrusts me with.

I guess he decided he liked the canvas he'd be workin' on today.

"I said I'd finish Jessie's back piece off for him. It'll take two, three hours tops," I tell Tac as I set up the station next to him.

"So, I can count on you to lock up then. Me and Tinks are gonna go back to the club when we're done here." He snarls at her peachy ass, and I hear the muffled giggle come from where the bitch's head is buried between her arms.

"If you think I can work on Jessie without you being here, fine by me." I set up my gun.

"Ain't nothing more I can teach ya, kid... Well not about tattooing anyway." He winks again, swiping a paper towel over his work.

"Really?" I stop what I'm doing. I never saw this coming, especially since I haven't exactly been pulling my weight lately.

"Soon as you're done with the shit Prez's got you on, we can start getting you some bookings."

I feel the smile lift my face. This is what I've wanted for so long. My own clients, my own work. It's been a long time coming.

"I don't know what to say..." I look back at him.

"Well, you can start by quitting being a pussy and wrapping this up for me." Tac shakes his head as he slides off his stool. "Seriously kid, what's gotten into ya? You've been wetter than a whore's cunt last few weeks, you got summit on your mind?" he asks, stubbing out his cigarette.

"Nah, nothing," I shake it off.

"You've even eased up on the attitude, I hardly recognize ya," he calls out while I go out back for a new roll of cling film. "And whatever it is seems to be workin'." He turns his back on the girl and steps closer to me. "Prez is callin' a vote next week," he drops his voice, "Looks like you're getting your patch, kid."

"I got to get the vote first," I remind him. Tac has no idea about the arrangement I got with Prez, and I don't know how he'll work it if I don't get the unanimous vote I need from the others.

"You got mine, Jessie, and Troj's for sure. The only one who might have fucked it up for ya was Chop, and the only one he shafted was himself... I'm proud of ya, kid." Tac slaps me hard on the arm. The feeling of pride only lasts a few seconds before dread overrides it. I've wanted this for so long. It's everything I've been working towards since the days I was getting spat at and being forced to sniff shit.

The problem is, I want Ella just as much... I want her fuckin' more.

Jessie turns up about half an hour after Tac leaves for the club. He straddles the chair and I set to work on shading the final touches into the portrait of Hayley that's being added to his back piece.

"So how's it goin' with the girl?" he asks me, knowing we're alone.

"As well as it can go. She hates her Pa, I'm certain of that now. I'm still tryin' to figure if there's anything to it though, maybe she just hates him the same way every other teenager hates their parents."

Jessie nods in agreement. "You know, it was massive for Prez to trust you with this," he reminds me, doing nothing to make me feel any better about betraying him for it.

"Yeah, and I don't wanna let him down. I wanna prove to everyone that all that stuff Chop used to say about me was shit. I don't know what he ever had against me." I wipe over Hayley's face before dipping back my gun back in the ink. It's crazy to think Ella had a sister, one she may never know about. Now that Hayley's gone I regret not giving her more of my time. I was rude to her a lot, always saw running her around as an inconvenience that took me away from doing real club stuff. Now, in a weird kinda way, I miss her. Life at the compound's not quite the same without her sarcastic comments.

"Speaking of shit, has anyone actually got information on Tommy?" I distract myself from the thoughts in my head, Jesus Christ, Tac's right, I'm turning into a fuckin' pussy.

"Mads is workin' night and day trying to find something. One thing we do know is that whoever buried Chop's file for him originally, buried a lot of shit, way more than Skid or Prez ever knew about. Chop told Prez he was wanted on suspicion of murder when he first came to the club. He never mentioned that it was for the murder of his wife. There are other cases too, all of them brutal.

We ain't got no one on the inside anymore. Prez used to have someone working for the gov, but he disappeared three years ago. I'm starting to wonder if that had something to do with Chop too.

I just hope Maddy burying it all again is enough to buy us time to find him before the feds do. There's not much we can do about the paper trail, not without someone on the inside."

I chuckle to myself, and Jessie looks over his shoulder at me suspiciously.

"Ella's Dad's a fed judge," I remind him. "The person we need is right under our nose, and there ain't nothin' we can do about it."

"Mads thought the same thing. But there ain't no way Prez is gonna get into bed with Judge Jackson. Justice will catch up with Chop soon enough. In the meantime, keep ya head on and focus on what you're doing. It won't be for long. Just 'till we know she's safe. Prez just wants reassurance that the judge ain't treating her bad."

"I'm on it, Jess," I assure him, getting back to inking him and letting the focus of work take over any thoughts of Ella and the deep shit I'm getting into.

Jessie leaves the studio as soon as I finish. He invites me to eat with him and Maddy tonight and I decide to pass on the offer. I've checked my phone a few times and Ella hasn't messaged so I'm gonna ride out and check she's okay.

I'm out the back putting the last of my kit in the sterilizer when I hear the shop door open. "We're closed," I call out. Tac is always reminding me to lock the shop door if I'm working outback. I stub out my smoke and walk out into the studio.

My body freezes when I look to the other side of the desk and I'm greeted with a shy smile. The same one that's etched in my thoughts 24 fuckin' 7. And one that doesn't belong here.

CHAPTER 20
ELLA

After a silent journey home with my father, I'd gone straight to my room. Mom had come up a few hours later, her face fully covered with makeup, dressed like she's about to walk the runway.

"Your father and I have been invited to the senator's for dinner," she tells me. I manage to hide my excitement, this is perfect, it means I can see Nyx again tonight.

"Penelope will be here if you need anything," she chimes as she leaves my room, already applying the fake act she'll have to keep up all evening.

"Have a good time," I call out, burying my head back inside my textbook. The sooner they leave, the sooner I can message Nyx and tell him to come over.

I pick up my phone, but instead of typing a message to Nyx I open the internet app and search local tattoo studios. I'm a little shocked that there's just one that's remotely close. It's over in Manitou springs. A town my father seems to have a real issue with. I went to a party there once and when he found out, he drove over and dragged me out in front of everyone. It was so embarrassing. All he's ever told me is that the town is bad and that the people who live there are bad too.

I write down the zip code of the studio, and change into a

pair of jeans and the hooded jumper, that I still haven't returned to Nyx. Then putting on a confident face, I head down the stairs and prepare myself to lie to Penelope.

"Where are you going, Miss Jackson?" Penelope calls out from the kitchen without showing her face. It takes a lot to get past her.

"Over to Abby's, we need to finish our English assignment, it's due tomorrow." I hold up my folder and a copy of the Great Gatsby.

"Your father says you're grounded." She appears in the door frame, drying her hands on her apron and looking unconvinced.

"I don't think assignment writing applies." I grit my teeth.

"And why can't Abby come here?" she questions.

"Because Abby has to watch her little cousin, her parents are out too." I make up that one right on the spot and surprise myself at how convincing it sounds.

"Okay," she nods eventually, and just as I'm about to open the front door I hear her again.

"Don't worry, Miss Jackson, I won't tell your father." I spin my head around quickly.

"About your assignment… just be back before ten-thirty." She smiles me a knowing smile, and I run and give her a hug before heading out to my car.

I type the zip code into my sat nav and it gets me straight there. Of course, I know there's no guarantee that this will be the place Nyx works, but seeing as it's the closest place for miles I stand a good chance.

I watch a hot looking blonde guy leave and get on a bike, and know I'm in the right place when I notice he's wearing the same hooded skull on the back of his vest as the person I'd seen the other day at the top of our street. And I wait till he's ridden out of sight before getting out of my car. I watch Nyx through the window from the other side of the street for a while. He's wearing black plastic gloves, and looks like he's being thorough as he cleans everything over.

When he disappears into a room behind the desk, I take my chance and quickly cross the street before I lose all my confidence and change my mind.

"We're closed," a rough voice calls out from the back room when I open the door. I step inside and stand still, in front of the desk. I'm unsurprised when I see the hooded skull on there too, and the words 'Dirty Souls MC' curved above it.

Suddenly everything clicks into place. Everyone's got a story to tell about the Souls, I've even heard my father talk about them.

When Nyx appears in front of me, he looks shocked to see me and I can't make out if it's a pleased kinda shock or the furious kind.

"What are you doing here?" he asks, his jaw tensed tight.

"My parents went out, so I decided to come find you." I bite at my bottom lip.

"How did you know to find me here?" It's the furious kind, he's definitely mad at me.

"It wasn't difficult, this is the only tattoo studio in miles." I half smile, hoping to lighten him up a little.

"You shouldn't be here, Ell." He quickly rounds the desk, barging past me to get to the entrance and check outside. When he's satisfied that no one's seen me, he snaps down the blinds and locks the door.

"What's the problem?" A nervous giggle comes out with my words because the way he's acting is actually scaring me a little.

"This just isn't the kinda place for you to be, I thought you were grounded anyway," he says, sounding on edge.

"I am, but I was curious, Nyx, you never talk about yourself, your family, or even your friends. I just want to know more about you... I didn't mean to get you angry." I suddenly feel pathetic, *Jesus, he doesn't tell you shit because he doesn't want you to know shit, Ella, get a grip…*

"I'm sorry, I'll leave." I make for the door, but he stops me, grabbing my wrists and pulling me back to him. So close that I feel his broad chest sag as he lets out a long, frustrated sigh.

"I ain't angry, not at you," he assures me, still sounding agitated. "Did anyone see you come in here?" he asks, and I shake my head.

"Take a seat, let me finish out back then I'll make sure you get home, okay?"

"I don't want to go home, I wanna stay here for a little bit." I stand my ground, fed up of all his mixed signals. "You can't make me feel bad for coming here, not when you were watching me in my room from that tree behind my house for god knows how long," I remind him.

Nyx looks at the floor and twists his mouth into something that resembles a smirk, I know he likes it when I stand up for myself, even if it's against him.

"Just give me five," he says disappearing into the back room again, leaving me so my eyes can wander. The walls are all black, but the bright lighting in the room and all the mirrors give the illusion that the place is much bigger than it is. There are sketches and photographs stuck all over the walls, and two tattoo stations that both look sterile.

Nyx is watching me from the doorframe when I turn back around. I don't know how long he's been staring, but I know it's long enough for him to see how nosey I've been.

"Do you do their tattoos?" My head points towards the Dirty Souls emblem on the desk.

"Yeah," he admits, stepping around the desk, and coming towards me.

"Is that why you didn't want me to come here, you didn't want me to know that you know them?" I ask as he gets closer and he shakes his head, his thick lips pouting.

"My dad hates them, says they're evil. Are they really as bad as everyone says they are?" Nyx nods back at me this time and I notice how his eyes are focusing on my lips like he wants to kiss me, and I just need a little bit more information before I can let that happen.

"You don't need to keep anything from me, Nyx, nothing's gonna change the way I feel. I've told you that."

He lunges for me and our conversation ends the moment his lips touch mine, he kisses any more questions I have for him out of my head and I don't even care that he's using it as a tactic.

His tongue slides between my lips, while his hands force my jeans and panties off my hips. I wriggle out of them until they're a pile on the floor and Nyx lifts me up by my ass, holding me tight to his waist, while his lips remain pressed on mine. He crushes me between his body and the nearest wall, his hands desperately fumbling between us to loosen his belt and take out his cock. I feel it press against my entrance, and he growls into my neck as he slowly pushes it inside me.

It burns like a hot rod but it's nowhere near as painful as it was last time, and it doesn't take me long to adjust to him again.

He pushes in and out of me, attempting slow and soft but I can feel he's holding back on me.

I grip at his T-shirt, my legs trembling around his waist as he buries his head into my shoulder, and I watch our reflection in the mirror opposite. His tight ass cheeks hang over the top of his jeans as he rolls his hips into mine and I feel something start to climb inside me. Reaching higher and higher, until I can't contain it. I call out his name as I feel myself tighten around him, my fingers scratching at his skin… and that seems to trigger him.

He stops treating me like glass and slams into me deeper, his hands gripping clumsily at my skin and his fingers digging into my flesh. Sweat trickles from his skin onto mine as he fucks me into the wall so hard, I swear I feel it shaking. A long agonizing groan comes from his throat as he empties inside me. And he holds me still, his shoulders heaving up and down as he keeps my thighs tight around him and steadies his breathing

I can't tell if it's my heart thumping so fast against my chest or his, and I wrap my arms around his neck and hold him even closer.

"I'm sorry for coming here," I whisper. And he pulls his head away and looks at me confused.

"You got nothin' to be sorry 'bout," he tells me with his strong arms clutching around my waist, and his still hard cock rooted deep inside me.

"I just wanted to feel closer to you," I admit, my words seem to make his whole body tense and he clings to me for ages in silence, his body pressed against mine and his forehead touching the wall over my shoulder. Eventually, his hands slide up from my waist to cradle my face, his body the only thing keeping me pressed into the wall. He looks straight at me, his face serious.

"You're the closest anyone's ever got," he promises, pressing his forehead against mine this time, the bridge of his nose lining up with mine.

"When you're ready to let me in, I'm here," I whisper, and I notice how the smile he gives me back doesn't quite make it to his cheeks. He backs away, pulling out of me, and works on doing up his jeans while I pull mine back on.

"It suits you," he says gesturing his head to the hoodie I'm wearing.

"Oh, this. It's real comfortable." I'm about to take it off and return it but he shakes his head at me

"Keep it. I prefer it on you." Coming at me from behind he wraps his bulky arms around me. The light kiss he presses just below my ear sending a shiver rippling all over my skin.

"So, this is where you work?" I shrug out of his arms and sit on one of the chairs. "Nyx Anderson, student by day, tattooing bad boy bikers by night."

"Something like that," he breathes out, straddling the stool beside me.

"Don't you need a special license to tattoo people, I thought you'd have to be older," I shrug, still taking everything in and realizing that my boyfriend is super fuckin' cool. If that's what he even is. We haven't really had that discussion yet. Maybe we should?

"The club kinda make up their own rules, no one argues 'em." Nyx laughs to himself.

"Just don't tell Abby about this for Christ's sake, last thing I need is for everyone to know. The club prefers to keep things private," he says, suddenly sounding serious.

"Pinkie promise." I giggle, holding out my little finger for him. He narrows his eyes and stares at it like he doesn't understand.

"Don't tell me you've never made a pinkie promise with anyone before." I laugh even louder, and Nyx looks back at me blankly. I show him, using my other hand to lift his, and wrapping my little finger around his.

"I pinkie promise that I won't tell a single *soul*, that you're a badass tattooist," I vow.

"And what happens if you break it?" he flicks his chin at me, creasing an eyebrow curiously.

"Oh Nyx, no one ever breaks a pinkie promise. It's the secret eleventh commandment."

"Ell, I don't know what the fuck you're talking about with this pinkie shit, But I trust ya," he smirks as he pulls our linked hand to his mouth and places a kiss on my knuckles, he must know how much I like it when he does that.

"Come on, I'll get ya home." Standing up, he makes his way to the back room. I'm about to tell him that I'm perfectly capable of getting myself home, but decide that I like the fact he cares enough to ride home with me.

When he turns off the back room light and comes out with

his bag on his shoulder, I'm still sitting on the chair with my legs stretched out.

"Promise me something?" I ask him, and he stops to look at me, his head tilting suspiciously.

"If I can give it to you, I will," he says, making me melt, just like all the times before, because I know that he means it.

"Promise me that you'll tattoo me." Nyx strides over to me, caging me into the chair by resting his hands on the armrests either side of me.

"Not a chance," he leans down and whispers in my ear.

"Why not?" I protest.

"Because there ain't no way I'm spoiling an inch of this skin. God made you too perfect to be tampered with, Ella Jackson."

"I'd just really like a little piece of you that I could keep with me when we're not together." I realize how ridiculous that sounds. I really need to stop saying my thoughts out loud.

"Ain't gonna happen darlin'." Taking my hand and pulling me up off the chair, Nyx leads me to the door, then he checks the coast is clear before we step outside.

He locks up the shop, pulling down the huge roller front effortlessly before walking me over to my car.

"I'll follow behind you," he says as he opens my door for me, then once I'm inside he closes it and leans his arms over the roof.

"You don't have to do that." I look up at the handsome face that's staring back at me from between his strong arms. Nyx takes another glance around the street before he dips his head inside my car window and steals a kiss from me.

"I want to," he whispers, showing me those dimples again before he taps his palm hard on my roof and makes his way over to his bike. I pull out of my parking spot and watch him in my rearview mirror the whole way home, breathing a sigh of relief when I pull up on the drive and my parent's car still isn't back.

It seems I've managed to pull off my little escape unscathed. I get out of my car and glance over the street to Nyx, who nods back at me before taking off. And I realize that it doesn't matter who he is, or how bad his secrets are. Nyx Anderson has the potential to break my heart beyond any repair.

Chapter 21

There's a strange feeling in my gut when I leave Ella to go inside, one that has me turning my bike around when I get to the top of her street and heading back. I park out of sight and follow the wall behind her house towards the tree I always climb.

The light's on in her bedroom and I watch her wiggle out of my hoodie. There's something I love about her wearing it. She's just in a tank top and panties now, and she stands in front of her mirror, looking at her reflection. Her fingers tracing over her skin, and when she holds up the hair off her back and twists slightly to look over her shoulder. I know exactly what she's doing.

She's trying to decide where she wants me to put her ink.

I meant what I said. It's ain't gonna happen. There's no way I'm gonna mar that flesh. No matter how much the thought of a huge Property of Nyx stamp where everyone will see it appeals to me.

I lose track of how long I watch her, but when she turns out her light I decide to leave. I need to get back to the club and somehow maintain living in both the worlds I want, until I'm forced out of one of them… or worse, both.

My girl was right about one thing from the start, I am reckless. Fucking her like that tonight in the studio proved it. It would have been safer starting a fire at a gas station.

I'm about to climb down from the tree and head off, when I notice the light to the judge's office come on, and I decide to stay and watch. He marches into view, dragging his wife behind him and I can't see all too clearly from back here, but his body language suggests that he's mad. I begin moving before my brain can keep up with my body. Jumping off the wall into the garden and keeping tight to the fence all the way around. I avoid the lit-up pool and manage to tuck myself under his window.

"We were being judged all evening thanks to your slut of a daughter. And don't you pretend you don't know that he's one of them, it's obvious."

"No Vincent. He can't be, Jimmer made me a promise, he would never." I hear the loud thwack that silences her, and I don't have to see his palm connect with her cheek to know that Vincent Jackson just struck his wife.

"You don't mention that bastard's name in my home. Slut. I wouldn't be surprised if you wanted him to be one of them. Is that what you want for your girl, for her to belong to them? Like you should have… Are you sad you weren't wanted, Joanne? That you weren't good enough even by their lawless standards."

"Vincent, please," Ella's mom begs.

"You were nothing, and I gave you everything. A home, a reputation, even a pretty pair of tits."

"We had an arrangement. He wouldn't go back on his word," she sobs, and the judge laughs at her.

"He's a fucking outlaw, you stupid bitch. You can't trust his kind of people, that's how you got into your situation in the first place." There's silence, and I can't risk looking in case I get seen.

"You fix the shit she caused. Get her back under control and start getting back our reputation. You'd think she'd have a better teacher."

"I'm sorry," Ella's mom cries.

"Not as sorry as you will be if your little bastard whore

makes any more mistakes," he warns, tempting me to smash my way through the window and kill the fucker with my bare hands.

"Don't hurt her, please."

"I don't have to hurt her, darling… that's why I have you." His final words settle a little relief in my chest but chill me at the same time. I got no fuckin' patience for a man who abuses his wife, but for now, it seems Ella is safe from his hand. For as long as he has his human punch bag.

I wait for it to go silent before quickly scaling the wall and heading straight back to the club.

Now I really do have something to report to Prez, and I got a feelin' it ain't gonna go down well.

When I arrive back at the club, I go straight to the bar where Prez always hangs. He sees me enter and pulls the bitch giving him head straight off his cock by her hair.

"Clear the room," he orders the others sharply. Thorne and Grimm get up without question, passing me on their way out. Followed by Cassie who kisses her lips at me as she passes.

"Thought I'd try her out for myself, see what everyone makes all the fuss about," Prez explains, getting up and standing behind the bar. He tops up his glass and then fills a fresh one for me, nodding at it as he places it in front of me.

"Whatcha got for me, kid?" he asks as I pick it up and tip it back.

"Your judge is an asshole," I tell him, placing the empty shot glass back on the bar. Prez immediately tops it up for me.

"You're gonna need to tell me somethin' I don't already know?" He stares at his own shot before he swallows it and pours himself another.

"He beats on his wife." I notice the way Prez's tattooed fingers stiffen around the bottle he's holding.

"But I don't think he's hurt Ella, he uses hurting her mom as a way of getting to her, and it works. She's already told me how much she hates him, this has to be why."

Prez nods his head thoughtfully, but I still got more.

"Don't know if you know this, but Judge knows Ella ain't his kid. I heard him and his wife talking tonight. He knows she's yours and he resents her for it."

"I figured," Prez admits sighing heavily and staring at his empty glass. "There's been too much Fed shit happening these past few years. That warrant for the raid a few months back was in his name."

It makes sense. The Judge has pulling power, he can get away with pretty much whatever he wants if he has the right people on his side.

"Look kid, I know the job sucks, and I appreciate the work you're putting in. A few more months and she'll be going to college. She's applied for Albuquerque and I got Maddy making sure that happens. I want her out of here, away from him. You think you can see this through for me till then?"

I don't have to think about it, a few more months will give me the time I need to figure out a way out of this mess.

"Sure thing, Prez," I agree, and he comes from around the bar and slaps my back.

"The moment she's safe, you get your patch. I've spoken to the brothers individually, ain't one of them that don't think you deserve it. You get my girl to college and you get a graduation of your own. I'm proud of ya."

He's the second person today to tell me he's proud of me. I only remember ever hearing it once before. It was a few years ago when one of the Bastards came to the studio late one night and pulled a gun on Tac. Cunt thought Tac was on his own, he was wrong. I was out back, and I knew Tac kept a gun under the desk. I was quick enough to pull it out and hold it to that Bastard fucker's head. And I felt no shame for pulling the trigger. He threatened a person I cared about and for that reason, his time was up.

I head out the room, making my way into the bigger, much

noisier bar where everyone hangs out. There're enough club whores working the bar to keep the guys topped up, and plenty this side to keep them entertained. So, I reach over and help myself to a bottle of vodka, then sit on one of the leather sofas and start to drink. After a head fuck of a day, I've just been thrown a lifeline by the man I'm betraying and I feel like shit for how grateful I am for it.

This time last night, I'd been balls fuckin' deep, taking my Prez's daughter's virginity. I'd sentenced myself to the death penalty, and just a few hours ago I'd shown my repent by taking her all over again. I'm pretty sure all this shit is gonna fall down around me and crush me in the middle. But right now, I have Ella, and I have time. I'll figure everything else out somehow.

Chapter 22
ELLA

This morning I'm allowed to drive myself to school, which I'm convinced is more out of laziness on my dad's part than forgiveness, but who gives a shit.

"You wanna tell me what you're finding so funny, princess?" Nyx asks when I find him waiting for me by my locker.

"I was just thinking about something," I shrug playfully, I'm in a ridiculously good mood today, and seeing him waiting for me has just made it even better.

"Tell me." He rubs his lips together and gets comfortable, resting his shoulders back against my locker and crossing his arms across his chest. Clearly, he's not gonna budge until I tell him. So I fess up.

"The other day out on the quad, when you were talking to Luke, you called me your girl," I point out, and I feel like an idiot when his face suddenly turns serious. "It's just I've never been anyone's girl before." I nudge him out of my way and open my locker. He doesn't say anything, just watches me as I dump my bag and pull out the stuff I need for calculus. "It's no big deal, okay. Forget I said anything."

"No." He slams my locker door shut and presses me into it. "I'm not gonna forget it." He looks deadly serious now. "You're not just my girl, Ella, you're my fuckin' everything, and right now would be about the time that I'd kiss you and prove it to every fucker watchin'."

"I think you're making it pretty obvious." I pull my eyes off his to glance around us at the audience we've acquired. Mainly, girls who are looking like they want to scratch my eyes out.

"Good," he nods his head satisfied, pulling my textbook out of my hand and placing it under his arm with his, before walking me to class.

What he'd said sticks in my head all afternoon. Now that Nyx is in my life, I can't imagine it without him. After graduation, we have to find a way of being together. I figure he won't want to go on to college. He loves to draw and seems to be doing what he wants already, tattooing.

It's a job he can do anywhere in the world, and that gives us options.

I know there's still so much about Nyx that I don't know but even secrets can't come between us. They can stay buried for all I care because I trust him. In the short time I've known Nyx, I've fallen in love with him. I want a future with him, away from my father, and away from Luke Robinson.

I meet Nyx in the library after last period, just like he texted me and asked me to, but I really can't see us getting any studying done.

"Stop looking at me like that, it's distracting." I tap my finger into his open textbook to remind him why we're here. We've been in the library half an hour and Nyx hasn't even picked up a pen.

"I'm allowed to look at you, you're mine." He takes a quick glance around the room before tilting his head towards mine and kissing my lips. How can him kissing me make my whole body react? I ache for him in places I never knew existed until I experienced Nyx Anderson. I can feel my pulse thumping between my legs and all I wanna do is have him inside me again. Under the desk I feel his hand slide onto my thigh, and he strokes me, the tips of his fingers teasing and almost touching me where I want him.

"Nyx," I warn, and the smirk on his face suggests he knows exactly what he's doing to me.

"What ya thinking about, darlin'?" he asks, closing up the book in front of me and snatching the pen out of my fingers with the hand that's behaving above the table.

"I'm thinking that you're gonna get us into trouble." My eyes wander over to the reception desk where the librarian is watching us suspiciously. He follows my glare over his shoulder briefly and is still smiling when he looks back at me.

"Maybe we should give her something to look at," he suggests, his finger pressing tight against my center, applying the perfect amount of pressure as it slips through my slit with just the fabric of my panties standing between us.

"Shit," I whisper, my body shivering under his touch while he watches, licking those damn lips at me.

"You still hurtin'?" he asks, and I don't recall him asking me that last night while he was power driving me into the wall of his tattoo studio.

"A little." I clear my throat. How the hell are my nipples reacting to this? He's nowhere near them.

"You know where my art class is?" He leans in closer to my ear, his voice giving me goosebumps.

"Yeah," I manage, clenching my thighs and crushing his hand.

"There's a storage closet for supplies next to it. I'm gonna get up from this table and you are gonna meet me there in five minutes." He doesn't give me a chance to answer him, removing his hand from between my legs and then sliding his book off the desk before he pulls his bag on to his shoulder. I watch him leave, my stomach doing a tiny summersault as I smile sweetly at the librarian, and then check the clock behind her desk. I wait four minutes before I grab up my stuff, then I try and stay calm and inauspicious as I head out into the corridor, towards the art block.

I know exactly what will be waiting for me I when I get there, and I can't believe I'm even considering it. If we ever got caught, Principal K would be sure to tell my father. And I'm in enough trouble where he's concerned. But… just the thought of Nyx inside me again keeps my feet moving forward.

I pause when I get to the door, checking left and right before I push open it but I don't get the chance to take the breath I need, before a tattooed hand reaches out from behind the door, snatches my wrist and drags me inside.

It's pitch black, I can't see a thing in front of me and when I feel his lips slam hard on to mine, he must swallow the gasp I make.

"I've been thinking about doing this all fuckin' day, Ell," he tells me grabbing my wrists and forcing them above my head. His body grinding into mine and making sure I feel how hard he is. "You wanna try something with me?" He flicks the lock on the door, and turns my body so my front presses into it. He's standing behind me now, his teeth scraping over the skin on my neck and making my nails dig into the wood.

"Sure," I whisper, petrified we're gonna get caught, despite the door being locked. I can hear him loosening up his belt, and my panties dampen with anticipation when he shoves up my dress and his cock slides between my thighs.

His strong arm wraps around my waist, and I almost yelp in shock when he spins me back around and drags us both down to the floor. His back rests against the door to prop us up and he places me on his lap. I see the benefits of it when his hand delves into the front of my panties, setting butterflies loose in my stomach when he rubs a finger tight against my clit.

"Reach between your legs and take my cock, Ell," he orders, sounding desperate and authoritative all at the same time as he forces my panties over to one side. Using my feet against the floor, I lift my hips off his body and do as he's asked, reaching between my thighs and taking a hold of his huge, firm cock.

"Fuck," he growls, rolling his hips as I pull him through my fists a few times. "Put it inside you," he commands, thrusting to meet the rhythm of my palm. Fisting my hair in one of his hands, he pulls me so my back is taught with his chest, I feel his tongue roll up my neck, his mouth against my ear and every part of me aches for him, I'm a desperate wreck as I fumble between us and line him up with my entrance.

"You sit your tight little pussy on my cock and get yourself off like you did in the woods when you rode my face," he whispers, and the memory of being back there and how good it felt that first time he made me come has me bringing him closer, and edging his thick cock slowly inside me.

I cry out when his strong hand grips at my hip and forces me down onto him. Pleasure shooting up my spine as Nyx pulls on my hair, keeping me tight to his body and his mouth tight to my ear.

"I'm sorry for making you hurt," he says. "I hate it." The hand he has on my hips controls how fast and how much of him I take, right now it's slow, agonizingly slow but I know it won't last, we're both too desperate.

"I wish you'd let me protect you the way I need to," he tells me, his teeth gripping at my lobe and keeping me in place. Both his hands move, sliding under my thighs, taking my weight off the floor and spreading me open wider.

He's in full control now, his strong hands gripping tight at my flesh and controlling the thrusts he's putting into me. He feels so big from this angle, he's consuming my whole body and I can't resist the temptation to reach inside my panties and touch my clit

Nyx fucks me hard while I rub my fingers against my sensitive flesh and it doesn't take long for that feeling to start building up inside me again.

"You fuck me up, Ella Jackson," he tells me, slamming me on to his cock harder. "You make me go against all my instincts." His words touch my skin, sending heat through my body. That, combined with the pressure of him deep inside me and the pulsing of my clit against my fingers cause my stomach to tense and my muscles to go rigid.

I scream out loud, past caring if anyone hears us, and when Nyx's hand slams over my mouth to keep me quiet I bite down on his fingers.

"Holy fuck," Nyx groans, hitting me with one last powerful thrust before his body stills too and his fingers clutch at my thighs. I feel him warm me inside and I lean my head back until it's resting on his shoulder.

"You got all the control, Ell. You're the one with all the power. I'll be yours for as long as you'll have me. I'll fight for us. And…" he nips at my ear lobe again making my pussy shudder, "Luke Robinson only breathes for as long as you want him to." I hear the chill in his voice but I haven't got the time to let it haunt me, not when he grabs my jaw and forces me to face him, his lips landing firm on mine and making me forget every bad thing that ever happened to me.

After we straighten up, Nyx casually walks me back to my car. "I've been thinking, you still wanna get that tattoo?" he asks when we get to my driver's door.

I nod back at him enthusiastically, excitement lifting my lips into a huge grin.

"Come by the shop after eight, park up the street and use the back door. Don't get yourself seen," he warns, releasing my hand so he can open my car door for me.

"What made you change your mind?" I ask, managing to refrain from jumping on him with excitement.

"I thought about it, and I like the idea of *my girl* wearing my tattoo," he tells me, his touch gentle as he tucks my hair behind my ear. It's hard to believe he's the same guy who just fucked the life out of me in the art cupboard.

"See ya later." He pulls away from me and walks over to climb on his bike and I watch him rev up his engine and pull out. Knowing things will never be the same again.

Chapter 23

I leave school already knowing exactly what I'm gonna ink on Ella. I see the way the other guys at school look at her. Luke pretends to hate her when everyone knows he'd give his right nut to have her the way I do. My sudden change of heart comes from the possessive asshole streak inside of me that can't resist the opportunity to put a permanent mark on her skin.

It feels pathetic, to need that kind of reassurance. But, then it might be all I have if I can't figure a way out of this shit I'm in.

The compass I've got on my forearm was the first tattoo I ever got. I'd drawn it over and over in my sketch pad when I was a kid and trying to figure out how to find my dad. I'd been stupid enough back then to convince myself it would help me.

Maybe it was fate or irony but it was that compass that got me where I am today. Tac saw my sketch pad when he took me in. Told me I had some real talent and although I was far too young at the time, he offered to tattoo it on me.

"You've drawn it enough times, figured it must mean something to ya," he'd said to me.

That's what I love about Tac, he never asks questions, but he sure knows how to read people. Now I want Ella to have it too, my way of telling her that no matter what happens I won't give up on finding a way for us to be together.

I know Tac will be leaving the studio before eight. Troj has a big fight in Denver tonight, most of the brothers are riding out to watch him. I'm out the back sketching when I hear the studio door open and some loud ass kids enter the shop. I leave Tac to deal with them, we're quiet so he'll either send them on their way or decide to make a quick buck out of them.

I put my earbuds in and carry on with my sketch. I want to make the compass I'm putting on Ella perfect.

"Yo Nyx," Tac shouts over my music and I flick out my earphones and look up at him.

"Got some kids out here wanting a team tattoo." Tac rolls his eyes.

"You wanna take it so I can shoot off?" I look up at the clock, it ain't even six.

"Hey don't be judgy, I've been working my ass off while you been playing golden boy to Prez."

"Ain't judging." I hold up my hands in surrender as I squeeze past him through the door and make my way out onto the shop floor. I pause when I see Luke and two of his football buddies, all looking pale-faced and shit scared in the waiting area. They all look like they're gonna bottle it, bouncing their knees and sweating from their pores.

Pussys.

"I booked you some stuff in for tomorrow too, can't have the shop shut all weekend." Tac slaps my back on his way out the door, paying no attention to the boys as he leaves. Luke waits until the door has shut after him before he speaks. His face finding a little color and a sly grin picking back up on his lips.

"Anderson, what the fuck you doing here?" he asks standing up and striding towards me with newfound confidence.

But this shithead's on my territory now, where club rules apply and shit like his ain't tolerated. Let's see how long that confidence lasts

"Looks like I'm about to tattoo you boys your lame-ass football tattoo," I shrug cockily.

"I dunno, Luke, I think I might wait till after graduation." Drew places down the motorbike magazine he's been flicking through and makes straight for the door.

"Yeah, me too." His other buddy goes after him, leaving just me and Luke in a stare-off.

"Got yourself some solid friends there, Luke," I smirk to myself sarcastically, making my way over to the station to start setting up.

"So, this is you?" Luke looks around the shop. "A bitch boy in a biker tattoo studio," he laughs.

"Loads of people get nervous their first time. Take a seat." I ignore his attempt to provoke me, tapping the leather chair with my palm.

"Aren't you supposed to do a stencil first?" I detect a hint of worry in his voice and smirk.

"I specialize in freehand unless you came here to get the transfer?" I check.

I can see how much Luke wants to back out, but I know he won't. He's got far too much pride for that. So, I snap the black latex glove over my hand ready to get started.

"Where's this going?" I ask.

"Arm." He pulls up the sleeve of his shirt, revealing a real lame excuse for a bicep. Seriously, this is the guy they chose to captain the football team. He flinches when I spray the area with anti-bac, and I shake my head and laugh as I wipe it over with a paper towel. There's only one type of person who gets his collage tattoo done before he's even left high school. Luke Robinson is the definition of the word Douchebag.

"You know guys like you don't keep girls like Ella Jackson," he tells me before I have the chance to start up the gun. "You're a phase. A rebellion, the bad boy that her folks warn her to stay away from." I ignore him and flick on the gun, hoping the hum will drown out his voice.

"If anything, you're doing me a favor." He crosses his arms

over his chest, preventing me from pressing the needle to his skin. "I'll tell you something about the guys that do end up with the Ella Jacksons of this world." He smirks. "They're ambitious, clever. They know how to get what they want, and they succeed in everything they do." This cunt really is going all out to try to taunt me.

"When you fuck up, and you will, Ella will realize what's good for her, and then it'll be my cock that horny little bitch is getting herself all choked up on."

It's all it takes for me to lose my shit, dropping the gun from my hands and lifting him off the chair by his neck. I throw him into the nearest wall, holding him in place with my forearm pressing tight against his throat.

"Now, let me tell you about the kind of guy I am, Luke," I warn him through my teeth. "I'm callous, I'm reckless, and I don't give a fuck who I have to hurt in order to protect what's mine. Guys like you, get to keep fuckin' breathing because guys like me are having good days." I press tighter into his neck feeling his Adam's apple quake against my tense arm.

"And as long as I'm still breathing, you will not get a touch on Ella Jackson. You may have her all scared, but you don't scare me." I take my knife out of my back pocket, holding it millimeters away from his eyeball, and watch with deep satisfaction as his pupils dilate with panic.

"I warned you that I specialize in freehand." I let the blade touch his skin, sliding it down his cheek without breaking the skin. "Tattoos are as permanent as scars, there ain't no room for slip-ups. You should ask yourself if you really want one before you commit." Pushing myself away from him I watch him pick up his jacket, his eyes remaining fixed on mine as he calmly strolls out the door.

There are only so many times I can threaten the kid before I'm gonna have to start taking action. Ella can't protect him forever, not when he brings his shit to my doorstep.

I pull down the blinds and lock up the studio door, then get back to sketching while I wait for Ella to get here.

I can't wait to get my hands on her when she finally arrives and Ella launches her hot little body onto mine as soon as I open the door. I catch her in my arms, holding her tight against me as I carry her inside.

"You sure you wanna do this?" I check, placing her ass down on the leather chair.

"Absolutely, I'm excited." She's practically bouncing, and I love being responsible for the sparkle in her eyes.

"You wanna see what you're getting?" I ask.

"Wait. I don't get to pick?" Her mouth drops open, and I shake my head back at her watching her skin turn white.

"Nope, if you want me to tattoo you, it's my pick." I reach over to my sketchpad and open it up to the page I've been working on. Ella's dainty fingers reach out and brush over my sketch and her lips pull into a smile.

"It's just like yours." Her fingers slide over to my arm and trace over the compass that's now part of my sleeve.

"I love it, it's perfect," she says with a smile, one I wish I could tattoo into my memories and keep forever.

"Do I get to decide where it goes?" she suddenly looks worried again. "It has to be somewhere my father won't see it"

"I was thinking here," I touch my finger to the inside of her thigh, it will be private there. Our little secret. I seem to lose her for a little while, her thoughts going somewhere else for a second, maybe she wants to back out.

"Yes," she snaps out of whatever it is that was troubling her fast, her hands clapping together excitedly.

"Okay then." I pull on some fresh gloves. I wasn't lying earlier when I told Luke that I specialized in freehand. I've been drawing this compass for years, I could do it with my eyes shut. It's on my skin and soon it will be on hers too.

"You nervous?" I check.

"Please, I've taken a lot worse than this." Her eyes lower to my crotch and beam back cheekily at me before I reach for the anti-bac and spray area.

"You ready for me, darlin'?" I ask, firing up the gun, and noticing how she jumps at the low buzzing sound it makes.

"I'm ready, Nyx," she nods, giving all of her trust over to me.

I watch her flinch when the needle touches at her skin, her face trying to be brave as I do the outline. I want to get it over for her quickly, but at the same time, I want to take my time and make it the most perfect thing I've ever done.

"So, what's with the compass?" she asks screwing up her face when I scratch over another sensitive nerve.

"You didn't want to ask me that before I started permanently inking it on your skin?" I look up at her and smirk.

"I trust you," she tells me, resting her head back and looking up at the ceiling.

"Well, if you trust me, do you need to know?"

"I don't need to know, I want to know, there's a difference." She gives me that clever look she does, and fuck, don't I love it when she gets smart with me.

"I'll tell you one day, pinkie promise." I humor her, the sound of her sweet giggle travelling all the way to my dick and doing nothing to help me focus.

After a few hours, I'm done, and I sit back and I admire my masterpiece, impressed with my shading work, even if I do say so myself. When I show Ella in the mirror, she squeals with excitement, wrapping her arms around my neck and pressing kisses all over my face, and I watch our reflection wishing that everything could be as simple as this.

Making Ella happy has rapidly become my latest addiction, and I wonder how much longer I'll be able to keep up the habit.

I'm just finishing wrapping her up when my cell buzzes. I pull it out my pocket and see it's Jessie calling. I want so much to ignore it. Hanging with Ella like this feels so fuckin' good.

But when it comes to the club, you can never be sure what shit's gone down.

"I got to take this," I hold up the phone to Ella, then step into the back room, pressing it against my ear.

"What's up?" I answer.

"Nyx, we need you to drive a cage out here," Jessie instructs me, sounding serious.

"Everything okay?" I check, wondering what the hell could have happened.

"For now, Utah brothers need us to help them take care of something with them after the fight. I got a hunch it's gonna get messy," he says, and I detect the thrill in his tone. Jessie lives for this kind of shit.

Most of us do.

Even settling down with Maddy ain't stopped his thirst for mayhem.

"I'll be there in a couple hours," I watch Ella through the door, she's still checking out her tattoo, looking real happy with it. I hang up the phone and go to her, my hands sliding up the back of her skirt and squeezing her ass cheeks in my fists as I pull her onto me.

"I need to lock up and get goin'. I gotta drive to Denver."

"Denver? Now? Why?" she asks, suddenly looking worried.

"I got some friends who need my help." It's the closest answer to the truth I can offer her. "Come on, I'll get you home." I make my way towards the back room, and push my prospect cut into my bag before she sees it.

"I can get myself home, you should go help your friend," she tells me when I come back out.

"They can wait."

"Nyx, I live in the opposite direction to Denver, I made my way here on my own I can make my way back." She reaches up on her toes and kisses my cheek.

"It doesn't look like I'll be around tomorrow, maybe you can sneak out and see me Sunday?" I slide my fingers just above her hip bone where I know she's ticklish, and she giggles, nodding back at me in forced agreement.

"Thank you for my tattoo," she says after I walk her to the back door, her arms hugging my neck while her fingers cross over the back of my head.

"You are welcome. Make sure you text me when you get home." I kiss her lips, then keep hold of her hand when she tries walking out of the door, I'm not ready to give her up yet.

She laughs, using a lame attempt of a tug to get away from me. Eventually, giving up any resistance and letting me pull her back on to me, her lips crashing onto mine and kissing me with that sweet little desire that never fails to make my cock a lead fuckin' weight.

"I love you, Nyx," she whispers with her lips still attached to mine. The arm I've got wrapped around her waist squeezes tighter, and I bunch up the light cotton dress she's wearing in my fist. I pull my head back because I mean what I'm about to say and I want her to fucking know it.

"I love you too," I tell her back, looking her straight in her hazel eyes and in that moment, I fail to see how we could be wrong together. How anyone could keep us apart.

Ella Jackson owns every part of me.

"I'll see you Sunday," she smiles as I place her back onto her feet.

"Sunday," I promise her, reluctantly letting her go. I watch from the door as she gets in her car. The wide grin not slipping from her face, not for even a second. I wait until she's driven away before heading back inside and pulling on my prospect cut. Some poor fuckers are about to get taught a lesson for fucking with the club, and something really bad in my gut tells me I'm not far from learning that lesson myself.

I must be fuckin' crazy. I know what I'm doing is dangerous, but I'm too far gone to stop it.

Soon as the business in Denver is dealt with, I'm gonna man up and tell Prez the truth. Hope that honesty will be enough for him to forgive me, and if it isn't, well…

I'll cross that bridge if I have to.

I can't keep lying to her.

I ride back to the club and pick up the cage. No doubt there will be casualties tonight, and as I drive to Denver all I can focus on are all the what ifs…

What if all this all works out for us? What if I actually get to keep her… and what the fuck will I do if I don't?

CHAPTER 24

ELLA

I get home to an empty house again and practically skip up the stairs to my room. Lifting up my dress I take another look at my new tattoo in the mirror. It's perfect, and I love that it links me to Nyx. A permanent mark that will tie us forever.

I blank out how much trouble I'll be in if Father ever sees it, and I try not to imagine the ways he might discover it.

Today has been too good a day to let thoughts like that loose in my head.

I hadn't planned on dropping the L bomb on Nyx and I'd expected awkwardness after the words tumbled out my mouth, but what I got back were honest words that made my heart flutter.

He meant it when he said it back. I heard it in his tone, I saw it in his eyes and felt it in the way he held me. I should never have ever doubted him. The way Nyx protects me is fierce, how much he cares for me has been evident since the day I caught him hanging outside my house in a tree.

Nyx may be wrong for me, he may have his secrets, but I've fallen in love with him, and I've fallen too deep to give him up now.

I change into an oversized T-shirt and settle on my bed. I want to text him goodnight, tell him to drive safe, and that I can't wait until Sunday. But I don't want to seem needy, especially not when he's with his friends. I'm just about to turn off my sidelight and try and get some sleep when my cell lights up.

I meant what I said. X

I can't help smiling to myself as I type out a reply.

Can't wait until you tell me again Sunday. Drive safe xxx

I cuddle into my covers and close my eyes, and let my heart float with a little bit of hope.

Saturdays in our house are always dull, Father either goes to his precious club or works in his office, while Mom commits herself to whatever the latest fitness fad is. When I come down the stairs, I find Mom with her body distorted in the same way as the woman on the TV, and as predicted, to my relief there's no sign of Father.

I'm on my way to the kitchen to grab some breakfast when the door to his office opens and a tower of a man steps out in front of me. He looks nothing like the usual type of person who would visit. A long unkempt beard covers up most of his face, and his narrow, spiteful eyes examine me thoroughly when I freeze in front of him. He wears black jeans with rips that clearly aren't for fashion purposes and a hooded top that look as though it hasn't seen a washing machine in a long while.

Father follows him out and reaches up to place a hand on his shoulder as if they're familiar with each other. I watch a smirk lift beneath the stranger's thick bush of facial hair as his focus lowers on to my tits.

"Well, this must be Ella," he says, causing my father to look unnerved. He rushes to usher the man towards the door. It's the only time in my life I ever recall feeling remotely protected by him.

The guy's head turns over his shoulders, his eyes continuing to assault me.

"Ain't she a pretty little thing, Judge Jackson," he taunts as Father opens the door. "Can't blame you for keeping that little treasure locked away."

I feel dirty just from his glare, and as much as I want to run to the kitchen, my feet are rooted to the spot I'm standing in.

"I'll be in touch," Father promises him, and if I wasn't so unnerved it would make me laugh at how submissive he's being. A man built like this one could crush my father without breaking a sweat and he knows it.

"Who was that?" I ask after he closes the door.

"No concern of yours," he snaps, passing me on the way back to his office and slamming his door.

While Penelope prepares my pancakes, I can't help but wonder about the man. He didn't look like the type to have business with my father. Maybe he was threatening him. The way he'd looked at me had been a warning in itself. Maybe he's someone who Father has sentenced in the past. Whoever he is, he's wrong if he thinks he could get to my father by hurting me.

Mom steps into the kitchen, red-faced, and breathless. She heads straight for the fridge, pours herself a long glass of water, and drinks it down as quick as her throat can take it.

"Darling, I'm just gonna take a shower. Then I thought we could go to the mall, maybe get some lunch?"

"Who was that man?" I ignore her suggestion.

"What man?" she plays innocent, and her oblivious act pisses me off.

"The man, who was just in our house, Mom." I tilt my head sideways and pull a face that shows I'm not going to play up to her bullshit.

"You know how focused I am when I exercise, darling. He was probably one of your father's associates. So, are we going to the mall or not?" she asks.

"He looks scary, you don't think Father's in any kind of trouble, do you?" I impress myself with how I make curiosity sound a lot like concern.

"Of course not. Your father is a clever man, Ella, he doesn't mix with people like that," Mom assures me.

"Right," I nod, pretending to be convinced.

After an hour at the mall, and Mom trying on countless outfits, all of which I've assured her she looks great in. She buys me a handbag that most girls my age would offer up a kidney to own, but all I can get excited about is the thought of seeing Nyx tomorrow.

When we get home, Mom needs to go for a lie-down. All the excitement of shopping and the four glasses of wine she had with her salad at lunch must have really taken its toll on her. I chat to Penelope while she waxes the floor in the dining room, and she tells me what her plans are for the vacation time she has coming up. She's going to visit her brother and his family and can't wait to spend some time with her nieces and nephews.

"And how about you, Miss Jackson, how will you spend your summer?" she asks, working her hands vigorously against the floor.

"Maybe I've met someone," I whisper, feeling heat spread to my cheeks. Penelope looks up at me, her big brown eyes spreading wide with excitement.

"Sounds interesting," she smiles. "Tell me, is he handsome? Does he treat my girl well?"

"He's perfect," I tell her, feeling my body sag dreamily.

"Ella, can I see you in my office," Father's voice bellows from behind me before I get the chance to fill her in. It immediately brings me back down to earth again. Dread pooling in my stomach as I stand up and make my way towards him. He marches ahead of me, holding the office door open, and then closing it behind me with a thud that makes my bones rattle.

I close my eyes and take deep breaths as he stalks around me, remembering what had happened the last time we were in this room alone together. The scream collects in my throat, but I swallow it back down thickly.

I'll be brave, showing him that he scares me only feeds his power.

"Last night while we were at the Millers, where were you?" he asks calmly, settling himself in front of me so our toes almost touch.

"I was here, at home finishing an assignment." It's a lie but if he knew where I really was, I'd have been in serious trouble way before now.

"Are you sure about that?" He twists his head to the side and I nod back, nerves tight and heavy in my stomach, turning over like an over-crammed washing machine.

"See, while you were grounded I took the opportunity to have your car fitted with some software," he explains, his finger brushing my shoulder and making me shiver.

"Software?" I question, feeling my lips beginning to wobble. *Be strong, Ella, don't show weakness.*

"Ella, you're my daughter, it's natural for me to worry." There's a chill in his tone that makes my eyes blur with tears. "So, do you want to explain to me why you were in Manitou Springs last night between 6.45 and 9.30?" his finger slides over my clavicle and down between my breasts and I feel the first tear spill on to my cheek.

"I was visiting a friend."

"A friend," he repeats, unconvinced.

"Uh, huh," I nod, praying that he believes me. He has to believe me.

"Are you lying to me?" he growls, his hand reaching up to clasp my jaw, and I lift my head to look at him. He's so angry.

"You know, if I find out you were with that boy. I'll kill him," he threatens. The look in his eyes forces me to believe him. Nyx may be strong and seem invincible, but my father is a man who always gets what he wants. Jesus, that's what the man could have been here today for.

"I wouldn't lie to you," I assure him, crossing my fingers behind my back and praying that he believes me.

"Who was the friend?" he asks.

"Olivia, Olivia Fellows. Her Mom owns a nail bar in town, she helps out some evenings. I was just giving her a hand." I know that if he checks he'll find that the nail bar actually exists. I just hoped it's enough for him to not question me being there.

"You must be punished for lying to me, Ella, do you understand that?" he asks me, pretending like he isn't going to enjoy what he's about to do.

My head nods back at him like an obedient puppy because I'm too scared to respond any other way.

"Good girl, move to my desk, and rest the front of your body against it," he commands, stepping out my way. I look back at him in horror. Fear wrapping itself around my throat, and strangling me into silence.

I take the five steps towards the desk and cautiously lean over it. Petrified of what's coming next as I press my chest against the wood surface. I shudder when I feel his hands rip my jeans over my hips, immediately panicking that he'll see my tattoo. Whatever punishment this is will be a whole lot worse if he sees that.

So I press my thighs tight together to try and keep it concealed.

Closing my eyes, I grit my teeth, and wait to hear the click of his belt, expecting the same punishment he gave Mom the day I rode off with Nyx. I guess I should be grateful he's actually punishing me this time instead of her.

What I get is much worse. His open palm comes down hard against my ass cheek. His flesh against my flesh, and his low satisfied grunts torture me with each harsh impact. I try so hard not to react, to hold in my disgust as his fat fingers grapple and imprint my skin. Salty tears seep over my cheeks and slide between my lips as I bite down on them to stop myself from wailing.

"Look at you, your thighs tensed together. Is your pussy wet, you filthy little whore?" he grunts from behind me, causing bile to clog my throat. I close my eyes and try to think about Nyx. I imagine all the things he'd do to my father if he knew what he was doing to me now. And I know without a single doubt that he would kill him, and then he'd be locked away from me forever.

My ass feels like it's on fire when Father's finally finished with me, and as he grabs a fist of my hair and pulls me flush to his body, I feel his spit land on my cheek as he serves me one final warning.

"Don't lie to me again, Ella, I will always know." He releases me suddenly, sending me flying forward onto his desk with a thud. My cheek slamming against the polished mahogany and anger coursing through me like a wildfire.

"I hate you," I manage to lift myself up to scream at him. "You're sick, the way you touch me, the way you look at me. You shouldn't be allowed to judge other people. I'm gonna tell everyone what a sick pervert you really are." I march past him to the door but I don't make it. He yanks me back by my hair, almost ripping clumps from my scalp as I resist, and then he forces me forward so hard that the front of my body slams hard into the door I was just trying to escape from.

His chest presses into my back, heavy breathes landing in my ear, and his hard cock pressing against my spine.

"I doubt that darling," he warns. "Your mother is fragile to say the least. How would she cope with the scandal? She can't lose me, Ella, not without sinking right back down into the gutter she crawled out from." His fingers soften, massaging my aching scalp.

"You will keep those pretty lips closed…" he whispers into my ear, "and I might just let you stay intact." He pushes himself off me and I fumble to find the door handle, finally locating it and somehow managing to scurry out into the hall.

I race up the stairs and lock my bedroom door before pulling myself under the comforter. Only then do I finally take a breath. My whole body shivering from his threat, and my ass stings from his filthy handprints.

I want Nyx, I want him to come and take me away from this hell and protect me. And as thick tears leak onto my pillow, I form a plan in my head. Tomorrow when I see Nyx, I'll ask him to take me away from this place. To start afresh with me. Fuck College, fuck my mother, fuck everything. All we need is each other.

CHAPTER 25

JESSIE

Resting on one ass cheek the whole way back from Denver is no fuckin' fun. We're a little behind the other brothers, and I'm hating every minute of riding shotgun in the cage, instead of riding my bike. Nyx has been quiet the whole journey, eyes focused on the road ahead of him, but then the kid never does have much to say for himself. Even I can tell that something's been eating him up lately though. I know that look, the doubt, the frustration. He's fallen hard, and I pray for his sake it ain't with who I think it is.

Luckily, Walker from our Utah Charter was an army medic back in his day. He removed the slug from my ass and stitched me up before we put my bike in the back of the van and set off a little after the others.

Having some distance between me and Squealer right now is probably a damn good idea.

Nyx looks across at me and sniggers. And yeah, I see the humor in the fact I've been shot in the ass by one of my own brothers. It was an accident on Squeal's part, and he apologized, but it's still a fuckin' inconvenience.

"Who thought it was a good idea to arm that idiot with a gun anyway?" I ask, leaning forward and swiping up my smokes from the dash. I light up what must be my twentieth since we left.

"I'll bet you ain't the only one who's got shot in the ass by Squealer," Nyx laughs, and I balance my cigarette between my lips so I can slam a fist into his arm hard enough to make him swerve.

"What's gotten into you lately? You're all happy and shit," I question.

"Nothing." I pick up on how defensive he sounds and stare back at him unconvinced.

"You gotta be looking forward to patching in." I let him focus back on the road.

"Yeah of course."

"So, nothing to do with that little project you been workin' for Prez," I dig deeper.

"Do I look fuckin' crazy?" Nyx bites back at me.

"Bitches can make the best of us do crazy shit," I tell him, thinking back to how much my life has changed since Maddy.

"Yeah, well we ain't all pussy possessed, but thanks for your concern," Nyx tells me flatly, glancing me a warning shot from the corner of his eye.

I wince as the truck bounces up the dirt track that leads past the club and up to the cabins. When the truck pulls to a stop outside mine, Maddy comes rushing off the porch and swings open the passenger door. She doesn't give me chance to climb out of the truck before she's straddling her tiny little body onto my lap and landing her mouth firm on mine. The pressure of her pressing my wound into the seat hurts like hell, but I take it. It's been 48 hours since I've had her and an ache in my ass ain't gonna stop me from being reminded why I miss her so bad.

"Put him down will you," another voice comes from my porch.

"Busted," Maddy's lips giggle against mine, and when she pulls away, I can't help but stare at her and wonder how the hell she became mine.

"Will you give the man a chance to get inside." Maddy's Mom, Marilyn, trudges off the porch towards us.

"Marilyn," I tip my head at her.

"How's the ass?" she asks, her brows knitting together with concern.

"It's been better," I answer, slyly rearranging my cock when Maddy lifts herself off my lap so I can get out.

"I always said that Squealer was an idiot, I mean who manages to shoot their own friend in the ass," she rolls her eyes.

"It was an accident, Mama," Maddy reminds her, pulling my arm around her shoulders to help me out.

"Well anyway, I'm gonna make sure you're fed properly, I'll have dinner with you tonight, cook you up something really nice."

Since we brought her to the club, Marilyn and Maddy have been building on their relationship. Both of them are under our protection now. The club has given Marilyn a job in the clubhouse, one with different expectations to her last position at the Bastard's club. She seems to have taken to the whole nurturing thing and is making up for lost time.

I like that Maddy has someone when I'm busy with club shit. In the time we've been together, I've seen her lose two people she was close to. But she's by no means fragile. Maddy Summers is a fighter.

"That sounds great Marilyn. In fact…" I reach into my back pocket for some bills. "Why don't you have Nyx here take you into town so you can pick up some steaks." I hand her some cash.

"Really?" Nyx leans over the steering wheel to throw me a 'what the fuck' kinda look. And I scowl back at him.

"Whatever," he throws up his arms in defeat. "Get in," he tells Marilyn who kisses my cheek, then her daughter's before hopping into the passenger seat.

"You should join us, you look like you could do with

cheering up a bit," I hear her telling him before he speeds out the yard.

Maddy wraps her arms around my neck and I lift her off the ground, guiding her legs around my hips, and ignoring the jolt of pain in my butt.

"Jessie be careful," she giggles when I dig my chin into her neck and tickle her with my jaw.

"I have no intention of being careful, not when I figure we got about forty minutes before your Mama gets back and I'll have to share you until she goes to work tonight." I carry Maddy inside and rest her ass on the kitchen counter.

"I Missed you," I whisper, pressing kisses against her throat.

"I missed you too, VP." She smiles, popping the buttons on her denim shorts and lifting her top up over her tits. Fuck, my woman is incredible. I only have to think about her, and my dick turns to rock. I'd spend my life inside her if I could, and that's exactly where I intend on being in the next couple of seconds.

A loud angry rap slamming on my door halts me from sucking one of her pink pert nipples into my mouth.

"Fuck off," I call out, throwing the closest thing I can reach, my boot, at the door, and hoping whoever it is will do one. I swear if it's Squealer come to apologize again, I'll shoot him in both his fuckin' ass cheeks so he won't sit down for weeks.

"Jessie, it's urgent," Prez's voice sounds strained.

"Fuck." I press my forehead against Maddy's, and she looks up at me through those long lashes.

"To be fuckin' continued," I growl.

"Come in!" I call out as I pull down her top. Prez smirks at me when he steps inside and catches Maddy sliding off the counter doing up her shorts.

"Sorry to interrupt." Prez looks over my shoulder. "Maddy," he tips his head at her.

"How's the ass?" he asks, pulling the same face as every other fucker who's asked me.

"Is that what you came here for, to check on my ass?" I love the man like a father, but I'm fucking deprived here.

"Actually, it's you I came to see," he speaks directly to Maddy.

"Oh right." She steps around me and I pull her back by her waist. Mostly to hide my raging hard-on, but also to tease her with what she's missing out on.

"What can I do for you, Prez?" she smiles sweetly, twisting one of her plaits around her finger. She knows exactly what she's doing to me, and it earns her a little more pressure against her back.

"I've had a tip."

"On chop?" I ask.

"No, this is about…" Prez takes a long breath before he speaks. "It's about Ella. Apparently, she's been attracting the wrong kind of attention."

I fuckin' knew it. I warned him, stupid fucking kid. I scrub my hand over my face trying to figure how the fuck Nyx is gonna pull himself out of this.

"Bastards got their eyes on her," he says, and my shock just about hides my relief that Nyx is in the clear. But it's short lived.

This is bad, real fucking bad.

"There ain't no way Bastards could know 'bout her Prez, you told me that yourself."

"That's what I thought, but they've been seen watching her house, we all know that's way out of their territory. It's too much of a coincidence." Prez is worried, I can tell from how he's standing; his eyes are doused with that anger that only comes when there's a threat on someone he cares about. "I was wondering if there was something you could do, some way you could see if they're on to her."

"Sure." Maddy quickly moves away from me to go to him, placing her hand on his shoulder reassuringly.

"If they've been sniffing, I'll find out about it," she promises. Passing him to no doubt pick up her weapon of mass destruction.

"Seriously. How's your ass?" Prez tips his head, faking sympathy.

"Fuck off." I flip him off.

Minutes later we're both on either side of Maddy looking down on to her screen.

"I've done a name search, put in a hundred-mile radius to see if anyone has tried to pull up a search on her that goes deeper than social media," she explains. I look to Prez and when I catch his eyes I grin smugly, my girl is totally kick ass.

"Oh, wow," she says pausing her fingers from their constant tapping.

"What?" Prez stiffens beside me.

"It looks like someone's put some kinda GPS on her car," she tells us.

"And can you tap into that thing?" Prez asks.

"Yeah sure, here it is," she pulls up a map on the screen with pinpoints dotted everywhere Ella has been, it's detailed down to how fast she travelled between destinations.

"Can you find out who this feeds to?" I ask Maddy. She nods and in a few more clicks some weird numbers come up on the screen, when she clicks them it reveals an address.

"That's her home address," Prez says under his breath. "Jackson is keeping tabs on her."

Maddy clicks back to the map where it shows the car is stationary at her home.

"What's that?" Prez presses his finger to the screen, where two green dots stand out from all the others because they are set further away. Maddy zooms in on them, and I look up at the ceiling, cussing Nyx in my head when I see where they're located.

"That's here in Manitou Springs," Prez leans closer to the screen. "Closer, move that thing closer."

Maddy does as he asks, and he clutches the back of her chair when he sees where the dots are situated.

"What the fuck was she doing at the studio last night?" he asks.

"Nyx," the name comes off his mouth like venom. "What was he thinking bringing her there?"

"Well it looks like she took herself, it's her car," Maddy points out chewing on her nail, she knows as well as I do that this is bad for Nyx too.

"Wait, something else just flagged up," she says, clicking a few more times until another number comes up on the screen, then an address that makes both me and Prez freeze.

"What's that address showing up for, Mads?" I ask nervously.

"There have been a lot of searches on her name that have come from that IP address in the past week or so, advanced kinda searches." She turns around to look at me, and my worry matches Prez's.

"What is it?" she asks, concern clouding her pretty features.

"That's the Bastard compound address," I breathe out, my eyes darting to Prez and watching his rage build.

"What have those searches uncovered?" he asks Maddy through his teeth, one hand resting on the table while the other looks like it might lift the chair she's sitting in and throw it.

"Well not a lot, the judge is registered as her father on her birth certificate, he's next of kin on her medical records. According to the World Wide Web, she's legit his daughter."

"Good," Prez nods, swallowing his bitterness, and I sense his sadness as he straightens himself back up.

"What do we do now, Prez, you want some of us to go pick her up, bring her in for protection?"

"No," he shakes his head, breathing through his nostrils.

"I want you to bring me Nyx."

CHAPTER 26

Seriously, does this woman have an off switch? Marilyn has rambled all the way into town and she's still going strong. I find it hard to be rude to her, she may be damn annoying, but her heart is in the right place. I don't know much about Maddy's mom, other than the fact she was a whore for the Bastards before shit went south. And that she must feel bad for the way she neglected Maddy back then, because she sure overcompensates for it now. She acts like a mother to everyone. Even Prez.

The whole drive back from Denver I've thought about ways of telling Prez about me and Ella. It's a huge risk, and there's no telling how things are gonna go off. I have no plan in place, nothing I can reassure her of. But it's something that has to be done. I'm a lot of things bad, but I've decided I really fuckin' hate being disloyal.

I pull up at the compound, and drive Marilyn back to Jessie's cabin, promising after her three-mile lecture about me needing to eat better, that I'll come over after a shower and join them for dinner.

I'm just about to step inside my own cabin when I hear Jessie calling me across the yard.

"Nyx." I look over at him, not liking the worried look he's got on his face one bit.

"Prez wants to see you, he's down at the club." He hobbles closer and lowers his voice in case anyone's listening.

"It ain't good, man. Prez got a tip, The Bastards have been lookin' in on Ella, and the Judge has been tracking her car."

Panic hits me first, followed quickly by raging anger that feeds the instant need to cause pain. My hands curl into fists, my jaw locks and all my muscles tense.

"Look, just a heads up. Prez got a look at the tracker, so he's seen where she's been." It's a warning from Jessie, but at this point, I don't give a shit. I just want to get to Ella and make sure she's safe. I storm over to my bike and speed off down the track to the clubhouse. I'll speak to Prez first, but it'll be brief. Ella is my concern, my only fuckin' concern. I'll deal with the amount of shit I'm in once I know she's safe.

I know exactly where to find him, and when I barge through the door of the member's bar, he's sitting in one of the leather armchairs drinking alone. His face scowls when he sees me, guaranteeing that this ain't gonna be a pleasant conversation.

"Sit," he orders, flicking his head towards the chair opposite. I take the chair, staring right back at him, hoping he's gonna make this quick because the thought of those Bastard cunts watching her is making me murderous.

"Years ago, this place used to be a real family unit," he starts, stubbing out his cigarette. "We have the perfect set up for it, right?" He's speaking so calmly, taking too much time. I need to get out of here and go to her.

"We'd have BBQs on a Sunday, our kids would play together, our old ladies helped each other out." He sniffs to clear his airways

"Ya know why we don't got that anymore, Nyx?" he asks, all the creases in his forehead pulling together. Of course, I fucking know, everyone knows. This Charter halved its members after Prez's old lady got killed, all the brothers with families moved across states to safer Charters.

"Yes sir," I respond, the quicker we get this over with, the quicker I can leave for Ella.

"I've lost Hayley, Skid's lost Carly, we got Jessie's old lady trapped here like a goddamn prisoner. And all those bitches ever did to deserve it was love us.

Being associated with this club makes our enemies their enemy too. It puts them at risk. You think I want that for my little girl?" he asks, the frustration slowly building in his voice.

"No sir." And I sure as fuck don't want that for Ella either.

"So be it the Bastards, the Irish, or the fuckin' Triad. Any enemy of this club knows that the only way to get to us is through them. That makes them a target."

"I get it," I tell him impatiently, needing to get the hell out of here and check my girl. I'll kill any fucker that thinks it's okay to watch her.

"No, I don't think you fuckin' get it, Nyx. I asked you to keep your eye on her, to talk to her at school, to be her friend."

"Yeah, and I did all those things. Ella trusts me, I look out for her."

"You made her a fuckin' target," he bellows at me, slamming his fist into the arm of his chair. "You may not wear the full cut yet, but you wear the prospect jacket. You work at the studio, you've done shit under the club's name and if you're a part of this club, the Bastards want to hurt you. They want to hurt the people you care about. You showed 'em you cared about her. You fucked up."

"What?" I shake my head back at him, confused. "You asked for this, you asked me to be her friend."

"I asked you to put yourself into her life temporarily, Nyx. I never asked you to bring her into mine. Into all this shit." He stands up and charges at me, his fist shaking with rage as he wraps it around my collar and drags me onto my feet. "What the fuck were you thinking, bringing her to the studio? That's Souls' fuckin' territory, Nyx, she shouldn't have been anywhere near it."

"She got curious, she came and found me," I shout back at him.

"That wasn't part of the plan, you were meant to be getting curious about her. Do you realize what you've done? The Bastards find out she's my daughter, they'll kill her. Hell, even if those cunts think she's someone *you* care about they'll kill her. That's what they do. They hurt us through them. It's the only way the spineless dicks know how to fight."

"Then bring her in, I'll fetch her now. We can protect her, same way we do Maddy," I yell, just the thought of her being close relaxes some of my tension. Telling Prez how much Ella means to me has suddenly become the least of my concerns.

"You think I want that for her? Constantly looking over her shoulder? 24-hour protection? What about her college plans, who's gonna protect her when she leaves town?"

"I would." It's the easiest answer in the world. I'll go wherever she goes just so long as I get to take care of her.

"You," Prez shakes his head and laughs at me. "Nyx, you're just a stupid assed kid and the whole reason we're in this mess. Bastards have seen your interest in her and now you've just put a target on the head of the only thing I got left." He throws me back, releasing me at the same time and sending me crashing into the bar. His words hit me much harder though. I don't argue back with him, how can I? He's speaking the truth. Besides I'm too angry with myself for fucking things up.

"We're at war, Nyx, and the only thing that comes out of war is death and destruction. I won't have her be a part of that, she can't be a part of this. It's time to back off."

"No." I quickly straighten myself up, I can't let that happen. "The judge, he's shady, Prez, we can't trust him."

"Well thanks to you, I haven't got a fuckin' choice now. Being associated with us is a far greater risk to her." I hear the sadness in his tone, and I stand in front of him feeling paralyzed when it suddenly hits me.

I've seen it for myself. I watched them shoot Hayley, I see how protective Jessie is of Maddy. Hell, Skid hadn't even been able to trust his own brother with his wife. Threat is all around us and I've been an idiot to think Ella could be an exception to the rules.

"You need to get out of my damn sight, boy," he tells me.

"What about Ella? I need to say goodbye, we were... we're friends." I back out of telling him what we really are, what's the point? He's right, I can't keep seeing her, not if I'm putting her at risk, and I can't turn her life upside down either. I can't offer her an education or stability.

I can't offer her jack shit but trouble.

"I'll call up the Utah Charter, they need an extra pair of hands."

"What?" I rage. "You can't send me away, this is my home. I have a job here, Tac needs me at the studio." This can't actually be happening. I can't be losing my club too.

"I'm the god damn Prez of this club, boy, I get to do what the fuck I want. You are a threat to my daughter. I can't risk her coming and trying to find you. At least this way if she does, you'd have fallen off the face of the earth. And trust me when I say it, you're really lucky you fucking haven't. This is the only way to stop them from sniffing around her."

He's right again. Ella won't give up on me, or on us. She found me at the studio, she'd find me here too.

"So that's it, you're done with me, you're exiling me to another Charter?"

"Pack your shit, say goodbye to Tac, and get the fuck off my compound," Prez answers coldly and I back away from him. Heading towards the door with my body fueled with anger, some for him, but most of it for me and my stupidity.

"And Nyx..." he calls out to me. "You go anywhere near my

daughter ever again. I'll kill you myself." Prez warns before I kick open the door and storm outside to my bike.

Rogue is practically skipping her way across the yard towards the club, she's dressed up more than usual and looking pretty smug with herself.

"Jessie in there?" she asks as she gets closer.

"No, he's up at home. Squeal shot him in the ass," I growl back, not in the mood for a conversation. How am I supposed to leave town and trust that Ella's gonna be okay when I know the Bastards have been watching her?

"Shame. I got something for him," Rogue grins wickedly. She keeps her ears to the ground for the club, keeps us updated with a steady list of the people dealing nearby.

"If you're heading up there, you mind giving him this?" she pulls a folded up scrap of paper from her back pocket.

"Give it him yourself," I shake my head, straddling my bike.

"Wow who's yanked at your dick?" she bites back at me.

"Nobody," I shake my head. "Fine, just give me the fuckin' note. I'll pass it on." I hold out my hand to take it. I got to speak to Jessie before I leave anyway.

"This one's a real piece of work," Rogue grins as she hands it over. "He deals up at pines peak on a Saturday night. If Jessie rides out fast enough, he might even catch him in the act."

"How you know about this?" I question her, already hoping that Jessie will let me go with him. He's injured, he might need an extra set of hands. I could really do with kicking the shit out of someone before I head off to Utah, that's even if I bother going. Utah ain't far enough away to keep me away from Ella, I'll convince myself that I can be unseen and come back, even if it's just to watch her.

"Frankie sacked a girl for turning up wasted. So, I did a little digging," Rogue answers the question I forgot I'd even asked.

"Frankie. Black Pearl Frankie?" I check. Not many people know it, but the club have shares in the strip joint on the border of town, I can only think of one reason why Rogue would know inside information from there.

"The one and only."

"How would you even know this shit?" I stare at the folded up piece of paper in my hand.

"Show up on a Friday night and you'll find out. Look but don't touch, sweetie." She flicks my nose with one of her long pink nails before she heads back to her car.

I open up the piece of paper she's handed me, and all the blood rushes to my head when I see the name scribbled in front of me.

Luke Robinson.

"Rogue," I call after her. "You sure this is the name of the one supplying the girls?"

"They all gave me the same contact name and number when I asked where I could get a fix. Some cocky college kid who likes to get handsy apparently." She shrugs before getting in her car and speeding out of the yard.

I stare at the paper in my hand and feel all the heat in my blood start to simmer. I thought I was gonna be leaving Manitou Springs feeling completely helpless, but this right here is the one last thing I can do for Ella. Luke Robinson just became official club business, and hell if I'm about to let Jessie take this one.

I ride up to my cabin and stuff some clothes and my sketchbook into a duffle bag, then I slide my gun into my holster and clip my knife to my belt. I ain't gonna go be a club bitch in Utah, not when I've worked so hard to belong here. I'm gonna do what needs to be done tonight and then I'm gonna ride as far away from Ella Jackson as I can get. I slide my prospect cut back on ready to do one final job for the club, and the only thing I can for Ella. If kicking the crap out of Luke Robinson and getting away from her is all I can do for her now, then I'll make sure I do both properly.

"Guess you won't be joining us for dinner, huh?" Jessie catches me as I'm leaving my cabin.

"I fucked up." I kick my boot hard at the wood rafter that's holding up my porch roof.

"Prez is hurtin' he just needs time. It's a good sign that he's sending you to another Charter, it means he wants to keep you in the club. Who knows, you might even end up coming back here."

"I don't think so."

Jessie didn't see how mad Prez was.

"You care about her, don't ya?" he asks looking a little uncomfortable, brothers don't usually make a habit of talking about their feelings around here. I nod back without looking at him, there's no point denying it. Not to Jessie, you can't lie to that fucker.

"Then, getting out of town is the best thing you can do for both of you," he says sadly.

"We could bring her in, protect her like we do Mads," I suggest, if Jessie sees the sense in it, as VP he may be able to convince Prez.

"Yeah? And who's gonna protect you. You know club rules, you're lucky Prez hasn't picked up on your real feelings and just thinks you're a fuck up. He respects you enough to think you wouldn't be that stupid." He smirks at me.

"Ask yourself honestly, would you really want that for her?" His face quickly turns serious again. "I'm not ashamed to admit how much I love my girl, but I feel like shit every day for what she's had to sacrifice. Go to Utah, Nyx, make the best of what you can, and forget about her." Jessie slaps my back and offers me a pity smile before he moves back to his cabin.

I make my way over to my bike and tie my duffle on the back, then just as I'm about to kick start the engine I hear a female voice call out to me. Maddy runs off her porch, surprising me when she throws her arms around my neck.

"I'll keep an eye on her while you're gone," she whispers. I pull back and look at her. "Prez isn't gonna risk anything, Nyx. He's gonna want to keep an eye on her discreetly. I can do it without even leaving my cabin. We got a track on her car thanks to the judge." She holds her hands between us and wiggles her fingers, somehow managing to pry a smile out of me. And making me jealous that Jessie gets to be with the girl he's crazy about. "Trust me, Nyx, I'll do everything I can for her." I nod back at her gratefully, believing every word she says. "Take care, Nyx." She kisses my cheek before dashing back inside.

I pull away from the cabins, down the dirt track, and past the club. Then I ride the windy roads that lead into town and when I get to the fork on the road, I don't hesitate, pulling back my throttle and heading for Pines Peak.

It ain't hard to find him, his shiny red jeep sticks out in the empty parking lot on top of the hill like a dog's nutsack.

I park my bike a good distance away so I can move closer on foot. I see the silhouette of a girl next to him, no doubt some ditzy cheerleading bitch he brought up here to suck him off while she gets high. I should put a bullet in the back of his skull, make sure he can never hurt Ella again. Any jackass who'd get pleasure out of causing her pain deserves to meet his maker.

I take my hand off my gun, deciding that it wouldn't be enough. Luke Robinson needs to hurt, he needs to feel pain in a way he's never experienced before. And I need to be the one to serve it to him.

I hear them laughing, not a care in the fucking world. And that's when I feel it snap, all the anger inside me that's been festering since the first day I saw him be cruel to Ella, releasing in one powerful burst. I charge forward so fast that the asshole doesn't see me coming, and take him by surprise when I drag him out of his jeep and lay my first punch deep into his throat, with any luck I'll crush the fucker's windpipe, he can choke on his own breath and his little slut can watch him fucking suffer.

He falls to the ground, and I block out the screams that are coming from the bitch behind me as I lean over him and pummel my fists over and over into his face. The pussy doesn't even fight back, his hands trying to make a shield of his body as he tries to shuffle away from me.

"Stop! Please stop. I'm calling the police," the girl screams, but she doesn't stand a chance of getting through to me. I don't even let the voice in my head telling me that Ella wouldn't want this stop me.

Luke's blood splats my face as my knuckles dent his flesh. I've lost any control I had, all I can focus on is all the hurt this son of a bitch has caused Ella. Reaching down, I grab his throat in the arch of my hand before lifting him up and slamming him down into the ground. Smashing his head against the parking lot curb. I hear it crack, but it still doesn't stop me. I think about the asshole's constant jibes, the shit he wrote on my girl's locker, and all the stuff I know this slippery fucker has thought about doing to her.

I straighten up and stamp my boot hard into his face, over and over, and still the pain inside of me doesn't go away. Not even when his body turns limp and his blood runs onto the ground around my feet. One final hard blow of my foot into his face sends two of his teeth flying out of his mouth, and I know he's not gonna get back up. He won't ever hurt Ella again.

I back away slowly from the sorry fucker, ignoring the sobs and cries coming from the girl in his jeep, I don't even panic that she just witnessed the whole thing. I hope the cops fucking come for me. Locking me up and throwing away the key is the only way to guarantee keeping me away from Ella.

Every single part of me hurts when I think about being apart from her, in a way that makes me want to tear my heart out of my chest and stamp it into the curb just like Luke Robinson's head.

I pull out a smoke, and smell the blood on my knuckles when

I bring it to my lips, then when I get to my bike I think about where I'm heading next and instead of heading towards the freeway, I turn my bike and head in the opposite direction. I drive towards Castle Rock because I'm selfish, I'm reckless and I can't leave without seeing her one last time.

I park three streets away to be extra safe, taking off my cut, and tucking it inside my bag. I walk through the backstreets to get to her house, climbing the tree one last time and hopping over her wall. When I step through her balcony door, she's fully clothed, and sleeping soundly on top of her covers. I realize that I'm covered in Luke's blood, I didn't think about that while I was on my way here. I didn't think about anything on my way here except having to let her fuckin' go.

I don't want her to wake up and see me like this, I can't face having to tell her this is the last time she'll see me. So I keep my feet as soft as possible as I step into her room. I watch her chest as it gently rises up and down, and how her lips twist into a sleepy smile. This is exactly how I want to remember her. Peaceful, and so damn beautiful that it cripples me inside.

I reach out my finger and brush away a strand of her hair from her face and she takes comfort in it. Her soft skin so close to the bloodstains on my hands remind me of how stupid I've been. How did I ever convince myself that she could be mine?

My head automatically leans towards hers, my lips feel fucking starved of her and I allow them to touch against hers, hoping it might heal the pain ripping at my chest just for a few seconds.

She stirs a little and I quickly pull away, scared that I've woken her.

"Nyx?" Her fingers reach up, and she strokes my lips, her eyes still shut.

"Yeah baby," I keep my voice soft and low, managing a smile against her soft fingertips.

"It's late," she moans sleepily.

"I know, go back to sleep," I whisper, wrapping her hand up in mine and pressing her knuckles against my lips.

"What are you doing here?" she asks, still not properly awake.

"I got to go away for a little while, princess." I feel the cords of my heart snapping, I wanna drag her out of this bed and take her with me but I know that ain't an option.

"Okay." She nestles her head into her pillow. And the thumb from my free hand strokes her cheek.

I'm sorry Ell.

I can't say the words aloud, can't risk her hearing them. Leaving her is gonna be hard enough, without her trying to stop me.

I meant every word back at the studio. I've never been in love before but I know this is it because of how much it hurts. She's changed my life. And I wish there was a way for us to be together without sacrificing her safety.

Yesterday, I told her I'd always fight for us and I hate that I can't keep my word.

"Mmmm... love you Nyx," she sighs into her pillow. Whispering those words, like she's been saying them her whole life. She won't ever know how much it means to me that I was loved by someone like her. That for some crazy reason this beautiful, smart girl in front of me thought I was worthy of that.

Cupping her cheek in the arch of my hand I take her mouth and I pray to fuck knows who, that by some miracle it won't be for the last time.

I let my lips linger over hers for longer than I should, absorbing her taste and stealing her softness. And I wonder how the hell I'll be able to stay away, knowing that such perfection exists in the world.

"I love you back, Ella Carson." I make sure I use the name she should have been given. I got a lot of anger for Prez right now, but he ain't a bad man. As it turns out, we ain't so different.

He gave Ella up eighteen years ago because it was what was best for her, I'm giving her up for that very same reason tonight.

Finding the strength to pull myself up from her bed is the toughest thing I've ever done, and turning my back to walk away from her feels like stepping into flames. I stop at her balcony door and torture myself with one last look, I'd never have been able to give Ella Carson the world, but I'd have given her my life and that's exactly what it feels like I'm doing when I leave her, closing her balcony doors one last time behind me.

I head towards the studio, Tac's bike wasn't at the club earlier, so he's either working late or fuckin' in his apartment upstairs. The shutter is up and the lights are on. So I get off my bike and nervously fill my lungs with air before I walk inside.

I open the door and freeze when he comes firing out of the back room, his skin pale under his ink and a real scared look on his face,

"What the fuck you doin' here, kid?" he asks, racing towards the door and pulling down the blinds.

"Guess you spoke to Prez, huh?"

"Colorado Springs' police department got a warrant out for your arrest," he says sounding panicked. "Danny just called with the heads up, and Roswell's working on it but it looks like there ain't shit he can do about it. You need to get out of town." He opens the till and grabs a fist full of cash slamming it into my chest.

"I'm sorry I let you down," I tell him calmly, knowing that this was coming. Recklessness was bound to catch up with me sooner or later. The sound of sirens ring in the distance, getting louder and louder.

"Sorry, for what?" Tac shakes his head. "Kid, you need to split, use the back entrance and take my truck." He tosses me the keys from under the counter and I catch them in my fist before slamming them back on the desk surface. He looks at them, then back up at me, shock and confusion etched all over his face as the studio lights up red and blue and two patrol cars skid to a halt outside.

"Run," he screams at me as the door crashes open and a team of armed officers pile inside, their guns drawn and aimed at me.

"This is the only way," I tell him, I don't even know if he hears me over the sound of the police screaming their commands, but he looks betrayed when I place my hands behind my head and drop down onto my knees.

This really is the only way. Ain't nothing in this world gonna keep me coming for Ella if I'm free. I see that now. I still went to her tonight despite Prez's warning of the danger I could have put her in.

"Nixon Anderson." An officer steps up from behind me, grabbing at my wrists and snapping a set of metal handcuffs around them. "You're under arrest for the attempted murder of Luke Robinson." He pulls me up onto my feet and starts reciting me my rights. I pay no attention to the shit he's saying, just stare back at Tac and hope he knows how much I hate myself for letting him down.

CHAPTER 27
ELLA

Damn Nyx Anderson, it's bad enough that he's in every single one of my thoughts during the day, without him teasing me in my dreams during the night.

Last night's dream was kinda beautiful. He'd come to me through my balcony doors like always and touched me with that gentleness he seems to reserve especially for me. His lips were soft as they brushed over mine. His words just whispers, and it had all felt so real that his taste still lingers on my mouth.

Just a vision of him in my sleep soothed the bitter memory of what Father had done in his office last night, but it soon comes flooding back to me and has me running for the toilet.

Nyx probably partied hard with his friends last night, so I doubt I'll see him until this afternoon. I make no rush to get up and go downstairs, for that reason and the fact I'm trying to avoid my parents at all costs.

I take a long cold shower, the stream of water stinging my bruised backside as it sprays my tender skin. I take ages deciding what I should wear today and in the end, settle on the pretty white summer dress that I'd been wearing when he came for me at Father's club and took me to his secret hideout.

I haven't figured how I'll get past Father yet, no doubt he'll protest at the idea of me leaving the house. So, all I can hope is that he and Mom have something planned for this afternoon.

Lunchtime passes without me hearing anything from Nyx, so I decide to call him. When the call goes straight to answerphone, I figure he's out of signal or maybe he just forgot to charge his phone. Nyx isn't like the other kids our age, he doesn't have his cell glued to his hand all the time. I very rarely see him with it in fact.

I distract myself with some school work, then waste another hour scrolling through TikTok videos.

Something doesn't feel right, and the nervous feeling in my gut gradually builds as more time passes.

I wait until it gets to 6pm before I give up telling myself I'm paranoid and call Abby for her advice. She doesn't answer either so I try to imagine what she would say instead. She'd tell me that all boys are assholes and that I shouldn't worry about him. But with Nyx, it's never that simple. I know what people he hangs around with now, it explains a lot. With them, he could have got himself into all kinds of trouble. I can't help worrying about him.

I join my parents for dinner that evening, trying to put on a front and act like nothing's wrong, but my stomach rolls, threatening to eject its contents every time Father's eyes burn at me across the table. I finish up as quickly as I can and excuse myself back to my room and after checking my phone again, see that there's still nothing from Nyx.

The whole day has passed without me hearing from him. Something's wrong, and I pray to god whatever it is has nothing to do with my father and that man that was here yesterday.

He doesn't come to me in my dreams that night either, instead, I get trapped in a nightmare. One that makes my body break out in cold sweats and puts a rotten taste in my throat.

I'm in my father's office, his fingers touching the inside of my thigh and Nyx's tattoo. He's angry with me, and his fingers feel like sandpaper as they rub over the compass like he has the power to erase it from my skin. I wake up with a jolt. The cool air blowing through my balcony window and setting a shiver over my skin.

I fight to suck in air, my chest struggling to lift, but eventually, I manage to take some deep breaths when I remember that my bedroom door is locked. Father can't get to me. I fumble at my side unit until I locate my phone and check it again. There's still nothing from Nyx and despite it being 4am, I decide to try to call him again.

This time I leave him a message, asking… no, begging him to pick up because I'm worried. I tell him that I need him. That I don't care if he's missed our date today, I'm not mad. I just need to know he's okay. Then I stare at the phone, willing for it to ring as the sun creeps up and lightens my room.

My eyes feel heavy this morning, due to my lack of sleep and all the crying I've done. I try my best to freshen myself up before I make my way down the stairs for breakfast.

It's a typical Monday morning for everyone else, Penelope is whistling in the kitchen, while Mom takes her morning dose of 'vitamins' and Father sits at the table, his eyes scanning the morning news. He doesn't look up, but I can see the smug look on his face and the sweat dripping from his freshly shaved top lip.

He repulses me.

"It's such a terrible thing, what happened to the Robinson boy, we must send Denise and Roger flowers." Mom's suggestion to my Father suddenly turns my whole body rigid.

"What happened to Luke?" I ask, despite deep down already having a pretty solid clue.

"He's in the ICU, a victim of an unprovoked attack up at Pines Peak apparently, lucky there was a witness and they have arrested the person who did it. I can't bear the thought of someone like that being out there on the loose. Is anywhere safe these days?" She tuts before stabbing a fork into her fruit bowl.

I struggle to swallow as I eat up the eggs Penelope has prepared for me, and I quickly make up an excuse about getting to school early for some extra study time with Abby.

Father nods as if giving me his permission, and Mother gives me a lecture about working too hard. I kiss her cheek and leave in a hurry, hoping that Nyx will be at school with a perfectly good reason for not coming to see me yesterday. One that doesn't involve Luke Robinson.

Mine is one of the first cars in the parking lot when I arrive. And I sit in silence, convincing myself that I'm being silly worrying about Nyx.

Of course he didn't do this to Luke, he cares about me, the night before last he told me he loved me for Christ's sake. He wouldn't say that and then get himself thrown into jail. I'm just being a stupid, paranoid wreck. I'm distracting myself from a much more important issue. The fact that my father's behavior towards me is completely inappropriate, and that there is every chance he might do it again is what I should really be worrying about.

There's no sign of Abby's car in the parking lot and when I hear the bell ring, I get my bag and head inside.

There are whispers all around the hall, everyone's eyes seeming focused on me as I make my way towards my locker.

"I heard that Luke's eye popped right out the socket and he crushed it in his fist," one of the cheerleaders tells the crowd that's growing around her. All of them turning and looking at me judgingly.

"What's going on?" I ask one of the boys I share chemistry class with.

"You're kidding, right?" he laughs at me as he looks me up

and down. "The new kid beat the shit into Luke last night, almost killed him. Apparently they're still not sure if he'll make it."

"And what about Nyx?" I hear the shake in my voice as I ask him.

"He got arrested, that's all I know. Lucky escape for you, huh? I always thought that kid was dangerous." He strolls off towards class leaving me drowning in a sea of chaos and I can't take it for a second longer.

I turn and run back to my car, pulling out of the school parking lot. I contemplate heading to Manitou springs. There has to be someone in the studio who can tell me what's happened. And If not I'll find out where the Dirty Souls clubhouse is and go there instead. I need answers, I need to know why Nyx did this? If he'd really put hurting Luke over us being together?

I weigh up the consequences in my head. Father will be crazy mad if he finds out I've gone back there, and there's no doubt that he'll be keeping track of me now. His punishment will be brutal, but I can't not know that Nyx is okay. And so I head south to the quaint little town of Manitou springs, regardless of what it might cost me, and in desperate need for some answers.

I park in a space close to the studio and try not to be intimidated by the two guys sitting on the metal chairs either side of the door with their legs stretched out blocking the sidewalk. Both of them wearing leather cuts and smoking something that doesn't smell like a cigarette.

I smile at the one whose long hair is piled up on top of his head in a perfect man bun, his face looks a little busted up, but he's still jaw dropping handsome, not exactly what I was expecting from the brutal bikers Father talks about.

"Hey darlin'," the other guy acknowledges me and I give him a polite smile back as I pull open the shop door.

"You lookin' to get inked?" he asks, pulling his legs in and resting his elbows on his knees. His eyes assess me from my heels, all the way up to my tits and the cocky smirk on his face gets wider.

"I'm here to find Nyx," I tell him.

"Nyx. You hear that Troj? She's here for Nyx." The guy stands up on his feet, his powerful frame towering over mine as he steps up to me. "Nyx is otherwise engaged, but I'll happily assist you with your requirements." He places his hand against the glass behind me and cages me under his arms. Close up, he's kinda handsome too but in all the wrong ways. Just looking at him feels like a sin. His hair falls into his eyes, and his stern features don't quite suit the huge smile he's wearing.

"Back off, Squealer," the other one tells him.

"Come on, Trojey I'm happy to go twos." Squealer, if that's even a real name, glances back over his shoulder at the long-haired guy, who rolls his eyes and takes another long drag from whatever it is he's smoking.

"You best go on inside darlin', speak to Tac," the more sensible of the two tells me, and I use my hip to barge the door open and almost send the tower of a guy who's trying to overpower me hurtling through it. It earns me a snorty laugh from his friend.

"Jesus Troj, you on a fucking pussy sobriety pact or summit?" I hear him cursing as I step inside.

I know straight away who Tac is. The bald guy is covered from his neck to his wrists, sitting on a stool behind the desk and counting out dollar bills. He's got a smoke dangling from his lips that doesn't smell like it's got just tobacco in it either. When I eventually get his attention, he stubs it out into the skeleton hand ashtray that's resting on top of his desk.

"What can I do for you, lil' lady?" he asks, not taking his focus away from the wads of cash in his hands.

"I came to find out what happened with Nyx," I say. Praying that this guy has some answers for me.

"That's club business darlin'," he shakes his head back at me.

"What did Luke Robinson have to do with your stupid club?" I press for more, not prepared to accept that as a valid answer.

"I'd watch your mouth, little girl, people have lost their tongues for saying a lot less. It'd be a shame for you to lose yours," he looks up and warns me, his eyes accessing me in the same way the other guy did.

"Well do you know where he is, does he have a lawyer?" I ask, not willing to back down. Nyx can't go to jail, Not for the sake of Luke Robinson. Everyone knows he likes to provoke, I could tell the police all the terrible things he's done to me, explain that Nyx did it to protect me.

"Like I said, the club is dealin' with it," the guy shrugs, not a shred of sympathy on his harsh face as he stands up and makes his way through to the back, taking his cash with him.

"Well, if you get the chance to talk to him can you tell him I need to speak to him?" I call out. Pissed off at how rude he's being.

"I doubt I'll be seeing him for a while," he calls back at me. Then reappears a few moments later.

"But if I do, who should I tell him was lookin'?" he crosses his arms over his chest and looks at me suspiciously.

"Ella," I tell him my name, and I can't help feeling a little bummed that Nyx never took the time to tell his friends about me. Tac raises his eyebrows like he's expecting more. "Ella Jackson."

"Sure," he gives me a half-hearted grin.

"You wanna write that down?" I check, not having much faith in him remembering.

"Like I said, Miss, I ain't expecting him back anytime soon." Tac goes back to his business, and I stand helpless, my heart shattering.

I want to give in to my tears, but I manage to hold off, bursting out the shop door and almost tumbling into the bigger of the two guys outside. He catches me by shoulders, and I shrug him off, racing to my car and speeding away before the tears finally let themselves free. Tears of anger, tears of heartbreak, and tears of regret for being so damn stupid that I never saw this coming.

Chapter 28

NYX

County sucks. It only took me a few hours of being here to learn that. The guards treat you like scum, the place is filthy, and there are far too many assholes trying to throw their weight around to prove they're a threat.

In reality, half the people in here wouldn't know real danger if it smashed them in the face with an iron bar.

I use my first time out in the yard to observe, scoping out the different crews and separating the real threats from the lowlifes in here for scamming old folk out of their pensions.

It ain't hard to figure out who's who, most of the men here wear their colors on their arms. There's a few guys knocking around that I know mix with the club rivals, and some with blacked-out patches. Black ink jobs ain't often done by choice. And these men are the ones to watch. Those fuckers are prepared to do just about anything to get back in favor with the ones they've pissed off.

I've barely scraped through my first day before I notice my first threat. Some big fucker, hanging out on the Mexican side of the chow hall. He's been eyeballing me since I got in and I can't figure if he wants to fuck me or use me as a punch bag. I don't care how big the son of a bitch is, he won't be doing either. I never intended on throwing my shit around on my first day here but I also ain't about to let anyone here think I'm easy pickings.

I've watched the way Troj fights, he's taken out men twice his size by being smart. And I'll be smart before I get my ass fucked.

I finish up the crap that's on my tray and start making my way out, a quick glance over my shoulder shows that he and some of his buddies have upped from their table and are making their way towards me.

I dump my tray with the others and move into the corridor that leads back out onto the yard. Clocking the two wardens that are standing guard at the doors, and waiting for that first strike to come from behind me.

I keep my shoulders loose and my fists tight. Adrenaline rushing through my veins as I get closer to stepping outside.

And when something finally comes, it's not what I expected. Something solid and cool presses tight against my scrunched up fist and a deep voice speaks into my ear.

"Jimmer says keep ya head down, kid."

I side glance the Mexican who's standing beside me, and he nods me an understanding as I unclasp my fist and take what he's offering. Now that we're closer I recognize the ink on his hand *Soldados Malditos*. It looks like Tac's work, I've seen him do the emblem enough times in the past. Whoever this guy is he's a member of the cursed soldiers, and they are solid allies of the club.

I tip my chin at him, checking the guard to my left ain't watchin' before I tuck the weapon into the back of my scrubs. And once we're out in the yard we go our separate ways.

I wait until I'm inside my cell before I look at what he's given me. The shiv ain't all that big but it looks as if it could be effective. Its blade sturdy and sharp and the handle made comfortable to hold by bandages and book pages.

Prez can't be all that mad at me if he's put eyes on me in here. It still surprises me that he sent Monica the club lawyer for me after I got arrested. She brought with her a direct order from him for me to plead not guilty. Which pissed me the fuck off. But I get that Jimmer needs to cover the club's back. I'd forgotten about the fact I was wearing my prospect cut in front of a witness when I was kicking the shit into Luke. And because the club doesn't deserve extra heat on them because my temper made me get sloppy, I agreed to his request. I pleaded not guilty at my first hearing, despite having every intention on doing the time. And thankfully, due to the brutality of the attack, bail was denied. So here I am, waiting on a trial.

I'm sticking by my original plan. I have to protect Ella. I'm guilty, what I plead in a courtroom ain't gonna change that.

I'll stand trial. I'll do what's right by the club, but *I will* be found guilty. There's too much against me for it to be any other way.

The days and hours pass slowly. I spend myself looking up at the mattress above my head, and torturing myself by thinking about what she's doing. I wonder if she's hurting like I am. And if Prez has found a way for someone else to keep watch over her. I'm just grateful for that sharp-tongued friend of hers. Abby will tell her to move on, convince her I'm a jerk, and I'll bet she's already come up with a plan to help Ella get over me.

"S'up Nyx." One of the inmates I share my cell with strolls in from kitchen duty. He's one of the do-gooders, got himself enrolled in just about every program this shithole got running. He chats a lot of shit. He chats too much full stop and I'm almost certain he'll be the first one I lose my patience on.

I nod back at him and tuck my sketchbook under my ass. He's asked enough times if he can check out my work and my answer is always the same. I ain't about to share Ella with anyone inside these walls.

The guy that sleeps above me follows him in and hops straight up on to his bunk. He seems average enough, and I'm guessing the pictures he's got covering up all his wall space are of his wife and kids even though he never talks about them. Not even when do-gooder tries to make conversation and asks.

He keeps himself busy around here too, working extra hours in the kitchen. He just don't preach about it like the other guy does.

Our other celly is a huge fucker who doesn't say shit, and looks pissed off at the world and everyone in it. He avoids eye contact and stays out of everyone's business. Which suits me just fine.

I keep a low profile myself, get my duties done, and then either sketch or work out with my free time.

It's all I can do apart from fucking miss her.

I've been in over a month now, I'm no longer the new kid and I ain't made a single friend. I ain't made no enemies either, which in here is a fucking miracle. I step outside for morning yard time, letting the morning sun heat my face and stretching out my legs before I take a seat on one of the bleachers and notice some ruckus over in the corner A couple of the skinheads throwing their fists around, beating on someone who's probably looked at 'em wrong.

"New inmate," do-gooder slides beside me, nodding his head towards the scuffle. More men have piled in now, inmates who they have fed their bullshit to and recruited. "He came in yesterday, shares a cell with a guy I take an art class with. You should join us, you're always sketching in that book of yours."

The wardens manage to break it up but not soon enough to stop blood from spilling, and the last guy who gets pulled off is putting up one hell of a fight. It takes two wardens to pry him off the helpless body that's curled into a defensive ball.

I watch on as one of the wardens help him back on to his feet, even from over here I can see he's in bad shape. Without doubt, he's heading straight for the infirmary. And If he's got any sense he'll try and spend as much time in there as he can because he's just made himself an easy target for anyone wanting to blow off some steam.

As he gets closer, I have to squint my eyes together to block out the sun because what I think I'm seeing can't be real.

His hair is longer, and even though the scuffle has caused it to flop over his face. I'd still recognize him anywhere. And he has the balls to snarl at me as he gets escorted off the yard by the wardens. His mouth filled with blood and his face already starting to swell.

I smile to myself and stand up from the bleacher.

"You know, that's the first time I've seen ya smile," do-gooder tells me as I follow the sorry excuse of a fucking bitch off the yard with my eyes.

"Don't get used to it," I murmur back at him before I head off to make a phone call for the first time since I've been in here.

It takes two days after I make the call for Jessie to show his face and I got to admit, it feels good to see him.

"How ya holding up?" He speaks into the phone on the other side of the glass. From the state of him, he's had a rough night, he's got a black eye and split lip.

"As good as," I shrug back and he smiles back at me.

"Guerro and his crew lookin' out for ya?" he checks.

"Yeah, I'm covered," I assure him.

"So, what's with the call, you said you have something for me." Jessie looks at me through the glass curiously.

"I do," I confirm, leaning forward.

"Tommy," I say his name slowly and watch shock find its place on Jessie's face.

"Tommy, as in Chop's Tommy?" he checks and when I nod back, he smirks the same way I had when I realized that we had him.

"He came in a few days ago, shares a cell with the buddy of one-of my cellys."

"What's he in for?"

"Hell if I know, I ain't done no asking yet. I didn't want to make it seem like I care. He's in pretty bad shape though, barely been in a day before he got laid into by the skinheads." I glance my eyes to a booth a few down from mine where one of the Nazi fuckers is taking a visit of his own.

"Just say the fuckin' word and I'll make that little cunt squeak. He has to know where his dad is, Jess."

Jessie sits back in the plastic chair and gets that look on his face, the one he gets when he's cooking something up.

"How many's Guerro got in here?" he asks

"Twelve, maybe fifteen," I answer, confused.

"Enough to outnumber the skinheads?"

"I guess, they have a few new recruits, but nothing useful."

"Protect Tommy," Jessie lowers his voice into the phone, shocking the hell right out of me.

"You're kidding, right?" I slam my hand on the surface in front of me and earn myself a stern look from the warden guarding the door.

"No, make it your personal business to ensure no harm comes to him. You tell him he's got Soul protection and you tell Guerro and his boys the same thing."

"Have you lost your fuckin' head, Jessie?" I ask him, seriously concerned that he's taken a hard blow to his senses during whatever shit went down to cause those bruises on his face.

"No, sounds to me like Tommy is in an impossible situation and needs a friend. Someone who he can talk to."

"No way, I hate him. He's a sleazy little rat!"

"Exactly, and I'll bet it won't take him long to put his own ass before his loyalty to his papa. The club needs you to do this. Skid needs it."

"Am I even a part of that club anymore?" I ask, thinkin' about how mad Prez had been the last time I saw him.

"You think we'd be workin' so hard out here to get you out if you weren't?" Jessie asks me with a confused look on his face. I don't want out. Out there is nothing but temptation. I've put Ella in enough fucking danger.

"Mads got the name of the witness from your police report. We're thinking of a way to deal with her. Luke ain't a problem, he's still in hospital but he's gonna make a full recovery. We got enough evidence on Luke. I've already spoken to his old man, and he doesn't want his family rep ruined. So they ain't pushing to make charges. It's just the state you're up against.

"You're wasting your time," I tell him.

"Nyx, we're gonna get you out of here. Plenty of us been in worse scrapes than this and Monica's managed to get us off. This Abby bitch won't even make it into the witness box, some polite advice from Rogue should see to that."

"Abby?"

I repeat the name he just mentioned, hoping he's made a mistake.

"Yeah, the chick who was noshing him off when you went all cray cray on his ass. She was high when it happened, it even says so in the police report. Even if she don't heed Rogue's warning and decides to take the stand, Marcella will rip her a new asshole up there."

"No," I shake my head.

"What ya mean, no?" Jessie laughs at me.

"I mean no threats, you leave her out of it."

Jessie leans forward, the look on his face turning serious.

"You listen to me, Nyx. That little slut running her mouth to a jury could cost you hard fuckin' time. You don't want that."

"Who says I don't want it." I shrug.

"I say you don't want it. In here, even the worse of 'em got a chance of getting out. Nothing's permanent. You go to prison where some men got no hope, you're playing in a different playground," he tells me sternly.

"She's a friend of Ella's," I sigh, I should really let rogue loose on the two-faced little whore for betraying Ella like that with Luke but I know it's not what Ella would want.

"Can't you get Maddy to talk to her instead?" I suggest, knowing Rogue will lose her patience too quickly with a girl like Abby.

"I don't think it will have the same effect," Jessie sneers.

"Ella wouldn't want her to get hurt."

"The club doesn't make it their business to hurt women, Nyx, you know that. She'll just get a warning."

I nod back at him.

"I gotta get back, I got someone waiting for me downstairs."

"The fucker who did that to you?" I tip my head towards his fat lip.

"Nah, that fucker's six foot under in a place only Grimm knows. You just remember what I said, you cover Tommy's back in here and get him to talk. We get Chop, then we get Skid's focus back. That's gonna go hella way of getting you back in Prez's good books." Jessie goes to put down the phone back on the receiver and I manage to catch him just before.

"How is she, is someone…" I swallow the lump in my throat, "Has Prez got eyes on her?" I torture myself some more by asking.

"Prez's doing what he can. Maddy too. There's been no activity from the Bastards so that's a good sign." Jessie looks solemn and it makes me feel like such a fucking let down. Just the thought of her being out there unprotected makes me sick with worry. There have been nights I've wanted to rip the bars off the windows to go to her. I hate feeling so fucking helpless. All I can do from in here is hope the Bastards saw what we had as a stupid high school hook up and have backed off her now I ain't around.

"Stay outta trouble," Jessie reminds me with a sad smile before he places the phone back on the receiver and leaves.

I get up from my booth and make my way back to the yard. What I'm about to do ain't gonna be easy, especially since Tommy knows how much I hate him.

When I first arrived at the club he tried bullying me, just like the boys in the foster homes. I dealt with it the same way as I dealt with them. By going in hard and with no mercy. I kicked the shit out of him before I knew he was the VP's boy. Even if I had known, I doubt it would have made the difference.

I find Guerro first and tell him Jessie's orders.

"Any excuse to wet up a skinner," he smiles at me showing his grills, and I nod back before I make my way over to the bench where Tommy sits alone.

He looks in a bad way, the bruises in his face out in full color now and his cuts starting to scab over.

"Ya good?" I ask, taking a seat beside him.

"What do you fucking care." He shifts away from me, I can smell the fear in him though. Tommy always did make a shit job of trying to act tough.

"I don't," I shake my head, leaning forward and resting my elbows in my knees. "But for some reason the Souls do."

"I don't need the Souls," he mutters under his breath.

"Your funeral, I'll let the others know." I go to leave him alone, and just as I predicted, he stops me.

"What others?"

"Oh, you thought I was the protection?" I snigger. "I've always been the one out the two of us with the balls, Tommy, but even I ain't got the meat to go up against a gang of skinners. Not to save your weedy ass anyway. Nah, I mean I'll call off the others who were gonna watch your back."

"What others?" He sounds intrigued now, and sits up a little straighter…

"Guerro and his crew," I nod my head over at them, the other inmates show them respect, because all of them are well built and handy. They pretty much run shit in here. "Then there's that big fucker over there…" I gesture over at the dark-skinned mountain of a man on the other side of the fence. "Brax fucked up the man who raped his sister a few months ago. He owes the club a favor. And of course we got a couple of guards," I say casually.

"What guards?" Tommy really does look interested now.

"What does it matter, you don't need the club's protection so I'll just leave ya here to worry about yourself."

"No, wait. What does Jimmer want? Why would he do all this after…"

"…After your papa fucked and killed his brother's wife. And if I remember correctly, not in that order," I sneer back at him.

"What does he want from me?" Tommy asks again.

"You know what he wants." I lean down making sure my body overpowers his Skinny frame.

"I don't know where he is." He looks up at me and I know he's lying.

"We'll see. Perhaps getting double dicked by two skinners might jog your memory."

I walk away and leave him to think on that, taking myself to a quiet spot of my own out of everyone else's way. Where I can be alone with just my thoughts.

Thoughts of her, that cut deep and scar like a jagged knife. And memories that I refuse to blank out because as crazy as it sounds, I actually like the way they hurt.

Chapter 29 - Ella

"You are not wearing that, tell her, Penelope, she's not wearing that." Mother's face looks horrified when I go down for breakfast.

And Penelope looks at me awkwardly. "Perhaps, we could find you something a little more appropriate, Miss Jackson," she suggests tactfully.

"She has something to wear. We picked something out at the Mall last week," Mom informs her like I'm not even in the room.

"Correction, *you* picked me something out in the mall last week," I argue back.

A lot has changed since Nyx got himself thrown in jail four months ago. For a start, I no longer feel sorry for my mother. She chooses to live with a monster. She chose this life for us, and I hate her for it. As soon as I have enough money saved up, I'll be taking matters into my own hands.

If Nyx leaving has taught me anything, it's that no one can be relied on. You want to get shit done, you own that shit yourself. He wasn't my escape from my father, he wasn't the hero I convinced myself he'd be. The only person getting me out of this place is gonna be me.

"It's your graduation, the whole town will be there, the local news is doing a feature, you need to look presentable." A throat clearing interrupts the start of one of Mom's rants, and my stomach flips over on itself when I feel him enter the room behind me.

"What's the problem?"

"A misunderstanding, sir," Penelope chirps in, taking my hand and pulling me towards the hall. "Me and Miss Jackson are going to start getting ready for the ceremony." I let her drag me up the stairs, with a look of warning on her face.

She locks the door behind me when we get inside my room, and I'm about to protest when she shakes her head at me.

"Ella, I know your heart hurts," she starts, surprising me when she actually uses my name. I've spoken to Penelope about everything since I'd been old enough to put sentences together, but I haven't spoken to her about Nyx. I haven't spoken to anyone about him, not even Abby. It's too painful.

"I…" I start trying to explain but she cuts me off.

"I know your plans, and you can't afford for your father to get suspicious. You must make him think he controls you too if you are going to get away." I look at her, trying my best to fake confusion. The less people know about my plan, the better. I trust Penelope, but I also know how much she needs this job.

"But I…"

"Shhh. Now put this on," she pulls the smart knee-length dress Mom insisted would be the perfect graduation dress from my wardrobe. "Just a while longer, Miss Ella, and you will have all your heart's desires," she tells me, unlocking my door and slipping back out into the hall.

I huff in frustration because she's right. So far my plan isn't doing so great. I have about three hundred bucks from last month's allowance saved up in cash, and when I'd put the idea of getting a summer job to Mom last week she'd looked at me as if I needed a head check. "Why dear, you have everything you need?" being her response.

I have more money in my savings, but I can't access it without asking Mom for the savings book.

I need hard cash.

The door clicks open just as I'm stepping into my dress, no doubt it's Mom come to check that Penelope has convinced me to change.

"Just in time to zip me up," I roll my eyes sarcastically at her, but my eyes widen and my heart falls when I see my Dad step into the reflection of the mirror in front of me. Both his hands curl around my hips, holding me like a vice. I feel the sweat already starting to leak from my pores, my pulse quickening to keep my blood pumping around my body when my skin turns cold.

His eyes hold mine through the mirror and I get confirmation of how much he gets off on my fear when I feel him pressing hard into the base of my spine.

"Of course," he says calmly. One of his hands creeping over my ass cheek to where my zip starts.

He moves slowly, pulling the zipper higher up my back, his glare fixing on me through the mirror the whole time.

"Perfect," he says, looking at my reflection almost proudly, as he slides his palm down my back.

"Such a big, grown-up girl." He smiles and I close my eyes and suck in a breath, hoping it will calm the panic rising from the pit of my stomach. I flinch when I suddenly feel his hand wrap around my throat, squeezing tight as he twists me around and forces me back onto my bed. He looks down our bodies, red-faced, and with an angry vein throbbing at his temple as he climbs on top of me.

I've known this was coming from the day he put his fingers inside me. Up 'till now, he's been satisfied with just painful taunts but it's not enough for him. I had so hoped I'd get away before he took it this far. His grip on my neck tightens as he forces me into the mattress, his face resting against mine.

"Behave today," he warns. Pointing a podgy finger at my face. I'm desperate to smack it away and have to ball my fist tight in an attempt to stop myself. I don't want to anger him any more.

"Okay," I whisper, sucking back my sobs and reigning back tears. He doesn't deserve to see me cry. No one does. I've learned that these past few months.

"We'll be the happy family everyone in town expects to see, pretend you're not a little slut like your mother." It infuriates me when he speaks about Mom like that, the woman has devoted her whole life to keeping him happy, she puts him before everything, even me.

"Okay," I promise again, I need air back in my lungs and his heavyweight off my body. He releases me, but not without snarling a cruel laugh at me. One that makes me rage inside, and the urge to watch him hurt is the only thing that gives me the strength to sit up and straighten myself out.

"That's a good girl." He pets my head like I'm a puppy and I bite back all the frustration that's pulsing through me and think about my plan.

Father checks his reflection in my mirror, smoothing out a crease in his jacket, then running his hand through his thinning hair before he leaves.

I run into the bathroom and lock the door pressing my back against it for extra safety. Then pulling up my dress I let my fingers stroke over Nyx Anderson's parting gift to me before he left, the one thing that no one can take away from me. Looking at the compass on my thigh, it doesn't feel like a tattoo anymore, it feels much more like a scar, one that will remind me to never give up my heart again.

I hate Nyx for leaving me, I hate myself even more for allowing my heart to still ache for him. For allowing him to still be my comfort when I think about the problems that loom over me. The disgusting thoughts I know my father has repulse me, I have to get out of here before he puts any more of them into action. That's a damage that once done, will never be repairable.

I hold myself together through the ceremony. Then I pose for a family photo that will probably be featured in Monday morning's local paper. Father doesn't stay long after, insisting he has work to catch up on. Mother leaves with him, and I assure her I have a ride home with Abby when really, I just want to be alone. Away from the house, and away from him.

"Hey," Abby calls over at me, she struggles out of the group photo she's in with girls she never used to speak to.

"A bunch of us are going over to Julia's for a post-graduation party. You in?" Abby's changed a lot these past few months too. She's lost weight, so much that her skin's actually starting to look too loose for her body. She doesn't take care of herself the way she used to and she always looks tired. Still, who am I to judge. I'm a hermit who never leaves my room.

"Nah, I'm gonna head back," I tell her.

"How? I thought I saw your parents leave already. Come on it will be fun." She looks at me with those pleading eyes that are so used to getting their own way. They make me feel guilty, I've spent hardly any time with her lately, been far too busy wallowing in self-pity.

"Sure." I give up, it's pointless arguing with the girl. Besides, if I'm at a party, I'm not at home, and I should at least try to spend a night not moping about Nyx. I pile into Abby's car with some others, people who haven't taken the time during senior year to talk to me, but all of a sudden act like we're best friends. One of them even asks me to sign their yearbook.

Julia's parents live by a lake, and have really put in some effort, the place looks amazing, the grounds decorated with lanterns, and all the lights reflecting from the surface of the lake. It doesn't take long for the tranquility of the place to be invaded by horny, drunk teenagers, music pumping, and loud irritating giggles.

I manage to find a quiet spot under a tree on the other side of the lake. It's the perfect place for me to watch the party from and

I know it would be where Nyx would be hanging out if he were here.

While I sit alone, hiding away from the real world, the sky falls darker and the lanterns burn brighter. The sound of laughter and fun carrying over from the other side of the water where the house is.

"What you doing over here on your own?" I recognize the voice straight away, it's one that has given me chills for the past year, only these days it isn't as confident as it used to be.

Yes, Luke recovered physically from Nyx's assault, but it seems to have taught him a life lesson. Not that it makes the slightest difference to Nyx's sentence. Far as I know he's still in El Paso County and every visitation request I've put in has been automatically denied. I don't know if it's out of habit or sheer determination that I keep submitting them on a weekly basis.

"Go away, Luke," I tell him without turning around, wiping the back of my hand over my cheeks in case there's any trace of tears lingering on them. He doesn't do as I ask, instead, he slides down and sits beside me. I should be scared, Luke always did have a talent for stirring fear inside me. But there's nothing Luke Robinson can do to hurt me anymore. Not after what I've been through. Besides he's already taken away from me all that ever mattered.

"What's on your mind?" his tone sounds almost caring.

"What are you even doing over here?" I turn to ask him and I'm greeted with a guilty face.

"Honestly? I came over to apologize. I know I've been a shit to you this past year, you didn't deserve it. I guess I just don't know how to handle rejection." He picks up a rock and throws it into the water, creating a ripple over its calm surface.

"It's done, in the past, forgotten," I tell him. Hoping it will send him on his way. I'd say he's paid a fair enough price for it, two months in intensive care and the end of his football career. Maybe he'll think about how he treats 'rejection' in the future.

"It doesn't have to be," he says, sliding his hand gently over mine. I have to check I've heard him right. After all he's done, all he's said. His constant shit.

"I heard you turned down Albuquerque and that you're sticking around in Colorado."

"You heard correct," I tell him, cursing Abby and her big mouth in my head, she seems to have taken sympathy in him since his incident.

I had to make a college acceptance somewhere. I can't have anyone suspect what I have planned. And it still makes me cry every time I think that I'm gonna be leaving town alone. Crying seems to be all I can manage to do these days, and it pisses me off.

"Now that my college plans have fallen through, I'm sticking around too. And I know you'll think it's crazy, but we'd be good together, Ella." Luke shifts a little closer. "I know you've been hurt. But anyone can see he wasn't meant for you, you're better than him."

"You don't know anything about me." I stand up and start marching away. Then I feel his hands on me, pulling me back by my wrist, forcing me to crash onto his chest. His lips press tight to mine, starving me of oxygen. Making him the second person today who's touched me without my permission.

He holds both his hands around the top of my arms to keep me tight against him, and I react in the only way I can. By lifting my knee and slamming it hard into his crotch. He releases me instantly and falls to the ground clutching at his balls.

"You stupid bitch," he cries out through his pain. Relief washes over me as I see him squirming on the floor and suddenly, I get it. Nyx's need to cause pain. Luke rolling around in agony gives me a sick little thrill.

"Don't ever touch me, you were warned," I remind him of Nyx's threat.

"Yeah, well I don't see your guy here to protect you now,"

his words sting as he calls after me but I let them settle and merge with all the rest of the pain I carry inside me. I make my way back towards the party, dialing for a cab on my way, and then going in search of Abby to tell her I'm leaving.

I find her in the bathroom, sucking some white powder off the vanity unit up her nose. She looks out of her head.

"Come on I need to get you home." I grab her arm and start dragging her towards the door. Hell knows what I'm gonna do with her once I get her out of here, I can't take her back to her place in this state, her parents would flip.

"Elz, I need to tell you something," she slurs, trying her best to focus.

"Tell me on the cab ride home." I steady her on her feet and take her weight when she wraps her arm around my shoulder.

"Stop being nice to me, I can't stand it." She pushes me away suddenly, with way more strength than I expected.

"Babe, you're my best friend. I know I've been distant lately but I'm missing Nyx, come on you can crash at my place. My parents are out."

"It's my fault," she blurts out, I ignore her, trying to get her to move forward.

"It was me. I was the one in Luke's car the night Nyx…" she swallows hard, unable to say it. "I'm the witness. I told the police everything that happened and I'll have to testify when it goes to trial."

I take a step back, trying to figure out what I'm hearing. Abby wouldn't do this to me, she's my best friend. She knows all the shit Luke put me through. She would never…

"What were you doing in his car, Ab?" I ask, her betrayal starting to sink in.

"Me and Luke we kinda, we see each other out of school. He… I need…"

"You know what, I don't wanna know." I stop her from

continuing. "You knew what Nyx did was to protect me, why would you testify against him?"

"I saw what he did, Ella, it wasn't human. He was gonna kill Luke. Nyx is dangerous. I thought I was doing the right thing. But seeing you so sad. I feel awful for it." She buries her head in her hands and I notice the marks on her arms, deep purple bruises, and crusted over scabs.

"What the hell is this" I grab her wrist and stretch one out in front of me. "Abby are you…"

"She doesn't want to leave, Ella, do you, Abby?" Luke fills the bathroom door, reaching out for my best friend and dragging her on to him, she props her body against his. Her eyes looking up at him adoringly.

"Abby, we need to go," I warn her. I can't worry about all the shit between us right now. We'll figure it out. I just want her to be safe.

"Leave me here I'm fine," she slurs back at me.

"You don't look fine, you look buzzed," I point out, her eyes are practically rolling in her head.

"It's called fun, Ella. When you remember how to have it come back and find me," she giggles at me, her body curling into Luke's.

I push past the pair of them, rushing from the bathroom and into the cab that's waiting for me outside. I pull out my phone to check the time, I hope to god my parents are still out when I get back. I don't want to face them.

It's rare for me to check my phone these days, it's not like anyone bothers to contact me anymore. But I do notice that I have an email. It's sure to be another visitation denial. I submitted a new request a few days ago, same as I do every week. I click it open preparing for disappointment and then my fingers start to shake when my eyes read over the words in front of me.

VISIT APPROVED

It's been two days since the approval to visit Nyx came through and I sit and wait patiently in the visitors room.

My heart dropping into my stomach when the steel door opens and Nyx steps through it.

He stops moving forward when he notices me, his eyes staring at me through the glass that separates us like he's surprised to see me here.

And even in the bright orange scrubs he's wearing, he looks every bit as handsome as I remember him.

He turns to say something to the guard, I can't hear what it is because of the thick glass between us, but whatever it is, he doesn't look happy.

Eventually, his huge chest sags and he steps forward. Taking the seat in front of me and picking up the phone.

My stomach flutters wildly when I copy him, lifting up the phone next to me, pressing it to my ear, and waiting to hear his voice.

"Whatcha doin' here, Ell?" He looks like he's in pain, he sounds like he's in pain, and suddenly, I wish I hadn't come here.

"I had to see you," I whisper back feebly. I can't stop my hands from shaking and have to close my eyes to contain my tears.

"You shouldn't have come," he tells me blankly, before he lowers his head and rests his forehead in the palm of his hand.

I miss his hands, can remember how they felt on me. His touch alone could make everything right with the world again, and I sure as hell could use that right now.

I hate that there's a barrier between us. If we could just connect again. My skin against his skin, just for a moment, I know I'd feel less scared about everything.

"Why did you do it, Nyx?" I ask, covering my mouth with my hand when I hear my voice weaken. I don't want to fall apart in front of him. That's not why I came here. I have so much to say. So much that I need to tell him.

Despite all he's done, I know that Nyx loves me. There was honesty in his voice when he told me, I saw it in his eyes when he focused on giving me his tattoo and I felt it every time he was inside me. If he knew what was happening to me out here, he'd fight to get out. He'd protect me.

"I told you, and I warned him. Nobody hurts you." His voice is weak, his eyes refusing to look up at me and all the emotions inside me erupt.

"You hurt me." I break into a sob. "You're hurting me right now," I confess, far louder than I intended and when his head shoots up and his green eyes connect with mine, seeing that they're glazed with tears splits my heart straight through the middle.

"It was never my intention to hurt you, Ell, all I've ever wanted was to take care of you."

"I warned you this would happen, Nyx… Jesus." My eyes sting from trying to hold in my tears. "Luke Robinson is the least of my problems out here." I shake my head, trying to pull myself back together.

"What do you mean?" His eyes quickly narrow and he leans forward, his knuckles turning white as he grips the phone tighter to his ear. "What the fuck do you mean by that, Ell?"

My eyes fall on to my lap, and I consider telling him about the nightmare I'm dealing with. But Nyx looks far too broken to hear it.

I'm the daughter of a judge, I know about the things that happen in places like this. Nyx doesn't need extra stress right now. He needs hope.

"You don't belong here." I change the subject. "Luke isn't dead, he's made a full recovery. You did what you did to him to protect me. You have a strong case, Nyx. I'll be a witness."

"You're wrong, this is exactly where I belong," he utters, and all I can do is stare at his lips. Beautiful lips that used to kiss me so gently.

"You're a good person, Nyx," I tell him because it feels like he needs to hear it.

His eyes suddenly turn cold and those beautiful lips hook up into a cocky smirk.

"A good person," he laughs bitterly. "Ella, I only stopped stamping on that piece of shit's skull because I thought he was fucking dead." His pupils burn through mine, sending a shiver over my skin. "Everything you said about me before was right, I'm reckless. I needed to protect you and that's the only way I know how. I'm not the person you want to be with, Ella."

"No." I slam my hand hard into the glass that separates us. "You've shown me you care, Nyx, you've cared about me in a way no one ever has. You fight to get out of here. Fight for us," I beg him, but all it does is frustrate him and I watch on as he scrubs his hand over his face then tugs at his hair.

"I'm bad for you," he manages, pulling in a long deep breath.

"You're everything that's fucking right for me, Nyx. And I need you out here." I give up wiping away my tears, they're flowing too fast. And Nyx needs to see them, he needs to know how much he's hurting me.

"Don't come here again, Ell. I don't want to see you." My heart plummets into my stomach when he hangs up the phone and stands up.

"You don't mean that, Nyx," I yell through the glass at him. And he stares back at me looking wounded. I wish I knew what the hell was going on inside his head.

I should tell him now, scream it out loud enough for him to hear through the glass. He'd never leave me out here alone if he knew the truth.

But I don't know how to tell him. I can't bring myself to say the words out loud. I feel sick just thinking about it.

"Nyx," I say his name again, feeling any hope I came here

with shatter when he turns and walks back towards the guard. "Please don't do this," I scream, slamming my hand into the glass again. The door opens and Nyx looks over his shoulder at me. I can see it in his eyes, even if he's trying to hide it from me. His shoulders look like they're carrying ton weights on them. Nyx is hurting just like I am.

"I'm sorry," his lips move but I don't quite hear the words and then he disappears through the steel door, leaving me out here all alone.

Chapter 30

"What do you mean the case is dropped?" I slam my hand hard on the table that's between me and Monica, the club lawyer. She doesn't even flinch.

"I mean, the witness withdrew her statement and the Robinsons weren't looking at charges so there isn't enough evidence to hold you. There isn't gonna be a trial, Nyx." She pushes a file full of paperwork in front of me.

"I tried to kill the motherfucker," I point out, unable to believe what I'm hearing.

"Not according to the witness who is now claiming the attacker was a man in his late thirties, and since your alibi for that night came forward…"

"What alibi? I don't have a fucking alibi." What the fuck is going on here? I want to pick the table up and launch it, but it's bolted to the damn floor.

"It's all in the report, Nyx." Monica rolls her eyes at me. And all I can feel is panic. This can't be happening, I can't be being released. I've got my shit together in here, I'm coping. I can't go back out there, not where she is. I haven't got the strength to stay away from her.

"The CCTV evidence backs up the alibi's story, you were at the Black Pearl during the time of the attack." She opens up the file and sure enough there's a grey fuzzy picture of me, the date and time on the screen matching the date I set all hell loose on Luke.

"Monica," I straighten myself up in my seat and lower my voice. "We both know, that's horse shit. I was nowhere near that joint the night Luke got his ass handed to him. That's old footage probably taken when I went on collections with Tac."

"Well, I suspect you've got Jessie's old lady to thank for that," she says, a tinge of bitterness in her tone. Monica was a certified member of the Jessie Donavon fan club before he tied himself down.

"Who's the alibi?" I ask, looking down at the photo in front of me.

"A Miss Jenna Copley, apparently you and her had relations in one of the private rooms."

"She's saying I fucked her? I've never even heard of the girl."

"Does it matter? You're off the hook." She snaps the file shut and stands up. "I've set the ball rolling for an immediate release. You get to go back to your life, Nyx." Her words cut through me like glass as she struts on her high heels towards the door.

I don't want to go back to a world where I can't have Ella. In here, she's just a fantasy, an impossibility. Out there…

"Oh, and Prez says it's time to make Tommy talk," she mentions as the guard opens the door.

I wait for her to leave and for the guard to escort me back to my cell before I slam my fist hard into the wall. What am I supposed to do now?

"What's got into you?" my bunk mate asks jumping down off the top bunk.

"I'm being released," I utter, pressing my forehead against the wall and closing my eyes. All I see is her face, all I ever see is her fuckin' face. Soft skin, beautiful eyes, a smile that tears right through my soul and makes my heart wanna give up beating. I'm not strong enough for this.

"That's a good thing, ain't it?" He slaps me on the back on his way to the basin.

"No, no it ain't." I shove off the wall and head out of my cell onto the yard to find Tommy. He's sitting talking to some old fucker that's in for armed robbery. He's the only one around here who takes the time out to listen to his shit.

"A word." I loom over Tommy until he looks up at me. He doesn't hide his fear well, which in here, is a skill he's really gonna need to work on.

I grab a fist full of his T-shirt and drag him over to the chain-link fence. "I'm getting out of here in the next few days, if you want your back to still be covered, you better tell me where we're gonna find your dad."

"I told you, Nyx, I don't know where he is," he tells me, his eyes shifting, around us like he's waiting for trouble.

"I've had your ass in here, Tommy, if I call off those Mexicans, who knows what shit that's gonna bring. You see the way that skinner with the glass eye watches you. It's been a real long time since he's sunk his dick in something warm and tight."

"Nyx. I don't know where he is. If I knew, I'd tell you. It's his fault I'm in here. His fault all those assholes hate me."

"What?" I release my hold a little to give him a chance to speak.

"He needed to make some quick cash, I don't know how he found me but he did, and he made me an offer. He was shifting leng for the skinners, brought me in for a share of the cut."

"And?" I shove him hard in the shoulder, getting impatient.

"And some undercover agent busted us. Dad got away with the guns and I got caught. You think the Souls are his only problem. He's running from more than just the club."

"You expect us to believe that he let you get busted and took off?" I look over at the gang of skinners. Chop ain't an idiot, he knew Tommy would pay the price in here for what happened. It just goes to show how callous he can be.

"He's got a plan in place, he's gonna get me out of here," Tommy bites back defensively.

"Well, you better hope he comes through with that plan, Tommy, because if he screwed those fuckers on the outside, they'll screw you in here one way or another."

"Nyx, I swear to you I don't know where he is. I appreciate what you've been doing for me here but I can't give you what I haven't got." I slam him up against the fence, making fear stretch his eyes wider.

"The club are gonna find your backstabbing cunt pops, and make him pay. And if those skinheads leave anything left of you, you wanna hope that you end up going down for a really long time. Because once you're on the outside you'll be next." I back away from him and head straight back to my cell.

It only takes 48 hours for my release to go through. And when I walk out through the gates and step into freedom, it's Jessie and Troj that are waiting for me with their backs propped up against a cage.

"Feel good to be free?" Troj slams me hard on the back.

"Yeah," I even manage a smile as I lie to him.

"What's it been, five months? Bet you're ready to empty the sack."

"It's been six," I correct him, ignoring his question.

"Well, we got some new hangouts at the club, I think you're gonna like one of 'em. Pink hair, pouty lips, big titties and a whole heap of issues. She don't take it in the pussy."

"What's the good in that?" I shove past him and throw my bag in the back of the truck.

"Because she takes it everywhere else." Troj slaps me again before he rounds the truck and jumps behind the wheel. I slide in after Jessie, resting one of my feet on the dash and taking the joint he offers me.

"So you're gonna have to work fast if you want a sample before you head out to Utah," Troj says, pulling onto the freeway. And I don't like the side glance that Jessie shoots him.

"What do you mean Utah?" I ask, pulling a long deep drag through my lips, Christ this shit is even better than I remember.

"Look," Jess starts. "Prez appreciates that you took a hit for the club, but nothing's changed. He's still sending you to Utah."

"Fuck." I kick my boot into the dash.

"I tried to talk to him but he's still mad at ya."

"I don't get that shit," Troj speaks up, reminding me that the others don't know about Ella and how I fucked up the secret task Prez set for me. "I mean yeah, you were sloppy about taking the kid out, but you were trying to take the workload off Jessie here, he'd been shot in the ass for fuck sake."

"Yeah, well you know how Jimmer can be," Jessie adds.

When we get back to the compound there's no welcome home party like there usually is when a brother gets out. But, I ain't a brother. I fucked all that up for myself too. Troj drives straight up to the cabins and Maddy is sitting out on the porch waiting for us, at least someone looks excited to see me.

"Nyx, Jesus Christ, you've um…" she looks me up and down, a shocked expression on her face.

"Weren't much I could do inside but work out," I explain.

"Bet he's got himself one heck of a strong right arm." Troj grabs at my bicep and Maddy blushes.

"Mom freshened up your cabin for ya, and maybe you could have dinner with us tonight as it's your last…" She stops herself from finishing her sentence looking sheepishly at Jessie.

"He knows," Jessie puts her out of her misery and moves past us into his cabin.

"And does that invitation extend to handsome best friends who have to live by themselves these days?" Troj asks.

"If they remember to bring wine," Maddy smiles sweetly.

"I'll see ya at seven," Troj dips his head and heads back to the truck.

"Thanks for the ride," I shout out before he pulls off.

"Why did you do it?" I ask her when I know the others can't hear. There's only one way Ella's name could have made its way onto my visitors list that day she came to see me.

"Because you both needed it," she tells me, looking a little guilty.

"I've really hurt her, and no matter how many times I try telling myself it's for her own good, it don't feel right."

"You need anything?" Maddy asks me, pity all over her pretty face.

"As a matter of fact, I do"

I walk up to the front door of the big fancy mansion, there's only one car on the drive and it's the one that belongs to her. Not that it matters, I wouldn't care if her parents were home. I came here to have a conversation and there's no way I'm leaving for Utah without answers.

I knock hard and wait a few minutes. There's no answer so I try my luck and push down the handle, hardly surprised when the door opens. People who live in neighborhoods like this one don't need to lock their doors.

"Hello," I call out as I step into the hall. The place is as lavish as you'd expect from the outside. But when I find myself in the kitchen, I'm surprised by the state of the place. There are takeaway containers all over the sides, empty bottles and I hear glass crunch beneath my boot when I take my next step. I must have just missed the party.

I move out the kitchen and head up the stairs, where music is blasting out of one of the bedrooms and when I push open the door, I'm completely shocked by what I see.

"Did you bring it?" Abby struggles to prop herself up from being laid out on her bed, and if it wasn't her house I was standing in, I'd hardly recognize her. Her body is so much thinner than I remember, her skin like creased up paper stuck to her bones. I don't know if her head has shrunk or if her teeth have grown, but they seem far too big for her mouth.

"Nyx." She looks shocked to see me, and I quickly realize it's fear, not shock when she tries backing herself up the mattress to get away from me. "I did what they asked, I retracted my statement," she assures me.

"What the fuck happened to you?" I ask, stepping closer. I didn't come here to fuckin' hurt her. I came here for answers. I need to know why she betrayed Ella, what was she doing in that car with Luke when she knew how much shit he gave her best friend. And I need to know that she's gonna look out for her now I'm going away again.

"I ain't gonna hurt ya," I assure Abby, keeping my face stern. I mean what I say, but that doesn't mean I ain't mad at her.

"I need to know why you betrayed her like that. What were you doing in that asshole's car that night? You know how hard he's made things for Ella, she's your friend for Christ sake."

"Yeah, well not anymore." Abby scratches at her arm and tries wetting her lips. She's shaking like fuck, the sacks under her eyes suggesting she hasn't slept.

"Where are your parents?" I ask, realizing there's something very wrong here.

"I'd say probably Belgium right now, or maybe Germany. I gave up giving a fuck a month ago," she laughs bitterly.

"What?" I step closer. The girl's room is a state, clothes thrown everywhere. But the shit on the bedside table confirms all my suspicions.

"Shit, Abby, how long you been jacking up?" I check out the

empty syringe and slam it back down again. And all the stupid little bitch can do is laugh back at me.

"This isn't a joke, Abby. This is fucking serious. This shit can kill you."

"Well, I ain't dead yet." She smiles at me.

"This is him, he's giving you this shit."

"Does it answer your original question, Nyx?" she responds, her eyes barely able to focus on me.

"You need to stop this shit right now, Abby. Ella needs you."

Abby giggles hysterically loud and drags both her hands through her hair in frustration.

"That's all you give a shit about, isn't it, Nyx? Perfect Ella Jackson. Daddy's precious girl. You know why Luke Robinson was such an asshole to her?"

I ignore her for a second, bursting into the en-suite bathroom and starting up the shower. Then I head back to her room and lift up her weightless body, carrying her to the bathroom and shoving her under the water still fully clothed.

"He hated her because he wants her," she taunts me. The water catching in her throat as she speaks.

"Why did you betray her?" I grip at the girl's hair and force her to look at me.

"Luke gave me what she couldn't," she slurs.

"You're a mess." I release her. Standing back and trying to figure out what I'm gonna do about this.

"Who gives a fuck. My parents don't care about me. They didn't even stick around to watch me graduate. I'm not pretty like Ella, I don't have the Captain of the football team's attention, or the new bad boy at school obsessed with me. I've got nothing, Nyx." Looking at her now, I kinda feel sorry for her. How could someone change so much in such a short time. Abby was so bright.

"You owe me, Nyx. I lied and I got you off the hook. I did what that crazy bitch told me to do. You need to get me some shit because I'm all out and I need it." Abby tries to stand up but slips back down again.

"You need to get some help." I turn my back on her, resting my hands on the basin while I try and pull my head together. I shouldn't give a fuck. This girl ain't no friend of Ella's. Not really.

But I know Ella isn't like me. She's a good person, she's kind and forgiving and she would be heartbroken if anything happened to her best friend. And for that reason. I'm gonna have to help her.

I turn around and pick her up in my arms, holding her under the water and hoping to get some life back into her eyes.

"You don't deserve what I'm about to do for you, but I need someone to be there for Ella."

"Thanks Nyx," she breathes a sigh of relief. "You need me to give you what I gave Luke? I'm all out of allowance this month." Her limp hand reaches out for my belt and I shake her out of it.

"Abby, I ain't getting you your junk, I'm getting you help," I tell her, trying to think straight. I can't call anyone at the club, Prez is mad enough at me, besides, Abby needs to be away from any temptation. Anything you shoot up is a hard limit at the club but, other recreationals are freely available.

"Help? What do you mean, help? I need a fix, Nyx" She starts scratching at her arms again, desperation overriding the dead in her eyes.

I ignore her and pull out my cell. Realizing that this is a time when having a friend outside the club would come in real fucking handy. I scroll through my contacts and consider calling Roswell, I could come up with a lame ass excuse. He's bound to know where to take her. But Roswell don't keep anything from Prez.

There's only one person I can call.

"Hello?" he answers the phone cautiously. It's late and I suspect he's off the clock. Deputy's don't do graveyard shifts.

"Danny, it's Nyx."

"Tac's kid?" I don't bother to correct him.

"Yeah, you remember you owe me that favor," I remind him.

"Sure," he responds.

"Well…" I look at the helpless wreck that Ella's best friend has become. "…I'm calling it in."

CHAPTER 31
ELLA

Riding a bus over to Manitou Springs has become part of my weekend routine. There's a cute little library there where I get some studying done, and I always pass an hour away in the coffee shop over the street from the tattoo studio where Nyx used to work. It's rare that I get through a visit without seeing one of the men who wear the Dirty Souls patch on their vests, and so many times I've been tempted to ask one of them how he's doing.

I've never felt this alone, ever. I'm missing having Abby around. She left to join her parents in Europe last month without even saying goodbye to me, and despite me texting her and telling her I forgive her over the whole Luke thing, she's terrible at keeping in touch.

She hasn't even sent me photos of the French Riviera like she promised, and we've always spoken about going there together.

I gather my stuff and get ready to leave the coffee shop. I haven't got long before the last bus back to Castle Rock. I'm heading out the door, not really paying much attention when I crash into something solid and come face to face with the guy from the studio.

"Tac," I say his name out loud, and he looks down at me a little befuddled.

"Ella, Ella Jackson," I remind him.

"Tinker bell tattoo?" he scrunches up his face awkwardly.

"No, I came to the studio looking for Nyx a few months back."

"Sorry darlin'. What can I do ya for?" He still doesn't seem to recognize me, but I continue anyway.

"I was just wondering if you'd heard from him, if he's doing okay?"

"I ain't seen him since he rode out to Utah but if I know Nyx, he'll be doing okay."

"Utah?" I check I heard him right.

"You know what, I do remember you now. The girl with all the questions." His tattooed arms cross over his chest and he looks down on me like I'm a fly he wants to flick off his nose.

"Look, Nyx got a Charter exchange after he got out, that's all I'm gonna tell ya. You seem like a nice girl. Why don't you go blow a footballer or summit?" He wades past me towards the counter and all I can do is stare out the window onto the street in front of me.

Nyx is out of jail, he got released and he never came looking for me. I guess he really did mean what he said that day I visited him.

I thought he'd said all that because he had no hope. But he's free. He's out. And he never came for me.

I move forward out into the street and start walking towards the bus stop. My eyes threatening to burst with tears and my stomach wanting to empty all over the sidewalk. I make it to the bench and pull out my cell phone, scrolling through my contacts and finding Nyx's number. My thumb lingers over the call button but as I stare at his name on the screen, I realize that it's pointless. I laid everything out to him. I told him how I felt. And he chose to move states to get away from me. There's nothing I can do for us now. There is no us. There's only me and a world full of problems that I'm gonna have to fix myself.

Chapter 32

2 months later

"Yo Grunt, Prez wants to see ya," Levi pokes his head around the door and calls out at me from across the bar. It's late and I've just finished changing a keg because the place is still rammed. The clubhouse in Utah is so much smaller than Colorado's. There's no space, everyone seems on top of each other and it stinks of stale beer, sweat, and sex. I just want everyone to fuck off so I can throw myself into some sketching.

"You mind jumpin' back here?" I ask Angelica, I even try to sound polite for the feisty bitch. She snaps her head around at me, pulling her focus from Sylvan. the Charter's VP.

"Can't you see I'm busy." she snarls, thinking she's something special because she's moved her way up the rank a little.

"Prez wants me" I look past her to Sylvan, who nods his head, then taps her ass, and orders her off. She shoots me daggers as she steps around the bar, so I hit her with a smirk to piss her off even more before climbing the back stairs up to Prez's office.

"Come in," he yells after I've knocked, and I open the latch and step inside.

Declan is one of the younger Presidents of the club, he ain't an original Dirty Dozen, but that doesn't mean he doesn't get the same respect. His father had been the first Dirty Dozen to start up a sister Charter and when he died a few years ago, Declan stepped into his boots. He runs the small Charter well.

"I spoke to Jimmer today," he tells me, nodding his head to the seat on the other side of his desk. So I sit down and wait for him to continue.

"Things are busy down there at the moment. Tac needs some help at the studio," he continues, and what I feel is a weird combination of relief and dread. Utah has some good guys, but they ain't my people. I've actually started to miss Squealer and his twisted sense of humor, and awkward silences with Grimm. But at the same time I know that being that close to Ella again will be a burning temptation not even the threat of death can douse.

The need to see her, to touch her, and see her smile again will be agony. And I can't even think about how I'll feel if she's moved on with someone else. I don't think I could actually let that happen. Just the thought of anyone else touching her the way I did, makes me fucking murderous.

"They want me to go back?" I check, almost hoping he'll say I heard him wrong.

"You ride out tonight." Declan nods back at me.

"Tonight?" I repeat. It's past midnight, I won't be getting into Colorado till morning.

"You gotta problem with that?" Declan frowns back at me.

"It's just late is all." I shrug.

"Ain't like you're used to sleep, kid, up till god knows what time sketching in that book of yours."

I feel protective when anyone mentions my sketchbook. My work is private. Pages and pages of Ella's face. I swear I have a portrait for every single one of her expressions.

"I don't know what you did to piss Jimmer off, Nyx, but my old man always told me he was a fair guy. Hell, he's proved it to me enough times since I took over. The fact he's asking for you back, proves you got a second shot. Don't fuck it up."

I thank him for his advice, although it's not needed, before standing up and leaning across the table to shake his hand. My time here may have sucked but it could have been made a lot worse.

Never being one for goodbyes, I go straight to my room, pack up the small amount of shit I arrived here with, then avoid walking through the bar by making my way out the back exit to my bike.

It ain't such a bad ride back, the roads are quiet this late, and I pull into the compound around 6.30am. Everything seems quiet, smoke's still rising from the fire pit and there's a light on in the garage, meaning Rogue either came in early or she never left.

I ride straight past and up to my cabin, hoping that it hasn't been occupied by someone else while I've been gone. The door is unlocked, and there's a window propped open. I step inside and toss my bag on the table.

It smells clean and fresh, I figure Maddy or Marilyn have a lot to do with that. There's even supplies for me to make myself a strong coffee. I take it outside with me and light up a smoke on the front porch, waiting for any sign of life to stir from the other cabins.

Half an hour, and three cigarettes later two bitches let themselves out of Squealer and Screwy's place. Both of 'em lookin' worse for wear as they stumble back towards Sluts sanctuary. I recognize one of the girls from hanging around the club before I left, the other must be new.

"I swear that asshole's dick is gonna fall off one of these days." I turn towards the voice and shield my eyes from the sun. "Good to see you back," Maddy smiles down at me.

"Thanks for getting my cabin ready,"

"Welcome, I would have got you some food in but I only heard you were coming back last night."

"How's she been?" I ask, desperate to know. Maddy promised to keep an eye on Ella while I was gone and despite the fact she's confined to the compound, I know she'd have somehow stuck to that promise.

"She started College in the fall, I'm all tapped into their security system so I can check the CCTV from time to time. I have cameras on her place too," she tells me, looking smug.

"What?" I choke on the smoke I'm inhaling.

"I convinced Prez that it would be good to have some eyes on the house, you know, see who's coming and going."

"So?" I ask, needing her to tell me something, anything.

"There's been nothing to suggest the Bastards are still interested, not since you went inside. But that doesn't mean they're not watching."

"Is she okay, like, is she happy?"

Maddy slides down beside me and wraps her arm around my shoulder. And I'm surprised how it doesn't feel strange.

"There's only so much you can pick up on from watching CCTV, but she doesn't look close to being happy, Nyx. Kinda like someone else I know." She nudges me gently with her shoulder.

"It fucking sucks, Mads," I tell her, pressing the heel of my palms at the porch step so hard that I feel the wood splinter my flesh.

"It won't be forever," she assures me, and I know she's only saying that to make me feel better. The situation ain't changing anytime soon between me and Ella. She's still the Prez's daughter and I'm still a fucking criminal. I even got the mugshot to prove it now.

"You better go see Tac, he's missed you." Maddy stands back up and dusts off the back of her jeans.

"Really?" I manage a smirk. Tac ain't one for showing

emotion.

"He's been like a bear with a thorn in his paw since you left," she giggles, making her way back over to her and Jessie's cabin. "It's good to have you back, Nyx," she tells me before disappearing inside.

When I get to the studio, it's all locked up, so I go round the back and bang on the door. I still don't get an answer so I try calling Tac on his cell.

"What's up?" he rasps groggily when he eventually picks up.

"I'm at the studio, where are ya?"

"It's about fuckin' time," he chimes back, I can hear wet noises coming from the background.

"You're getting noshed off, aren't ya?" I shake my head to myself.

"Yep… and I'll be at the studio in 'bout half an hour so you better pick us up something for breakfast." He hangs up the phone and I check the time. 8:50.

Ella could be making her way to college now. Ironically, it's the same one Hayley and Mads used to go to and it's only a few minutes ride from here. So is Bernie's. The best food joint for miles.

It's a stupid thing to do, especially when it risks her seeing me. I guess I'll just have to make sure she doesn't.

I park my bike and pull up my hood before I start walking the route to Bernie's, which passes right past the College entrance. The chances of seeing her are low, I don't even know if she has an early Friday class anyway. Still, I find a tree with a thick enough trunk on the opposite side of the road to the entrance and allow myself five minutes.

Five minutes to catch a tiny glimpse of her, to see her again after all the time I've had to go without her, and when after seven I still have no luck… I decide to move on.

One last glance over my shoulder causes me to stop moving, and I have to check twice because I swear the person I'm looking at is Ella Jackson. Same height, same hair color, but this is not my girl.

Her skin is too pale, her eyes are dark and tired. My feet freeze onto the sidewalk, a heavy weight crushing at my chest. She's wearing the hoodie I gave her, it's at least three times too baggy for her tiny frame, and the jeans she's wearing aren't the usual ones that flaunt all her curves.

She clutches her folder tight over her front and keeps her head down like she doesn't want to be noticed. The impulse to run across to her and scoop her up almost has me moving towards her. But I'm helpless, and it hurts like hell.

Seeing Ella so miserable and broken is a stark reminder that all this is my fault. I did this. I broke her heart. All this is on me, and that causes me more pain than my body can cope with.

I turn away, running back to my bike, and I skid off, forgetting all about Bernie's.

I should never have come back here, now knowing that every day she'll be less than a few miles away from me. I'm not strong enough for that. What was I thinking? What was Prez thinking? None of this makes any sense.

It kills me that it will be left for someone else to drag her out of the hole she's fallen into. A pit I created full of darkness, that's left her hurt and in pain. And all I can do for her now is pray that in time she'll find her light again.

"Jesus, I thought you'd at least look happy to be back," Tac says after his last customer leaves. He looks up at the clock and steps out back, pulling two beers from the fridge. Popping the cap on one before handing it to me.

"That's us done for the day, kid. Back to the club for the welcome back party? I know Mel's gonna be happy to see ya," he winks.

"I don't know." I take a swig of my beer and busy myself clearing up Tac's mess.

"Whatcha mean?"

"I don't know how Prez is gonna react to me being back, and to be honest I'm tired from the ride back last night."

"Tired, are you shitting me Nyx, I raised you better than that." He slaps me on the back of my head. "You don't have to worry about Prez, you wouldn't be back here if he didn't want you."

"You're saying that me being back here got jack fuck to do with you?" I look back at him unconvinced.

"Hey, you know the Prez, once that man's got his head set, ain't anyone who can change his mind. You going to Utah was a lesson, not a banishment. You're an asset to the club, Nyx. You proved that when you got banged up."

I want to believe him. I want to believe him real bad. But he doesn't know how deep my betrayal lies. He doesn't know that I've failed the Prez in the worst possible way. Not only did I fall in love with his daughter, but I wrecked her in the process.

Maybe Prez does know about my real feelings for Ella, Jimmer Carson is a clever man. Perhaps this is my real punishment. Being this close is a torture I thoroughly deserve.

"It was a few months in county, Tac, hardly hard time." I distract myself from the thoughts in my head, I know Tac did a five-year stint for the club before I met him. I didn't go to jail for the club though. I can see how it would look that way. But he was much more a problem for me than he was the club.

"Come on, Prez wants us to do some bar runs before we head back to the club," Tac says, and I roll my eyes before finishing my beer. Doing bar runs with Tac is never a quick job.

The club have a lot of investments around town and on the last Friday of the month, we pick up our profits. That usually consists of Tac stopping by each one, checking up on 'business' while getting smashed, and me driving. I guess things haven't changed since I've been gone. Still, it'll keep us away from the club for a few more hours.

We're on our way to the fifth bar, and Tac is already half cut. His hand hanging out the window and banging loudly on the side of the truck to the beat of the music blaring out the stereo as we pull up outside Dillon's Sports Bar.

I follow him inside and he heads straight for the bar, Dillon sees us and lifts his head before disappearing out the back to get us our cash. Tac has already knocked back a shot in the time it's taken me to step up beside him, and I shake my head at the barmaid when she holds up an empty glass at me.

There's noise coming from a crowded booth in the corner of the bar, and I see the waitress sneering at the group of lads causing it.

"They givin' ya trouble, Zara?" Tac asks as she places her tray on the bar.

"Nothing I can't handle, Tac," she winks at him, and he slaps the denim covering her ass as she moves on. I turn my back on them and when Tac informs me this will be our last stop of the night, I order myself a beer.

"Well, fuckin' well," a voice slurs from behind me, and when I turn around to rest my elbows on the bar, Luke Robinson is standing right in front of me.

Either he thinks he's untouchable because of my charges, or I knocked that much shit into him that he forgot what happened last time we came face to face.

Things ain't looking good for him, especially not in the mood I'm in. After seeing Ella today, I ain't scared of going back inside. In fact, right now it feels like an easy route.

"So, you're back in town," he says, looking over his shoulder and huffing a laugh, at his friends.

"You seen your girl since you got back?" he asks confidently, sliding up beside me at the bar.

"And who the fuck are you?" Tac looks him up and down

like he's a rotten smell under his nostrils.

"This is the fucker I served time for. And it was totally fucking worth it." I don't pull my eyes away from Luke's as I answer Tac's question.

Tac checks Luke over again and laughs darkly before his attention moves on to Dillon and the envelope of cash he hands over.

"Yep, it's a shame you left your girl so cut up about it. It took her all the way 'till graduation to get over you," he says, the cockiness in his voice putting me right on fuckin' edge. "Julia Michelle's party, if I remember correctly." He looks up at the ceiling like he's recalling a memory. "Mmmm, I get now why you were always wound up so tight over her. There's just something about those soft lips… Cherry, right?"

He barely has chance to finish that sentence before I fist the back of his head and slam him nose-first into the bar. When I pull his head back up, his face is a bloody mess from the broken glass that's sliced him open, one of the gashes only just missing his eye. I grab him by his collar and drag him out into the parking lot, letting him drop on the floor in front of me before I kick my boot hard into his stomach. The coward curls himself up into a ball but I keep on going at him, feet and fuckin' fists until I feel strong arms wrap around my shoulders pulling me off him.

"Jesus Christ, kid," Tac yells as he holds me off. A crowd's gathered around us and Dillon wades through everyone.

"Get him out of here," he shouts at the small group of Luke's so called friends. Friends who were happy to stand and watch him take a beating without so much as cracking their knuckles. "I don't wanna see you boys around here again," he warns them.

They scrape Luke up from the floor and load him into the back seat of a Lexus, before the tires screech and they speed away.

"Show's over, folks," Dillon calls out and heads back in the bar, the spectators slowly filtering in behind him.

"Get everyone in there a drink on us," Tac dips his hand into the envelope and pulls out some bills. "No one saw shit."

"Gotcha," Dillon nods in response and heads inside.

"Hell, a few more blows to the head and you could have killed the kid."

"Nah, that fucker just keeps on bouncing back." I lean forward, resting my palms on my knees while I catch my breath. I don't know what the hell it's gonna take to knock the fucking confidence out of that asshole. He really must have a death wish.

"What he say to get you so riled?" Tac asks. "He dealin' shit round here again? If he is, you leave it to Jessie this time," he warns.

"He touched something that belongs to me," I answer, shaking out my wrist.

"Well now that you've hashed that out, you better go clean yourself up so we can head back to the club."

I look down at my hands, tacky with Luke's blood, again.

"Good idea," I nod, heading back through the bar and ignoring all the stares as I make my way to the restroom. I look at my reflection in the mirror, there are splats of blood sprinkling my face, and the eyes staring back at me hold enough fury to take out an army of Luke Robinsons. I'm hardly making a good start at getting back in Prez's good books.

My heart beats in my chest so fast, rage pushing adrenaline through my veins, and it burns under my skin so hot that I reach into my back pocket and take out my cell. My bloody fingers shake as I dial the number I deleted from my phone the night I decided to let her go, but already had memorized. When it comes to her, I can't let anything go.

"Nyx," she answers after the first ring, her voice sounding shocked and melodic at the same time. "Nyx, is that you?" I close my eyes and listen to her voice like it's a fucking fix.

Then I remember what had me calling her in the first place.

"Did you let Luke Robinson kiss you?" I ask through gritted teeth. My rage ready to erupt all over again if I don't get the answer from her I need. I need to know that prick was just provoking me when he said that he kissed her.

"Nyx, where have you been?"

"Did you let him kiss you?" I ask again. My knuckles slamming hard into the tiled wall beside me because I don't know how to handle all the pain I'm feeling. I need to feel something different.

"No, he kissed me, and I..."

"You did fuckin' what, Ell?" I growl, trying to speed her up.

"I kicked him in the balls," she tells me, and I swear I can almost hear the proud smile I imagine on her lips, it feels good to picture her smiling after what I saw today. It even causes my lips to tweak up into a tiny grin.

"That's my girl," I whisper, pressing my forehead to the mirror in front of me, letting relief cool my blood. Ella seems to have a way of instantly setting me calm.

"Nyx, please tell me where you are. I miss you."

"I got to go," I tell her, my voice turning colder. I shouldn't have called her, it's another selfish fucking act that could have major consequences.

"Please Nyx, don't hang up. I need you. I need you so bad that I can't even breathe," she breaks into sobs, and I have to bite down on my fist to hold in the noise my throat's threatening to make. I wanna scream and tear down the walls. But more than anything I wanna to comfort her, to wrap her up in my arms and tell her everything is gonna be okay. The fact I can't, sends my fist hurtling straight back into that damn wall again.

"Don't give up on me, Ell," I blurt the words out before I hang up and launch my phone at the wall. I shouldn't be asking that of her. I shouldn't have called, I shouldn't have reacted to Luke like I did. But that girl brings all the wrong out in me, and there just ain't no right without her.

Chapter 33
ELLA

It's been a week since he called, and hearing his voice was just as painful as it is reassuring. Since I heard he got released from jail and that the charges were dropped, I'd been waiting for him to come for me. And after two months of waiting, I was just getting my head around the fact that it wasn't gonna happen.

During dark times I'd wondered if something bad had happened to him. somehow managing to convince myself that Nyx loved me so fiercely that death would be the only explanation for his absence. It sure made it easier for me to accept him not showing up.

He hasn't called again, and he hasn't picked up any of the calls I've made to him either. But those final words he said before he hung up have stuck in my head.

"Don't give up on me."

I don't want to give up on him, but the inevitable is drawing closer and closer and I can't just sit back and wait for it to happen.

"Do you ever wash that thing?" Mom looks down at Nyx's hoodie in disgust, the same one I've been wearing almost every day since we've been apart.

"Of course I do," I snub her, burying my head back into my textbook.

"You should come to the mall with me, have you got anything from the winter collection yet?"

"Jeeez, Mom, there's more to life than fuckin' clothes," I snap, swiping up my books from the table and heading up to my room.

I lock myself in and take a long warm bath, then decide to have an early night.

Keeping up this pretense is exhausting, I've not put a foot out of line over the past few months, refusing to give Father an excuse to punish me.

The trick has been to stay out of his way, to become invisible. But he's just waiting for me to slip up. I can feel his tension brewing, he's just looking for that excuse.

I get into bed and have no trouble falling asleep. My body tired, and my mind worn out from over thinking.

Nyx comes to me in my dreams again, and it feels so real that I even shiver when cool air licks at my toes. A chill traveling all the way to my neck when he opens my balcony door and steps inside.

I wait for him to lie down beside me, but tonight he just stands, watching. I blink my eyes to try and open them. Then jump in shock when I realize this isn't a dream. My balcony door is open, and standing in front of it is a huge dark figure, his face covered with balaclava. And it's not Nyx, the eyes peering back at me through the holes are too evil to belong to him.

They take a few steps closer, and when my mouth opens to scream. I'm quickly silenced with a huge hand that slams over my mouth and pins me down.

"Good to see you again, Ella," the voice is low and scratchy as it sends fear quaking through my body. I automatically wrap my arms around my body for protection.

"You see how easy it was for me to get to you?" he whispers. "You should tell the judge that." The strong hand covering my mouth and nostrils starves me of oxygen and I thrash out in panic.

"Tell him to get me what I need, or it will be his pretty little treasure who pays the price." Suddenly, something he says connects in my head. Pretty little treasure, I've heard that before. And now I'm certain that the man who had come out of Father's office all those months ago and called me that, is the man threatening me now. I remember how nervous he'd made Father and it terrifies me. No one makes my Father nervous.

"I think I'd have fun with you, Ella," he tells me, and I shudder when his wet tongue slides against my cheek. He releases my mouth, and while I'm gasping for air, he disappears out the balcony doors he came through. I leap up and throw my dressing gown on, before rushing across the hall, and thudding my fist against my parents' bedroom door. Father swings it open furiously.

"What's going on?" He eyes me up and down and I pull my huge fluffy robe a little closer to my skin.

"That man, who was here. The scary looking one, he was just…" I try to form the words as tears spill down my cheeks and the shock of what just happened hits me all at once.

"For Christ's sake, spit it out," he bellows at me and Mom surprises me when she pushes past him and wraps her body around mine. But I turn my back to her, I don't want her comfort.

"He was just in my room, he came in through my balcony, said if you didn't give him what he wanted, I would pay the price." I watch Father's face turn a brilliant shade of white and his eyes set to stone.

"What does he want, Vincent? Whatever it is, just give it to him!" It's the first time I can ever remember Mom raising her voice to him, and he must be really worried, because he doesn't respond to it.

"Back to bed, I will deal with this in the morning," he tells us both, looking haunted. "We'll hear no more about it. You keep your balcony door locked in the future." He points his finger at me like all this is somehow my fault.

"But Vincent…"

"Back to bed," he warns Mom, his glare silencing her and telling me I should do the same. I make my way back across the hall without argument, and for the first time in a long long time, I make sure my balcony door is locked firm.

CHAPTER 34

I can't stop thinking about her and how much she's changed. Her sad eyes haunting me every time they look back up at me from the paper I've sketched her onto, and all I can focus on is how I can make her better.

It's what brings me to Castle Rock and why I'm sitting in my truck, opposite a nail bar on Main Street.

I watch Joanne Jackson through the window, chatting happily to the woman working on her hands, with a plastic smile wide on her face. I remain patient until she leaves and then I get out of my truck and cross the busy street, following her down the sidewalk towards her Mercedes.

"Mrs. Jackson," I call out as I catch up to her, she's about to pull the driver's door open and already has a prepped smile on her lips as she turns her head. A façade that quickly drops when she sees it's me.

"What do you want?" she whispers through tight lips, her eyes scanning around us to make sure no one is watching.

"I'm worried about Ella."

"You've got some nerve coming up to me," she warns, making it hard to believe this is the same woman who I just watched from the truck.

"I care about her, I just need to know she's okay. Tell me that and I'll leave you alone," I promise.

"No, she's not okay." She looks back at me like I'm an idiot. "She's broken, has been for months now. And I warned her, I told her all about your kind." Her eyes turn into slits as a newly manicured finger jabs me right in the center of my chest. "You think I don't see it? That I don't know what you are… Who you are? Walking away from my daughter is the best thing you ever did for her." She turns her back to me, fiddling frantically with her door handle.

"And was walking away from Jimmer Carson what was best for you?" I ask her. She pauses instantly, and when she spins back around, she catches me completely off guard with the harsh swipe her palm makes across my cheek. I rub my hand over the sting and smirk back at her. It's a shame she can't find that kinda fight in her when her husband comes at her.

"Don't you dare. I did what was best for my daughter." Her voice shakes with anger, but her eyes are too heavy with regret for me to buy what she's saying.

"And that's what your husband is, what's best, right?" I check, watching her chest sag as she releases a long, tired breath.

"We've all made our mistakes, we live by them." Her voice turns a little softer, and the scowl on her face lets up a little too. "You've done right by Ella, leaving her alone. I'll give you that much credit." She checks around us again for witnesses. "I trust you will continue to do so."

"I love…"

"Don't," she cuts me off. "Don't you fucking say that. Ella was fine before you came along. She was happy and now look at her. My daughter's become a shell because of you. If you mean it and you really do love her, leave her alone."

"I just…" I stop myself from saying what I'm about to. It ain't gonna do me no favors, but fuck it. What do I have to lose? "I just got this feeling in my gut that me and Ella are repeating the history of two people who loved each other eighteen years ago. Two people who deep down have been miserable ever since.

Jimmer Carson loved you enough to let you go and I'll do the same for Ella, but I won't have her be miserable. I'll have eyes on her until the day I know she's happy and that there's nothing left for me to do for her."

"Go back to your stupid club, Prospect." Joanne Jackson looks down at the prospect patch that's sewn into the leather of my cut. "You come near my daughter again, I'll break the promise I made myself all those years ago and I'll go see Jimmer myself. I'm sure he'll be interested to know how close you've become to his daughter."

With that said, she gets inside her car and backs out onto the street. I stand and watch her drive off, hoping to god that I ain't staring into Ella's future.

I get back to the club and help Jessie out at the garage for a few hours. I ain't much use, but everyone's got to pull their weight and I need to keep myself busy. Maddy brings Jessie down some lunch, and I smile at her gratefully when she tosses me a brown paper bag too. I can't help feel a pang of jealousy when I imagine how it might be to be with Ella like this. Together every day. No secrets or sneaking around. And no fuckin' heartache.

"You ever regret bringing her here?" I ask Jessie after she's left.

"Not for a second," he tells me as he slides out from under the Honda he's working on. "I hate what she's had to sacrifice for me. But every day I keep livin', I'll be sure to remind her why she did it. Why d'you ask?" He takes the spanner out of my hand and disappears back under the car.

"No reason," I say quietly. Mine and Ella's story ain't like Jessie and Maddy's. Ours is much more the fucked up tragedy type. No happy endings.

"You're off duty, asswipe." I feel a shove in my back and turn to see Rogue smiling at me.

"Finally, someone who knows what they're doing around here," Jessie's voice comes from under the car.

"Out the way, let the big boys get to work," Rogue barges past me. "Maybe you could hook us up with a coffee or summit before you leave." She blows an impressive bubble out of the gum she's chewing, and winks at me before stepping into her bright pink overalls. I ignore her, shaking my head.

Rogue's hot as hell, but no one around here's brave enough to touch her.

Anyone can see that the girl's got issues. Deep invisible scars that she tries to cover up with sass.

"Are you gonna move or not?" she asks, taking her thick blonde hair and piling it into a rough bun on top of her head.

"Sorry," holding up my hands, I shift out of her way. Figure I'll use the time to grab a shower before I start working the bar in the clubhouse. Prez has been running me ragged since I've been back. There's been no talk of me getting patched in, which I predicted anyway, due to the major fuck up I made of the task he set for me.

When I get to the cabins, instead of heading into my own I knock on Maddy and Jessie's cabin door. Maddy is the only person who can help me, and as much as I don't want to bring her into this by asking. I need to know my girl is okay.

"Is Jessie okay?" Maddy asks the instant she opens the door, and I nod reassuringly. "Rogue just took over from me so I can help out at the club. I was wondering if you could help me with something before I start?"

"Sure." She opens up the door wider so I can step inside, then heads straight for the fridge and pulls out a beer, placing it on the table for me.

"What's that for?" I stare at the bottle.

"You're asking someone for help, so I figured you must need

it," she says curling up one side of her mouth, and I snatch up the bottle and take a mouthful.

"I saw her," I confess. "She looked so…"

"Unhappy," Maddy finishes for me.

"Yeah. I know you said before that you were watching her. I just wondered…"

"You want me to use my kick-ass superpowers to check in on her," she smirks back at me, looking as if she's up for the challenge.

"Yeah." I can't believe I'm asking her for this. Why do I constantly insist on torturing myself?

"Okay." Maddy opens up her laptop, her fingers clicking the keys faster than I can blink.

"So… I have CCTV footage from the parking lot at Colorado College. Ella takes classes on Monday, Tuesday, and Friday mornings, the rest are afternoons. So, if I cross-reference those times with the GPS on the car. Yep, there it is… She arrived on campus around 8:45 yesterday and pulled out around 11:15. Do you want to see her arriving or leaving?" She takes her eyes off the screen to look up at me.

"Wow, you really are kick-ass," I tell Maddy, excited at the idea of seeing Ella again, even if it is gonna break my heart. "Ummm, leaving I guess."

"Okay." She sets back to work for a few seconds and turns the screen. My eyes find her straight away on the grey, blurry picture. She's walking across the parking lot, wearing the same jeans and hoodie she'd been in when I saw her last time. She's lost all the confidence from her walk, it's like watching a stranger and it stabs my chest so deep I almost choke.

She gets inside her car and pulls off. I'm about to spin the laptop back to Maddy when something catches my eye in the corner of the screen. Someone I recognize resting against the chain-link fence and watching her leave.

"Can you rewind this thing?" I ask Maddy.

"Sure." She uses the keys to run the footage back a few seconds and I watch the slippery little fucker's head turn as he watches Ella's every move.

"There, in the corner of the screen, you see that?" I ask Maddy, and she pulls her glasses down from her hair and leans in a little closer.

"Tommy," she gasps out loud when she she's what I'm seeing. "What would Tommy want with…" she pulls her hand over her mouth in horror.

"I don't know, Mads, but I don't trust that fucker to be anywhere near her. He was deep in shit with some bad people when he was in county."

"We need to go to Prez," she says.

"And say what? We were just checking in on your secret daughter because Nyx got his heart all torn up over her and we found…"

"I knew it," Maddy interrupts me. "You absolutely love her," she laughs to herself.

"What does it even matter? I can't have her." I shrug, feeling my cheeks burn red, and I hate that Maddy looks so sorry for me.

"But I sure as hell ain't about to let anything happen to her." I add, getting up and running my hands through my hair, I need to think straight about this.

"Nothing's impossible, Nyx," Maddy tells me, the dreamy smile on her face proving she doesn't have a clue how brutal Jimmer Carson can be.

"Come on, let's go save your girl." She snaps her laptop shut and scoops up my truck keys. "We'll tell Prez I was checking in on her, and that I came to you for confirmation that it was Tommy in the video. It'll all be fine."

Prez shakes with fury as he watches the CCTV footage. Maddy sets to work scanning through the cameras positioned outside the judge's home, and taps into some more on campus. Sure enough, Tommy pops up in the distance often enough for it not to be a coincidence. Prez scrubs at his face, pacing the floor of the small bar room while he tries to figure out what he can do about it.

"Maddy, go out to the garage and get Jessie, he's gonna have to take a ride out to pick Tommy up, at least we know where he will be. I figure we got about an hour before he'll be back there watching her leave," Prez orders

"Sure thing, Prez." Maddy jumps to attention, rushing out to get Jessie and leaving us alone.

"I could call her, ask her to meet me somewhere. We should bring her in and keep her safe," I suggest, hoping that Prez is on my level now. That he'll let me take care of her the way I need to. Having her here is the only way I can guarantee she's safe.

"The Bastards and now this." Prez slams his fist hard onto the bar, making the optics behind it rattle. "Why? What could Tommy possibly want with her…"

He slumps down onto the bar stool and I watch all the color drain from his face. "Fuck," he whispers.

I don't like the sound of that fuck.

"Chop." A chill slips over my skin when he says the name out loud, I never watched the video of what he did to Carly but we all know about it. He's merciless and if he was capable of doing that to his own brother's wife…

"Let me go get her," I stand up. "This is bigger than your old secrets, this is about making her safe. We can do that here. I can keep her safe. You trusted me before, trust me now," I plead.

The door bursts open and Jessie strolls in still wearing his dirty overalls and wiping the oil off his hands with a dirty rag.

"We got eyes on Tommy," Prez quickly brings him up to speed. "I want him brought back here, and I want to know what the hell he's doing following my daughter." I watch Jessie's face tick with satisfaction.

"Nyx, go with him. And I don't want a fucking scene, not like the last disaster you pulled." Prez looks at me when he says that, making Jessie smirks. "You bring him back here quietly and once he's here, Jessie can do his shit and get some answers," he orders.

"What about Ella?" I protest.

"Don't fuckin' argue with me, boy. I know what's best for my girl. Right now, that ain't you. I need someone I can rely on." He looks back at Jessie. Have Screwy and Squealer tail her in one of the trucks. They are not to approach her unless it's an emergency and I don't want her out of their sight until she's home."

"Got it, Prez." Jessie is already stepping out of his overalls, and Maddy takes them, passing him his cut.

"Gotta go to work, baby." He raises his eyebrows at her, a dangerous glint in his blue eyes as he kisses her hard on the mouth.

"Come on, kid. Time to go catch us some rat," turning to me he jerks his head towards the door. And I snarl as I follow him out, pissed that it's the fuckin' temper twins that are being sent to protect Ella, when it should be me.

I jump into the driver's side of the truck and wait for Jessie to finish relaying Prez's instructions to Screwy and Squealer, noting that he doesn't explain to them who she is to Prez. When he hops into the passenger seat he reaches down to his ankle and pulls out his knife, twisting the handle in his palm.

"I've been waiting on this one," he tells me, his lips twitching darkly.

"Yeah, well don't think you're getting all the fun," I warn him, starting up the engine and pulling out the yard.

CHAPTER 35
ELLA

I don't go straight home after college. Instead, I drive to the bank.

This morning I tricked Mom into giving me my savings account book, I told her I'd been saving my allowance and wanted to deposit it. Knowing that she's leaving for her woman's retreat today, and won't have time to deposit the money herself. I also lie when I tell her I want to treat myself to a visit to the salon in town. And she's far too delighted at my eagerness to pick myself up, that she doesn't even question handing it over to me.

I'll have to withdraw the entire contents of my savings. Dad will do something to stop me from accessing the account once he realizes I've run away. He'll think he can use money to control me, the same way he does Mom. But me and my mother are two very different people. Money is one power he can't hold over me.

I explain to the clerk at the bank that I wanted to pay off a chunk of my college fees as a surprise to my parents and half an hour later, leave the bank clutching an envelope that contains my entire life savings.

I get home and head straight up to my room, quickly stuffing the money into the suitcase that's packed ready to make my escape. I have everything planned out in my head and I can feel my nerves building as the time ticks closer. Thanks to Father's tracking device I can only use my car to get me so far. I'll drive to the nearest train station and dump my car there. Then I'll get a taxi to a bus station a few miles away and head for the furthest destination I can reach.

I'm not stupid, I know the money won't last me very long. I have no one I can depend on to help me. But I've come to the conclusion that I can't be in any more danger out there than I am staying here.

Satisfied that I have everything prepared, I hide my suitcase back in my wardrobe. I'll wait until Father is in bed before I make my escape, I just hope he doesn't take advantage of us being alone in the house together. My bedroom door taps and Mom lets herself in just as I'm closing my wardrobe doors.

"Adaline will be here to pick me up soon, I wanted to come and say goodbye," she says.

"I hope you have a good time." I head for the bathroom to avoid her.

"I thought you said you were going to the salon." She follows me and stands inside the door.

"They were fully booked, so I'm going back with Abby tomorrow," the lie rolls off my tongue easily. I haven't seen Abby since graduation. But I've mastered deceit just lately.

"Darling, when I get back, I want us to sit down and have a proper talk, okay?" she smiles at me sadly.

"There's nothing to talk about, Mom, I'm okay, really," I assure her, faking a smile. Anything just to get her the hell out of here.

"I love you, Ella," her voice wobbles like she's on the verge of crying, and I wonder for a second if she senses that this is the last time that she'll see me for a while.

"I love you too, Mom," I tell her, managing to fake her a smile. She leaves me in the bathroom, closing the door behind her, and I wait until I hear her leave my room before I flick the lock on the door. I used to sympathize with my mother for what she went through, despite how unhappy Father made growing up for me, I never doubted that she loved me. Just lately though, I've been forced to think differently.

I pull Nyx's hoodie over my head and stare at my reflection. My stomach's grown so much these past few weeks it's becoming almost impossible to hide, and it won't be long before he or she decides to make their appearance into the world. As desperate as I am to meet the little person growing inside me, I'm petrified about what will happen when that time comes.

I stroke my hand over my stretched-out skin and feel a wriggle beneath my palm. My special little secret, proof that what me and Nyx had was real. I haven't seen a doctor since I found out I was pregnant, couldn't risk anyone else knowing but me. But instinct tells me it's going to be a boy.

A beautiful boy, with eyes like his daddy's.

I've kept him a secret, shielded him for this long, and in just a few more hours we'll be out of this town and free from my father. Things are gonna be tough. I have no idea how I'm gonna manage being a single Mom. But what I can be sure of is that I'll do everything I can to give my child a good life and protect it. It's what makes me question everything about my own mother.

I often wonder if Nyx would have still left if he'd known about our baby. How different things might be if I'd taken the opportunity to tell him that day I visited him in El Paso County. Nyx doesn't seem like the kind of guy who'd run away from trouble. In fact, over the past eight months, I've often imagined Nyx as a father. It's crazy given how reckless he can be, but I can't help wondering if he'd have been as protective of our child as he was of me. If he'd love him unconditionally the way I already do.

Then I stop myself because it makes me feel sad and stupid. I pull myself back to reality and remind myself that if Nyx really loved me, he would be here with me and we'd be running together.

I run myself a bath and lie back in the warm water. Letting my body soak and my tummy stick out from the bubbles. I swish the water around it with my fingers. Checking myself over for stretch marks. I'm lucky enough not to have any yet, but then I'm not exactly big. I've been able to hide under baggy clothes up until now. Even my parents and Penelope haven't questioned me. I only started to show a few months ago and so far, no questions have been asked. Though I have noticed Penelope staring at me a little curiously lately.

I watch my stomach ripple as he moves inside me, seeking out a more comfortable position, and I press my hand protectively over the hard ridge he makes on my left side. Hoping he knows I'm here for him. That I'll do anything to keep him safe. And for the first time in months, I smile a smile that isn't fake, because something in my gut tells me that everything is gonna be okay for us.

Chapter 36

Tommy quivers in his seat like a shitting dog. His face already busted up, due to my lack of self-control, and his eyes wildly flick between Jessie and me waiting for what comes next.

Tommy was once part of this club, he's fully aware of what Jessie is capable of down here in his basement. He's even cleared up after him. He has every reason to be nervous.

"Tommy, Tommy, Tommy." Jessie pulls out a chair from beneath the table and straddles it in front of him. "You know why you're here?" he asks

"Because my Pa killed Carly," he answers, not a shred of empathy in his voice.

"This club doesn't judge men on another man's actions," Jessie reminds him. "What me and Nyx here wanna know, is why you've been following Ella Jackson around since you got released from county last month?"

"Ella Jackson." The prick must have picked himself up some fucking balls since I left him cowering in El Paso because he looks up at the ceiling acting like he's trying to recall the name. I can already feel myself running out of patience.

How the fuck does Jessie pull this shit off?

"Pretty hazel eyes, wavy hair, tight little ass. I think I know who you're talkin' about." He smiles. I launch at him, knocking

RECKLESS SOUL

the fucker back to the floor on the chair he's tied to. Pressing the heel of my boot into his throat, I apply enough pressure for him to start choking.

"Nyx," Jessie warns. "He ain't gonna be any use to us fuckin' dead."

"He won't be a threat either," I point out, removing my foot, and grabbing the front of his hair with one hand, dragging him and the chair back into an upright position.

"You tell us what the fuck you were doin' following her. Or I swear to god I will make you eat your own nutsack," I warn. His confidence seems to have suddenly vanished, and he looks at the floor trying to avoid eye contact with me.

"Why do you care about her anyway? She's just a girl." I can't hide the way my eyes quickly flash at Jessie, and if he's as surprised as I am, he doesn't show it. Either Tommy doesn't know Ella is Prez's daughter, or he's a good fuckin' liar.

"You workin' for your old man?" Jessie asks him calmly, pulling his knife and letting it dangle in the hand he has resting over the chair he's sitting on.

"I'm not gonna rat on my dad, you might as well kill me now." Tommy shakes his head definitely.

"Ahhhh loyalty, Nyx." Jessie looks at me and laughs darkly, "You must have inherited that from your uncle Skid." He leans forward, sliding the tip of his knife under Tommy's chin and using it to force his head up, so he's looking him in the eye. "Because you sure as fuck didn't get it from that cunt Daddy of yours," he tells him in a harsh whisper.

"Do you even remember your uncle Skid?" he asks, sliding the blade over Tommy's throat without breaking the skin. "The uncle whose wife your Pa raped and fucking murdered.

Do you remember how Carly used to take care of you when you were younger, making sure you were fed and looked after while your Pa fucked his way through every club slut on the compound?"

"Don't talk about him like that." Tommy's voice comes out weak, and I'll bet he sounded like that while he was getting his ass pounded inside county.

Tommy sucks at making good choices.

"And was your Pa there for you when you landed up in jail. He knew how tough things were gonna be for you in there with all those Skinners he betrayed and no protection. Did he try and help you? Where is he now, Tommy? Is he trying to get you out of the shit you're in? If I called him up right now and told him that we have you, do you reckon he'd risk his life comin' here to get you?" Jessie kicks the chair he's been resting on out of his way, stabbing the knife into Tommy's shoulder. "I think we both know the answer to that question. Don't we?" Jessie shoves his face into Tommy's once he stops screaming.

"You're wrong," Tommy shakes his head. "You really don't know who that girl is, do you?" he laughs hysterically through the tears that have started to film over his eyes.

"That bitch is Judge Jackson's daughter," he says with pride. "And my Pa has had that man in his pocket for years."

"You really expect me to believe that?" Jessie chuckles at him.

"My Pa's smarter than any one of you, even Prez. You really think he spent all his time at this club out of loyalty. He was here for his protection. He gave the judge the information he needed and in return, he got to keep his ass out of prison," Tommy sticks up for his father. I side glance the mastermind that is Jessie Donavon, and somehow manage to mimic the cool reaction he's applying to the information he just bled out of Tommy.

This is huge, Chop has been ratting to the judge this whole damn time. Prez is gonna want more than blood when hears this new information, but for Ella's sake, me and Jessie have to keep our cool.

"So, what about the girl?" I ask through my teeth, and when

Tommy remains silent, Jessie adds a little more body weight to the knife making Tommy scream in pain.

"The... the judge, he ain't been sticking to his side of the deal since the Carly incident." Tommy strains against his pain, referring to his auntie's death like it's nothin' but an inconvenience. Not the brutal murder that rocked this whole club and left Skid a broken man. "Pa wanted him to put us in some kinda witness protection program for protection, and he's trying to make out like he can't pull it off. The girl is just insurance that he'll make it happen." Jessie shoots me a stern warning not to react, and I click my knuckles to stop myself from killing the weedy little prick with my bare fists.

"And where's Chop now?" Jessie asks calmly.

"Like I said. I won't rat." Tommy shakes his head.

Jessie laughs at him, then gestures with his head for me to follow him outside to the corridor. Dropping the act and looking serious the minute the door closes behind us.

"Go relay all that to Prez. Ask him how far he wants me to take this shit," Jessie orders, lighting himself up a smoke.

"What do you mean, how far? We go all the fuckin' way," I fume back, my shit close to being fucking lost.

"That kid in there is the only family Skid's got left. I won't do permanent damage without his say so." Jessie sucks hard on his smoke, and I feel his tension.

"And you think Chop will think like that if he gets his hands on Ella?" I argue my point back at him in a whisper so Tommy won't hear us.

"That's what separates bad from evil, Nyx, now go talk to Prez and ask him to get a hold of Skid."

"This is bullshit." I shake my head and as I'm about to storm off, Jessie grabs the scruff of my cut and pulls me back.

"Jesus Nyx, what's wrong with you? You're getting blindsided by a bitch. The Prez's fuckin' daughter outta all of 'em," he points out harshly, and I throw my fist into the solid stone wall and let out a loud frustrated growl as I pull my hair from my scalp and pace the cold, damp corridor.

"You really do fucking love her, don't you?" he shakes his head at me. "Fuck Nyx, what are you thinking?" Jessie scrubs his hand over his face.

"I don't know how to love," I assure him. A blatant lie, because if loving someone feels like your heart is slowly being torn out of your chest, I'm fucking feeling it. I've been feeling it since the first day I started that shitty high school and she smiled at me.

"I'll go relay all that shit to Prez," I tell him, avoiding any more judgment and needing to get some air.

"Go careful, Nyx," Jessie calls out from behind me, and I stop and take in a deep breath before carrying on up the stairs.

When I get up to the foyer. I look out of the double doors onto the yard. It's dark outside and when I notice Squealer and Screwy's truck, the first thing I wonder is who has eyes on Ella now.

I find Prez in the lounge bar on his own, looking like he's got the weight of the world resting on his shoulders and I tell him what Tommy just spilled. I watch his face turn to shock, the same way mine and Jessie's had when we heard it.

"All this time he's been ratting to the Judge." He slumps back in his chair. "He's been a member of this club for sixteen years." Prez sounds hurt as he pours himself another drink and downs it in one.

"You think Skid was in on it too? You know before the whole Carly thing happened," I think out loud, though I struggle to believe that Skid could be a part of all this. Barring Tac and Jessie, that guy's the loyalist person I know.

"You watch your fuckin' mouth, boy. Skid was just a kid when Chop brought them here. I'd slice out my own tongue before I doubted him. And I'll take out yours if I hear you say shit like that again," he scowls.

"Chop betrayed him worse than anyone," Prez adds and I nod my agreement, I should never have doubted Skid, but everything's so fucked up around here these days.

"I'll try and get hold of Skid, Jessie's right, we can't hurt Tommy till we've spoken to him. He's lost enough." Prez's answer makes my blood boil, but I ain't in the position to argue with him. Truth is, right now I don't give a fuck what happens to Tommy, all I'm worried about is Ella.

"Who's watching Ella?" I ask.

"You care an awful lot 'bout something that's none ya business, boy." Prez looks at me suspiciously.

"She's safe," he tells me eventually, putting me out of my misery. The boys followed her into town and then back home. We got Tommy, and there ain't no way Chop is brave enough to come that close to town knowing the club's out for his blood."

"What about the Bastards? They were watching her too. You really think she's safe out there?"

"She's a damn sight safer out there than she would be here," he says sadly, pouring himself another drink.

And I fucking hate that he's right.

CHAPTER 37
JESSIE

"How d'you want me to handle this?" I ask Skid when he comes flying down the stairs into the basement. He doesn't answer me, just pushes past me and opens the door to get to his nephew.

"Where is he?" he grabs hold of Tommy, lifting him and the chair he's tied to off the floor and shaking him.

"I don't know," Tommy cries out, and Skid launches him at the wall so hard that one of the wooden legs snap off the chair and Tommy lands sideways on the ground.

"You tell me right now where I can find him, Tommy, or I swear to Satan I'll kill you." Skid pulls his gun out his holster, slides back the chamber and presses the barrel tight on Tommy's temple. "Don't fuckin' test me," he warns. His heavy hands shaking as he holds the weapon into his nephew's face with such force, I swear his skull is gonna shatter.

"I don't know." Tommy must realize what serious shit he's in now because the little weasel starts to cry. Tears streaming down his face and dribble running on to his chin. He's scared and hell, I would be too. Skid's got nothing to fucking lose these days.

"I don't know where he is," Tommy screams out, and all my instincts tell me that he's telling the truth. I've heard fear many times, what I'm hearing now is helpless fear. If Tommy knew where Chop was, he'd give him up. The kid doesn't wanna die.

"You gotta believe me, Uncle Skid. I don't know. He just told me to keep my eye on the girl for him. I haven't seen him since the Skinner's deal went wrong." Tommy sobs but Skid doesn't let up. He's still got a whole lot of tension in the finger that's resting on that trigger.

"I don't wanna die," Tommy cries out. "I'm fucking scared, Uncle Skid."

"And how do you think your auntie Carly felt?" Skid forces the gun even deeper into his nephew's flesh and I swear he's gonna do it. He's gonna pull that fuckin' trigger and end Tommy's sad pathetic life.

"He fucked her, Tommy," Skid's voice weakens to a whisper, and tears stream out of his anger filled eyes.

"She was good and pure. She never did a thing to harm anyone and he fucked her like she was a whore... Jesus, fucking Christ." Skid launches the gun out of his hand, throwing it across the room and then falling back with his back against the wall.

"Jesus. fucking. Christ." He slams his palms on to his knees a few times before throwing his head back and covering his face with his hands. Then he breaks down.

Tommy lies paralyzed on the ground, catching his breath, and I hope the son of a bitch realizes how lucky he is to still be breathing

"I can't live without her, Jess," Skid's voice croaks as he looks up at me like I got some answers for him. But I got nothing. Not a damn fucking word to say. I don't know what I'd do if anything happened to Mads. I can't even think about shit like that.

"Listen," I crouch in front of him, grabbing his head between my hands. "We are gonna find him and he's gonna pay for what he did," I swear, and I mean it. I won't rest until it's done. Skid needs this. He's lost his way, but I refuse to believe that we can't bring him back.

"It ain't gonna bring her home, Jess." He sounds so helpless, tears drowning those big kind eyes that used to be filled with such contentment.

"No, it ain't," I admit, almost choking on the lump in my throat, that's a hard truth that even I struggle to fuckin' swallow. "But it's gonna help ya heal. We're all gonna help ya heal, brother," I assure him.

"There ain't no healing when you've lost your soul, Jessie." Skid closes his eyes and it causes more tears to stream down his cheeks.

"I'm broken, I got nothing left in me no more," he admits staring forward into space. "You wanna know how many times I've held that gun to my own head?" He's looking at me now, like that's a serious fuckin' question.

"Every night, Jessie," he tells me seriously. "Every damn fucking night since she's been gone. And I can't fuckin' do it. I can't pull the trigger. Just like I couldn't pull it on him." His eyes slide over to where Tommy's still lay, cheek down against the concrete floor.

"That ain't the answer, Skid, I don't know what is," I level with him, "But it ain't that."

"I just wanna be with her again." Skid scrunches up his fists. "I wanna walk into my cabin and have her waiting there for me with that smile that owned my fucking heart. I wanna argue with her over what shit we watch on TV."

I move so I'm sitting beside him, my back resting against the wall now too, and I look up at the ceiling and can't help but think about all the things I miss about Hayley.

"I wanna know what our kid would have looked like. If it had been a boy or a girl? I torture myself with that shit over and over," he admits, using his arm to wipe away his tears.

"You all think I'm hell bent on fucking up my brother. That getting him back here so I can tear him apart is gonna heal me, but it ain't. She's the only one who's gonna put the heart back in my chest."

We sit together in silence. Tommy so still I wonder if he's still breathing. I got nothing useful to say to Skid, and I hope that me sitting here beside him is enough to let him know that I feel his pain.

"I gotta get away from this club, Jessie," he tells me eventually, like he's been thinking on this for a while. His face is blank as he stares forward. "Everything here reminds me of her. I feel like I can't fucking breathe."

"Fine, we'll move you out the cabin, Tac's got some room above the studio," I suggest, I know Skid avoids going home at night; he's always the last one to leave the club. I get that. I see Carly laying out lifeless on the floor the way I found her every time I walk through his door.

"It ain't just the cabin, Jess. She's fucking everywhere. Who stitched that patch on your cut for you?" He looks over to where my cut's hanging on the back of the chair.

"Carly," I smile to myself when I think about her.

"I go to the garage and I see her sitting behind my desk, nagging at me for not keeping the books better for Thorne. I step in the clubhouse and see every fucking memory we ever made there play out in my fucking head. His finger slams hard into his temple and his body tenses. Hell, I can't even look at squeal without seeing that star shaped scar she put in his cheek.

I snort a laugh when I remember the time we were all fixing up the bar room a few years ago. Carly was taking down a board from the wall and Squealer did the one chivalrous thing he's ever done in his life. He tried catching her when she slipped off the stool she was standing on, and she thanked him for it by accidently stabbing him in the face with the screwdriver she was holding.

"She felt real bad about that," Skid smiles sadly and looks up at the ceiling.

"You can't leave, Skid," I tell him seriously. "This club needs you."

"I ain't me no more, VP. I don't know who I am. I used to wake up and feel like I was the luckiest man in the whole fucking world, now I don't feel anything but hate."

"I gotta find out who I'm gonna be without her," he adds

And as much as his words ain't what I want to hear, I totally get them.

"What do you need?" I ask him.

"I need you to not tell the others until I'm gone. They'll try and stop me and I can't deal with that shit, Jessie, I've made up my mind."

"What about Prez?"

Skid reaches into his jacket and pulls out an envelope handing it over. "I been carrying this around for a few weeks now. It explains everything, and I filled out my transfer request to the nomads."

"Wait, no. You ain't going nomad." I can't believe what I'm hearing and I won't let it happen. "Take time out, Skid, however long it takes, I got ya on that. But you ain't going fucking nomad." I turn my head to face him, don't give a shit if he sees the fucking tears in my eyes. I arrived here when I was just a kid. Skid's been like an older brother to me ever since.

"Nomad means you're alone out there, that you don't belong no place." I remind him. "You can't be a nomad when you got a family, Skid. And we're your family. When you get your head straight, you're coming home to us, your brothers. Hell, Carly would take me out with more than a fucking screwdriver if I didn't make you see that."

"I hear ya," Skid nods his head, smiling back at me bravely.

"Look out for Rogue. I've let her down this past year and that crazy bitch may not give the vibe she needs anyone, but she does."

"It's done, brother," I assure him, standing up and holding up my hand to help him up off the floor.

"And what do we do with him?" I tip my chin at Tommy, who's still laying in silence.

"I want you to keep him here, to get him fucking straight." Skid looks down at his nephew.

"You want a shot at being a decent man you'll listen to this one," Skid tells him firmly. "You got one chance to prove yourself to this club, don't fuck it up."

Tommy nods his head and looks at the floor.

"You can start by telling me what you were doing in your uncle's cabin the day of the lake party," I focus on him. This is the first of many fucking tests. I got no hope of talking Prez into letting him stick around if he ain't gonna be honest.

Tommy looks deflated but he speaks up. "Dad needed the USB drive from his trunk," he says. "And before you start hitting me again. I have no idea what's on it. Just that he was real desperate to get hold of it and that he didn't want anyone else to know about it."

"And did you get it for him?" I ask.

Tommy's eyes fill with tears and he looks up guiltily at his uncle.

"He wouldn't have come back if I did."

CHAPTER 38
ELLA

I wait full clothed beneath my covers until I hear Dad's footsteps on the landing and hear his bedroom door close. He'll spend some time reading before he falls asleep, so I time another forty-five minutes before I brave moving from my bed. My heart beats frantically in my chest as I go over and over the plan in my head and I can't help thinking all this would be so much less scary if Nyx was coming with us.

I can't deal with those kinds of distractions right now though. The moment I've spent months planning is finally here, and I can't afford to mess this up.

Creeping out of bed, I grab my suitcase from inside the wardrobe. I've decided to travel light, just my cash and a few changes of clothes. I leave my regular cell on my bedside table and slide the burner phone I bought a few weeks ago inside my back pocket. I can't trust Father not to have some kind of tracker on that too, especially since he pays the bill.

My case isn't heavy so I don't risk wheeling it down the hall, and carry it instead. My heart thumps against my chest and my stomach twists in knots as I open my bedroom door and step out into a pitch-black hall.

I make slow silent steps until I reach the top of the stairs then take each step carefully, memorizing where each one creaks.

I'm almost at the front door, relief slowly replacing my anxiety, when suddenly the room lights up and a calm voice chills my bones

"Going somewhere, Ella?" Seeing Father staring back at me with that wicked glint in his eyes leaves me with only one option.

To run.

I bolt towards the front door, trying to yank it open, but it's locked. Of course, it's fucking locked, I even thought about that when I evaluated all the things that could go wrong with my escape.

His heavy footsteps thunder towards me and I quickly reach up to the hook where the key is hanging. He catches up to me and I yelp in pain when he fists at my hair, slamming my face hard into the heavy wooden door in front of me.

My head throbs in agony and I taste copper as blood trickles from my nostrils on to my lips.

"Trying to run from me," he chuckles against my ear, causing my entire body to shiver. It isn't just me he can hurt now, the risks are so much greater.

"Please let me go," I beg, as softly as I can manage. "I won't tell anyone about what you've done."

"Let you go." He spins me around so I'm facing him. His dark grey eyes alight with sick thrill. "I haven't got what I want yet." He presses his body tighter into mine, and I smell the alcohol on his breath.

"I've waited a long time for you, Ella," his voice sounds almost tender and my stomach rolls with disgust. I can't fight him from here, there's no space between us. The moment I've been dreading all this time has come and there's no escape. I'm never gonna survive what he's about to do to me.

"It'll hurt less if you don't fight," he whispers me a petrifying promise. His hand squeezing at one of my tits through the thick sweater I'm wearing. When his hands lower over my body I know it's only a fraction of a second before he discovers my secret, and feeling his body relax against mine I strike. I move fast, ducking under his arm and running towards the kitchen to try my chances with the back door. But he comes after me, and while I'm looking over my shoulder my foot gets caught on the rug and I trip, landing hard on my front.

A sharp pain slices through the pit of my stomach, and a loud wail escapes my throat. But I don't have time to panic, not when his fist is back in my hair, dragging me towards the living room.

"You won't get away from me," he yells at me. "All these years, I've taken care of you, I've given you everything you needed. What have I ever got in return?" He pulls me to a stop and crouches in front of me. "It's time you paid your dues." He leans over my body, grabbing my arms and pinning them on either side of my head. I struggle beneath him, fighting to be free, and then fear I'll pass out when his heavy fist slams into my cheek.

My face feels like it's shattered in two, but somehow I manage to keep on fighting as he shifts both my wrists into one hand and starts to loosen his belt with the other. My growing panic seems to give me a sudden surge of strength and I look up at him with all the hate I can muster, pull up my knee, and smash it straight between his legs.

His heavy weight falls onto mine, and I quickly roll him off me, scurrying onto my feet and take advantage of the distraction.

I rush for the front door, my fingers shaking as I reach for the keys and managing to grasp them. I cry out when they fall from my trembling hand, checking over my shoulder as I scoop to pick them up, I see him lifting on to his feet.

By some miracle I manage to unlock the door, but I don't have time to grab my suitcase, I don't have time to think about anything other than running for safety. And that's exactly what I do. I run, out into the black, cold air, and I keep on running until the stitch in my stomach forces me to stop.

I hide behind a tree to rest a few blocks away from my street, my heart slamming in my chest while I try to catch my breath. I can't worry about not having any money or my car. I just need to get as far away as possible. I'm about to make another run for it when I feel another sharp pain slice across my stomach. One so strong that it makes me double over.

I breathe out, holding on to the tree until the pain subsides. The fall I took back at the house could have hurt the baby. A lot of things could have happened back there that I can't bear to think about, and now I'm really screwed because I have no money and no vehicle. What am I supposed to do now? I can't even go to the hospital to get checked out. My father will find me and drag me back.

I manage to stumble another few blocks, constantly checking over my shoulder, before another pain wracks through my body. I'm not an idiot, I know exactly what this is now, and it's really bad timing, the worse in fact.

I've read about giving birth. I've even been brave enough to watch a few YouTube videos.

But now I can actually feel it happening. I'm more scared than I ever imagined, and I figure I only have one option left. One that I'm scared enough to have to try. I'm relieved when I feel in my pocket, and my cell is still there. Pulling it out, I click on the one number I bothered to store. The only number that matters, and the only person who can help us now.

I just pray that he'll answer this time, because now we need him more than ever.

Chapter 39

NYX

I'm hanging out at the fire pit by myself. Wondering how the fuck things have come to this.

Ella out there, her life being threatened, and me being able to do fuck all about it. Prez finding out how I feel about her and me getting what's coming all seems irrelevant.

I wish I could convince him to trust me again. To let me take her away from here, I'd die before I let anything happen to her. Do anything to keep her safe. I flick my cigarette into the flames and stand up. It's time to come clean, I'm gonna speak to Prez, admit that I've fallen in love with his daughter. Consequences be damned.

I'm heading back inside when my cell starts vibrating inside my jacket and when I pull it out, I see a number I don't recognize. Everyone around here uses burner phones, it could be anyone.

I press the phone to my ear and block out the music booming out from Tac's truck by slamming a hand over my other one.

"Nyx… Nyx. Oh thank god." I recognize her voice straight away, and hearing her sound so fucking scared cuts me up so much that I almost choke.

"Ella, you okay? What's wrong?" She doesn't answer, all I can hear is heavy breathing, followed by tiny whimpers that petrify the fuck out of me.

If Chop or any of those Bastard cunts have her, if they've laid a finger on her. I'll kill them.

"Ella, where are you?"

"At that park, four blocks from mine," she manages, struggling between stuttered breaths.

What the hell is she doing there?

"You alone?"

She doesn't answer me and hearing her cry down the phone is unbearable.

"Ella are you alone?" I shout down the phone.

"Yes," she manages, and it eases me up but only until her next painful moan.

"Ella are you in trouble?" I ask.

"Yeah Nyx… I'm in real fucking trouble," she says, her voice so weak I hear the shiver in it.

"I'm coming for you, just sit tight, okay?"

The phone goes dead and I waste no more time. Heading straight for my truck, and skidding out the yard.

I drive to the park without looking at my speedo or stopping for any reds. My mind racing with all the things that might have happened to her. I could be walking straight into a trap, but getting to my girl is all that matters

I hop out of my truck and scan around the park for a sign of her. Then a loud painful wail that comes from the toilet block points me in the right direction. I sprint towards her, almost ripping the door off its hinges to get to her. Then when I find her crouched forward on her hands. Her body struggling for breath and rigid with pain, I sink on my knees beside her.

"Ella, what's wrong?" She's crying so hard, her eyes are swollen and there's blood seeping from her nose. She looks up at me guiltily when I brush away the hair that's stuck to her face with tears and sweat.

"Ell, tell me what it is so I can fix this." I'm doing my best to stay calm, though I'm ready to beat the shit out of whoever's done this to her. Her pain seems to ease, and her body relaxes slightly. Enough for her to shift her body to sit back on her knees. Her tear filled eyes lower down her body, and when I follow them I feel my own double in size. Her hand is pressed tight against her sweater, and her usual flat stomach is now much larger and round.

"Holy fuck." I stumble backwards. Hitting the ground with my ass.

"I'm sorry, I didn't know who else to call. I didn't think it would hurt this much. Please help me, Nyx, I'm so scared," she begs and I can't even respond, I'm still staring at her, my fingers trembling as I push them through my hair and try to fuckin' think straight.

"Nyx," she cries out my name, tears rolling over her cheeks and causing me to snap out of it. Somehow, I push all my shock to the side, and suck in the panic. Then launching forward, I take her in my arms and scoop her up, rushing as fast as I can to get her to my truck.

There's a comfort in having her close, and despite the urgency of the situation I can't resist placing my lips to her temple and appreciating how it feels to hold her again. When I reach the truck, I place her carefully on the passenger seat, then race back around the front of the truck to jump in beside her.

"It's gonna be okay," I try my best to reassure her, despite the crushing panic in my chest when she clutches at the handle of the door and screams as I start pulling away. I swear whatever it is she's feeling, it's crippling me just as much, because I have no idea what I can do to make her feel better.

"I'm gonna get you to the hospital. They can help you," I tell her, my hand stroking her thigh while I drive, as if it's gonna make any fuckin' difference to the pain she's in.

"No!" She looks up at me, her pretty eyes full of fear. "No hospitals, please. My father can't know about this. He'll kill me.

Please Nyx." She should know I'd never let that happen. But the fact she's scared enough to be distracted from the pain she's in, makes me swallow the lump in my throat.

"'Kay darlin'. No hospitals," I promise. Lifting my hand off her leg and holding it out so she has something to squeeze when I notice her face tensing with more pain.

"Where you taking me?" She throws her head back against the seat when her pain passes again, and I hadn't even realized where I'm headed myself until I have to give her an answer.

"Home, Ella… I'm taking you home." I lean over and press my lips against her sticky forehead.

"I'm so sorry, Nyx," she sobs, "I thought I could sort something out. I had money saved, I was gonna run, and then he caught me."

"Wait… what, who are you talkin' about?" My fingers grip tight at the steering wheel.

"My dad, he flipped when he found out I was gonna leave home. I tripped over trying to get away from him and then he hit me." She fights to hold back her tears, so she can finish what she wants to tell me. "Do you think it'll be okay? The baby I mean…" I look down to where she's stroking a hand protectively over the neat little bump. "…I thought I had at least a few more weeks before it came"

"Your dad did this?" I check, my blood boiling under my skin.

"It was gonna happen at some point, Nyx," she says reaching out and gripping my arm, as her body gets attacked with more pain.

"Ell, I should really get you to a hospital, he could have hurt you, or the…" Fuck, I'm too much of a pussy to even say it out loud.

"I've managed to hide this from him for all this time, I'm not gonna have him find out now. Please," she pleads me with her eyes, and there's no hope of me saying no to her. Even knowing that a huge shit storm is about to hit.

At least at the club I know she'll be safe. We can call the Doc, he's always fixing people. He'll fix this.

When we get to the compound there's no one outside the clubhouse, so I head straight up to the cabins, parking the truck outside mine and rushing to help her out. I barge open my door and hurry us inside. We don't even make it to the couch before she bows over in agony again. I ease her on to the floor, do my best to comfort her while she cries out in pain but I'm useless to her. There's no way I can do this by myself. I need help. And I know exactly who to get it from.

"Stay there. I'm gonna get help," I tell her, prying my hand out of hers.

"Don't leave me, Nyx, please, not now." She tugs at my arm when I go to get up, and I quickly grab her face in both my hands, anger rushing through me all over again when I see the mess the judge has made of her.

"I am going next door to get someone to help us. I. am. not. leaving you. I'll be right back. I promise. Just stay here." I slam a kiss onto her forehead, and just about manage to stand up on my wobbly legs.

"Well, it's not like I'm gonna fucking run anywhere, is it?" she calls out after me as I rush out the door.

I race to Jessie's cabin and hammer on his door, calling Prez from my cell while I wait for him to open. Prez sounds groggy when he answers. I yell at him to call the doc and get to mine, hanging up before he has the chance to ask questions. It seems to take forever, but Jessie eventually opens his door, his hand ruffling through his unruly hair. "Someone better be fucking dying," he tells when he sees me.

"I need you and Mads, at mine, right the fuck now," I tell him, already moving to get back to Ella, and Jessie must see how panicked I am because he doesn't question me, just calls out to

Mads, who comes out of the bedroom, wearing one of his band shirts.

"Get some bottoms on, Nyx needs us," he calls over his shoulder, jogging out behind me.

He halts in my doorway when he sees Ella on the floor. The look on his face, similar to my reaction when I first saw her.

"What the fuck?" He turns his head to me, and if he hadn't quite been awake before, he sure is now.

Ella is doing her best to steady her breathing, her face red and scrunched up in pain.

"Jesus Christ, Nyx, tell me this ain't your problem," he says sliding another hand through his hair and scrubbing at his face.

"Holy fucking shit," Maddy's shocked voice screeches from behind us.

"Great, you're here," I sigh in relief when I turn around and see her standing in shock. "You need to do something."

"Do what?" She looks at me as if I've lost all senses. "I'm a hacker not a frickin' midwife." Maddy gives herself a few seconds to process before she steps around me and Jessie to get closer to Ella.

"I'm Maddy, Jessie's old lady," she speaks soothingly, slowly crouching down in front of her.

"That's nice," Ella nods her head trying to be polite. "Can you make the pain stop?" she begs

"Get her some vodka or something, that should take the edge off." Jessie rushes over to my cupboards and pulls out a bottle.

"She's pregnant, Jessie, you can't drink when you're pregnant," Maddy reminds him, already trying her best to get Ella to relax by breathing with her.

"Well by the looks of things, she ain't gonna be for much longer," Jessie points out, unscrewing the top and knocking back a mouthful himself. "Here darlin'." He steps closer and hands Ella the bottle.

She takes it from him and launches it at the wall before

clutching at her stomach and screaming again. Seeing her like this, so scared and in so much pain fuckin' kills me.

"You need to look down there and see what's going on," Jessie says pulling an awkward face at Maddy, his head nodding to the space between Ella's legs.

"Why do I have to look?" Maddy argues back, her voice all high pitched and panicky.

"What in the hell is goin' on here?" We all turn when we hear Prez's voice. And Jessie marches straight at him, forcing his palms into his chest and holding him back.

"The girl called Nyx 'cause she was in trouble, and as you can see… She needs our help." Jessie throws Prez a look that begs him not to react the way we all know he wants to, and I'm surprised that my head was still attached to neck when Prez nods back begrudgingly in a silent agreement.

Maddy pulls the throw off my couch, draping it over Ella's knees before she helps her out of her leggings, and all I can do is stand out the way, useless, as it finally dawns on me that a person is about to come into this world. A tiny helpless person that I'm 99.9% sure is half mine.

"Oh my god, I feel so sorry for you." Maddy holds her hand over her mouth and looks at Ella sympathetically after she's finally braved the looking between the leg situation.

"Babe, I don't think you're helping much," Jessie points out. "Ain't you supposed to be boiling water and getting towels?" He steps around Ella, avoiding looking down.

"What the fuck is that gonna do?" Maddy asks, looking up at him confused. "Boiling water is not gonna help what's going on down here. Just take off your shirt." She holds out her hand.

"I don't think now's the time, darlin'." He winks back at her, then quickly drops the cheeky grin off his face when Ella cries out in more pain.

"Just take it off, Jessie. The baby is literally coming. Where's the doc?" Maddy looks over her shoulder at me.

"Grimm rode out to get him, he should be here soon. Just try keepin' it in a bit longer," Prez answers, his face failing to mask the concern he has for his daughter.

"I don't think she's gonna be able to do that," Maddy snaps at him. "Oh Jesus, there's something protruding out of it." Maddy starts to gag, and Jessie steps up bravely, placing his hand on his old lady's shoulder and cautiously checkin' it out for himself.

"Right darlin', you listen to me." He looks up at Ella, his skin turned pale but somehow holding it together. "Women all over the word been doin' this shit for years. And without doctors. You're gonna be fine. Ain't nothing gonna happen to you on my watch." He takes the black band from round his wrist and uses it to tie back his hair before he slides down behind her. Placing a leg either side of hers, he pushes his arms under hers, and grabs hold of both her hands. I look over to Prez, and I'm certain that we're both thinking the same thing. That we should be the one comforting her right now.

"Now I got up here covered," Jessie speaks to Maddy over Ella's shoulder. "And well, you're just gonna have to pull your shit together down there. 'Cause I can't fuckin' deal," he tells her.

He turns his attention back to Ella, who's gripping his hand so tight her knuckles have turned white. "You listen to what my girl tells you and we're all gonna be just fine," he assures her.

"I feel something real heavy down there. Like I need to push," Ella strains.

"It's the baby's head, sweetie." Maddy looks up, trying to hide the disgust from her face. "I think you should push."

"I can't, I'm too scared," Ella shakes her head in protest.

"Ain't no use being scared, this baby is coming. Think you gotta just do what your body's tellin' ya," Jessie tells her, and I have no idea how he's being so calm.

"But my dad. What if he takes it away from me?" she

wails through tears. My eyes flick over to Prez again and I watch his stare turn cold as he focuses on his only living daughter.

"Your daddy ain't gonna do shit. I'll promise you that. Listen to what Maddy tells you," he says, his authoritative tone a little softer than usual.

"I can't… I can't even take care of myself. I can't do this on my own." The pain doesn't seem to be affecting her anymore. She's so fuckin' scared and I can't stand back here and watch her fall apart a moment longer.

"You ain't gonna be alone," I tell her, stepping forward, and crouching beside her. I take one of her hands from Jessie and hold it tight mine, hoping she doesn't feel how unsteady it is.

"I'm here, and I'm gonna take care of you. Of both of you," I promise, the thumb from my other hand wiping away the tear from her cheek.

"You promise?" She snuffles a tiny smile,

"Yeah," I nod my head, looking her right in her terrified eyes so she knows I mean every word.

As long as I got a breath in my body I'll take care of her, but judging from the way Prez's eyes are drilling into the back of my head right now, I doubt it will be for very long.

"Me too," I hear his low voice rumble from behind me. "I'm gonna take care of you," he pledges, and my heart fills with relief.

"You hear that, darlin'?" Jessie tells Ella, his eyes looking past my shoulder up at Prez. "That there's the President of the Dirty Souls MC and if he makes ya a promise, I can assure ya it's as solid as steel. You're here now, you're both under our protection. So you do what you need to do. Fear ain't never been welcome on this compound. None of us would be here if we let that get in our way." I notice how his eyes fall on to Maddy and a dopey smile sets on his face.

"Oh my God," Ella screams. Her hand crushing mine, and

her whole body tensing as she finally gives in to her body's demands.

"That's right," Maddy encourages her. "You're doing it. Whatever you're doing is working. It's gross, but it's working."

"I'm so sorry, Ell," I whisper, kissing her knuckles to my mouth, and watching helplessly as she screams like her body's splitting in two.

"The head and shoulders are out. Next push I think it could all be over if you make it a good one," Maddy tells her, starting to sound a little excited.

"You hear that? One more. You got this," Jessie tells her as another contraction rips through her. Ella howls like a fucking wolf and Maddy reaches between her legs. A hint of a smile on her focused face.

"You did it, it's here," Maddy tells Ella pulling this tiny, pink body up in her hands, a faint snuffling noise coming from its mouth.

"I thought kids are supposed to cry when they come out?" I look at Maddy, hearing the panic in my own voice. Something ain't right.

"Here, pass him up here," Jessie says calmly, reaching out his hands and taking the little slimy figure that still ain't fuckin' crying out of Maddy's arms. He places it in Ella's shaky arms, then hooks a finger inside its tiny mouth, pulling out a finger full of slimy mucus. And I finally exhale when I hear the loud high pitched screech release from its throat.

"There ya go, darlin', looks like you got yaself a little boy. And being born here on the compound pretty much guarantees this little fella a patch, watcha reckon, Prez?" Jessie looks up at Prez, and when I follow his line of vision, Prez's eyes are brimming with tears.

"Hey," Ella, looks down at our kid with this huge beam lighting up her face, placing her finger inside his hand, and I dare myself to take a proper look at him.

He's fucking perfect.

I catch Prez watching me, his eyes clutching rage now, tears still unshed. And a loud rap at the door pulls his focus from me. Grimm pokes his head around the door. Doing a double take when he sees the scene in front of him.

"Prez, doc's here," he announces, opening the door wider for the doc to step inside. Doc doesn't ask any questions, he never does. He just goes straight to Ella and starts tending to her with the baby still in her arms. I move out of his way with Maddy, my whole body trembling like a leaf. I'm fuckin' petrified, and not because of Prez or the club. I'm scared for the tiny little person who's just been born into the world, with me as his father.

Jessie hops up from behind Ella, popping a kiss on her cheek.

"Congratulations darlin'." He smiles down at her and she grabs on to his arm and thanks him, over and over.

"You too." She looks to Maddy "I don't know what we would have done without you both," she smiles.

Jessie nods me over to the other side of the room as he pulls Maddy under his arm. "We fuckin' nailed that, babe," he tells her proudly, landing a kiss onto her forehead.

"You were incredible, and so calm. The way you helped him breath like that, honestly, Jessie, you were amazing." Maddy's right. I can't even think about what might have happened if he hadn't been here and thought so fast.

"You want the truth? I was fuckin' terrified," he blows out a breath before he looks at Mads and smiles. "But I figure it'll be good practice." He tugs her in a little tighter.

"Um, Practice for what?" she raises her head up at him.

"For when I knock you up." He places a hand over her flat stomach. "You know we're gonna have to let it happen sometime, darlin'." He smirks.

"After seeing what I just saw, you'll be lucky if I ever let you near me with your dick again," she warns.

"You sure about that?" he checks, a glint in his eyes.

"I seriously need to wash this shit off my hands," Maddy says, cutting the conversation, and quickly heading for the bathroom.

I take a look over at Prez, he's standing and staring at his daughter and new grandson. I can feel the heat radiating off him as he gives Jessie a grateful pat on the back when he passes him on the way outside for some air.

"That's the cord cut," Doc says. "Does someone wanna hold this little guy while I deal with the mother." Shit, that sounds weird, someone referring to Ella as a Mother. It's another huge wakeup call. I'm about to step forward and hold my son for the first time. Hoping that it won't be the fuckin' last. But Prez's voice stops me.

"I'd like to… if that's alright with you?" He looks down at Ella, his hard face suddenly softening into a smile.

"Sure," Ella smiles back at him, carefully stretching up her arms and passing over our kid to Prez, and having no idea that she's passing him a grandchild. He takes the tiny bundle in his arms so gently you'd think he was handling a grenade.

"He's beautiful," he tells Ella, who nods back gratefully before her eyes dart over to me. Prez moves steadily to take a seat on the couch cradling his grandson in his arms, focusing on him and nothing else. And I listen to the doc instruct Ella.

I don't know how long I stand there and watch the scene in front of me. Trying to hold myself together and figure out how I'm gonna protect them if Prez can't forgive me.

"Nyx," Ella's voice snaps me out of my trance. She's sitting in one of the arm chairs now, our son wrapped up and in her arms. Her skin's still flushed and covered in bruises, but she looks so much better, now she's smiling.

"He's perfect, isn't he?" she says dreamily as I rest my ass on the arm of the chair and wrap an arm around her.

"I'm so sorry I wasn't there. That you went through this all by yourself," I tell her. I know Prez can probably hear me, but if he hasn't figured it out by now, I doubt he ever will.

"Where did you go, why did you leave after you got out of jail?" She looks up at me, her eyes filling back up with tears that I can't handle seeing again.

"Because I'm an idiot." I take her chin in my hand and kiss those lips that I've been craving for months. I don't care that Prez sees, right now, giving Ella reassurance is more important than anything he's got planned for me.

"I'm just happy he's okay. After what happened. I was so scared." Guilt strikes me in my gut like a lit match, burning rage through my entire body. None of this would have happened if I'd have been taking care of them like I should have been.

Prez gestures his head towards the back door of my cabin before he storms out onto the deck.

"Give me five. I'll be right back," I promise Ella, kissing her on her head and placing my hand over our baby boy's chest. How is it possible that an hour ago I didn't even know he existed? And now I'd lay my life down for him.

I follow Prez out onto the deck that overlooks the lake.

"Look Prez, me and you can hash out whatever we need to. But right now…"

"Did he do this?" he asks, cutting off the speech I had prepared. "Did the judge hurt her?" He pulls the door closed behind him so Ella can't hear. And I nod my head back at him, clenching my fists.

"I should have…"

"She needs you." He shocks me, and I see how much it hurts him to admit. "That girl's been through enough tonight. So, you get back to her and give her whatever she needs." He stares at his daughter through the glass door. "But if you ain't waiting for me at church tomorrow morning at 9am. I swear to fucking god, Nyx, you'll be Grimm's next problem."

"Prez I…" I try to start explaining.

"Save it for tomorrow." His eyes bore into my angrily before he steps back inside.

Chapter 40
ELLA

I can't believe my little boy is here, or that a baby could be so beautiful. He has Nyx's eyes and the same pouty bottom lip. I'm just grateful that he's okay after what happened back at the house.

The older guy who everyone calls Prez steps back inside the cabin after speaking to Nyx outside.

"Make a list of what you need for the kid. I'll send one of the boys out to a 24 store," he tells me.

"Thanks," I smile gratefully, suddenly feeling shy. I'd been in too much pain to notice the cut he wore before, but I see it now, He's a Dirty Soul. These people aren't supposed to be hospitable, they're outlaws. Yet despite his harsh expressions and the flair of danger in his pupils. This man has shown me only kindness.

"We take care of our own round here," he tells me huskily, before walking out the front door into the darkness.

"You both warm enough?" I hear Nyx's voice and turn my head towards him. He's standing resting his shoulder against one of the wood beams, watching us.

"We're fine," I smile awkwardly. I don't know where to even start explaining all this to him. I've just sprung a kid on him for Christ's sake. And yet, he doesn't seem mad at me. Quite the opposite in fact.

He steps closer and crouches in front of us.

"If I'd known about this." his huge tattooed hand strokes over our little boy's back. "I'd have come back."

"I tried calling you, Nyx, I came looking for you but when I heard your charges got dropped and you vanished off the face of the earth… Why did you leave?" I feel tears starting to slide down my cheek and I'm about to wipe them away but he beats me to it.

"Ell, there is so much I got to explain to you, stuff I can't tell you right now. But you need to understand that I would never have left you unless I had to." I nod because despite what he's done, a crazy part of me trusts him. Or maybe I just need to believe what he's saying is true because I'm all out of options. Either way, I feel safe here. Safer than I have in a long time.

"How have you managed this all by yourself?" He shakes his head in disbelief, His hand moving so gently to cradle the back of our baby's head.

"I found out I was pregnant about a month after you got arrested. I was so scared, especially with everything that was going on at home with my father." I ignore his puzzled look and continue. "I thought about my options. I even drove all the way to Denver to a clinic, but when I got there I couldn't even get out of the car to go inside." I clutch the bundle in my arms a little tighter.

"So, I decided I had to keep him. Figured I had a few months to get my shit together before it would be a problem. I was gonna make a new life for us both, get out of town and start somewhere new, just me and him."

"Shit, you shouldn't have had to go through all that, Ell." He shakes his head, angry at himself.

"I don't regret it, Nyx, now he's here and I've got him in my arms. I could never give him up."

"Hey, hey." Nyx wraps his strong arm around me and tucks

me into his chest. "I may have only just found out about this, but I'm glad you did what you did. How could I not be?"

"Babies change lives, Nyx, we're both too young. When I decided to keep him, I took that responsibility on myself. I don't expect you to do the same." I want to be with Nyx more than anything in the world, but not by trapping him. I'm convinced that's what Mom did to my father and I refuse to repeat history, not after growing up and seeing what it does to a family.

"You ain't got a choice," Nyx tells me. "I love you, Ella, and there is so much that needs explaining to you. But as of right now, you guys are the only thing that matters to me. I'm not going anywhere, and I know I haven't given you many reasons to trust me on that, but you have to believe me."

"I believe you," I assure him, because, call me naïve and stupid but how can I doubt him when he's looking at me and our son with so much love in his eyes.

The baby starts to wriggle in my arms, his tiny little whimper quickly turning into a full-blown cry. Nyx pulls back, eyes wide and panicked as he stares down at him.

"He's probably just hungry," I try to reassure him.

"We ain't got the shit around here for babies." He stands on his feet, looking helpless again.

"Relax, I think I got it," I tell him. "Here, take him a sec." Nyx looks scared as hell as he reaches down and slides his hand under our little boy's head carefully and slightly trembling he scoops him up and on to his chest.

"I got him," he nods at me reassuringly, with a sweet grin on his handsome face that melts my heart.

I pull up my top and unhook my bra, then hold out my hands to take him back.

Nyx carefully places him in the crook of my arm, and we watch his tiny little mouth rook until it finds what he's looking for. It takes a while for him to latch on properly but he soon stops crying.

"See, problem solved." I wince at the weird sensation of him sucking.

"You're fucking incredible, you know that?" Nyx shakes his head and watches with deep concentration.

"I watched a lot of YouTube tutorials. I actually thought it was gonna be a lot harder," I confess.

Nyx pulls off his hoodie and covers us up with it. And despite all the trauma of tonight it makes me relax being close to him again.

"You must be shattered," Nyx says after the baby's finished feeding and has fallen back to sleep. He's right, despite my blood still pumping full of adrenaline, the overwhelming mixture of emotions and all the questions I have swirling in my head are exhausting. I can feel my eyes getting heavier.

"Let's get you to bed," he says, taking our sleeping boy out of my arms and pulling him up onto his bare chest.

"You need a hand getting up?" he asks, and I shake my head, using the armrests to pull me onto my feet. Nyx somehow manages to hold the baby in one of his arms and wraps the other around my waist, aiding me on the small journey to his room.

There's a double bed, and a chair set in the corner that's covered with clothes. I get straight into bed, taking comfort in the sheets that smell just like him as I sink into them and he places our baby down on a pillow beside me.

"We haven't got anything for him to sleep in," I say, suddenly realizing how unprepared I've been through all this.

"I'll watch him while you sleep," he assures me, laying down on the bed behind me, sliding his arm under my shoulders while his other wraps over us both protectively. "Just close your eyes, everything's over now. I got you both." I feel my eyes starting to droop and let myself fall to sleep, for the first time in months feeling content.

I hear a tiny knock on the door and feel Nyx slide away from me. Still, I keep my eyes shut, I'm not ready to wake up.

"Are they okay?" I hear the female voice whisper.

"They're fine, thanks Mads," Nyx whispers back.

"I googled the essentials you'll need and sent Jessie out. It's all on the table," she keeps her voice low.

"I owe you guys," Nyx tells her.

"You spoke to Prez? Maddy asks him, sounding concerned.

"He wants to see me at church tomorrow."

"Try not to worry, Nyx, the man's not a monster."

"You've only seen his good side. He's fucking furious, Mads. You saw the way he looked at me. He ain't gonna forgive me for this, and I can't lose them. They come first now. Look what happened the last time I left."

"It'll work out," I hear Maddy assure him. "I'll stay with these guys, why don't you go take a shower?" I feel the mattress lift as Nyx gets off the bed.

"Just promise me that no matter what happens tomorrow, you and Jessie will look out for them," he says.

"I promise," Maddy whispers before I hear the door close again. I try to piece everything I've just heard together in my head. It sounds like Nyx is in trouble. Maybe that's why he left in the first place? But if that's the case, why is he back? I decide to take this time alone with Maddy to try and find out. Faking a stir, I open my eyes and see Maddy sitting in the chair in the corner of the room. she smiles at me when I focus.

"Hey, where's Nyx?" I ask, pretending I hadn't just heard their conversation.

"He's just grabbing a shower, do you need anything?" she asks.

"I'm good. Thank you."

"Jessie got you some stuff from the drive and buy, we're gonna have to send Nyx out to grab more stuff tomorrow though. I didn't realize how much stuff such a little person needed," she says, lifting her head to peek fondly at my little boy.

"You really think we're gonna be able to stay here?" I ask hopefully. Crazy as it sounds, I feel safe among these people.

"Oh, Hunny, you can count on it." She wears a huge smile. "It's about time I had some decent female company,"

"And Nyx, you think he's gonna struggle to deal with all this?" I ask, seeking out assurance as I find a more comfortable position in the bed.

"Hey, you don't need to worry about Nyx, that guy's crazy about you," she tells me, moving closer and touching her hand over my baby's chest. "He's gonna be crazy about this little guy too, even if he was a shock."

"What's he been doing all this time? Why did he just vanish, when he got out, why didn't he come for me?"

"That's not my story to tell," Maddy says softly, sliding her hand over to mine as she sits beside me.

"But I promise you that if he'd had a choice about it, he wouldn't have and I can tell you he's been hurting real bad the whole time you've been apart. You guys need to talk about a lot of things."

"I'm worried he's gonna do something stupid," I admit, trying to hold back tears.

"Stupid?" Maddy looks at me confused.

"He knows who did this," I lift up my fingers to stroke at my sore cheek, it all seems so long ago now. Yet it's only been hours.

"That could be bad," Maddy admits, the look on her face, suggesting she knows how Nyx can be. "You wanna talk about it?" she tilts her head sympathetically,

"I can never go back," I tell her. "And if I told Nyx everything that happened, no one would be able to stop him." Tears slide onto my cheeks and I use the back of my hand to wipe them away.

"You're safe now. Whoever did this can't hurt you anymore."

"I was trying to run away. I knew I had to before this one came along." I look down at my sweet little boy.

Maddy nods like she understands,

"I knew it was coming, he'd been looking at me weird for years, and then…" I suddenly stop myself from saying any more. The words are too sick for me to say out loud.

"Ella did he…" Maddy sits up a little straighter, and I see how she's trying to prevent the disgust from finding her face.

"I managed to get away," I assure her, "but there were times before… times when he'd touch me. I knew it was wrong, but he knew how to threaten me. My Mom isn't exactly stable. He abuses her, I still shouldn't have let him do what he did to me." God, it feels good to finally tell someone about this, and I don't know what it is about Maddy but I'm drawn to trust her.

"None of this is your fault," she tells me, tears welling in her eyes as she wraps her arms around my shoulder.

"It makes me feel sick whenever I close my eyes and I think about his hands on me. How could he have done something like that to me, I'm his daughter." I look at Maddy for answers, and all she can do is shake her head.

"Whatever happened, it's over now, you're safe here. This place may not be a mansion in Castle Rock but we all take care of each other. We'll take care of you too, both of you."

"And Nyx, is he safe? I heard you talking before, he's in trouble, isn't he?" I throw everything at her. I'm past trying to be discreet.

"Don't worry about any of that," she smiles at me, but I'm not convinced by it. It's far too sad.

"Why are you doing all this for me?" I'm a stranger to these people, if I'm right and Nyx is in trouble with this Prez guy, why are they helping me?

"Get some rest. Nyx will be back soon and you guys have a

lot to talk about. Just don't doubt for a second that he didn't mean what he said earlier about taking care of the two of you."

"How can you be so sure?" I ask, my eyes heavy and struggling to stay open.

"Because of the risk he took tonight," she tells me, and I don't have the strength to ask what she means, because here, in a place I've never been before, surrounded by strangers, for the first time in a long time I feel safe.

Chapter 41

NYX

I head back out onto the decking for some fresh air after Maddy takes over watching Ella. For me, the whole game's changed now. Two people need me, two people that I ain't prepared to lose. I have no idea what is gonna go down with Prez tomorrow, but before whatever shit storm he got planned for me hits, I have to be sure the person who tried to hurt them will never touch them again.

I'm gonna head out to Castle Rock and I'm gonna slit Judge Jackson's throat.

"Tell me that ain't your fuck up," a voice comes out of the darkness, catching me before I can head back through my cabin and get on my bike. When I look over my shoulder, I see Brax standing in the shadows of my deck.

"What you say?" I look him up and down, confused as to what the fuck he's doing out here.

"Fuck Nyx, you stupid cunt!" He slams his boot hard into one of the pillars holding up the roof.

"I did everything I could to protect you from this." He talks through his teeth, shaking his head at me like I've let him down or some shit. I barely know this guy. Nobody fuckin' knows this guy. He's just a nomad who stuck around little longer than usual, and right now I don't have the time, or the energy to be dealin' with his crap.

"What do you mean you tried to protect me?" I shake my head at him, clearly, he's snorted too much of Tac's shit up his nose.

"I watched you, saw how close you were getting to her. Fuck Nyx, you were thinking with your dick instead of your head. Gettin' really sloppy about hiding it too." Brax is clearly frustrated. I try to take in all he's saying, but none of it makes any sense.

"Do you wanna tell me what the fuck is going on here?" I step closer to him. I don't care about his reputation, I'll kick his ass into that lake if he don't start talking some sense.

"Jesus, Nyx. The Bastards weren't after her, they don't even know she exists. I was the one who told Prez they had eyes on her. I even stole a laptop and snuck onto their compound to do all those searches on her to back up my story 'cause I knew he'd have Jessie's bitch check it out."

"What?" Heat flares under my skin as I lunge forward and fist the front of his T-shirt.

"I needed to have Prez pull you off the job. I wasn't gonna stand back and let you get yourself killed over some bitch."

"She wasn't just some fuckin' bitch, she meant something to me." I shove him hard against the cabin wall and wait for him to fight back, with all the rage I got contained, he'd have to be some kind of titan to match me right now.

"Yeah, Nyx, and feelings for bitches like that get you fucking dead." He looks back at me without a single trace of fear in his eye.

"She was pregnant, alone, and scared for months. Thinking I'd left her through fuckin' choice," I yell at him.

"Yeah, well I didn't know about the kid, did I?" Brax looks at the floor as if he's regretful for that part at least.

Not fuckin' good enough.

"The judge hurt her. I almost lost the only thing in this world I ever cared about." My grip gets tighter, and still, Brax doesn't flinch. "I got no clue why you feel the need to interfere in my business, but next time, do me a favor and stay the fuck out." I don't have time to deal with him tonight. He's only fueling my frustration. I'll deal with this crap when I know the judge isn't a problem anymore.

I release the grip I got on Brax's T-shirt and go to head back inside.

"Because you're the only fucking thing I ever cared about," he says calmly before I make it through the door. My body spins back around just to check I just heard him right.

"What you say?"

"I couldn't just sit back a watch you fuck everything up, Nyx. You don't know it but I've been looking out for you since you were born and our mama left a twelve-year-old kid in charge of his baby brother while she went out earning money to feed us."

Shit this guy really must be high.

"What the fuck you talking about?" I step back out towards him.

"When she died, I was too young to take care of you, and I couldn't go into the system, Nyx, not when I knew what had happened to her. I had to find the guy who killed her, so I ran before they could find me."

I slump down on the chair and pull my hand over my face while I try to take in what he's saying.

"I never stopped watching out for you. I tracked you down a few times in those shitty foster homes they put you in. I felt bad as hell about it. Then I lost track of you until I showed up here a few years ago on a run and found you prospecting. Hell Nyx, I don't know how the fuck it happened but we've somehow ended up on the same path."

I try to piece everything together in my head, looking back to the first time I'd seen the patch, the rider who visited my foster home. I've spent all this time looking for a Father, not a Brother

"You were the guy that came to that home all those years ago, you threatened Bill and Toby"

"You knew about that?" Brax looks back at me surprised.

"It ain't a coincidence that I came here. I came looking for you. I saw you that day... not your face, but the cut. I thought you were my dad."

"Well looks like you found me, kid, and I'm sorry to disappoint ya."

"Wait, you said something about our mom, what happened to her?" These are the answers I've been searching my whole life for.

"Look, we can talk about this another time, Nyx. Right now, we need to figure out how to get you out of this shit. And if it helps... I'm sorry, okay?" His attempt at an apology looks like it cost him some fucking pride, but it's gonna take a lot more than that to make up for what Ella has had to endure. "I guess I didn't realize what the consequences would be when I was trying to save your fuckin' life."

"Jesus." I look up at the stars and shake my head. A kid, a fuckin' brother, the threat of an impending death. How many more surprises can land on me today?

"I hear you got a meeting with Prez in the morning," Brax looks at me focused.

"Yeah," I nod, taking the cigarette that he offers out to me.

"I'll have a truck ready for you, the girl, and the kid in case that shit goes south. I have enough cash to see you through for a while, and if you can manage to stay low for a few days. I can try and sort you out something more permanent."

"You can't betray the club, you know what the consequences are," I remind him.

"I may be a part of this club, Nyx, but I've always made my own rules," he tells me, before taking a sharp inhale on his own smoke. "I'll admit it, I fucked up. I was trying to protect you and this is on me. Get back to your girl and your kid, and know that I got your back if that's what it comes to."

I nod at him before I head back inside the cabin. I can't deal with all the questions in my head right now, and I like the idea of having a plan in place if shit goes wrong tomorrow.

I head to the bathroom and take a quick shower before returning back to my room. I don't know what I'm gonna do about the judge, but if my conversation with Brax has taught me anything it's that I got to think things through better before I act on 'em. I got no space in my life for mistakes now. No more being reckless.

Ella is fast asleep with our little boy beside her when I step inside, and it physically hurts me when I think about what could have happened to them. Brother or no brother I can't see that I'll ever forgive Brax for what he did.

Maddy is sitting watching them from the chair, chewing on her nails with a real worried look on her face.

"What?" I ask her, wondering how much more I can take tonight.

"How much did you know about the judge, Nyx?" she asks me nervously, grabbing my arm and quickly ushering me out of the room.

"I knew he hurt her tonight. That he hit her and I doubt it was for the first time. That's why I'm so mad at myself I should have been there…"

"Nyx, if I tell you something you got to promise me that you won't react straight away."

"Jesus, Mads, what is it?" I look up. There can't be more, not tonight.

"Promise me," she insists.

"I promise," I shrug, telling her whatever she needs to hear so she'll spit out what she's holding back from me.

"The judge has done… more," Maddy closes her eyes, trying

her best to be tactful. "He touched her inappropriately, I think he even tried to rap…"

I'm already heading for the front door.

"Nyx, wait," Maddy calls after me and somehow manages to get herself in my way.

"Move out of my way, Maddy," I warn her, Jessie's bitch or not I'm getting out that door and serving the judge his justice.

"You promised," she tries reminding me.

"Then why fucking tell me," I snap at her. "All that man has done, did you really expect me to let that go?"

"I told you because we need to convince the Prez to tell her the truth." Maddy lowers her voice to a whisper. "The girl thinks she's been being touched up by her father, Nyx, get your thoughts off killing people for a second and try and think about how that might feel."

I take a step back, clenching my fists to stop myself from punching something. Maddy's right, How the hell must Ella be feeling about this, she doesn't know the truth.

"Tomorrow when you speak to the Prez, you need to make him understand how important it is that he takes that away for her. But right now, this moment Nyx, you need to be there for her. She's trying to be brave but she's petrified. Trust me I've been in her shoes. This place, you guys, you're a lot to take in. and it's not just her she's got to think about. You got responsibilities now, Nyx, you can't act first, think later, you got to be smart. Committing murder, as just as it might seem right now, ain't smart."

I let out a long, frustrated sigh when I realize she's right.

"Go get some sleep, Mads," I tell her, calming my voice. "I promise I won't do anything stupid," I assure her. She nods back before stepping out of my way and opening the door.

I head straight back to my bedroom, sitting in my chair, and watching them both sleep soundly on my bed. Ella's arm wrapped protectively around my son. My chest feels like it could split open for all the love I got for them. Gently, I place myself on the bed beside her and wrap my arm around them both.

"You came back," Ella whispers sleepily.

"Always," I assure her.

"Ell," I try to catch her before she drifts off again because as much as a huge part of me doesn't want to know. I have to.

"Yes?"

"The judge did he ever…" I try to keep the tension out of my body at the thought of it. Ella needs calm right now.

She twists her head around, her eyes wide open and slamming me straight in the heart.

"That night after you took me to your shelter, he thought we'd been together… He checked." I watch the huge wet tear slip between her lashes.

"What do you mean, he fuckin' checked?" My fists tighten.

"He examined me," she looks horrified at her own words. "Threatened to hurt Mom again if I didn't let him, and Nyx, she'd taken such a thrashing that night for what I did." Every part of me wants to get out of this bed and go make that fucker pay but seeing Ella broken keeps me right here beside her.

"There were other times too, it was only a matter of time before he did it. It makes me feel sick and dirty…" she starts to sob again

"Shhhh," I silence her with a kiss, unable to hear anymore. Not tonight.

"All that's over now, go back to sleep. He can't hurt you anymore." I snuggle her closer and let her body against mine douse some of my rage.

I ain't gonna react tonight, not while I got my whole world safe and encased in such a small place. A place I want to hold them in forever. And before I close my eyes, I promise myself that I'll die before I let anyone keep us from being together.

CHAPTER 42

ELLA

I wake up with Nyx's arm wrapped around me, and his tattooed fingers resting over our son's tummy. Yesterday morning I'd never have imagined waking up like this, all of us together.

The baby woke twice during the night, I fed him and we both figured out together how to change him, and get him back to sleep again. I've let myself slip into such a state of contentment that I've somehow blocked out all the horrors of what happened. That's how I have to move on. They are just bad memories now. My father can't hurt me anymore. I got us away from him. I survived, and now with my little family by my side I can work at getting over what he did to me.

After my talk with Maddy last night, I realized there's someone I need to speak to today, and I'd be lying if I said I'm not nervous about it.

I managed to wriggle out of bed, careful not to disturb Nyx or the baby. They both look so peaceful and I feel the dreamy smile find my lips as I stand and watch them for a few seconds.

I pull on the leggings that Maddy folded up on the chair for me and find a clean shirt of Nyx's to put on. Then reaching into Nyx's jeans pocket, I pull out his cell phone, relieved that it doesn't have a lock code. I search through his contacts until I find Maddy's number and then hit call.

"Please tell me you haven't done anything stupid," she picks up, and I feel a little guilty when I hear how tired she sounds, it's still really early.

"Um not yet," I whisper.

"Ella, I thought you were Nyx, is everything okay?"

"Yeah, everything's fine. Nyx and the baby are still sleeping. I just need to ask a favor."

"Sure, what can I do?"

"I need you to take me to that Prez guy who was here last night," I tell her, getting a long silence as a response.

"It's early. Prez ain't really a morning person," she tells me.

"Please Maddy, I need to talk to him before he sees Nyx," I beg, then after another long pause she gives in.

"Fine, I'm on my way around now. I'll get Jessie to give you a ride up to the lodge."

"Thank you," I say gratefully before hanging up the phone.

Maddy walks in the kitchen a few minutes later, an oversized Dirty Souls T-shirt, covering her thighs as she heads straight for the kitchen.

"Jessie's waiting in the truck. I'll take care of Nyx if he wakes up," she smiles, before heading straight for the coffee machine.

I waste no time heading out to the yard. I'd been so preoccupied with pain when we arrived last night, the place looks so much bigger than I remember. There are at least sixteen cabins all set next to each other in a horseshoe that curves around a lake. It's actually really beautiful here.

Jessie smiles at me from the truck as I make my way over to him as quickly as my sore body will allow.

"Mornin' darlin' how ya feelin'?"

"I'll feel better when I've talked to Prez." I smile back at him, managing to pull myself into the passenger seat. The ride up to the lodge is bumpy, and as much as I can tell Jessie is trying to drive steady, I can't help wincing at certain points of the journey. Luckily, the drive is short and a few minutes later I find myself standing on the Prez's doorstep while Jessie waits propped up against the hood of the truck.

"Good luck," he nods at me before I knock and nervously wait for an answer. The door flies open and I can tell by the look on Prez's face that he's shocked to see me.

"Morning, I hoped you and I could talk about something," I smile awkwardly, trying my best to hide my nerves.

"Should you be up? Where's the baby?" he asks, scratching at his chest. It's obvious I've dragged him out of bed, he's still only wearing a vest and some boxers.

"Come in," he pulls open the door and steps out of my way welcoming me into his kitchen. I look around the room, surprised at how brightly decorated and clean it is.

"You want a coffee or summit?'" he growls at me, switching on the coffee machine.

"I'm good thanks. I haven't got long. I'll need to get back to…" we really needed to come up with a name for the little guy, I can't keep referring to him as the baby.

"So what brings you up here?" he asks, gesturing for me to sit at his table.

"I came to talk to you about Nyx." I don't take the deep grunt he makes under his breath as a good sign but carry on regardless.

"I don't know what kinda trouble he's in, but I came here to ask you not to hurt him… See what you don't understand sir, is that Nyx is all I've got." I feel tears building behind my eyes, but push through, determined for this man to hear me out. "I can't go back to my family. Not after the things my father did to me, and my mother… well, she's a wreck. My father has hurt her for so many years I don't think she knows the difference between right or wrong anymore."

Prez scowls at my words but remains silent, allowing me to continue.

"Nyx is the only person in this whole world I can depend on.

And I know that I'm nobody to you, sir, you and the people here have been so kind to me I shouldn't ask any more of you. But I'm begging you to cut Nyx a break because…" I sniff back more tears and swallow the lump in my throat. "…because I love him."

The man wears an odd expression as he listens to my rambling plea, surprisingly he looks sympathetic, maybe even a little sad himself.

"You love him, huh?" he narrows his eyes and I nod back at him enthusiastically.

"And the kid, it's his, right?"

"Yes sir, he didn't know until last night. I didn't find out until after he was arrested, which was all my fault by the way. Luke Robinson was bullying me and Nyx just wanted to protect me. I get that he took it too far but that's Nyx." I shrug.

"And Nyx had no clue about the situation you were in?" he checks

"I thought it was best to hide it from everyone. Nyx disappeared after he got released. I would have told him if I had any way of finding him. But now I just want to put it all behind us and be a family, and I know that's what he wants too. I trust him. I can't lose him again, not now." I manage the whole sentence before I break into a helpless sob.

"Don't cry," Prez commands, a little softness breaking through his harsh tone.

"You have to understand that this club has rules. Nyx broke a fundamental one of those rules. I trusted him with something. Something real fuckin' special to me, and he betrayed me," Prez explains, giving away a whole lot more than I expected him to.

"Nyx is a lot of things bad, sir, but he's loyal. I don't know what happened to make him leave me, but it must have been important. Since the day we met, he's protected me, he's made me feel safe. I need that right now and I want it for my son too. Please."

Prez scratches at his beard.

"And what do you think the rest of my members would think of me as a leader if I let him get away with what he's done?" he asks me thoughtfully.

"The people who I've met from your club so far have been so kind to me. I'm sure they'd understand that sometimes we get forced into situations beyond our control, we make mistakes. And that good men can sometimes forgive."

When he doesn't answer me, I think it's a good time to leave. He looks lost in thought, like what I've said might have actually struck some kind of cord inside him. But then, the man doesn't seem the type to back down from a decision. I've heard some pretty ruthless things about the Dirty Souls and if they're true, the man who leads them can't have much of a conscience.

"I should get back to the baby." I stand up and make my way towards the door before I actually throw myself at his feet and beg him not to take Nyx away from me. I doubt he'd be very tolerant to that. I see myself out of his kitchen and make my way back to Jessie's truck.

"So, how'd it go?" he asks me gritting his teeth.

"It went okay, I guess," I shrug. "I just wish I knew what Nyx had done that was it so terrible."

"Nyx didn't do anything that we all ain't been guilty of," he tells me cryptically, starting up the engine and making the journey back to the cabins.

When we step inside Nyx's, Maddy has already laid the table for breakfast and there's no sign of Nyx and the baby.

"They're still asleep," Maddy looks up from the grill, and Jessie goes straight to her and hugs her from behind.

"How'd it go?" She gives me the same hopeful look Jessie had when he'd asked me that question.

"I just wish someone would tell me what Nyx is in trouble for."

"Don't worry about it," Nyx's voice comes from behind me

and when I turn around, he's standing in the doorframe, our tiny son resting over his shoulder, and cradled in one of his huge hands.

"I think someone got hungry again." He makes his way over to me and carefully places him in my arms. Something is comforting about having him back, I couldn't have been gone very long, but I've felt like a part of me was missing. Stroking my finger over his soft little cheek, I make my way over to the couch so I can feed him.

"Listen, I don't want you worrying about me, okay?" Nyx tells me. "Just focus on you and this little guy."

I nod back at him, hoping that Jessie or Maddy won't bust me about going to see the Prez, something tells me Nyx wouldn't be happy about it.

"So is someone gonna give the lil' guy a name?" Maddy says as she blows the steam off her coffee.

We all look at the door when it bursts open, and I recognize the guy covered in tattoos who barges through it.

"Nyx, what the fuck!" he roars.

"Tac, right on time, we're trying to think up a good name for my son. You got any ideas?" Nyx asks cockily.

"Maybe you could name him after his Pappy, it'll be a good fucking tribute," Tac bites back. Nyx suddenly senses how anxious that makes me, and tries soothing me by stroking my arm. I still don't miss the look of worry that's settled on his face. I'm missing something massive here and I can't stand everyone being so secretive.

"Tac, a word." Jessie shoves the man back out the door, and Maddy looks at me awkwardly. "I'll give you guys a minute," she says before quickly following them out.

"Nyx, what did you do?" I ask him as soon as the door closed behind her. "You need to tell me right now how bad this is."

"I broke club rules," he says, dropping his head.

"How? It has to be bad, everyone around here is acting like

you're gonna end up dead for Christ's sake. Did you hurt someone?" And then a terrible thought enters my head, "God, did you actually kill someone, Nyx?"

"No," he shakes his head, but in a way that doesn't give me much confidence. "Nothing like that. I did something that I shouldn't have, but I don't regret it."

"What's gonna happen to you now?" I ask, petrified of his answer.

"I'm gonna talk to Prez and try to sort it out."

"And if you don't?"

"That ain't an option. Because the three of us are gonna be together no matter what." He stands up and pulls on his leather cut. It's the first time I've seen him wearing it, and he looks so damn hot it almost makes me forget what I'm worried about.

I notice the word Prospect written in white along the bottom.

"What does that mean?" I ask, and he looks over his shoulder and follows my eyes to the patch.

"Prospect means you're workin' at becoming a member of the club."

"And that's what you want, to be a member of this club?"

"It's all I ever wanted…" he crouches down in front of me "…'till I met you." He grabs at my hand and strokes his finger over our little boy's cheek. "Now, there ain't nothing more important than this," he tells me.

"Why did you want to be one of them?" I'm curious as to why anyone would choose the lifestyle of an outlaw.

"Because they're the only family I've ever known. I came to them searching for something and then I found something else." His eyes focus on me as he smiles.

"Is it still what you want? To be a Dirty Soul?" I ask.

"If it comes down to a choice between them and you, it's an easy one." He places a kiss on my forehead before he stands back up.

"Ell, if a guy called Brax comes and tells you to go with him.

Don't question him okay, you get the kid and you leave." I hate how serious he sounds all of a sudden.

"Nyx…"

"Don't ask, Ella, just promise me you'll trust Brax if he comes for you."

"Okay," I agree and he kisses our little boy's head.

"You make sure you come back to us, Nyx." I look up at him, trying to sound threatening.

"Pinkie promise," Nyx holds out his little finger, and I hook mine tight around it.

The promise is sealed now, I just have to trust that he won't break it.

Chapter 43

I fucking hate leaving them, and when I get out on to the yard. I feel the eyes of every brother on me. Jessie has his hand on Tac's chest, stopping him from launching at me and I get why he's so angry. Tac cared about me enough to give me a shot and I've let him down.

Prez called a church meeting late last night, so everyone will know who Ella is now, and that I betrayed him in the worst possible way. I walk straight past them all and get on to my bike.

Brax steps out of his cabin and rests his shoulder on one of the porch pillars, crossing his arms over his chest. The subtle nod he gives me assures me that he has everything in place if things go wrong, and I can't believe I'm having to put all my trust in him right now.

I start up my engine and take the ride down to the clubhouse, parking my bike beside the only other one that's down here. Then I make my way up the path that leads to the chapel, my heart pumping out of my chest as I knock at the door. I hear Prez call out for me to go inside, and I take a deep breath before I push the door open.

It's been almost a year since he called me in here and set me my task. Trusting me to watch out for his secret daughter, to get close and find out more about her. The kid I was back then wasn't capable of caring for anyone but himself. I'm a man now, with responsibilities and a heart that beats fiercely for my family.

Prez waits for me at the head of his table, his eyes narrow and focused on me as I step up towards him.

"Look, Prez…" I start when I reach the opposite end of the long table. I figure a safe distance between us is a good idea.

"You stop those pussy lips running when you're in my church, boy," he shouts me down, his expression cold and the long, drawn-out silence that follows having me even more on edge.

"You know what the consequences are for a brother who fucks with another's old lady?" he asks me.

"I do, sir."

"And that those same consequences stand for daughters, right?" he checks.

"Yes, Prez." I look down at the worn wooden floor beneath my feet.

"So what I'm tryin' to figure, Nyx, is how anyone who held the nerve to fuck the president of their club's daughter, while he was lookin' him right in the fuckin' eye every day, wouldn't want to be getting outta town real fuckin' swiftly." He sits forward in his chair and slams his palm hard into the table. So hard it sounds like it might crack under the impact.

"I understand that, Prez, but…" A loud scrape echoes around the room when he stands up from his chair.

"You either gotta be a real dumb fuck, Nyx, or have balls bigger than Texas," he adds.

"I ain't running, Prez, I'm standing here and I'm owning my shit. I didn't just fuck Ella. I fell in love with her." I realize fuck is probably the wrong word choice a little too late and Prez's lack of reaction to that unnerves me.

"I wanted to make her mine from the moment you first handed me her picture. I tried really hard not to fall for her, but I couldn't do a thing to stop it. And now that it's happened and we got him here too. I refuse to fuckin' regret it." I suck in a breath. "So I'm gonna make this real easy on ya," I tell him, swallowing back the lump in my throat.

"If you want me dead for loving your daughter, you'll know exactly where to find me. 'Cause you were wrong, she belongs here with her real family. With you. And with me now. I ain't goin' anywhere."

There's another icy silence, this one lasting even longer than the last one. Maybe he's thinking of all the ways he could kill me, and I just hope to God he doesn't intend on Jessie doing the deed.

If he's thinking of exiling me again, death would be his better option because I ain't going nowhere, not without my girl and our kid.

"You bet your fuckin' ass you ain't." Prez looks at me sternly before closing his eyes and dropping his head. "Jesus, Nyx. I swear to Satan, you got one chance not to fuck this up, or so help me god I will not think twice about making my own daughter a widow. You got that?" He looks back up at me, his hard eyes scowling me a warning.

I stare at him for a while, going over in my head what I just heard.

"I got it," I say, in far too much shock to feel any relief just yet.

"Now hand over that cut," he nods his head at the leather I'm wearing, and it stabs at my chest having to pull the cut off my back and lay it out on the table. Yeah, it was just a prospect vest, but wearing it made me feel like I belonged somewhere. I've worked damn hard to be a member of the club. These guys have been my family and I can't think about how I've let Tac down. I just hope I get to keep my job at the studio.

I get what Prez is doing, and I'm grateful for it. He has to stick by the club's rules, and if I ain't a member, I guess that means I can be with his daughter. He needs to keep his respect around here. I understand that.

"You can get the fuck out of here and go 'own that shit', boy," he throws my own words back at me, with zero tolerance in his voice. I nod back at him, turning to walk away.

"And Nyx," he calls out just before I get to the door I turn my head, and my hand automatically reaches out and snatches what he just tossed at me.

Black, soft, leather, it makes hairs lift up off my skin when I look down and realize what I'm clutching in my fist.

A Dirty Souls cut.

"I don't ever wanna hear you chatting that cunt struck nonsense again, ya hear me, brother?" he tells me, almost smirking.

"Prez?" I look up to him, confused.

"The President of the Dirty Souls can't have his daughter marrying no fuckin' prospect," he points out.

I have no words to say back to him. I'm speechless.

"And let me fuckin' tell you something, Nyx, there will be a fuckin' wedding," he adds a firm warning in his tone

"Sure thing, Prez," I manage, allowing a smile to hook at my lips.

"What about the others?" I ask.

"They all voted you in last week, that's why we called you back here. They'll understand that sometimes the rules have to be adjusted. And as someone recently told me, it takes a good man to forgive."

"Thanks." It seems such a small word for what he's giving me, but I don't know what else to say.

"Nyx, I'm angry as hell at you, the only reason you're alive is because for some crazy reason my daughter is in love with you, and I ain't about to be the one who breaks her heart."

"Never know I might grow on ya," I shrug, hoping to lighten the mood.

"Don't fucking count on it," he stares back at me, his expression blank.

"I'm gonna speak to the girl in a few days, tell her the truth about where she came from," he explains, and I nod in agreement, it's gonna be a hard secret to keep from her, especially now that I know the full extent of the judge's abuse.

"What we gonna do 'bout the judge?" I ask, needing to make him pay.

"That's gonna be your first order of business as a fully patched member. You, me and Jessie are gonna go pay him a visit." Prez manages to keep his cool but only because he doesn't know the things I know.

"I wanna see that fucker burn for what he's done to Ella, the sick bastard needs to suffer."

"He'll suffer, Nyx," Prez promises. "You just put all your focus into protecting my girl. She's all that fuckin' matters. We ride out tonight, I'll call for you when we're ready."

"I gotcha, Prez," I agree, taking it as my cue to get the hell out of there, and getting straight on my bike.

Ella's pacing nervously when I open the door. While Maddy sits squashed between Tac and Jessie on the couch. I have to do a double-take when I see Brax sitting in the armchair awkwardly holding my son. I'd doubt the guy is capable of being gentle with his own dick let alone a newborn baby.

"Nyx," Ella throws her body onto mine, her arms wrapping around my neck and squeezing me tight. "What happened?"

Everyone else in the room looks tense while they wait for me to speak.

"He patched me in." I put them out of their misery, still not believing the words coming out of my mouth. "It's gonna be okay. Prez made me a member," I explain to Ella.

She looks confused for a second, but then when I smile at her, her lips crash onto mine.

"So we can stay here?" she looks up at me hopefully.

"Yeah, darlin' we can stay," I tell her, placing her back on her feet and heading over to Brax.

"Who thought it would be a good idea to let Brax hold my kid?" I ask the room.

"Actually, he's really good with him." Ella takes the baby out of his arms.

"Right, Uncle Brax?" she jokes,

Me and Brax both look at each other. There's no reason to keep the fact we're brothers a secret, but now ain't the time to drop that grenade, not when Ella is about to get the shock of her fucking life.

"Well, we should leave you guys to it." Maddy slaps Jessie's knee and stands up.

"Yep," Jessie gets up and heads for the door, squeezing my shoulder on his way out. "I'm glad it all worked out, best get Brax outta here before he gets broody." His lame joke earns him a scowl from my brother, but he still gets up and follows him out.

"Me and you are gonna talk about this," Tac whispers as he pulls me in for a hug. "Gotta say it though," he rolls his eyes over Ella. "I'da risked it too. Welcome to the family, darlin'," he places a kiss on Ella's cheek.

I wait for him to leave before I go to my girl, wrapping my arms around her waist and pulling her and my boy in close.

"I told ya it would be okay." I kiss the top of her head. Still not believing what's happening myself.

"And you got the cut." She looks so happy for me. "Jessie explained that it's kinda a big deal."

"I'd give it all up for the two of you," I tell her honestly. "Being at this club, being associated with us puts you in danger, but I promise I'd die before I ever let anything happen to either of you."

"I like it here, I feel safe," she tells me sweetly.

"He's everything I thought I didn't want, and now that he's

here I can't imagine not having him." I look down at our sleeping little boy, and Ella nods back, she completely understands what I'm saying.

"I wish I was there for you, all that time. I missed out on so much that we should have gone through together."

"We're here now." Her eyes remain on him, and I place my hand on her chin and lift up her head.

"I love you, Ella."

"I love you too, Nyx." She smiles at me sweetly, and I just have to taste those lips again.

My lips, my family, my fucking everything.

CHAPTER 44

JESSIE

I'm checking we got everything in the cage ready for our trip out to Castle Rock when Skid comes out of his cabin. I watch him tie his duffle on the back of his bike, and know that this is it.

"You sneaking out the back door on us?" I walk towards him, wishing there was something I could say to make him stay. "Me, Prez and Nyx are headin' over to Castle Rock to beat Judge Jackson's ass if you wanna come?"

"Nah, I wanna hit the road before it gets dark," he replies.

"Where ya heading?"

"South, I think." He checks the ropes tied around his bag are firm by tugging on them.

"What if we find Chop?" I ask, thinking about what he said down in the basement.

"I won't be far enough away that I can't come back and make him pay." His answer satisfies me enough to know we ain't lost Skid completely.

"And Tommy?" I check,

"He's staying in my cabin while I'm gone. I spent some time with him last night, Jess, he doesn't know where Chop is. That fucker's let him down just as much as he has us. All he's done is use the kid. I know the club ain't ever gonna trust him again, but he needs to be put on some kinda straight path."

"You know he's gonna get bitched around," I warn.

"Yeah, I warned him about that too, Chop's made a lot of enemies out there. I've explained that we're his best shot. You won't get no shit from him."

"I'll work on it," I assure him, I've never had much time for Tommy, even before all this shit. But for Skid's sake he'll get a shot at redemption with me. Just one. I just got to figure out how to talk Prez into it.

An awkward silence falls when there's nothing more left to say.

"You better hit the road," I tell him, wiping the dust out of my eyes.

"Yep," Skid nods back before wrapping his huge arms around my shoulders.

"Take care, Jess." He pulls away and saddles his bike.

"Don't leave it too long."

"I'll be back, Jess, like you said, you crazy assed fuckers are my family." He kick starts his engine and with a tip of his chin, takes off down the track.

"You okay?" Maddy creeps up from behind me, sliding her arms around my waist.

"Yeah, I'm good." I spin around and tuck her under my arm.

"I'm gonna sit with Ella and the baby while you boys do your thing tonight," she smiles up at me, and I can't help laugh to myself.

"What's so funny?" her hand slaps my chest.

"You make it sound like we're going bowling or some shit. You're too fuckin' cute," I tell her.

"Ella doesn't know what you're doing, does she?" The smile suddenly drops off Maddy's face.

"It's down to Nyx to decide how much he shares with his old lady," I remind her.

"I don't think I could bare you keeping anything from me."

Her fingers play with the lapels of my cut as she rests her head against my chest.

"As if I could, you know more about what goes on around here than I do these days." I bend down and scoop her up, making her squeal when I throw her over my shoulder. I slam my palm down on her ass and carry her back inside my cabin, intending on making my woman come on my tongue at least twice before I go make that judge suffer.

"So how we doing this?" I check with Prez before we bust into the Judge's mansion and reign hell. I'm behind the wheel as neither of these guys were in any fit state to drive, the tension is steaming off them. And Nyx looks like a hungry wolf about to tear into his prey.

"We gotta try and get a location for Chop." Prez's eyes focus forward. "That's gonna be on you, Jess, and you won't have long. I ain't feeling patient." He takes off his Dirty Souls ring and places it on the dash, then slides his knuckle duster over his fingers. There doesn't need to be a vote to determine if this man lives or dies. He put his hands on Jimmer Carson's daughter. Grimm is already a few blocks away, waiting for the call.

"We let Jessie do some talking, we get some answers on the Chop situation. Then we make him pay," Prez goes over the plan.

"Jesus, Jess, I hope you ain't got a fucking speech planned," Nyx leans forward to tell me.

"Front or back door?" I ask, stubbing out the joint I've finished and feel my blood start to pump a little faster.

"Oh, we're charging straight through that fucker's front door," Prez nods towards the house and I watch a dark smile pull on Nyx's face.

"Here," Prez reaches under the seat and hands me one of the guns we picked up from the Russians last week, not that I'm gonna need it for this piece of shit. Then he reaches back under and pulls one for himself.

"Don't I get one of those?" Nyx asks.

"You got a gun don't ya?" Prez points out.

"Yeah, but so's Jessie, why don't I get one of those fancy new ones?"

"Because Jessie here didn't knock up my daughter," Prez answers simply, checking he's got a full mag before he slides it back in.

"How long you think he's gonna hold that against me?" Nyx asks me under his breath as we're walking across the street.

"A lifetime." I laugh to myself before we step up to the judge's front door. His Porsche is on the drive so I'm guessing he's home, and according to Ella her Mom's away for the weekend. I attempt to count to three but don't get past one before Nyx's boot goes through the door and him and Prez pile inside.

It's dark, all except for the flicking lights that are coming from the room at the back and when we step inside with our guns drawn, the judge is sitting on his couch staring back at us in shock with his cock in his hand. I look at the screen and realize we've just caught Judge Jackson jacking off.

"I'd put that slug away before you lose it," Nyx says, firing the first round of the night right at the judge's cock. I don't know if he missed on purpose to fuck him up, or if he's just a shit shot. But there's a neat little bullet hole in the judge's pelvis to show for it.

Nyx launches forward and drags him off the couch on to his knees and presses his barrel into the back of his head.

"Judge Jackson," Prez nods his head at him like he's greeting an old friend. He's coming off as calm but I know better.

"I came here to tell you that you won't be seeing Ella or

Joanne again," Prez continues, slamming his brass knuckles hard into the judge's face, then wipes under his nose with a bloody fist. It's rare for Prez to get his hands dirty these days but I know the old man still breathes for this shit.

"You can't hurt me, I'm a federal judge," Jackson mumbles back, I'm pretty sure his jaw is busted and if it ain't it will be.

"You really believe that." Prez crouches down so he's eye level with him. "You hurt my little girl, I don't give a fuck what you are," he growls at him, before spitting at his face. "You're gonna pay a heavy price for that motherfucker. But first, you're gonna tell us where Tobias Saunders is."

I move behind the judge, grabbing his arms behind his back and forcing him on to his feet. Nyx stands beside Prez and waits for an answer.

"I don't know where he is," Jackson says, still wearing a brave face.

"If you got any sense, you'll tell us. We brought Jessie here for a reason," Prez warns him.

"I don't know where he is. He's a ghost. He's been trying to get me to hide him away for months," he says.

"Let's see shall we," Nyx storms off and when Prez follows him, I shove the judge forward and we go too.

We turn his office upside down. There are files and files of shit he's obtained over the years on the club, all information he could only have got from an insider. It seems Tommy was telling us the truth after all.

"You can spend all night looking, I don't know where he is," Jackson says after Prez asks him for the tenth time. They've battered his face unrecognizable and his body hangs limp in his office chair. "The last time anyone heard from him was when he came here and threatened that little slut daughter of yours," he manages. I watch Nyx pause from searching in one of the cabinets, lightning in his eyes as he thunders forward and rips the judge out the chair by his collar.

"What you just say?" he pushes his face hard into Jackson's. The flames in his eyes scorching down on the judge's.

"You heard what I fucking said. A slut just like her mother." Prez tosses the papers in his hands and steps up behind Nyx and I know that my interrogation is over before it even got started.

"You know last night while I was laid next to my girl, she told me a story," Nyx says and my eyes flick between Nyx and Prez because I know what's coming, Maddy spend all last night crying about it. Prez don't know about it yet though, and shit ain't gonna be pretty when he does.

"Which hand did you use?" Nyx asks the judge calmly, his nostrils flaring as his hand arches around the dirty fucker's throat.

"I don't know what you're talking about," Jackson answers him with a huge smug grin.

"I'm talking about the hand you put on my girl when you gave her your fucked up little examination, you sick bastard."

Prez remains still, but the look on his face switches from dangerous to fucking murderous.

And when the judge laughs, blood spraying all over Nyx's face. I decide to help the kid along.

"This one's a dominant lefty, Nyx," I point out, I can tell from the ink stains on his left pointer finger and that's the hand he was shaking his cock with if I remember right.

"Left it is." Nyx drags Jackson out of the office through the house and Prez gives me a look as we follow him into the kitchen. We watch on as Nyx smashes the bastard's head hard into the kitchen work surface beside the sink. Holding him down by his throat and pressing his gun into the side of his face.

"Ella thought you were her father, what you put her through was really fucked up. And I'm gonna make sure you feel every bit of pain she felt when you hurt her." He leans over the judge's body and flicks on the switch to start up the garbage disposal unit. I feel the smile creep on my face as Nyx takes the judge's left arm and moves it into the sink.

"No, please don't. Don't... fuck... ahhhhhh," the judge screams as Nyx forces his fingers in to the grinding chamber, pulverizing his flesh and filling the white porcelain sink with blood.

"I bet you got off on my girl begging you to stop. I could put a bullet in your head right now and end all your pain. But you don't deserve that. You are gonna feel every ounce of pain possible before we end your sorry life, Jackson." Nyx tosses the gun out of his hand and slams the asshole's head back into the marble kitchen surface.

It's finally over for Vincent Jackson an hour later. Prez struck the final blow, but not before Nyx practically caved his skull in.

"Call Grimm in," Prez steps back from the lifeless body that's bloody and broken on the kitchen floor and I flick my eyes across the room at Nyx, he's sitting on the floor, his arms resting over his knees, just staring at Jackson's body. The cigarette he's smoking dangling from his lips and his face, arms and hands covered with blood. I've always known the kid had a fiery streak but what he just unleashed on the judge was brutal even by my standards.

"It still don't feel like enough," he says darkly, keeping his eyes focused.

"It never will be," Prez tells him sadly. "But it will sure make it easier for me to look my girl in the eye."

"Now clean up ya hands, and go get anything you think she'll want from her room. You can come back to the lodge and take a shower before you go home to her and the kid." Prez holds out his hand and pulls Nyx back on his feet. Then sliding his hand behind Nyx's head, he pulls his forehead on to his.

"No one ever hurts our girl again," he promises and Nyx nods back.

"Now go clean up," Prez orders him. I wait till Nyx is out the room before I smile at my Prez.

"Wipe that look off your face, VP," he warns me.

"I think this Grandpa shit is turning ya soft already," I point out.

"Fuck you," he smiles back at me, laying his boot into the judge's stone dead face one last time.

Chapter 45

Ella

Me and Nyx spent the whole weekend together, he came back with a heap of my stuff the other night and went out yesterday and brought everything we needed for the baby, as well as loads of stuff we didn't.

We've spent hours building the crib and baby furniture, we even eventually settled on a name for the little fella.

"Dylan's out for the count," Nyx tells me as he creeps out of the bedroom, and lifts me up onto the kitchen counter. He's about to kiss me when the door knocks, and he lets out an annoyed sigh against my mouth.

"Come in," he calls out, unable to hide the frustration in his tone.

Jessie and Maddy step inside, Jessie looking serious, while Maddy bursts to hide a smile.

"Just got back from speaking to Prez," Jessie starts. "Chop's lodge has been cleared, and seeing as I'm officially VP, the place is mine now," he tells us.

"That's awesome." I can see now why Maddy is so excited, the place looks stunning from the outside, it's next door to Prez's lodge and looks out over the whole compound.

Jessie opens his mouth like he was about to say something else.

"We want you guys to have it," Maddy interrupts, blurting out the words like they've been burning inside her mouth.

"What?" Nyx asks, shocked.

"You guys need the space more than we do," Jessie says looking around the cabin at all the stuff we've accumulated over the past few days.

"You don't have to do that," Nyx tells him.

"It's done, I've already spoke to Prez about it. Here," he hands the key to Nyx who takes them out of his hand before he pulls Jessie in for one of those weird half man hug things.

"Where's Dylan? We thought we could watch him while you guys head up and take a look round your new place," Maddy says, still bubbling with excitement.

"He's asleep, and that would be great," I say, starting to feel excited myself. Nyx's cabin is cozy, but it's getting a little tight around here. The places were obviously designed to be holiday homes.

"Well get goin'," Maddy practically forces us out the door and Nyx looks at me and shrugs with a helpless smile at me before we leave them in charge and make our way up to the cabin.

The place is beautiful and even more perfect on the inside. A nice bright kitchen, just like the Prez's with a long window that looks out onto a balcony that spreads along the whole front of the house. There's a living room, three bedrooms, and a good sized bathroom.

"This is incredible, I can't believe Maddy and Jessie would give this up for us," I say to Nyx as we stand on the balcony and look down at the lake. From up here it feels like we're standing on top of the world. I can see out for miles.

"Beautiful ain't it," a rough voice comes from behind us, and when I turn around, Prez is standing in the balcony door, he nods his head to Nyx, who places a kiss on my cheek.

"I'll be inside if you need me," he tells me, leaving me on the balcony, and getting a slap on the back from Prez as he passes him.

It feels weird, like something's going on and the way Prez is looking at me has me feeling uneasy.

"I wanted to talk to you about what Nyx did," he says, his voice softer than I'd ever heard it.

"You want to talk to me about it?" I ask, surprised, everyone has done everything to avoid talking about what Nyx has done with me

Prez looks torn for a second, like he might change his mind.

"You deserve to know," he says eventually, leaning his arms over the balcony barrier and looking out at the stunning view in front of us.

"Nineteen years ago, I loved a girl, exactly the way that kid loves you." He starts. "The club was much smaller then, we ran it out of a bar down in town. There were no other Charters, we only had twelve members."

I can't help but look around and think how well he's done for him and his club.

"I cared about that girl so much, I'd have moved the fuckin' earth for her," he tells me, his voice so low that it's a growl.

"But we weren't meant to be together Ella, she was far too good for me, but hell if I could stop myself from fallin' for her. I kept her away from the club, mainly to protect her, but also because I wanted to be a better man for her." I nod back at him letting him know that I understand.

"One night she turned up at the club, she was a mess cause she'd found out she was pregnant. The girl was petrified about what her folks would do."

"I can relate," I interrupt him, and he gives me a hint of a smile back.

"Well, I stepped up, sure the situation wasn't ideal. I had other commitments. The club, a kid with another woman, but secretly I was fuckin' happy about it. I told her I'd take care of her and the kid and I really fucking meant that, Ella. I would have given them anything."

"Would have?" I ask, wondering what happened to them.

"Yeah, turned out she only wanted one thing outta me.

She wanted me to let her go.

She wanted to keep the kid, but she didn't want to raise it with me. And that really fucking broke my heart," Prez admits sadly.

"I'm sorry that happened to you." I ignore any barriers and reach out for his hand. I don't know why he's telling me this but I don't like seeing him sad.

"You know what it's like to lose someone you love," I say my thoughts out loud, wondering if this is the reason he'd been so easy on Nyx for whatever rule he broke.

"I know all too fuckin' well," he says, his eyes glassing over.

"So what happened to them?"

"I did as she asked, I stayed away. And it turns out I had a baby girl. I already had another daughter. Her name was Hayley. And every day that I watched her grow I thought about the daughter I never got to meet. I wondered if she looked like me, if she had attitude like her big sister had. I'd heard that her Mama got married before she was born, that she was doing alright for herself. And I accepted that for a lot of years. But then I lost Hayley," he tells me, his voice breaking slightly.

"Oh my god. I'm so sorry." His story is tragic, no wonder he's such a hard man.

"She was so young, I didn't know how to deal. And I reacted to it by doing something real fuckin' selfish," he admits.

"What did you do?" I ask him intrigued.

"I looked my girl up. I went back on the promise I made her Moma and I found out what I could about her. On paper she had the perfect life, everything a girl her age would ever want. But I had this niggle in my gut that she needed more. That she needed me."

His eyes well up and I squeeze his hand in mine.

"I fucked things up so bad with Hayley, and I guess I needed to be needed. So I set a plan in motion, one to help me get to know her better. I put someone in her life, so he could tell me about her. I just wanted to know simple stuff, like what food she liked, and if she got good grades. I just wanted to fucking know her."

I look over my shoulder for Nyx, wondering why he's opening up to me like this, Prez doesn't seem like a talk about your feelings kinda guy, especially to a stranger.

"I got word that the people who killed Hayley, knew the club were interested in my daughter, and I panicked. I was so mad that he'd fucked up, when really, I should never have asked him to be in her life in the first place. I blamed him for my fuck up, and I punished him by sending him away. And I didn't realize I was breaking my girl's heart by doing that." He looks at me guiltily, and I swallow thickly when I start to link everything together.

"You sent him away," I check.

"Yeah."

"Why are you telling me this?" I ask, suddenly feeling off guard, with a strong suspicion there's more to this story, something that involves me.

"This club is protective of its family. Daughters are off limits," he tells me. "Nyx broke the rules."

I take in a stuttered breath and my eyes turn blurry with tears.

"The woman you were in love with, the mother of the child. What was her name?" I ask him. Pretty sure I already know the answer.

"Joanne," he says, watching my reaction as I back away from him.

"You're… my…" His head nods back at me slowly, and I feel tears pinching between my eyes.

"I'm ya dad, darlin'," he tells me, and I'm totally unprepared for the huge wave of relief that crashes over me, I close up the space I've made between us and throw my arms around him.

This is all so messed up. I've been lied to for my whole life. Yet all I can focus on is the fact that monster who has tormented me for so long isn't my real father. Prez is clearly shocked at my reaction and remains still for a few beats, before his arms tighten around me and I feel him release a relieved breath.

"I thought you'd be mad," he muffles into my shoulder.

"I don't know how I feel. Honestly, I'm just relieved that I didn't come from that evil man," I sob and smile at the same time.

"Look, you don't have to answer this now, think on it for a while." He pulls me back, holding me by my shoulders so he knows I'm listening to him. "I want more than anything for you and the kid to stay here for us to make up for all the time I missed out on. But you gotta know, I've got enemies out there, darlin'. People who'd want to hurt you if they knew you meant anything to me. I'd let Nyx take you somewhere else, anywhere you wanna go."

"I lived under the same roof as someone who wanted to hurt me," I explain. "I've never felt safer than I have here. I want us to stay here." I wipe away my tears and smile at him.

"You have no idea how shit I feel 'bout what happened to you, if I'd have known what he was capable of I would have got you out of there a long time ago," Prez tells me looking disappointed.

"I had a sister," I distract him from his guilt. I don't want to talk about my past now.

"You did, and I think Hayley would have really liked you," he tells me with a proud smile and eyes full of tears.

"I'd really like to get to know you better, tell you more about her if that's what you want," he says.

"I'd really like that," I nod back. "And Dylan, shit, he's your grandson." It all makes sense now. The way he'd treated me that night I came here. The way he'd held my little boy.

"Yeah, and I'd really like to get to know him too," Prez tells me. "Look, I'm right next door, any time you wanna talk. We can take it slow, we got time now."

"Thankyou…" I grab his hand again, "…for not punishing Nyx"

"Just 'cause he ain't dead don't mean he won't be punished," Prez tells me with a wicked smirk.

"I got to get down to the club, you need anything you let me know," he tells me, and I nod to him as he backs out the balcony door.

I look out on the view, breathing in the fresh mountain air as I take everything in. Vincent Jackson isn't my real father, my whole life has been a lie, but standing here looking down on the Dirty Souls compound, I can't seem to feel mad about that. What I do feel is excited, excited for a future. My family's future.

Hands slide onto my hips and lips touch my neck, and I take Nyx's hands and pull them around my waist.

"I wanted to tell you," he says.

"I get why you didn't. You were trying to protect me"

"I knew you hated the judge, but I didn't think he was a threat to you. If I did, I would have got you out of there, fuck the consequences."

"I don't want to think about the past, Nyx, I want to look forward now."

"You know I'm gonna give you everything Ella Carson," he promises. And hearing my name for the first time feels really weird, a good kinda weird. I turn in his arms to face him, his nose brushing against mine as I stare up through his eyes straight into his reckless soul.

"You already did," I whisper, before our lips touch and I lose myself to him again.

EPILOGUE

The ice in my whisky has melted, and I'm starting to wonder if she's gonna show.

I'd picked this place to meet her for a reason. And I'm sitting in the very same booth I watched her from that night. The night her and her preppy friends decided to live wild and visit a biker bar in a different town. I'd known within seconds of setting eyes on her that I'd have to have her. And I did, for at least a whole summer. She was the only girl I needed during that time. I didn't touch a club slut, and I wasn't touching Mary-Ann anyway.

Joanne looks around the bar wearily when she steps through the door. She hasn't really changed much over the years. She's still fuckin' heart-stopping stunning, and she still carries herself like she knows it. Her heels clip across the sticky wood floor as she heads straight for me.

I wonder if she's gonna slap me, and I'm almost disappointed when she doesn't. Though what she does do is far more fuckin' painful. She looks me straight in the fucking eyes. Making it impossible for me to ignore how they're on the brink of breaking. Her lips wobble, desperate to sob, and I do all I can to ignore the painful wedge she instantly puts back in my chest.

"Thanks for coming," I gesture for her to sit opposite me.

"I didn't have a lot of choice, did I?" she bites back, turning up her nose as she slides into the booth.

"You want a drink?" I ask, and she shrugs, acting like she isn't bothered either way.

"Can we get a vodka and lime ova here," I call out to Shelly who's working the bar.

"Sure thing, Prez," she calls back over, as eager to please as ever.

"I'm not the same person I was back then," Joanne tells me, though I can tell she's impressed that I remembered her drink by the small curl in her lips.

"You're right about that, how ya finding it being a widow?" I ask smugly, before lighting up a cigar.

"You know why I asked you here?" I start.

"Ella called me, she told me about the baby. Jesus, Jimmer, how could you let this happen? We had an agreement," she snaps at me under her breath looking around to check she isn't causing a scene. I huff a laugh at her and exhale smoke across the table.

"Did you speak to your husband like that, JoJo?" I ask, watching her cower slightly. Truth is, no one speaks to her husband. Not anymore. And I'm guessing from the way she's looking at me that she knows exactly what happened to him.

"Yeah, didn't think so, darlin'. See it turns out all those years ago when I thought I was doing the right thing by my daughter, I really fucked up. I relied on you, her mother to put her first. I trusted you enough to let her go.

Turns out, she'd have been better off with me the whole time."

"Don't you dare…" Joanne starts, but I soon cut her off.

"Did you know what your sick fuck husband's been doing to her? 'Cause I do. She told me everything, and I'm here to warn you that I'm taking care of shit now."

"Are they okay? Ella and the baby," she asks, her angry act dropping quicker than a whore's panties.

"They're fine. Safe, happy and I ain't about to admit it to him, but Nyx is a good kid. He'll take care of them."

"That's exactly what they are, Jimmer, kids," Joanne says, knocking back a large mouthful of her drink before Shelly even has chance to place it on the table.

"That may be so, but they seem to have it together. Better than we ever did," I remind her of the mistakes we made.

"I did what I thought was right at the time, Vincent had money, he gave us security. He was legitimate." She looks around the bar that was once the Dirty Souls Clubhouse like it would never have been enough.

"I thought he'd give us the life we needed," she adds.

"When did he start beating on ya?" I ask, fisting my hand at the thought.

"Soon as Ella was born, I never hid from him who she belonged to. I thought it might protect us in case you ever came for her."

I laugh again.

"If I'd have known what that sick bastard was about, I'd have come for you both, and there would have been nothing that cunt could have been capable of doing that would have stopped me."

"Why did you bring me here, Jimmer?" she cuts me to the point.

"I just wanted you to know that our girl's safe. That you are welcome in the compound to meet your grandson anytime you want, and that if you ever need club protection you got it. You always fuckin' had it, which is why I'm so mad at you for not coming to me."

"Ella must hate me," Joanne's hand shakes as she lifts the glass up to her lips again.

"She just doesn't understand, especially now she's got Dylan. She's a good Mom, she'd protect that boy with her own life."

"I tried to protect her," Joanne tries to convince me.

"All you had to do was leave," I shrug.

"For what, Jimmer? A shot at being your old lady?" Her

voice is tinged with bitterness and it lights up a new rage inside me.

"Would that have been so bad? At least I'd have respected you." I manage to catch her hand as it comes at my face.

"Let's not forget who I am, Joanne," I warn her, gripping hard at her wrist and releasing her when she slowly starts to back down.

"Ella and Dylan are gonna spend the rest of their life surrounded by people who care about them, she's got friends and a family, and they'll be happy."

"Can you tell her I'm sorry?" Joanne asks.

"You should tell her that yourself."

"I can't face her," she admits shamefully.

"Just make the call if you change your mind." I stand up and move to walk away, but freeze in my tracks when her hand curls softly around mine.

"I'm sorry," she says. "Do a better job taking care of her than I did." The tears in her eyes prick like a thorn in my heart.

"You just worry about taking care of yourself," I tell her, walking away before I give her any more of me. Troj stands up from the bar, nodding a goodbye to Shelly and follows me out into the ice-cold evening.

He doesn't ask me any questions as I saddle my bike, and then he follows me in the short ride back to the club.

It's late, but there's still one more person I have to see before I can wind down.

"Where's your brother?" I ask Nyx when I find him in the main bar. It still feels strange, how Brax could have kept the fact they were brothers from him for so long.

And Brax has more secrets, I'm fucking sure of it. I just can't worry about that right now.

I have a job that needs taking care of, a favor for a friend that I never expected to be called in, and Brax is perfect for the job.

"He's here somewhere," Nyx stubs out his smoke in the ashtray. "Ella speak to you about Sunday?" he checks.

"Yeah, I'm in."

Ella likes to do the whole Sunday family dinner thing, and I have to admit, I kinda look forward to it.

"I met up with her Mom earlier," I confess. Nyx knows as well as I do how Ella is missing her Mom, despite her not having a lot of respect for Joanne right now. She's confused, and I may not have a lot of respect for Joanne myself but I want her to be part of Ella's life.

"How'd that go?" he asks, signaling for Haven to bring us a drink by raising two fingers.

"I don't think she'll be stopping by anytime soon," I say feeling disappointed for Ella.

Nyx shakes his head.

"Her loss."

The shots land on the bar and we both neck them in one.

"If you see Brax tell him I'm in the members bar," I tell him moving on.

"Gotcha Pops." Nyx's smart mouth earns him a firm clip across the head, with any luck it'll knock some sense into him.

"I'll see ya Sunday then," he calls after me as I make my way out into the foyer and into the quieter bar.

I help myself to another drink. It's just me in here, which works well because I haven't told the other brothers about the task I'm setting Brax.

I hate having to keep stuff from my brothers, but this shit is heavy, the fewer people that know, the better, which is why I'm worried about putting all my trust in Brax.

The guy can handle business. He's been a nomad ever since he patched in at the Utah Charter. He's visited us over the years, helped us out whenever we needed him. But I've always wondered what his deal is.

Hearing Nyx was his brother came as a shock to all of us.

Why he'd kept something like that to himself and chose now to tell the kid, makes no sense or reason. I'll get to the bottom of it eventually, but right now I got bigger shit to deal with.

The door knocks and he steps inside. "You wanted to see me, boss?" he says, marching straight to the bar to help himself. I'm slowly starting to see it now, the resemblance between him and Nyx, both of them have that same arrogant walk. The same chip on their shoulder. Their eyes may be different, but they share the same pouty mouths.

"Take a seat," I tell him.

He gets himself a drink and balances his ass on one of the stools before knocking it back. Things kicked off between me and him when I learned he'd lied to me and told me the bastards were watching Ella to protect Nyx.

I'm human, I got why he did it, he was protecting his brother, but there had been consequences to his actions, and my girl spent months dealing with shit she shouldn't have had to alone. I saw his guilt, and he's made his redemption by becoming a good uncle to my grandson. It's only been a few months but I've noticed a slight change in him already, and I wasn't shocked when he asked me last month if he could become an official member of our Charter.

"You spoke to the boys yet?" he asks, knowing that I'm gonna have to call a vote on that decision.

"Not yet… There's something I need you to do first. A nomad kinda job."

Brax turns down his bottom lip and nods.

"Chop?"

"Nah, no more leads on that one. He's sitting quiet for now but we're waiting for him to resurface."

"So, who is it? Hell Prez, if you're hiding another secret daughter, I'll warn you now, you're sending the wrong guy. I don't play nice."

"She's not my daughter," I tell him and watch his face suddenly turn serious.

"She's a she though?" Brax looks fucking judgy back at me. "You know the rules Prez. No women, or kids," he reminds me, knowing that there's only ever one service I usually require out of him.

"Jesus Christ, Brax, I'm not asking you to kill anyone." I snatch the bottle out of his hands and take a swig.

"It'll be a first," he smirks back at me arrogantly.

"I just need you to take her," I ignore his comment and explain.

"What, like kidnap her?" Brax looks confused at the concept, which comes as a shock considering how many times he's pulled that shit off.

"If that's what you wanna call it, then yeah," I shrug like it's no big deal.

"What's all this about?" he asks, Brax is used to fucking shit up, he's an enforcer like Jessie who goes where he's needed. He tortures and creates pain, and if he needs to, he kills.

"It's about getting revenge, pride, and it's about protecting the people we care about by eliminating the threat."

"Oh, so this is Bastard shit?" Brax smiles darkly.

"This is a trade of promises between two very different people, and me upholding my word."

"The others know about it?" Brax looks back at me suspiciously.

"They'll know when they need to, but this happens tomorrow. I'll have the details ready for you in the morning."

"Wait, what about Sunday? I got the invite too," he looks smug.

"There will be other Sunday's. I'll cover for ya," I tell him shaking my head. I'll deal with Ella, the two of us have grown closer than I could ever have imagined over the time we've spent together, bonding over Dylan and me telling her more about Hayley.

"Why me?" Brax asks, looking puzzled.

"Because something tells me you know a little something about chasing revenge..." He stares back, refusing to confirm or deny my assumption. But I don't need assurance, I see it in his eyes, it's in the pain he creates. Hate is what keeps Brax Marshall's blood pumping.

"...And I need someone who ain't gonna fuck up," I add as he slides his ass off the stool and keeps his eyes focused on me. I don't know who did him wrong in this world, but if they haven't already, they sure as shit are gonna regret it someday.

He looks me over for a while, like he's considering my request, but his answer is exactly what I expected.

"Consider it done." He nods, turning his back to leave.

"I gotta feeling this one's gonna be trouble," I warn before he reaches the door. "We can't afford distractions. You're the only person here I can guarantee ain't gonna fall for the smart little bitch." I tell him as he turns back around.

Brax winks, and toasts the bottle in his hand.

"Sounds like a challenge, Prez,"

The End

ACKNOWLEDGMENTS

The first thank-you I need to make is once again to Sharon, for always being on the other end of the phone and for standing outside my house in the freezing cold to celebrate the first Dirty Soul release with me. You are a LEGEND!

Secondly, I have to thank my amazing Beta's Andrea, Angela, Aliana, Corrine, Erin, and Karen, for being so supportive, making me smile with your notes, and generally being fantastic people.

To Sarah, I've never met anyone as smutty, impatient, and honest as you are. Thank you for making me laugh every single day and for your amazing beta skills.

To Apryle and Lucy for never failing to be wine ready, and loving my Dirty Soul boys as much as I do.

And to Emily, Erin, Jenni, and Lana for being the best book friends a gal could wish for.

Once again I'm super grateful to Kerry at Rebel Ink Co for making another excellent cover and putting everything together for me. And to Sarah at Sassi's Editing Services for still putting up with me and making the editing process so easy on me.

Linda, You're a mother-in-law like no other, thank you for being so supportive of everything I do, and for being fantastic support through the lockdown. We will get that girls holiday we deserve!

And to every reader, blogger, and author who show me your support, I'm so grateful to you all

Last but not least thank you to my amazing little tribe. For making the best out of our Covid19 lockdowns together. We've had crazy days, lazy days and most importantly we've made each other giggle. Rob, Mikey, Ben, Max, and Layla, you guys are my entire world xxxx

ALSO BY EMMA CREED

HIS CAPTIVE

US: https://amzn.to/35GxYDf

UK: https://amzn.to/3klppSc

CA: https://amzn.to/33CXPJr

AU: https://amzn.to/2ZN2Q0Z

LOST SOUL

US: https://amzn.to/3rxkPF5
UK: https://amzn.to/3aOKenS
CA: https://amzn.to/2KVeoL7
AU: https://amzn.to/2JtMPbw

COMING AUGUST 2021

VENGEFUL SOUL

ABOUT THE AUTHOR

Come find/stalk me on the following social media platforms.

Newsletter
Facebook Group
Facebook Page
Twitter
Instagram
TikTok
Goodreads
Bookbub

ABOUT THE AUTHOR

Come find/stalk me on the following social media platforms.